Standing on a ridge looking out over the dry lake bed of Mareotis, Bonaparte knew that the rest of his army was still coming ashore at Marabout but it was towards the north-east that his gaze was drawn, towards Alexandria. He felt as though some kind of invisible magnetic force was pulling him towards its spires and minarets, towards the city named after and founded by the conqueror he sought so desperately to emulate and eventually eclipse. He wondered if all those many hundreds of years ago Alexander had stood here in this same spot, anticipating his own coming conquests, aware of his own destiny and so eager to fulfil it. He was aware of the questioning gazes of his companions, of a certain restlessness among them, but even that could not disturb his meditative attitude and an unshakeable belief that what he had already embarked upon would bring him even greater glory.

It was another ten minutes before he spoke and gave the order for the advance to begin, watching as the commanders dispersed. Despite the cloying heat, Bonaparte felt a shiver at the back of his neck. The troops were beginning to form into a large column, ready for the journey. He smiled to himself. The time had come.

Bonaparte's Invaders

Richard Howard

WARNER BOOKS

A *Warner* Book

First published in Great Britain in 1998
by Little, Brown and Company

This edition published in 1999 by Warner Books

Copyright © 1998, Richard Howard

The moral right of the author has been asserted.

A CIP catalogue record for this book
is available from the British Library.

ISBN 0 7515 1812 3

Typeset by Palimpsest Book Production Limited,
Polmont, Stirlingshire
Printed and bound in Great Britain by
Clays Ltd, St Ives plc.

Warner Books
A Division of
Little, Brown and Company (UK)
Brettenham House
Lancaster Place
London WC2E 7EN

Bonaparte's
Invaders

One

The ship lurched violently back and forth, then from side to side, the waves battering it with such relentless force that Alain Lausard was convinced the frigate would capsize.

It was a conviction the dragoon private had held ever since the thirty-six-gun *L'Esperance* had left Toulon harbour twenty-two days earlier. He was amazed that the vessel had not been sunk by the turbulent seas or overturned by the powerful winds that had followed the French fleet as surely as the flocks of seagulls, which even now swooped and dived overhead. They were like living clouds, constantly undulating and shifting position as they travelled above the ships, often diving to sea level to feed.

The realization of what they were feeding on brought fresh contractions to Lausard's stomach, and he gripped the side of the main deck rail and closed his eyes, trying to fight back the sickness that afflicted him.

It was a battle he could not hope to win and, finally, with a despairing, even angry groan, he leaned over and vomited once again.

Half a dozen seagulls sped down towards the water, anxious to feed on the regurgitated contents of Lausard's stomach, just as they had been doing for the entire voyage. It was a common scene in the choppy water around the ships of the French armada, and one, Lausard had no doubt, that would continue, although for how long no one knew as no one knew their ultimate destination.

He remained leaning limply over the side of the frigate for a moment longer then slowly straightened up, wiping his mouth with the back of his hand. To his right and left, in front and behind him, all he could see were sea, ships and sky. His world had been reduced to those three sights during the course of the last twenty-two days. Plus the merciless rocking of the frigate on the water, the sound of the wind in the rigging, the flapping of sails, the stench of salt air and vomit, of thousands of unwashed men crammed together throughout the fleet. The daily routine of eating what passed for rations, trying to find water that wasn't stagnant, only to bring everything up again an hour or so later. The constant bickering with the crew of the frigate; the boredom, the smells. The sheer misery of sea travel. His entire existence had been transformed into this floating purgatory that showed no sign of ending. And he knew it was the same for every one of his colleagues, for every single man aboard every ship in the entire vast fleet.

Led by the flagship *L'Orient*, on which Napoleon Bonaparte himself was sailing, the massive collection of vessels had sailed out of Toulon harbour what seemed like an eternity ago. The flagship herself had towered above them like a fortress, a vast floating citadel bristling with three tiers of forty cannon each and crewed by over a thousand men. For those who had watched from shore the sight was breathtaking. Thirteen ships of the line, some carrying anywhere between seventy-four to one hundred and ten cannon, forty-two frigates, brigs, avisos and other smaller vessels and over one hundred and thirty transports of all kinds had left the harbour. Aboard were seventeen thousand troops and as many sailors and marines, over one thousand pieces of field artillery, a hundred thousand rounds of ammunition, over five hundred vehicles and seven hundred horses.

The fleet had been further swelled by three lesser convoys from Genoa, Ajaccio and Civita Vecchia, bringing the total of men to about fifty-five thousand and the number of sail to almost four hundred. On the open sea, the armada covered four square miles. Looking around, Lausard could see no end to the massive flotilla. The world consisted of sea, ships and sky.

L'Esperance was typical of its class. Crewed by three hundred men, it boasted an impressive array of firepower. On its main deck it sported twenty-six twelve-pounder cannon, and on the quarterdeck were eight six-pounders and two carronades, while the forecastle boasted two six-pounders and two carronades. The men had marvelled at the size of these weapons and the thirty-six-pound projectiles that they fired. The ex-schoolmaster Bonet had guessed that it would take four men to carry each of the missiles when the time came to unleash them.

Bonet's curiosity had not been shared by the other men of the unit, who were by turn puzzled, indifferent or irritated by his interest in the workings of the ship. Like Lausard, they had other things on their minds – namely their destination. Although even that seemed to have taken on secondary importance as they struggled to cope with life aboard ship.

'Personally, I don't *care* where we're going,' the forger Roussard declared, clutching his stomach. 'In fact, if we're on this stinking boat much longer I doubt if any of us will survive to see land again.' He looked pitifully at Lausard then bent double over the side of the ship and retched, his stomach offering up no more.

Carbonne wiped his bald head with his forage cap and exhaled wearily. 'Where do *you* think we're going, Alain?' he asked Lausard.

'I wish I knew. It isn't England, I know that.'

'Someone said Naples,' Charvet offered, loosening another button on his thick woollen tunic, aware of the heat as well as the uncomfortable motion of the frigate.

'I heard Sicily,' Rocheteau said.

'Wherever it is, I hope there's plenty to eat.' Joubert rubbed his shrunken but still huge belly. 'I'm starving.'

'You're always starving, fat man,' Delacor snarled. 'How can you even think of food at a time like this? The last thing I need is a meal.' He tried not to think about his lurching stomach, hoping the contractions would subside.

'It must be a rich country where we're going,' Sonnier said. 'After all, Bonaparte promised we'd all have enough money to buy six acres of land each when we returned.'

'We'll be lucky if we ever see land again, never mind be lucky enough to *buy* any for ourselves,' Rostov snapped. The big Russian was sitting cross-legged on the deck, his head bowed as if in prayer. He had found that staying off his feet reduced the effects of the seasickness a little but not enough to bring him any lasting relief.

'I thought being in prison was bad,' Giresse bemoaned, 'but this is worse. The food there might not have been fit for pigs but at least we could keep it down.'

'Six acres,' Bonet sighed wistfully. 'That's a lot of land. I think I'd build my own school. I enjoyed teaching.'

'Until they locked you up for it,' Delacor reminded him.

'They locked me up for not teaching what the Directory ordered. They locked me up because I taught the truth.'

'They still locked you up. You're still a criminal like the rest of us.'

'We're not criminals any more,' Lausard corrected Delacor, 'we're soldiers.' There was a note of pride in his tone.

'Soldiers belong on land,' Rocheteau told him, still clutching his belly. 'What the hell are we doing here, anyway? We should be back in France drinking wine, eating bread and enjoying our victory.'

'*And* the women,' Giresse added.

A ripple of laughter rose from the green-clad dragoons; it had become an unfamiliar sound in the past weeks.

However, their laughter was soon stifled as a wave slammed into the side of the ship, sending some of the men toppling over like human skittles. A great spray of sea water covered the deck and the men, but it was dried almost immediately by the hot sun. Lausard looked down at his tunic and saw the wool was covered by a thin white crust of dried salt; he brushed some of it away in disgust.

As the men picked themselves up and brushed themselves down they heard laughter.

Lausard looked round to see two seamen emerging from a nearby hatch.

One was stripped to the waist and barefoot, his black hair tied back in a long ponytail. The other was dressed in a dark blue tunic and white trousers. The black bicorn he wore marked him out as being of a certain rank but there was little else to signify his seniority. Both men regarded the dragoons with ill-disguised contempt. It was a look the troops had become well acquainted with during their time on the frigate. Their presence was resented by the sailors with a vehemence that matched their own distaste at being aboard the ship.

'Still not learned to stand up?' the man in the blue jacket teased.

The dragoons knew him as Marek, a gunnery sergeant who commanded a battery on the main deck. Like most of his colleagues, he was deeply tanned, his skin rough and pitted, his hands like ham hocks. His companion was in his early twenties, a scrawny specimen with long, thin fingers, one of which was missing. He wore gold earrings in both ears, clearly visible where his unwashed hair was swept back. As Lausard watched, the sailor climbed into the rigging and made his way swiftly up it, moving as surefootedly as a chimp until he was thirty or forty feet above the deck. A number of his fellow sailors already moved around up there, scurrying back and forth with an assurance Lausard found it difficult not to admire.

'That's landsmen for you,' Marek said, pointing upwards at the men in the rigging. 'They work the yards. I say they're the most skilled men on the ship.'

'Why do you call them landsmen?' Lausard asked. 'They're sailors like you.'

'No they aren't.' Marek snorted disdainfully. 'I'm a professional. I have a rank. They're untrained. They couldn't work a cannon or plot map co-ordinates. You need a brain for that.'

'Then what are *you* doing here, you glorified fisherman?' Rocheteau said.

Some of the other men laughed, but once again their amusement was stifled by a jolt to the frigate, which caused it to lurch uncomfortably in the churning water.

'Have you got any idea what our final destination is, Marek?' Lausard asked.

'If I had why should I tell *you*?' The seaman smiled.

'All we want to do is get off this stinking boat,' said Lausard. 'We don't want to be on here any more than you and your men want us aboard. Besides, *you* might be used to smelling like a pig but *I'm* not. I haven't even been able to change my uniform for weeks.'

'That's the trouble with you soldier boys, you're pampered,' the gunnery sergeant jibed. 'Too much soft living. When it comes to *real* hardship you start crying.'

'We fought our way across most of Italy,' Rocheteau told him. 'We sent the Austrians running before us. We've seen things you couldn't even dream of.'

'Don't try to impress me with your tales of war,' Marek sneered. 'I fight in darkness, down there.' He pointed towards the main deck below. 'Choked by smoke, blinded by fire and with enemy guns only feet away from me. That's *real* war. And out here there's nowhere to run. We can't just turn and flee when things turn against us. Not like you.'

'Considering how many times the navy has been beaten, perhaps you'd have been better off running,' Lausard retaliated, glaring at Marek.

There was more laughter from the other dragoons.

Marek opened his mouth to say something but thought better of it, and simply raised a hand and stalked off across the deck in the direction of a group of sailors manhandling a twelve-pounder into position.

Lausard watched the retreating figure, then turned

back to the choppy water to watch the other ships. The powerful wind billowed in their sails, sending them speeding along, cutting through the choppy water with ease, but the smaller craft, *L'Esperance* included, seemed to feel every single bump and swell of surf.

'You're a friend of the Almighty,' Roussard said, nudging Moreau. 'Can't you have a word with him and get him to calm the sea?'

Moreau glared at his companion.

'Better still,' Rocheteau added, 'ask him if he knows where we're going.'

Some of the men laughed, but Moreau was unamused. He continued to clutch the side of the deck barrier, his face milk white.

'I wonder how the horses are doing,' Tabor murmured.

All the animals, pack mules and cavalry mounts alike, were on separate transport further back in the great armada. They had been herded into stalls below deck, around twenty animals to each ship. The farriers travelled with them, fed them their meagre rations and tended to them as best they could. For the animals the voyage was even more arduous than it was for the troops. Stuck in the holds in perpetual darkness, many of them died of thirst, and were either hurled overboard or, in some cases, eaten by the starving crews.

'To hell with the horses,' Delacor rasped. 'What about *us*?'

'I wonder what our new captain thinks of all this?' Lausard mused aloud.

'I think he's enjoying himself,' Rocheteau said. 'Captain Milliere is a dedicated gambler it seems. Which is just as well because the only things to do on this ship are gamble or be sick.'

'You should know about the gambling,' Lausard reminded him. 'You organized it.'

The men laughed.

'Perhaps it's a good job we haven't had any pay for so long,' Rostov offered. 'If we had we'd all be broke by now.'

'I wonder what old Deschamps would make of this?' Giresse said.

'He was a good officer.' Lausard looked around at the men. 'I hope he's well.'

'Where *are* all the officers, anyway?' Roussard enquired.

'Below deck, gambling or trying to sleep,' Rocheteau informed him.

'A boat took some of them over to *L'Orient* this morning; Desaix went with them, I saw him,' Bonet observed.

'It would be difficult to miss someone as tall as General Desaix,' Charvet noted.

'He was wearing that old blue jacket of his,' Bonet continued. 'Without the lace. You'd never know he was a general.'

'Perhaps *he* knows where we're going,' Giresse wondered aloud.

'Him and Bonaparte,' Delacor said. 'You can be sure that *they'll* both have enough to buy more than six acres of land when all this business is over. I heard that most of the generals were feathering their own nests during the Italian campaign.'

'Like some others I could mention?' Rocheteau chuckled.

'What did we get out of that?' Delacor challenged. 'A few pieces of gold and silver. Some officers had enough to buy houses, entire estates. The Bourbons were removed because they had too much wealth and now they've been replaced by men even more greedy.

Even the Directory are no better. They are only rulers under another name.'

'Every country must have rulers,' Lausard said. 'Whatever shape they take.'

'I thought we fought to free people from their rulers,' Delacor continued.

'We fight because we are ordered to,' Lausard told him. 'Nothing more, nothing less.'

'So who will we fight if we ever get off these stinking ships?' Roussard wanted to know.

Lausard merely gazed out to sea, at the huge armada of vessels as far as the eye could see. He wished he knew. He wished he could answer Roussard's question, but as yet, like everyone else in the army, he was clueless. He had already spilled Austrian, Piedmontese and Italian blood. But whose blood he would spill next, he couldn't begin to imagine.

Two

As Lausard descended the narrow wooden stairway that led down into the Stygian depths of the main deck, he gripped the handrail tightly. Buffeted by a wave, the frigate rocked uncertainly for a moment and Lausard feared he would be hurled off the narrow walkway, but the tremor passed and he continued on his way, struck, as ever, by the foul stench that permeated this nether region. Exactly how many men inhabited this part of the ship he didn't know. He guessed two or three hundred: a combination of the sailors who normally called this their home and the men of his own unit who had been assigned this black hell-hole as living quarters for the duration of the voyage.

The troops slept on the bare boards of the deck while most of the naval personnel had hammocks slung from the beams, many of them above the cannon. The crews slept around their guns as if the bond between them was unbreakable. Six to a crew, they were, almost without exception, squat, powerful men who spoke little, even to each other.

Among the crew was a number of young boys, some in their teens, some even younger. Lausard had learned that during a battle these boys would rush from gun to gun carrying powder where it was needed and, in some cases, even tending to the wounded as best they could. Life at sea seemed unpleasant enough for grown men, thought the dragoon, but what it must be like for these children he could only imagine. One of them, a boy of about twelve, dressed only in a pair of threadbare knee-length *culottes*, was scooping water into a ladle from one of the barrels at the foot of the wooden steps. Lausard watched as the boy rinsed out his mouth with the rancid fluid then spat it out on to the deck close to the dragoon's boots. The boy looked at him then ambled off back towards a nearby twelve-pounder.

Lausard stuck his hand into the water and scooped some on to his face, washing away the sweat. The water was slightly warm and smelled rancid. But it was all they had. There were two barrels at either end of the deck, for drinking, washing and cooking. It was rumoured that there was fresh water in the hold but they had received nothing resembling fresh water for more than a week now.

Lausard made his way slowly along the deck, stepping over sleeping men, ducking to avoid hammocks where he had to. He could see barely two feet in front of him in the gloom. At various points on the deck candles were burning, offering tiny islands of illumination in this sea of blackness, but for the most part the deck was funereal. Occasionally the gunports would be opened to allow in some much needed fresh air and some natural light, but on the whole the main deck was lit just by these few candle flames and it became impossible to tell day from night.

There was a number of cabins towards the rear of the ship where the officers of both the army and the navy had their quarters. These, so it was rumoured, were well lit and comfortable, but Lausard found it difficult to believe that anywhere on *L'Esperance* offered much in the way of respite from the hideous day-to-day existence he and his colleagues endured. Like most, this was his first time at sea and he hoped it would be his last.

He tripped over the outstretched legs of a sleeping dragoon but the man didn't even stir. He was lying with his head on his saddle, his face hidden by the blackness, only his low breathing indicating that he was still alive. His tunic was undone and open, his hands clasped on his chest. Many of the men had divested themselves of their uniforms because of the stifling heat but also because the material was in such an appalling state. Without the benefit of sanitation, many men, crammed together in such restricted conditions for so long, found the stench of their own clothes, never mind those of their comrades, intolerable. Dried sweat, urine and vomit were the overpowering odours that filled the foul air. As oppressive as the darkness, their combined smell hung like an invisible cloud over the men.

Many of the men had retreated to the dank, reeking abyss of the main deck over an hour before in an attempt to get some sleep. It seemed that only when sleep claimed them were they free of the ravages of hunger, thirst and seasickness.

Lausard had stayed topside for a little longer, looking out over the churning sea, watching the seamen at work and thinking. His thoughts had turned to France. He didn't doubt for a moment that there was purpose in this mission but what it was he could not comprehend. Why had the men not been told their destination? Where could Bonaparte be taking them that would hold so much fear? Had that been the reason for the secrecy? he pondered. And yet, most of this army, dubbed 'The Legions of Rome' by its commander, were veterans of the Italian campaign. Men who would not show fear easily. Men, like himself, who had fought their way through battles like Mondovi, Lodi, Arcola, Rivoli and Castiglione. But Lausard had no fear of the final destination, wherever it may be. Whatever awaited them had to be better than the hell they were living aboard ship.

The frigate listed again and Lausard cursed as he almost overbalanced. A candle was burning just ahead of him and he could see some of his comrades gathered around it, heads bowed in some cases.

Joubert was lying on his back, his face slick with sweat, his belly spilling over the top of his breeches. He had removed his tunic, as had Tabor, who was lying curled up in a foetal position, his head resting on the jacket.

Sonnier lay on his side, one hand clamped across his mouth, the other ineffectually clutching his stomach. Lying against his legs was Gaston. The young trumpeter had suffered a little less violently from seasickness than his older colleagues and now, as he saw Lausard approaching, a smile creased his youthful features. The private tried to return the gesture but it faded as he became aware of his stomach contracting and thought that he was going to be sick again. To his relief, the tremor passed and he sat down, cross-legged, next to Rocheteau, who was chewing cautiously on a piece of salt biscuit he'd found in his pocket. He offered a chunk to Lausard, who shook his head.

'No water,' Lausard muttered, 'and yet all they give us

to eat is salt beef and salt biscuits. Salt makes you thirsty.'
He shrugged.

'Bonaparte might know how to organize an army,'
Delacor said indignantly, 'but he doesn't know how to
feed one.'

'It isn't his fault,' Lausard argued. 'It's the contractors
who supply us. They're a bunch of crooks looking to make
a fast profit.'

'So they sit on their fat backsides in France, while we
starve to death on this stinking ship,' Roussard hissed.

'Us and everyone else in the army,' Sonnier echoed.

'I don't care about anyone else,' Delacor told him, 'I
care about *me*.'

'We'd noticed,' Rostov responded, rubbing both hands
across his sweat-drenched face.

Bonet seemed oblivious to the bickering of his companions; he was looking fixedly at a copy of *Le Moniteur*.

Lausard could just make out the date of the newspaper
in the odorous blackness of the main deck. 19th May,
1798. 'The news in there will be a little out of date,
Bonet,' he said.

Bonet smiled. 'I bought it just before we sailed. As a kind
of keepsake. There are reports in here about the fleet leaving
Toulon. But they have no idea where we're heading either.'

Lausard held out his hand and Bonet passed him
the paper.

'"Officers and soldiers,"' Lausard read aloud. '"Two
years ago I came to take command of you. At that time
you were on the Ligurian coast, in the greatest want,
lacking everything, having sold even your watches to
provide for your needs. I promised to put an end to
your privations. I led you into Italy. There all was given
you in abundance. Have I not kept my word?"'

'Who said that?' Tabor asked vaguely.

'Bonaparte, you half-wit,' Delacor snapped.

'According to the newspaper, we all answered with a single shout of "Yes",' Lausard continued.

'What he said is true, isn't it?' Sonnier offered. 'Napoleon *did* lead us into Italy.'

'And nearly got us all killed,' Delacor qualified.

'Napoleon?' Giresse said, smiling at Sonnier. 'Are you on first-name terms with our commander now, Sonnier?'

The men chuckled.

Lausard held up a hand for silence then continued reading.

'"Well, let me tell you that you have not done enough yet for the fatherland, nor the fatherland for you. I shall now lead you into a country where by your future deeds you will surpass even those that now are astonishing your admirers, and you will render to the Republic such services as she has a right to expect from an invincible army. I promise every soldier that upon his return to France, he shall have enough to buy himself six acres of land."'

'Is that why you kept the paper, schoolmaster?' Rocheteau wanted to know. 'So that you could show that to Bonaparte in case he tried to cheat any of us?'

'It says here the speech was followed by shouts of "Long Live the Immortal Republic" and by patriotic hymns,' Lausard said, flicking the newspaper with his finger. He passed it back to Bonet. 'It seems it is easier to be patriotic on dry land.'

'Have you stopped believing in Bonaparte then, Alain?' Rocheteau questioned. 'I thought you were the patriot amongst us.'

Lausard shrugged. 'I've never had the monopoly on

patriotism. But you tell me, would a speech like that have been as well received by this army had Bonaparte given it two days ago?'

Rocheteau shook his head. 'I for one would not have applauded it.'

'And yet, when we land, we will fight if he tells us to fight,' Lausard said. 'We will charge if he tells us to charge, and we will do it because we are soldiers, not because we are patriots.'

'I fight for God.' Moreau's voice came from the gloom.

'Then I hope he takes care of you,' Delacor said. 'Me, I'll trust myself, no one else – and certainly not your God.'

Moreau crossed himself.

'Is that what you would build on your six acres, Moreau? A church?' Carbonne prompted his colleague.

'I would build a fitting monument to His majesty, to His power and goodness,' Moreau said.

'I'd build a bakery like my father's, and every day I'd awake to the smell of freshly baked bread, just like I did when I was a child,' Charvet said wistfully.

'Do you have to mention food when I'm so hungry?' Joubert complained.

'We're all hungry, Joubert, not just you,' Delacor snapped.

'I'd build a farm in the Urals where I was born,' Rostov declared.

'I'd build a brothel and fill it with the most beautiful women in France.' Giresse chuckled. 'Then I'd make sure the only customer they ever had was me.'

A wave of laughter came from the men. The sound was subdued; swallowed and stifled by the impenetrable blackness.

'Shut up!' shouted an anonymous voice.

Lausard turned and tried to peer into the umbra, attempting to pick out the source of the shout.

'Can't you shut up and go to sleep,' the voice said again, more insistently this time.

'Are you such a coward that you shout at us from the darkness?' Lausard called back. 'Show yourself.'

'Be quiet, soldier boy,' a voice called from much closer.

Several of the dragoons could see one of the sailors sitting up in his hammock smoking a pipe, thick smoke billowing around him.

The man was huge. Fully six feet tall and sporting thick muscular arms and a torso that looked like granite. His face was almost hidden by the gloom, only portions of it illuminated by the sickly candle light. Lausard could make out a thick moustache and beard but that was about all.

'The sooner we reach land the better,' the huge sailor said. 'Then we can all be rid of you. You don't belong here.'

'Do you think we *want* to be here, you idiot?' Delacor snarled.

There was a loud thud as the sailor slid from his hammock and dropped to the deck floor. He rose to his full impressive height and took a step towards the dragoons. Several other seamen joined him as he advanced towards the troops.

Lausard got to his feet, Charvet and Rocheteau flanking him.

Rocheteau's hand fell to his belt, his fingers touching the hilt of the small knife jammed there.

All around the deck men were moving, voices rising in volume. Curses and threats were exchanged.

Delacor stood close to the gigantic sailor, forced to look up into his face.

'What's going on?' a familiar voice asked, and both soldiers and sailors saw Marek approaching through the darkness.

'I think these little men need to be taught a lesson,' the big seaman said.

'Ah, so you've met Legros?' Marek chuckled. 'You should stay away from him. You might upset him.'

'What will he do?' Lausard remained unimpressed. 'Suffocate us with his stench?'

Legros took a step forward, lunging at Lausard, who stood his ground.

Marek stepped in front of the sailor. Charvet blocked Lausard's path.

'The time will come, soldier boy,' Legros snarled. 'You and all of your babies will be food for the fish. I'll kill you.'

'You're welcome to try,' Lausard said calmly.

Charvet raised his hands into his boxer's stance, his eyes boring into those of Legros.

'A fighter,' Marek said. 'You would dare to fight Legros?'

'I'll fight all of you,' Charvet said.

Marek looked at Rocheteau, who nodded.

'There could be money in a fight like that,' Marek observed.

Rocheteau smiled. He pushed the last piece of salt biscuit into his mouth and chewed.

Three

Napoleon Bonaparte raised the glass of red wine in salute, looked around at the other men who had joined him in his cabin, then drank. Those who surrounded him did likewise, some against their better judgement. Despite the relative comfort enjoyed by the higher-ranking officers on the voyage, many of these fighting men were still experiencing their first taste of sea travel, and the seasickness that afflicted so many of their troops had also struck them.

Bonaparte himself had escaped the worst ravages of the long voyage. He sat on the edge of his bed, which had been fitted with gimbals to counteract the effects of the repeated dips and rises of tide, and looked around at those who had been summoned to his cabin aboard *L'Orient.*

'Gentlemen, we dock at Malta tomorrow. The first part of our great adventure. The first chapter in a catalogue of deeds that men will talk about for years to come.'

'Why Malta?' a quizzical voice from close by asked and Bonaparte looked up to see General Dumas looking down at him. Dumas was a giant of a man, a mulatto who towered over most of his colleagues.

'The island has strategic value,' Bonaparte informed him. 'But at present it is necessary for us to take it to replenish our supplies. Especially water. Orders have already been sent to the Grand Master of the island informing him that we wish to dock to take on water. Whether or not that permission is given we will land troops to the north and south of the capital, Valetta, and also on Gozo, the neighbouring island. We will then encircle Valetta, and wait for the knights to surrender.' He took another sip of his wine, satisfied that his explanation was clear enough.

'This Grand Master of whom you speak,' Dumas continued, 'who is he? Grand Master of what? And who are these knights?'

Bonaparte chuckled but Dumas frowned in bewilderment.

'His name is Baron Von Hompesch,' the cavalry general was told. The answer came from Louis Alexandre Berthier, Bonaparte's chief of staff. 'A German. He is Grand Master of the Order of the Knights of St John of Jerusalem. The Knights Templars. It is an ancient order.'

'An outdated order,' Bonaparte added. 'It no longer serves a purpose and it will fall because it *has* to fall.'

'The knights rule the island,' Berthier continued, 'and the island rules the Mediterranean. The English, the Austrians and the Russians all wish to acquire it. The Russians in particular. It would give them a foothold here. The Tsar has publicly declared himself to be a protector of the Order.'

'If we do not take it then our enemies will,' Bonaparte said.

'If not the Russians, then the Austrians. Von Hompesch is sympathetic to their cause.'

'These knights, will they fight?' The question came from General Caffarelli. He was a lean, thin-faced man who had lost a leg in Germany fighting for the Republic. As he moved slowly about the cabin, his wooden leg bumped loudly against the floor.

'Some of them might,' Berthier replied. 'More than half of them have always been French but our intelligence tells us that many have somewhat conflicting attitudes towards the Republic.'

'If they will not accept us then they should be destroyed,' Caffarelli stated.

Bonaparte smiled. 'Your loyalty to the Republic is admirable, Max,' he said. 'But, at times, perhaps a little over-zealous.'

Some of the other officers laughed but the engineer general turned and glared furiously at them. 'All who oppose the Republic should be destroyed,' he hissed. 'As were those Bourbon leeches we carried to the guillotine.'

'I agree with Caffarelli.' General Desaix sipped at his wine. 'If these knights oppose us then let us eradicate them.'

'There *are* Republicans among them,' Berthier said. 'Intelligence reports have revealed as much.'

'What intelligence reports?' Desaix demanded.

'In December of last year, I myself despatched two emissaries to Malta,' Bonaparte informed the other man. 'One of them was sent as a spy, the other, Citizen Poussielgue, on official business. One of his cousins is Guardian of the port of Valetta. He remained for four months and he spoke to many of the French knights. He found Republican sympathizers. Among them Bosredon de Ransijat, the Treasurer of the Order, and also a man called Fay, the Commissioner of Fortifications. The other knights said that they would resist any invasion unless they were assured of compensation.'

'It would seem that diplomacy rather than force is what is required,' Berthier added.

'You would have us held to ransom by these dogs?' Caffarelli snapped. 'Why pay them when we can simply destroy them?'

'Do you think I doubt my own men?' Bonaparte hissed. 'Men who have subdued and conquered half of Europe will take this island without weapons if they have to.'

'Even if they do decide to fight there should be little problem,' Berthier said. 'There are enough supplies in Valetta to withstand a siege for four months but the defences are poor. There are nearly a thousand guns but they have not been used for a century. The powder supplies, according to our reports, are rotten and unusable.'

'What about troops?' Desaix enquired. 'How many are there on the island?'

'About ten thousand Maltese militia, poorly armed and not eager to fight. There is a native garrison of about fifteen hundred men and three hundred and thirty-two Knights Templars, fifty of whom are either too old or too sick to fight. The others have no heart for it.'

The officers listened to the news in silence, occasionally swapping glances with each other.

'We know that our men will fight,' said Desaix. 'But what of these "pekinese" you have brought along with you? These architects, surveyors, chemists, studiers of animals and rocks. What place have they on a military mission?'

'Ask Caffarelli, he helped to pick them,' Bonaparte said, smiling.

The engineer turned on his colleague, looking up at Desaix. 'These civilians are men of great knowledge,' Caffarelli said earnestly. 'All have their purpose.'

'I heard that there were singers and poets among them,' Dumas commented. 'How will *they* help us?'

'They will all be needed when the time is right,' Caffarelli insisted. 'There is a need for brains as well as brute force on this mission, Dumas.'

The cavalry general snorted dismissively and reached for the decanter of wine, refilling his glass.

Bonaparte looked around the room at one of the men who had not yet spoken. He was dressed in a dark blue, long-tailed tunic, dark blue breeches and short leather boots. The bicorn he held sported a huge white feather plume. Admiral Brueys sipped his wine and listened distractedly to the conversations of the army officers, his mind seemingly elsewhere.

'What are your views on this landing, Brueys?' Bonaparte asked finally.

'I have no view, General,' said the admiral. 'The business of which you speak is military. My concerns are for my ships.'

'What concerns do you have?' Bonaparte wanted to know. 'Have you no faith in your men or in your own abilities?'

'I don't doubt my own abilities, General,' said the admiral. 'Just as I don't underestimate the abilities of my opponent. Nelson has ships in the Mediterranean. We only avoided him leaving Toulon by luck.'

Bonaparte waved a hand dismissively. 'That one-eyed, one-armed Englishman,' he snorted. 'Don't try to frighten me with tales of Nelson.'

'It is not fear that I feel for him, but respect,' Brueys responded. 'A respect you would do well to share, General.'

Bonaparte glared at the seaman. 'You were assigned this force because of your ability, you *and* your colleagues. You have in your charge over forty thousand of my men but you also have something else. You have the destiny of France in your hands. That destiny, like my men, must be protected. Against Nelson or whoever else comes against us.'

'If he catches us in open water he will destroy us,' Brueys said flatly. 'The British ships are faster. They will move through a fleet of this size like a knife through butter.'

'It is your job to see that they don't.'

'That may be easier said than done if he catches us.'

Bonaparte poured himself another glass of wine and returned to his bed, even though the ship was relatively stable as it moved through the night-shrouded ocean.

The uneasy silence was interrupted by a knock on the door of the stateroom and Berthier crossed to open it.

He found himself confronted by an aide-de-camp, dressed in an immaculate uniform, who saluted smartly and handed the chief of staff a piece of paper. Berthier scanned it, returned the salute, then closed the door, listening to the ADC's receding footsteps. Finally he walked back towards Bonaparte, the piece of paper held before him.

'From Grand Master Von Hompesch himself,' Berthier

said. 'No more than four ships at a time are to be admitted to Valetta harbour.'

Bonaparte's expression darkened. 'Send a communication back to the Grand Master now. Take this down. General Bonaparte will secure by force that which should have been accorded to him freely.'

Berthier crossed to the small writing desk in one corner of the room and hastily scribbled down the message, the quill scratching noisily across the paper as he wrote.

Caffarelli smiled.

Desaix finished his wine.

'We land tomorrow, gentlemen,' Bonaparte declared.

'And after Malta?' Desaix asked. 'Where then?'

The Corsican smiled. 'The place where Alexander found his greatness. The place where all men of destiny are drawn. Egypt.'

Four

It was a beautiful day in Paris. The kind of day that made men and women want to feel the sun on their faces. The kind of day that made them feel glad to be alive. The sun was high in the sky, a burning circlet in a blue firmament barely trimmed with wisps of white cloud. In the gardens of the Tuileries the smell of roses was strong in the air. A heady aroma that symbolized summer as much as the buzzing of bees that floated on the calm breeze collecting pollen. Flowers throughout the huge gardens were in full bloom, each, it seemed, competing with the others to display the most brilliant colours and tempting scents. A network of wide gravel paths twisted and turned through the gardens, passing ornamental fountains, rockeries and flower beds.

Charles Maurice de Talleyrand paused beside one of the rose bushes, snapped off a bloom just below the head and sniffed it approvingly before attaching it to the lapel of his long frockcoat.

'A day like this makes a man appreciate God and all his works, don't you think, gentlemen?' he said, smiling, looking round at his companions.

'What chance do I have?' Paul Barras sighed. 'I am surrounded by priests.'

He looked first at Talleyrand then at the older, taller man who accompanied them. Emmanuel Joseph Sieyès was in his late forties but appeared older, the ravages of so much childhood illness having wrought its damage on his features.

'You discredit me, Barras,' Talleyrand said. 'Sieyès was formerly a priest. *I* was Bishop of Autun.'

'Eventually defrocked,' Sieyès reminded him triumphantly.

'This is true,' the younger man conceded. 'But I like to think that God's loss has been France's gain.' He chuckled.

They continued walking, their feet crunching the gravel beneath. Seated ahead of them on one of the ornamental benches that were dotted around the impressive gardens was Gohier, another member of the Directory. He was gazing at the massive edifice of the palace itself, his eyes narrowed.

'When the Bourbons were executed we should have destroyed this place,' he said, nodding towards the building. 'As long as it stands it remains a monument to their corruption. To the obscenity of born rulers.'

'What are we if we are not rulers?' Sieyès challenged.

'We were not born to these positions,' Gohier retorted. 'We gained them by our ability, not by our breeding.'

'You cannot judge a man by his breeding. We have already proved that talent, sensitivity and character were not the property of the so-called upper class. Did it help them to survive? No. *We* are the ones who survived.'

'Men of the people,' Talleyrand said, a smile touching his features.

'You find that description amusing?' Barras snapped.

'Come, my friends, you have the privilege and wealth of those born to fortune. Are you any better than those you replaced?' Talleyrand asked.

'For a minister of state, Talleyrand, you speak with the words of sedition,' Barras told him.

'I thought this country was one of free speech now. Am I not entitled to voice my opinions? My position as Minister of Foreign Affairs doesn't prevent me from having my own thoughts, even about those whom I serve.'

'We are not here to discuss the workings of this government.' Gohier's tone was dismissive. 'We are here to discuss General Bonaparte and his latest venture.'

'His latest folly would perhaps be more appropriate,' Barras said sardonically. 'This Oriental expedition is doomed to failure.'

'Then why was it sanctioned in the first place?' Talleyrand demanded. 'You all know that if it succeeds it will yield vast dividends. It will swell France's coffers even more than the Italian campaign did and it also has untold strategic value.'

'What is to be gained by seizing a country so far away?' Gohier wanted to know.

'The policy of any country should be expansion,' Talleyrand informed him. 'Preferably into territories it can colonize and use for its own benefit, whether those benefits be military or economic. The colonization of Egypt offers both.'

'We already have merchants there,' Sieyès reminded his colleagues.

'And a consul general in Cairo as well as consulates in Alexandria, and Rosetta, the two principal ports,'

Talleyrand added. 'We have a larger interest in Egypt than any other country in Europe has.'

'French trade with Egypt amounts to less than six million livres a year,' Barras said. 'It isn't a very impressive figure.'

'But that is from only fifty or sixty merchants dealing in coffee, rice, sugar or cotton,' Talleyrand said. 'And they are constantly harassed by the Mamelukes, the rulers of the province. I think they would welcome outright *seizure* of the country.'

'What do you know of these Mamelukes?' Barras enquired.

'They are a warlike people,' Talleyrand said. 'When they are not fighting amongst themselves they battle the Turks, our allies. They are little more than thieves but very successful ones and their horsemanship is legendary. They live in luxury at the expense of those they rule.'

'Like any monarchs,' Gohier interjected.

'The current rulers, Ibrahim and Murad Bey, have signed a trade treaty with the British,' Talleyrand informed the other men. 'If they gain a foothold there then our problems will multiply ten-fold. In short, gentlemen, if *we* do not take Egypt, someone else will. The Ottoman Empire is the "sick man of Europe". I think it is up to us to administer the cure.'

Sieyès nodded sagely. 'I agree. The loss of our colonies in West India would be lessened by the acquisition of Egypt and its surrounding lands.'

'Egypt is the link joining Africa, Asia and Europe. If General Bonaparte can take it then the possibilities are endless. Trade routes to Arabia and India would become ours. We could deal a crushing blow against England's Asian trade. For, after all, is England not the real enemy?'

'I fear we are throwing away money that would have been better spent elsewhere,' Barras said.

'An invasion of England would be far more expensive than what it has cost to send General Bonaparte and his men to Egypt,' Talleyrand explained. 'By establishing France in Africa, we shall guarantee the peace of Europe.'

'Should we not consider another reason too?' Sieyès broke in. 'The freeing of the captive people of Egypt. If we can restore to them some measure of self-rule then we will be following the ideals of the Republic.'

'An admirable sentiment,' Barras commented. 'But I think there is a reason for us to rejoice in this expedition – a reason that exceeds any financial or cultural considerations.'

The other men looked at him in bewilderment.

'It frees us of the presence of Bonaparte,' Barras explained. 'How long will he be gone? Six months? Longer? It gives us time to consolidate our power against him.'

'The man is a hero,' Gohier snapped. 'He conquered Italy for us. Why should we fear him?'

'Because there is nothing more dangerous than an idle hero,' Barras said quietly. 'Especially when he has control of the army. He is an ambitious man. How long do you think it would be before his ambition extended to the Directory? To us. I tell you now, he would have settled for nothing less than that.'

'You may be right,' Sieyès agreed. 'I fear he would as easily turn against us. Without an enemy to confront he would seek one out.'

'This expedition gives him the chance to pursue his own dreams of glory while helping the Republic,' Barras said.

'Your suspicions, it seems, have no end where our General is concerned,' Talleyrand offered. 'Perhaps it would be better for all of you if he simply did not return.'

'We wish no harm against him,' Sieyès assured him.

Talleyrand shrugged.

'He is a very able general,' Sieyès continued. 'But make no mistake, he wanted to lead this expedition. With the Austrians subdued he has no war to fight. He is merely another general kicking his heels waiting for action, waiting for the chance to be a hero again. We allowed him that chance.'

'You try to hide fear with nobility now,' Talleyrand countered. 'But I myself know how keen he was to set sail. General Bonaparte seeks Egypt for as many complicated reasons as we ourselves.'

'He thinks he's on some kind of mission of liberation and education,' Barras said. 'That's why he's taken so many civilians with him. He has a hundred and sixty-seven members of the Commission of the Sciences and Arts with him. Astronomers, botanists, antiquarians, mathematicians, chemists. He even has a poet with him, Parseval-Grandmaison. What does he hope to do, conquer Egypt or educate it?'

'A little of both,' Talleyrand said.

'He will soon tire of these *savants*,' Barras snapped. 'Bonaparte knows only battle, he will not be interested in their teaching when the time comes.' There was a note of scorn in the Director's voice that Talleyrand found distasteful.

'You seem to harbour a strong dislike of the General, Citizen Barras. Could it be because he stole your mistress?'

Barras shot Talleyrand a vicious glance, aware that the eyes of the other men were also upon him.

The look turned to a sneer. 'He took nothing that I was unwilling to release.'

Talleyrand smiled and began walking along one of the other paths, followed by Gohier and Sieyès.

Barras glared at the statesman's back for a moment longer then strode up alongside him.

'When Alexander conquered Egypt he took thinkers as well as soldiers with him,' Talleyrand said. 'Forty centuries later our own conqueror does the same. Bonaparte and Alexander are very alike in nature.'

'Then I hope our General remembers that Alexander died during his time in the Far East,' Barras chided.

'I'm sure he knows that,' Talleyrand said. 'And much, much more.'

Five

'Tell me I'm not seeing things,' Joubert murmured. 'I'm so weak from lack of food that what I see is not real, is it?'

'It's there, fat man,' Delacor assured him, gazing out across the water, a wan smile on his sallow features.

Lausard too was beginning to wonder if the sight before them was imagined. The result of too long at sea, of too little food. Had the ravages of their terrible journey finally caused them all to begin seeing things, imagining what they *wished* would be there? He felt his stomach contract slightly as *L'Esperance* was rocked by a large wave, but the sight before him – a sight he had begun to doubt he would ever see again – seemed to make even the misery of seasickness dissipate slightly.

Land.

The arrival of the leading ships in the armada had been presaged by a swarm of activity amongst the sailors aboard the frigate and, no doubt, aboard many other ships of the fleet. Up to an hour earlier they had been rushing about above and below deck, for the first time during the voyage seemingly unconcerned by the presence of their unwanted passengers. Intent only on completing the duties assigned to them prior to dropping anchor.

At first Lausard and the other dragoons who had been on deck had watched, bemused, as the sailors had set about their tasks wondering what had precipitated such furious industry. Others were languishing below, either unable or unwilling to drag themselves up, but as the ferocious actions of the sailors grew ever more intense, nearly all of Lausard's unit had managed to find their way up on to the quarterdeck, into the hot sunshine that bathed the fleet, where they now surveyed the glorious sight before them. Even the officers had left the relative comfort of their cabins to watch the flurry of activity.

Lausard found himself standing beside Lieutenant Royere, who was gazing around him at the sailors, at the land and at the other ships that lay anchored a few hundred yards offshore. Men clambered with incredible speed and purpose through the maze of rigging above them, tying and untying ropes, securing or releasing sails. Some of the watching troops didn't know what was more amazing, the *sight* of land or the preparations necessary to reach it. Sails were furled, pennants fluttered from mizzen masts, each carrying a different message, but what those messages were Lausard had no idea. Men high up in the crows' nests of ships signalled to each other with flags. To the army it was another silent and foreign language, but all that they cared about was the sight of land. Their journey was over. At last they would be able to leave the ships that had carried them so far and caused them so much suffering. Wherever they were, whichever foe they were to face had to be preferable to the hell they had experienced since leaving Toulon.

'I had an uncle in the navy,' Royere muttered, watching the dizzying array of flags that streamed from the leading ships. 'He used to tell me about sea voyages when I was a child.'

'Did he tell you how uncomfortable they were?' Lausard wanted to know.

Royere grinned. 'Somehow he neglected to mention that.'

'Do you know where we are, Lieutenant?' Lausard turned to Royere.

'I have no idea.'

'Weren't even the officers told of our destination? Is it *that* important? I don't understand the need for mystery.'

'Perhaps if we'd have known where we were going before we sailed, we'd have all deserted,' Sonnier offered.

'Well, you'd know all about deserting, wouldn't you?' Delacor riled him.

Sonnier turned away.

'Do the naval officers know our destination?' Lausard pressed.

'We have had little contact with them, Lausard. We occasionally eat our meals together but they tend to keep to themselves, as do we. There is no love lost between the army and the navy.'

'We've noticed.'

'They see us as unwanted baggage,' Royere continued. 'Nothing more. If they could cast us all overboard I have no doubt they would.'

Lausard looked around and saw Captain Milliere making his way slowly along the deck, peering towards the outcrop of land that so many of the French ships were anchoring close to.

Milliere was in his early thirties. He was a slim but powerfully built man who sported a thick moustache and a swarthy complexion, giving him the appearance of having some Italian or Spanish blood in him. The most striking thing about him were his eyes. Emerald green, they seemed to glow as if lit from within by a searing iridescence.

He joined Royere and Lausard and gazed out at the land.

It was inhospitable. A tiny stretch of beach was abruptly halted by towering cliffs that seemed to form a sheer face, lowering down at the French as if challenging them.

'How do we get horses up there?' Royere contemplated.

'We don't,' Milliere told him. 'I received orders this morning that we are to stay aboard ship. Cavalry will not be needed for this landing.'

Those men within earshot groaned audibly.

'So we're to be left on these stinking ships while the infantry take all the glory?' Charvet bemoaned.

'*And* all the booty?' Delacor hissed. 'By the time those bastards have finished, there'll be nothing left for us. No gold or silver, no food or water.'

'Two hundred of General Bonaparte's guides will be going ashore,' Milliere continued. 'Apart from that, it's an infantry job according to orders.'

'Orders from whom?' Lausard demanded.

'General Dumas himself,' Milliere explained. 'Believe me, *he's* not too happy about it. He always was impatient. I served under him back in 'ninety-three.' The captain smiled wistfully. 'The first thing he did when he took over as General was to tell his staff officers to strip off their gold and silver rank badges. He said they smacked of luxury and corruption.' Milliere chuckled. 'He said they should replace them with wooden items.'

'So, when do *we* get off these stinking ships?' Roussard wanted to know.

'When we reach our final destination,' Bonet offered. 'This obviously isn't it.'

'So where the hell are we?' Delacor insisted.

Milliere looked up towards the forecastle of the ship and saw a group of blue-uniformed naval officers poring over a map.

'That's the captain.' Milliere pointed to a small man in a long frock coat. 'Verdoux. He would know where we are.'

'Could you ask him, sir?' Lausard enquired.

'Does it matter? We're stuck on this ship until General Bonaparte says otherwise.'

'But if we know where we are, why we are anchored here, we might have some idea of *why*?' Lausard persisted.

'To take on fresh rations and fresh water, I should think. We can do nothing, men, except wait.'

'And suffer,' added Royere.

'Look,' Rocheteau said, grabbing Lausard's arm and pointing towards one of the other anchored ships.

As they watched, a rowing boat was lowered over the side of the ship into the water below. The small vessel rose on a wave then seemed to settle momentarily, and the men watched as the sailors in the boat retrieved oars and pushed them into the water. Next rope ladders were hurled over the side of the ship and, as the dragoons looked on, blue-jacketed infantrymen began to make the unsteady descent into the waiting boats. Elsewhere, lengths of thick hemp were tossed over and the foot soldiers climbed down as best they could, gripping on to the rope for dear life, afraid to look down at the sea for fear of falling into it.

The sailors tried to keep the boats steady as the first of the infantry reached the bottom of the ladders, but the surf was choppy and it was an almost impossible task. The first two men reached the boat with relative ease, the third jumped from the bottom rung of the ladder and landed heavily, but a fourth man misjudged his footing and toppled into the water. Sailors dragged him from the water and left him gasping in the bottom of the boat. Another man fell in, losing his musket in the process. He too was dragged aboard after a struggle.

Those climbing down the lengths of rope seemed to be having even less luck.

Lausard watched as a man inched his way down the thick hemp only to lose his handhold. He plummeted fully twenty feet into the dark sea, his shriek of terror rapidly silenced by the watery embrace of the ocean. He did not resurface.

More and more men were beginning to clamber uncertainly into the waiting boat and, elsewhere, other ships were disgorging their terrified cargoes into similar transports. Each of the boats took about thirty men and the dragoons watched as the first of them struck off for land, the sailors forcing the oars through the churning surf towards the shore. More boats gradually filled with infantry and followed the leading vessel until a flotilla of about a dozen of the small craft was heading through the choppy waters to the beach. Only by Herculean effort did the sailors manage to prevent some of the craft from overturning in the savage waves, and Lausard could see the infantrymen clinging desperately to the sides of the rowing boats to prevent themselves fall-ing out.

More men were pouring down the rope ladders, other unfortunates sliding down the ropes with varying degrees of success.

Another man went under but was pulled to safety.

An officer, trying to climb one-handed while he held his sword scabbard away from his leg to prevent it entangling in the rope ladder, slipped close to the bottom and fell into the water, knocking a sailor in with him. Both men disappeared beneath the water.

Efforts were made to rescue them but only the sailor emerged from the dark water, coughing and spluttering, helped aboard by his comrades.

Gaston shuddered as he spotted several pieces of equip-ment floating on the sea, but noticing the boy's reaction, Roussard put a reassuring hand on his shoulder.

'You're lighter than us,' he told him. 'You'll float.'

Gaston didn't seem particularly cheered by the thought and continued to watch the parade of infantry clambering uncertainly down the side of the ships into the rowing boats, which ferried them ashore, turned around and repeated their task.

The disembarkation of infantry continued for what seemed like an eternity, watched by the solemn dra-goons.

'Why the hell are we standing here?' Carbonne asked. 'If we're not landing, what's the point?'

'What else shall we do, then?' Giresse said. 'Go below and sing songs of victory? Count our back-pay? Cook ourselves a meal? What else *have* we to do?'

'I wish we *could* cook ourselves a meal,' Joubert com-plained.

'Do you think they'll bring back fresh water, Alain?' Rocheteau asked.

'Fresh water *and* food, I hope,' Lausard said, still gazing fixedly at the boatsful of infantry being buffeted by the waves as they were rowed ashore.

'They don't care about us; they're not going to bring us anything back,' Delacor whined. 'They'll be too concerned with their own well-being.'

'General Bonaparte will have sent commissaries ashore,' Bonet said. 'They'll take care of our food.'

'To hell with that,' Delacor said angrily. 'I want to go ashore.'

'Don't be ridiculous,' Giresse snapped.

'What's so ridiculous about wanting to get off this hulk?' Delacor challenged. 'What's so insane about wanting to find fresh water and food? Am I the only one who is sick of being on this floating dung-heap?'

A number of the other men shook their heads.

'We can't go ashore, it's against orders,' Tabor said. 'We have to do as we're told, don't we?'

'You half-wit,' snarled Delacor.

'You heard Milliere,' Rocheteau insisted. 'This is an infantry operation.'

'I heard him say that we weren't needed,' Delacor said. 'He didn't say we *couldn't* go ashore.'

'Then you'd better start swimming now.' Rocheteau's comment was accompanied by a burst of laughter from the other men.

'What kind of riches do you think are there?' Delacor motioned towards the mountains. 'We have no idea what country that is or what we might find there. We could find fortunes for ourselves if we went ashore.'

'We could also find death,' Roussard countered. 'We

don't even know where we are. We could be on the other side of the world for all we know.'

'I don't think we've been sailing *that* long,' Lausard observed, amidst a chorus of chuckles. 'But Delacor does have a point. We don't know how long the infantry are going to be ashore. We don't know how long we're going to be stuck here waiting.'

'What are you getting at, Alain?' Rocheteau pressed.

'Just thinking aloud.' Lausard looked around to see the dragoon captain climbing a narrow flight of steps towards the forecastle, followed by Royere.

The two cavalrymen were greeted with frosty stares from Captain Verdoux and his staff and Lausard watched the men gesturing over the map then towards the craggy outcrops of land, towards the cliffs rising from the sea like towering monoliths. After a moment or two the cavalry officers made their way back, Royere pausing against the guardrail as the ship lurched violently. Then he and Milliere rejoined their men.

'That,' said Milliere, gesturing towards the cliffs, 'is the island of Malta.'

'Where the hell is that?' Delacor wanted to know.

Bonet stepped forward. 'So, we're still in the Mediterranean,' he said. 'I thought we were.'

'Thanks for the georgraphy lesson, schoolmaster,' Delacor chided, 'but that doesn't mean anything to me.'

'Gozo and Malta,' Bonet continued, 'they're islands about fifty miles south of Sicily.'

'That's right,' Milliere told him. 'We saw them on Verdoux's map.'

'Does *he* know what's going on?' Lausard asked.

'If he does he isn't saying,' Royere elaborated. 'Troops are landing on both islands. We're here to capture them.'

'Not *us*,' Delacor hissed, 'just the stinking infantry.'

'Malta,' Lausard murmured under his breath.

As he watched, another of the rowing boats reached land, its occupants scrambling gratefully from it.

After another hour there were nearly two hundred men ashore. And still the ferrying of infantrymen continued.

'So, if Malta isn't our final destination, where is Bonaparte taking us?' Carbonne asked.

'Just shut up and throw the dice,' Rocheteau urged.

The men were seated in a wide circle on the quarterdeck of *L'Esperance*. Some had removed their tunics in the heat and were using them as makeshift seats. Carbonne had tied his shirt around his bald head to protect his shiny pate from the ravages of the sun, which was beating down mercilessly on the anchored French armada.

Lausard glanced overboard every now and then to see rowing boats still taking infantrymen ashore. He consulted his watch and noted that the French had been landing on Malta for over three hours now. The first men to land had long since disappeared into the interior of the island, not up the sheer face of the cliffs as Lausard had expected, but through deep ravines that cut through the granite façades like natural passageways. The actual journey inland appeared fairly easy, at least from the quarterdeck of the frigate. Lausard wished that he and his unit had been ordered ashore, not merely so that they could feel solid ground beneath their feet, but because anything, even the prospect of battle and possibly death, was preferable to the endless waiting he and his comrades had been sentenced to. He was also overcome by a feeling of worthlessness, as if he was superfluous to this operation. The blow dealt to his pride was almost as keenly felt as the ravages of seasickness and, in both cases, he was powerless to alter the situation.

The other men of his unit seemed to have faced the prospect of remaining ship-bound with varied attitudes. Some were relieved that they would not have to fight too soon, while others longed for the opportunity to vent their frustration on their opponents at having been cooped up for so long. Others coveted landing so that they could feel firm ground again and possibly find fresh food and water. But, as hordes of infantrymen were ferried ashore, all the dragoons could do was watch helplessly.

There wasn't much to bet with. What little pay the men had received before leaving Toulon had long ago been gambled away, won back and gambled away again. In fact, the money never left the ship. A man might lose his money and his watch one day and win the whole lot back the next, only to have it taken from him once more in another bout of boredom-banishing gambling. However, after twenty-three days, even the gambling had become monotonous. The men could muster little enthusiasm for the odd roll of dice, especially when the stakes they were playing for were so meagre. As Carbonne rolled, the kitty comprised two half-eaten salt biscuits, a gold earring, two buttons and a battered clay pipe that had no tobacco in it. It was hardly a prize to set men's pulses racing.

'Where did Milliere and Royere go?' Giresse asked, noticing that the officers weren't present on deck.

'Back to their cabins probably,' Delacor grunted. 'To sit in comfort while we all fry out here like fish drying in the sun.'

'So, even they don't know where we're going,' Rostov observed. 'I wonder why Bonaparte hasn't even told his officers what our final destination is?'

'Perhaps he doesn't trust them. I know *I* don't,' Delacor said. 'I don't trust any of these officers.'

'They probably feel the same about you,' Lausard told him. 'After all, it isn't easy to trust a rapist, is it?'

Delacor glared at Lausard menacingly, but Lausard held his gaze defiantly.

'Coming from a thief that's a bold statement,' Delacor snapped.

'I stole out of necessity,' Lausard countered. 'It wasn't necessary for you to rape a woman, was it?'

A heavy silence had descended over the circle of men, all eyes turned towards the two arguing troopers.

'That's all in the past now,' Delacor hissed. 'What does it matter? We're all criminals. No man here is better than any other.'

'Are we going to gamble or fight?' Rostov prompted.

Finally, Delacor waved his hand in Lausard's direction, aware that the younger man's gaze was still fixed on him. 'Give me the dice,' he demanded.

'This is a waste of time,' Sonnier grunted. 'Why are we gambling over biscuits and buttons?'

'Because we've got nothing else to gamble with,' Rocheteau reminded him.

'You can bet the infantry will have plenty to gamble with by the time these islands are taken,' Giresse observed.

'That's what I told you.' Delacor hurled the dice. 'They'll be able to take what they like and we sit here rotting and penniless.'

'Valetta has a higher percentage of prostitutes than any other city in Europe you know,' Bonet offered. 'Valetta is the capital of Malta.'

'More prostitutes than Paris?' Giresse's eyes lit up.

Bonet nodded.

'Even more reason to go ashore then.' Giresse chuckled. Some of the other men laughed too.

'You can bet the infantry will be having their fill of the women too,' Delacor said.

'And the food,' Joubert added, rubbing his huge stomach.

'Then perhaps we *should* go ashore,' Lausard said quietly.

The other men looked at him.

'When? You heard Milliere, we're under orders to stay aboard ship,' Bonet said.

'He said that he had received orders that the cavalry were not needed for this operation,' Lausard reminded his companion. 'He didn't say we *had* to stay on this ship.'

'But how do we get ashore?' Roussard enquired.

'The same way as the infantry. By rowing boat.'

'When?' Delacor asked.

'Tonight. We take a boat and we go ashore. We explore this place for ourselves. We find our own food, our own water, our own plunder and our women.'

'We'll be court-martialled if we're caught,' Sonnier said.

'I don't intend to be caught,' Lausard said flatly, his eyes scanning the ring of troops around him. 'Who is with me?'

Six

As Napoleon Bonaparte sat on the edge of his bed in his stateroom aboard *L'Orient*, he listened to the creaking of the massive flagship as it bobbed gently in the waters. Outside he could see the blackness of the night occasionally disturbed by lights aboard some of the other moored vessels. They twinkled like fireflies in the seemingly palpable gloom beyond. He cradled a glass of water in one hand and sat, head bowed, blinking hard, his room lit only by a few candles.

Major Jean Andoche Junot stood gazing down at his superior. He thought how small the General looked, sitting there in just a shirt, breeches and boots that looked two sizes too small for him. This wiry Corsican didn't look like the conqueror of Italy, the scourge of the Austrian army and the man who intended to subjugate Egypt. To Junot, a powerfully built man in his twenty-eighth year, he looked more like the man Paris society had so cruelly nicknamed 'Puss in Boots'. And yet, Junot, who had served with Bonaparte as his secretary at Toulon back in 1793, then as his aide-de-camp in Italy, knew that the

General had the demeanour not of a gentle cat but of a great predator.

Bonaparte's eyes darted around the room as he looked up, and Junot saw that familiar radiance and vitality in them. Junot had woken the General just minutes earlier, and the two men had since been joined by Berthier, who now stood close to the writing desk in one corner of the room, furiously scribbling on a piece of paper, the quill scratching loudly in the stillness of the room.

Junot had been ashore that day along with the infantry and his commander and he had been surprised at how easily the two islands had fallen. Gozo without a shot being fired, and then, but for a few half-hearted volleys from the local militia, Malta itself had been overrun. The major had felt something akin to disgust at how easily the Maltese had surrendered their homeland. He himself had been wounded three times in the service of France during the last nine years, the last time in August of 1796 when he'd been seriously injured but had managed to despatch six of the enemy during the engagement. He had no time for cowardice or for the men who sought refuge in white flags and raised arms. His dislike of the Maltese, therefore, had been instant and deep-seated. Two of them now waited outside the stateroom, patiently preparing themselves to be summoned before the leader of their conquerors. Junot hadn't liked the look of the men who had arrived at *L'Orient* seeking a truce. They looked like men whose only desire was to please their invaders. They came seeking peace not with resentment and bitterness in their hearts but with relief. For that he despised them.

Bonaparte got to his feet and buttoned his shirt. He looked at his two companions. 'What of these warrior knights, Junot? What do they want here?'

'They want peace, General,' the major told his commander. 'But they are not warriors. They are cowards. They didn't stand against our men today. They sought only to surrender. They have no hearts.'

'Did you expect them to stand against the army that conquered Italy so easily?' Bonaparte asked. 'Against the men who brushed aside the military might of Austria like so much dust? Perhaps you judge them too harshly.'

'They embraced our men as liberators, not as conquerors,' the major offered finally, a note of distaste in his tone.

'Surely that showed sense.'

'It showed cowardice.'

Bonaparte slapped him on the shoulder.

'The two men who are here were instrumental in helping us take these islands so easily,' Berthier interjected. 'But for their influence we might have faced stiffer opposition. They are Republicans, both of them. They told many of their colleagues how futile it would be to resist us.'

'So, they are traitors too?' Junot sneered.

'If that is the word you choose to use,' Berthier said. 'Their deceit proved to be a powerful weapon.'

'We do not need the help of traitors,' Junot snapped.

'Do not underestimate the value of deceit, Junot,' Bonaparte said, smiling. 'Sometimes deceit can be as powerful as fifty cannon.'

'We should thank them, not despise them,' Berthier observed. 'If the Maltese had resisted then we might have lost many men today. Men we cannot afford to lose.'

Junot remained unimpressed.

'Best show these men in,' Bonaparte said finally, watching as the major crossed to the door and opened it.

He ushered in two figures whose faces looked deathly

pale in the dull glow of the candles in the stateroom. They both stood sheepishly at the threshold, heads bowed, hands clasped before them like naughty children facing the wrath of an angry teacher.

'Come in.' Bonaparte watched as the men entered, Junot closing the door behind them. 'Would you care for some wine?'

Both men shook their heads.

'Which of you is de Ransijat?'

The shorter of the two men looked up. 'The Treasurer of the Knights of St John,' he said.

'We are aware of the position you held,' Bonaparte informed him. 'And of the history of your order. You have a noble tradition but you and your kind have no place in this modern world. You are relics of the past.' He sipped at his water. 'Where is your Grand Master?'

'He awaits you on the island,' de Ransijat said, 'to welcome you.'

'So you are his messengers. His errand boys. Well, then take some news back for your leader.'

'Grand Master Von Hompesch desires peace, General Bonaparte.' The other man, taller and more sturdily built than his companion, with a white moustache, spoke.

'And who are you?'

'My name is Fay. Commissioner of Fortifications for the Order.'

'All we ever wanted was peace,' de Ransijat added. 'We have no quarrel with France or with the Republic. We are Frenchmen ourselves.'

'And yet you ruled this island like monarchs. Like the Bourbons who ruled France. You are aware of *their* fate?'

Both men nodded.

'You shall have your peace,' Bonaparte continued. 'France and I would gain nothing by destroying you but we gain much by your allegiance. I am also aware of your efforts and those of some of your comrades in the months leading up to our arrival and I will not overlook your contribution.'

'What is to happen to the Order?' Fay wanted to know.

'It will be disbanded. All knights under the age of sixty will leave the island within three days. They may take money with them for travel expenses but no more than two hundred and forty francs.'

Berthier sat down at the writing desk, dipped his quill into ink and began writing.

'What of the Grand Master?'

'A principality will be obtained for him in Germany,' Bonaparte said. 'He should be happy to return to his homeland. He will be paid a pension of three hundred thousand francs a year. That is more than generous compensation.'

'And the other knights?' de Ransijat enquired.

Bonaparte shrugged. 'They will receive pensions dependent upon their age. Between seven hundred and one thousand francs. As for Malta itself, the island is to become part of the French Republic. A commission, headed by one of my men, will act as the government of this province. I will also expect a number of knights to join my expedition.'

'To where?' Fay asked.

'That need not concern you now. During the next few days I will detail men to make an inventory of your treasures. We will take what we need from you.'

'We have possessions beyond value, General,' de Ransijat

55

said, his expression darkening. 'I beg you not to touch those.'

'What are these things you value so highly?' Bonaparte demanded. 'Everything has a price.'

'We have a splinter of the True Cross,' de Ransijat said. 'The symbol of our Lord's death. I beseech you, do not deprive us of such a priceless gift. If you steal that you steal not just from us but from God himself.'

'I am no thief,' Bonaparte said sternly. 'I have no need of pieces of wood. They cannot buy me provisions. Keep your splinter.'

The Knights' treasurer bowed his head gratefully. 'May God smile upon you,' he said.

'God may wear whichever expression he pleases. It matters little to me.'

The only sound inside the stateroom was the scratching of quill on parchment as Berthier continued to write. Bonaparte stood in the dimly lit room eyeing his visitors, aware that Junot was also running an appraising, if somewhat scornful eye over the two men. Berthier finally finished writing, blew on the ink and handed the paper to Bonaparte, who scanned it quickly before passing it to de Ransijat. The knight bowed low and took it.

'Take that to your Grand Master. Tell him I will come ashore in Valetta tomorrow. Remind him how lucky he is that I do not come carrying a sword.'

The two knights again bowed then turned to leave the room as Junot ushered them out.

'There is still much to be done here, Berthier,' Bonaparte said. 'Only then can the true purpose of this expedition be fulfilled. Only then will we find our destiny.'

'And what of Nelson?' Berthier asked.

'He will not stop us. He has too few ships and is too far away.'

'How can you be sure? Admiral Brueys is convinced that—'

'Admiral Brueys is afraid of this one-eyed Englishman,' Bonaparte snapped, cutting his companion short.

'Perhaps with good reason.'

'Nelson and the entire English fleet will not prevent us from reaching Egypt. Nothing will stop me from treading in the footsteps of Alexander.'

Seven

The rowing boat was about fifteen feet long, suspended from a hemp cradle just above the quarterdeck of *L'Esperance*. Like the six others dotted around the ship it represented the only means of escape for the occupants of the frigate should it sink. It swung gently to and fro with the swell of the sea. The strength of the waves seemed to have grown with the coming of night and now, as the blackness covered the ocean in the early hours of the morning, the sea and the sky appeared to have merged into one impenetrable umbra. The smell of salt water, noticeable all through the heat of day, seemed, strangely, to be even more prominent in the stillness of night.

Lausard, Rocheteau and Delacor took hold of one of the ropes holding the rowing boat in position while, at the other end, Giresse, Carbonne and Rostov mirrored their movements.

Sonnier stood close by, eyes scanning the gloom, peering around for any signs of movement.

Gaston too was present on the quarterdeck, watching

and listening for any who might interrupt this *sojourn* by the men in the unit.

The lines were released and the men braced themselves, the boat heading for the churning waves that seemed to be slamming into the side of the frigate with unpleasant ferocity. Lausard looked over, down towards the black ocean, and saw the white crests of waves breaking against the hull. Every so often a drizzle of spray would fly up like a salty curtain. He wiped sea water from his face and nodded towards the thick lengths of rope the men had secured to the central mast.

These were guarded by Moreau and Tabor who looked on with a combination of bemusement and nervousness, watching as their six colleagues began their descent towards the rowing boat with nothing but their grip on the rope preventing them from falling twenty feet into the sea.

Lausard was the first to descend, moving hand over powerful hand down the rope towards the bobbing rowing boat. He could hear the sea churning beneath him, felt the tilts and sways of the frigate as it was left to the mercy of the tide. With infinite care he continued his climb down, looking below only when he was sure he was within sight of the rowing boat. It was ten feet below now, he guessed. He continued to climb down. With less than six feet to go he paused, wondering if it would be safe to jump this final distance, but somewhere at the back of his mind the thought nagged that the bottom of the rowing boat might give way beneath him. He may well plunge straight through the flimsy wood into the black water.

Above him, the other men were climbing down. He heard Delacor cursing as he eased himself down the rope. Rocheteau kept looking down and shaking his head. Giresse made the entire descent with his eyes closed, gripping the rope until his knuckles turned white. Like green-clad monkeys, the dragoons eased themselves carefully down the side of *L'Esperance*, past the closed gun-ports and the sailors inside who neither suspected nor cared for the antics of these troublesome soldiers. If they had known, they would probably have hoped that all of them ended up dead in the water.

Lausard saw that he was about three feet from the rowing boat. He let go of the rope and fell the short distance into the small craft, grunting as he hit the bottom, relieved when he didn't hear the sound of splintering wood. He looked up to see Rocheteau about to join him, the corporal also dropping the last couple of feet into the boat. Both men grabbed oars, steadying the vessel as their companions cautiously made their way down the ropes to join them. Carbonne hesitated as he dangled helplessly against the side of the frigate, afraid to let go of the rope.

The other men urged him to let go, to jump the final few feet as they had but the former executioner kept a strong grip on the rope, terrified to release himself to the forces of gravity or, more particularly, to the hungry sea. A wave struck the side of the ship, splashing water up and over him, causing the rowing boat to rise several feet into the air.

'Jump or you'll get us all drowned,' Rocheteau snarled.

'I can't let go.' Carbonne's huge hands were locked on the hemp as surely as if someone had sewn them to it.

'Come on, or we'll leave you there,' Delacor threatened.

'Let go, Carbonne,' Lausard said. 'Do it now.' As he spoke he raised the oar he was holding and prodded the big man hard in the ribs. The shock made Carbonne lose his grip and he fell from the rope, tumbling the last three feet into the rowing boat and landing with a thud.

'You could have got us all killed, you fool,' Delacor hissed.

'Shut up and row,' Rocheteau commanded, forcing another oar into Delacor's hand.

Each of the men took hold of a shaft and, on a signal from Rocheteau, they began to force the blades of the oars deep into the water. Waves rocked the boat and drenched the men with spray but they continued rowing, forcing their way through the surf towards the towering cliffs, which seemed to have thrust their way up from the sea like accusatory fingers. But beneath those cliffs was land, and it was the thought of reaching that land that gave the men the added strength to drive the boat on, fighting back that ever present feeling of nausea. Lausard fought back the all-too-familiar feeling, and soon, as he peered through the gloom he saw that the shore was mere yards away. He tapped Rochteau's shoulder and the corporal also saw the welcoming sight of dry land.

With renewed vigour the men worked the oars, their need to be free of the clutches of the sea reaching a state of near desperation now.

The rowing boat finally hit the beach with a thud, the impact causing Rostov and Giresse to topple from the stationary craft. The Russian fell on to the sand, a smile spreading across his grizzled features as he felt the grains between his fingers. Water lapped against his legs but it didn't appear to bother him. Carbonne too seemed oblivious to the tide washing ashore, drenching his already sodden uniform. He was crawling on all fours up the beach, squeezing the sand beneath his large fingers.

Lausard and the others leaped clear of the boat and dragged it up the beach, aware of an incredible dizziness sweeping over them. Lausard felt as if his legs might buckle at any second. He realized it was because they had not walked on firm ground for so long. He dropped down into the sand, a combination of relief and joy enveloping him. Twenty-three days had passed since any of them had been on solid ground and no one knew how many more days would elapse before they would be again. But at that moment, all that mattered was they were ashore.

Giresse rolled over and over in the sand, like a child freed of restraints for the first time in its life.

Delacor picked up a handful of the sand and kissed it.

The men hauled the boat further up the beach, noticing some bushes growing close to the base of one of the cliffs. Beyond that natural curtain of flora, Lausard could see one of the many narrow paths that cut through the cliffs. He glanced down at his watch, squinting in the gloom. It was just after one.

'It'll be light in less than five hours,' he said. 'Let's not waste any time. We have to be back aboard before dawn.'

'Let's find what we came ashore for,' Giresse said, smiling. 'Women.'

'And food.'

'And drink.'

'And booty.'

'Come on,' Lausard ordered heading towards the path. 'Let's move.'

The dragoons headed off towards the interior of the island.

The smell of oranges was overpowering and quite magnificent. Lausard was the first to detect the wonderful aroma, which seemed all the more intense in the stillness of the night. He realized that it was coming from a low-walled garden surrounding a house up ahead. The fragrance caused his mouth to water and, within seconds, all six men were running towards the low wall. They climbed over it with ease and found themselves surrounded by dozens of small trees, each bearing scores of the ripe fruit. Delacor pulled several of the oranges from a branch and bit into the first without even removing the skin.

Lausard tore open some of the fruit and sank his teeth into it, savouring the flavour, allowing the sweet juice to run down his chin. He ate one after another, gorging himself on this first taste of fresh food for almost a month. His companions were doing the same, stuffing the fruit they couldn't eat into their pockets.

It seemed as though succulent fruit trees stretched for miles, and as the men walked on they felt as if they were in heaven. The foul taste of salt biscuits and salt beef was forgotten, even the horrors of their voyage were momentarily pushed to the backs of their minds.

The grass that carpeted the tree-lined area was covered in a heavy dew and Lausard suddenly pulled off his jacket and shirt and rolled in the moisture, enjoying the cooling caress of the wet grass. It was the closest he had come to a wash since leaving Toulon and it was an opportunity he didn't intend to miss. Giresse copied him, smearing the dew over his torso and face. He even knelt to sniff the earth beneath, the familiar musky scent so welcoming after the constant stench of vomit, sea water and unwashed companions.

'I think we've landed in heaven,' he said, smiling. 'All I need now is a woman and my life will be complete.

I could die here and now and I would be a happy man.'

'I'm just glad to be off that stinking ship.' Delacor was nibbling at yet another orange.

'It's so beautiful here,' Carbonne commented, looking around him at the trees and blossoms.

About two hundred yards further on, half hidden by the thickly planted orange trees, was a house. A whitestone dwelling with a slate roof and olive vines entwined around it.

'Let's see if they've got anything worth taking,' Delacor said, getting to his feet. 'I'll bet the infantry have scraped everything clean on this island. I told you they would.'

Lausard finally got to his feet, slung his jacket over his shoulder and wandered after his companions, his pace unhurried. He wanted to enjoy the peacefulness and beauty of this place for as long as he could. He pulled a blossom from a low branch and sniffed it.

Up ahead, Delacor and the others had reached the house, where they could see that its back door was open.

'No sentries,' Rocheteau observed.

'They'll have pushed on into the interior by now,' Lausard said.

'How can you be sure?' Delacor questioned.

'Our troops were landed here to capture arms and supplies, not farms.' Lausard pushed past Delacor and strode through the door into the kitchen. There was bread on the table. Even a half-empty bottle of wine.

'Giresse was right,' Rocheteau said, joining his companion inside the kitchen. 'We *have* landed in heaven.' He snatched up the loaf and bit off a piece of it.

The other men entered the kitchen, their eyes widening with delight at the sight of the food and drink.

Rocheteau handed a piece of the bread to Rostov, who ate heartily, while Delacor snatched up the wine and downed several great gulps before handing the bottle to Carbonne.

Giresse began pulling cupboards open. He found flour, maize, biscuits and even cheese. The smell of the food was overpoweringly welcoming and he grabbed as much as he could.

'It's strange,' Lausard said, accepting a piece of bread from Rocheteau. 'There are no signs of a struggle. No evidence of fighting.'

'Who cares?' Delacor said, pulling open drawers with one hand while gripping a lump of cheese with the other.

'It looks as if the inhabitants fled,' Lausard said, wandering through into the other part of the house, noticing how immaculately kept it was. 'Let's move on, see if we can find our way to a village or a town, perhaps we can find out what happened.'

'What about the food?' Rostov wanted to know.

'We'll carry as much as we can. We should take some back for the others on the ship.'

'To hell with them,' Delacor growled. 'They should have come ashore themselves, let them go without.'

Lausard threw him a disdainful look then headed back into the kitchen. He pulled the cloth from the table and began stacking fruit, bread and other provisions upon it.

When he'd finished he pulled the four corners together and tied them, forming a makeshift sack. This he fastened to his belt.

Delacor had moved into the other part of the house and was searching for valuables. Unable to find anything he stormed upstairs and the other men heard him clumping about angrily. They heard a couple of muffled oaths and then he thudded back downstairs to rejoin his companions.

'I told you those bastards in the infantry would take everything,' he snapped. 'There's nothing to be had in this place.'

'Why didn't they take the food?' Rocheteau questioned. 'That would have been more important than riches.'

'Nothing is more important than riches,' Delacor said.

'Money's no good when you're starving,' Lausard reminded him. 'You can't eat gold, can you?'

'Joubert could.' Giresse chuckled. 'That fat man could eat anything. I've got some bread for him. It should stop him grumbling for a few minutes.'

'To hell with him,' Delacor hissed. 'To hell with all of them. They're not sharing any of *my* food.'

'Remember that when *you* want something of *theirs*, Delacor,' Lausard warned him. 'We are all comrades now, we share everything within the unit.'

'Not I.'

'There will come a time when you need the help of others.' Lausard took a step towards him. 'And when that time comes think back to this day.'

The two men glared at each other, until Lausard pushed past his colleague. The other dragoons followed, striding through the house until they reached the small front garden. Beyond it was a narrow road, little more than a dirt track. Lausard saw the marks of many boots in the dust and realized that the infantry had come this way earlier in the day. The road sloped up sharply towards a range of low hills, and above those hills he could see the reflection of many lights illuminating the night sky. The other men also noticed them as they walked along unhurriedly, passing more houses on either side of the road. All the dwellings were as untouched as the first one, and Lausard's suspicion that the inhabitants had fled without any resistance seemed to be correct.

'That must be Valetta up ahead,' he said, pointing towards the crest of the hill and the lights beyond. 'The capital.'

'I hope Bonet was right about it having so many prostitutes,' Giresse said excitedly.

'I hope there's a decent inn,' Rostov pondered. 'I want a drink.'

They were close to the top of the ridge now and they heard voices on the reverse slope. French voices.

The men crested the ridge and found themselves confronted by blue-clad infantrymen. They were sitting in a circle, some lying on the dewy grass, others sitting cross-legged, passing a bottle of wine among them. One man was smoking a pipe; two others were munching contentedly on pieces of bread. They were gathered around the dying embers of a camp fire that seemed scarcely necessary in the heat of the night. Beyond, the dragoons could clearly see down into the heart of Valetta, its streets well lit and swamped with French troops.

'Where did you lot come from?' a tall corporal asked, getting to his feet and running appraising eyes over the dragoons. 'I thought all the troops were landed this morning.'

'That's just like the cavalry,' another man shouted. 'They arrive only when the fighting is over.'

A chorus of laughter rang around the infantrymen.

'And what use would these have been?' another observed. 'They haven't even got any horses.'

'I see no horse but I see a horse's arse,' Lausard said, looking at the infantryman.

It was the dragoons' turn to laugh.

'Was the fighting so fierce you needed us, then?' Rocheteau asked.

'They hardly fired a shot, these Maltese,' the corporal informed him. 'Those that didn't turn and run got on their knees to greet us. Just as their women did.'

'Only most of them got on their backs to show their gratitude,' a soldier nearby called and more raucous laughter filled the air. 'There are some rare beauties here. Dark eyed and mysterious, like sirens.'

'Where are they?' Giresse wanted to know.

'In Valetta.' The corporal gestured towards the town beyond. 'You'd better hurry though, they've been busy.'

As the dragoons passed the infantry they heard more laughter.

'Is that why you've left your horses behind, boys?' called an infantryman. 'Do you plan to ride something else tonight?'

The closer they got to the outskirts of the town, the more troops they saw. Infantrymen were walking about, cooking, sitting talking, smoking and generally enjoying being back on dry land, however short their stay might be. Lausard saw one man sitting with his back against a house darning his socks. He nodded amicably towards the dragoons as they passed. Close by, five men were gambling and Delacor heard the unmistakable chink of coin on coin.

He turned around, looking longingly at the pile of gold coins in the middle of the men.

'See, I told you they'd have taken plunder,' he said. 'They must have got it here; they can't be using their own pay.'

'That's for sure,' Giresse echoed. 'I haven't had any pay since we left Italy.'

There was a church up ahead to their right, the doors open wide. Men were ambling in and out as if they were on some kind of pilgrimage. Lausard noticed that many were carrying bundles, which on closer inspection he could see ranged from candlesticks to pieces of altar cloth. Delacor quickened his pace, walking ahead of his companions.

'Those thieving bastards. They've even robbed the church.'

'Damn them for doing it before *we* got here,' Rocheteau said, also walking ahead.

'Alain, look.' Giresse was pointing towards a two-storey building with balconies outside its upper windows. A woman with flowing dark hair, dressed only in a diaphanous white robe, was leaning over the rail, looking down at the scores of French troops moving through the streets below.

As Giresse looked on longingly, the woman was joined by another, slightly younger woman who was holding a sheet around her slender body. She too gazed down at the Frenchmen, even waving to Giresse, who returned the gesture frantically.

'I'm going in,' he said, grinning. 'These women have obviously been waiting for a man of my charms, a man who knows how to treat them.'

Lausard smiled, watching as Carbonne joined his companion, wiping a hand over his bald head as he approached the door of the building.

'It looks as if it's just you and I, Rostov,' Lausard said to the Russian. 'Let's get a drink.'

Opposite the church was a large tavern, the pavement

cluttered with infantry either about to enter or in the process of leaving. Lausard could hear the sound of raucous singing and laughing coming from inside. He and Rostov entered, surprised to find the tavern less crowded than they'd expected. There were a dozen tables, eight of them occupied, the main one by a group of infantry from the Fortieth Demi-Brigade. It was they who were singing, led and conducted by a large man with a grey moustache and pitted skin. He was stripped to the waist to reveal a white, undernourished body. The result, Lausard reasoned, of so long a sea voyage and insufficient food. He would not, the dragoon thought, be the only one in that condition.

Dozens of bottles of wine stood on a table at one end of the room and Lausard and Rostov took one each and retired to a table in a corner, where they watched the drunken escapades of the other men, two of whom were dancing in the middle of the floor to the great amusement of their colleagues. On the far side of the room, Lausard could see the raven-haired Maltese women sitting with the French troops, quite prepared it seemed to put up with their drunken fumblings. Other women moved from table to table, grabbed intermittently by the drunken infantry and held like prizes.

'Do you ever wonder what our purpose here is, Alain?' Rostov was gazing at a particularly beautiful young woman in her early twenties, who was sitting on the knee of a corporal, kissing him.

Lausard looked puzzled for a moment. 'On these islands?'

'No, on earth. What is our purpose as men? What were we all born to do?'

'Has the sea turned you into a philosopher, Rostov?'

Lausard grinned. 'It's a strange time to be questioning the purpose of life.'

'We are born, we struggle through life and we die, few of us ever making a mark.'

'Then perhaps we should thank the army for giving us the chance to make that mark. If not for the army we'd all still be rotting in jail cells now.'

'Instead of facing death in battles? I'm not sure which I'd rather choose.'

'When my family was killed, I lost everything. Honour, pride, self-respect. I felt as if I'd lost my soul. At least the army has given me the chance to regain some honour, even if it does come with death.'

'Are death and honour not separate things to you?'

Lausard could only shrug. He sipped at his wine. 'If the two exist together, then so be it. If my death *is* the only honour then I accept that. Life has nothing to offer me any more apart from that chance to regain some of my pride and self-respect.'

'What did life offer you before? You were a thief living in the gutters of Paris. That was hardly fulfilment, was it?'

'So, what do *you* want from life, my friend?' Lausard was anxious to guide his colleague on to a different topic. He knew only too well what life had offered *him* before the deaths of his family. He had lost so much more than the men whom he now called comrades. None of them knew his true background: his rich and privileged upbringing, his wealth, the love of his family. It had all vanished beneath the bloody blade of the guillotine. The lives of those he loved extinguished as surely as his would have been. He shared a uniform with these men, he shared his food, risked his life with them and sometimes *for* them, but beneath the surface he was as different from them as chalk from cheese. He had been an aristocrat; they had been peasants. He had been educated; few of them could even read. He had known little hardship prior to the death of his family; they had known nothing but deprivation.

And yet he had slipped with frightening ease into their midst, had been accepted readily into a class he had never expected to encounter let alone live amongst. He did not see them as beneath him; he felt no contempt for these men he called comrades because now he was no different from them. They all wore the same uniform; they all fought for the Republic. They were united by their circumstances. Lausard noted the irony of the situation: these same men would probably, five years earlier, have helped carry him to the guillotine.

The Russian's voice interrupted his reverie. 'All I ever wanted from life was my own farm, a wife and children. Is that too much to ask?'

Lausard shook his head. 'All I ever wanted was to be a soldier. And now I am. Perhaps I should be grateful. Perhaps we should all be grateful to Bonaparte. It is *his* ambition, *his* purpose in life that has brought us to where we are now. We are merely the tools of his intent. Puppets in his hands to be used as he wishes. And I am content to let him lead.'

'But lead us where?'

'Your guess is as good as mine,' Lausard replied, downing more wine.

Two women approached the table, both in their early twenties. They were slim, dark haired and clad in simple dresses of green and brown muslin. The taller of the two smiled at Lausard, and he returned the gesture, his eyes fixed on her, taking in every detail of her face.

'You remind me of someone,' he said quietly, as she sat down beside him.

'Your wife?'

'My sister. How old are you?'

'Twenty-two.'

Lausard reached out a hand and gently stroked her cheek, relishing the softness of her flesh.

'Have you come to keep us company?' Rostov asked the girl sitting close by him.

'We have come for whatever you wish. My name is Louisa, this is Marie.' She nodded towards the other, slightly younger girl.

Lausard was still staring at her, apparently mesmerized by her darkly beautiful looks and her slate grey eyes.

One of the infantrymen at a nearby table had pulled a small whistle from his tunic and was furiously blowing a jaunty little tune that had several of the drunken infantrymen on their feet, dragging their Maltese companions and even their own fellow soldiers up to the centre of the room. They danced without grace but made up for that with their exuberance.

'Will you dance with me?' Rostov asked Louisa, getting to his feet. 'It's a pleasure I've long forgotten.'

She smiled and allowed herself to be led into the mêlée.

Lausard watched his companion for a second then turned his attention back to Marie.

'Do you want to dance?' she asked.

He shook his head.

'I will do whatever you wish,' she said, placing one hand on his thigh and leaning closer to him.

'Just drink with me, talk with me, that's all I ask,' he told her, gazing into her face.

'Most of the men who I've met today have asked me for much more than that. What makes you so different?'

'Does it bother you that I want you for something other than your body?'

She looked down a little shyly. 'I'm grateful,' she said softly. 'You said I reminded you of your sister. Where is she?'

'Dead.'

She reached out and touched his hand, a gesture of tenderness he had not experienced for longer than he cared to remember.

'Her name was Nicole,' Lausard said quietly. 'She was the same age as you when she died. Such a waste of life.'

Lausard felt her squeezing his hand more insistently now, and he looked into her eyes.

'Come upstairs with me. I want you to.'

'Why, because you have a living to earn and I am your next source of income?'

'No. So we can speak in peace. It's too noisy down here.'

Lausard looked across and saw Rostov merrily twirling his companion around the dance-floor, a smile fixed across his grizzled features.

Lausard got to his feet, his hand still held by Marie. He allowed himself to be led towards a staircase at the far end of the room. There was a table close to it where several infantrymen were seated. As they drew nearer, one of the men, a corporal, snaked out an arm and grabbed Marie around the waist, pulling her on to his lap.

She shook loose of him and tried to step away but he got to his feet.

'Come on, pretty rabbit, don't hide from me,' he said, slurring his words.

'Leave her alone,' Lausard said, stepping between the drunken corporal and Marie.

'This is none of your business. This is between me and the whore,' rasped the corporal, lunging forward.

Lausard grabbed the man by the lapels and pulled him closer so that their foreheads were almost pressed together.

'I said leave her,' the dragoon hissed then flung the corporal backwards. He crashed into a table, overbalanced and went sprawling, upsetting several bottles of wine that promptly shattered on the wooden floor. As the corporal staggered to his feet, he grabbed at one of the broken bottles, gripping the neck so that the jagged shards were pointing at Lausard.

'I'm going to gut you like a fish,' the corporal snarled.

'Try.' Lausard didn't flinch. Even as he watched three other infantrymen rise and surround their corporal his expression never changed from one of steely determination.

The corporal took a step forward, jabbing the broken bottle in the dragoon's direction. One of the other men picked up a chair and hefted it before him.

'Let's at least make this a fair fight.'

Lausard recognized the voice without looking round.

Rostov had joined him and the big Russian stood eyeing the opposition. 'Four against two seems fair enough to me.'

'Four against four is even fairer,' came a shout from close to the doorway of the tavern.

Out of his eye corner, Lausard noticed that two more green-jacketed men had entered.

Rocheteau and Delacor strode across to their companions and stood on either side of them, glaring at the infantrymen.

'Come on then,' Lausard said to the corporal. 'You and I, now.'

The corporal looked at the other dragoons then at his own men.

No one moved.

Every eye in the place was trained on the confrontation.

'It's just as well the Maltese *did* run,' Lausard said, his eyes never leaving the corporal. 'If you were the best that France had to offer they would have probably stood firm.'

With a shout of rage, the corporal lunged forward, the broken glass aimed at Lausard's face.

The dragoon side-stepped the clumsy movement, grabbed the corporal's wrist and snapped it sharply upwards, the sudden pain forcing the infantryman to drop the bottle. Lausard drove a fist into his stomach, watching as his opponent doubled up in pain.

One of the other infantrymen reached for his bayonet but stopped as he felt the needle-sharp tip of a blade against his throat. 'Leave it,' Rocheteau instructed quietly.

Lausard struck the corporal twice in the face, the second blow splitting the man's bottom lip. He fell backwards, crashing first into his men then into a table behind.

As the dragoon watched, the infantryman rose but only as far as his knees, blood spilling down his chin.

Lausard motioned towards the exit, and Rostov and Delacor began moving steadily through the watching infantrymen.

'I'll remember you,' the corporal hissed, wiping his mouth with the back of his hand. 'There'll be another time.'

'Perhaps,' Lausard said, a faint smile on his lips.

He took a step towards Marie and kissed her tenderly on one cheek.

'Take care,' he whispered, gently touching her face. Then he and Rocheteau spun round and headed for the door of the tavern.

'I'll find you somewhere and we'll finish this,' the corporal shouted after him.

Lausard ignored the bellow of rage.

'You should have killed him,' Delacor said as Lausard and Rocheteau emerged from the tavern.

'There'll be enough time for killing in the days to come,' Lausard said. 'Now, let's get what we need and head back to the ship. It'll be light in an hour.'

Eight

Paul Barras sipped at his glass of wine and shook his head slowly.

'What does Bonaparte think he is?' he said irritably. 'A politician? We sent him on this expedition as a soldier and he attempts to mediate and govern as a politician.'

'Is that so wrong?' Gohier demanded. 'And, as you so rightly said, it was we who sent him on this expedition with orders to capture Malta. He has succeeded. Why do these despatches trouble you so, Barras? He has been successful in the first part of our orders.'

'I feel you supported General Bonaparte in his expedition rather than sending him on it,' Talleyrand interjected, moving to the large picture window in Barras's office. He looked out into the gardens beyond, tiring of his position before the large table that accommodated the Directory members.

'What do you mean?' Barras demanded. 'We commanded Bonaparte to take Malta and Egypt.'

'Bonaparte would have done that anyway,' Talleyrand insisted. 'You know that he intended to leave for Egypt whether or not you and the other members of the Directory had backed him. There was no way you could have stopped him. Our General is on a mission of his own. To achieve spirtual as well as military control over this land he is so drawn to.'

'I can see nothing wrong in these reports,' Sieyès offered. 'Bonaparte has done nothing but good, for himself, for France and for the Directory.'

'I agree,' Gohier echoed. 'The measures he has implemented since his capture of Malta are further proof of his ambition and his ability.'

'I don't think any of us doubt his ambition,' Barras said. 'It is just a matter of how far that ambition takes him. What will satisfy it? Taking power from us?'

'Bonaparte is a soldier,' Sieyès insisted. 'He seeks glory on a battlefield, not in the political arena.'

'It seems to me we should be grateful to him for the amount of money he has secured for the Republic.' As he spoke Gohier looked at another of the pieces of paper before him. 'He confiscated almost seven million francs worth of treasure from the Order of St John.'

'And most of that has been transferred to the paymaster and taken on to Egypt,' Barras protested. 'This expedition has already cost over three million francs.'

'Money that came from the Vatican and from Switzerland,' Talleyrand reminded the other man. 'Not from the Republic.'

'And for the work he has done in Malta I feel he is to be applauded not villified,' Sieyès said. 'You only have to look at the action he has taken. He placed the island under the control of a nine-man governmental commission, eight of them native Maltese. By doing that he prevents the risk of revolt by the locals.'

'I think leaving General Vaubois behind with four thousand men to act as a garrison should help to prevent revolt too,' Gohier chuckled.

'He abolished slavery,' Sieyès continued. 'He freed nearly two thousand Turkish and Moorish slaves, isn't that the true code of the Republic? To free those who are oppressed?'

Barras nodded almost imperceptibly. 'I can read his list of achievements as well as the rest of you,' he said irritably. 'He has ordered that all Maltese men wear the French tricolour cockade, set up a military hospital, reorganized the island's postal service, reduced the number of monasteries and the number of priests ordained. As I said, I can read these and all the other schemes he has initiated. But why has he ordered that sixty boys from the wealthiest families on Malta be sent to Paris and educated here? And at the expense of the Republic, I might add.'

'He has also requested the Directory to send graduates of the École Polytechnique to Malta to teach mathematics, mechanics and physics,' Gohier added. 'I see nothing wrong with the children of Malta learning from the country that liberated them. Bonaparte has set up a new primary and secondary school system too and prescribed a new curriculum.'

'With emphasis on the sciences, French and the principles and morality of the French Constitution,' Sieyès added. 'It is an admirable piece of thinking in my opinion. In less than a week he has liquidated a state centuries old, out of touch with our modern world, and transformed it into a more worthwhile and vital part of the Republic.'

'What is your view on this, Talleyrand?' Barras turned to his colleague.

'As Minister for Foreign Affairs I see the expansion of the Republic as a good thing.'

'Bonaparte wishes *you* to travel to Constantinople; he is anxious to bolster our alliance with the Turks.'

'Our alliance with Turkey is strong enough without me undertaking such a journey. They will support General Bonaparte when the time comes.'

'Bonaparte has ordered you to go,' Barras insisted.

'As you constantly remind me, Barras, General Bonaparte does not rule the country, he commands the army of the Orient,' Talleyrand said. 'He has *requested* that I liaise with the Turks. It is a request I feel to be irrelevant. I am not answerable to our General.'

'Perhaps he fears the Turks will not offer their support when the time comes,' Gohier interjected.

'Turkey has nothing to gain by siding with the Arabs against us,' Talleyrand reminded him. 'They have suffered as much as any during the rule of the Beys.'

'Do the Turks know of General Bonaparte's expedition?' Sieyès asked.

'They have known about it since before he sailed,' Talleyrand said. 'I myself assured their ambassador here in Paris, in April, that France had no hostile intentions towards them.'

'I understood that they were concerned that Moslem territory should be occupied by a non-Moslem power,' Barras said. 'If Bonaparte conquers Egypt that is precisely what will happen. They may decide to fight our army on Holy grounds.'

'There is an old Turkish proverb,' Talleyrand began. '"An Ottoman hunter, if he wants to chase a hare, goes by oxcart."'

'Meaning what, Talleyrand?' snapped Barras. 'We haven't the time for games.'

'Meaning that the Turks will be in no hurry to break

their alliance with France and fight General Bonaparte. They will not side with the Mamelukes. They would be joining their own sworn enemies if they did that. However, even if such a thing *should* happen, I feel we must maintain our position, both military and political. All trade in the Mediterranean *must* pass into French hands and Egypt *must* belong to the Republic.'

'If Bonaparte performs as well in Egypt as he did in Malta then it is surely just a matter of time,' Gohier said, smiling. 'How long is it since he left Malta?'

'The fleet sailed five days ago,' Talleyrand informed him. 'He should reach Egypt in five or six weeks dependent upon the conditions.'

'And Nelson,' Barras added.

'Is Bonaparte aware of Nelson's presence in the Mediterranean?' Sieyès asked. 'He makes no mention of it in these despatches.'

'The Englishman's presence will not have escaped him,' said Talleyrand. 'But he is well ahead of the English fleet. For now.' The words hung ominously in the air.

'He has very able men commanding the fleet,' Sieyès said. 'Our ships are a match for anything the English have.'

Talleyrand scratched his chin thoughtfully.

'I wish I could agree with you,' he said cryptically. 'Let us hope, for everyone's sake, that assumption is not put to the test.'

Nine

It was getting hotter. There was no doubt about it. The men were all agreed that, aboard *L'Esperance* and every other ship in the massive French armada, the temperature was climbing, as it had been ever since they had left Malta. Each successive day at sea saw an increasingly oppressive rise in the level of heat, and men who had found the twenty-three-day voyage to Malta difficult were beginning to find life aboard ship close to intolerable.

Lausard noticed, through bouts of persistent seasickness, that the swarms of seagulls which had followed the fleet from the outset seemed to have thinned – as if the birds themselves could not stand the heat. Even the breeze that filled the sails of the ships and sped them through the water was warm. The air itself had turned stagnant, along with most of the water aboard.

There was little food left. That which the dragoons had retrieved from the island themselves was all but used up, supplemented now only by the usual ration of salt beef which, as before, only increased the men's raging thirsts.

The main deck of *L'Esperance* was like a huge coffin. Dark, airless and fetid it was a miserable place for the dragoons but offered their only respite from the sweltering sun. They could either spend time on deck retching miserably over the sides, seared by the blistering rays, or retreat to the reeking gloom of the main deck. Some of the men, those suffering most acutely from seasickness, were up on the quarterdeck, while Lausard and about twenty of the other men in the unit remained in the subterranean darkness below.

Lausard had hauled a bucket of sea water aboard and was attempting to wash his tunic. The stench of the green wool had become so overpowering that even *he* could barely stand it, and the salt water did little to help. All it did was make him feel sick when he smelled it.

'Why bother cleaning it?' Joubert's voice was low and gravelly, his breathing laboured. 'You'll probably be dead before you get the chance to wear it again. Dead from hunger, thirst or that infernal sun.'

Lausard ran a hand through his soaking hair, the long strands sticking to the back of his neck and his shoulders.

'If you're wounded wearing a filthy tunic then the dirt will get into your blood stream.' The big man suddenly looked concerned about the appalling state of his own jacket. Lausard grinned.

'I can't stand much more of this heat,' Moreau said, lying on his side on the wooden deck, perspiration running in rivulets from his body.

'Why not ask your God for a cool breeze?' Lausard enquired.

Gaston was also lying down, trying to sleep in order to find at least some temporary relief.

'Any ideas where we might be going, schoolmaster?' Rocheteau said, nudging Bonet.

'As far as I can tell, we're still travelling East. But for how much longer I don't know.'

'East,' Rocheteau grunted. 'Where will that take us?'

'Morea, Candia, Anatolia, Cyprus. Or Egypt.'

Lausard looked quizzically at the schoolmaster.

'I think we're sailing in circles,' Roussard offered.

'I'd give my soul for a bath,' Bonet said. 'Sinking into cool water up to my neck then—'

'Shut up, schoolmaster,' Rocheteau snapped. 'Aren't we suffering enough?'

'Still complaining?' The voice seemed muffled in the darkness, as if the rancid air was acting as an invisible blanket.

'What do *you* want?' Rocheteau said, realizing that the voice belonged to gunnery sergeant Marek.

'I was looking for you. I didn't know if you might be topside spewing blood with the rest of your babies.'

'Tell me what you want then leave me alone,' Rocheteau snapped.

'I want to talk about a wager.'

'We've done nothing but gamble since we got on board this hulk,' Joubert said. 'We're all bored with it.'

'I'm not talking about rolling dice or turning cards. I'm talking about sport.'

'What kind of sport?' Rocheteau took up the bait. 'What can we do on a ship?'

'You know how much we hate you land babies,' Marek chided. 'I think it's time to settle our differences once and for all and make some money at the same time.'

Rocheteau looked at the sailor expectantly.

'Boxing,' Marek said. 'A series of fights. Your best against our best. Bets to be taken on each contest.'

'What will the officers say?' Rocheteau asked. 'They'll find out where the fights are to take place. There's nowhere to hide on this thing.'

'The officers are as bored and in need of distraction as you. Don't worry about them. If you can find five men with the guts to face five of mine then we've got a contest,' Marek challenged.

'If they're to fight *you* the men will be queuing up,' Rocheteau said and a chorus of chuckles rose from the dragoons.

'I have no intention of fighting. I just need your help to organize this. What do you say?'

'I say yes,' snapped Rocheteau.

Marek smiled crookedly.

'We'll hold the fights here, on the main deck,' he said.

'Go and see if you can find five of your fishermen then,' Rocheteau chided. 'Let's begin as soon as we can. I'm looking forward to taking your money.'

Marek spun and disappeared into the gloom.

Lausard also got to his feet.

'Alain, where are you going?' Rocheteau wanted to know.

'To find Charvet,' Lausard told him. 'Remember what they locked him up for?'

The other men looked blank.

'Gambling in a church,' Lausard said, grinning. 'Gambling on fights that *he* was taking part in. We don't need five men. We *have* our boxer.'

Rocheteau wiped blood and perspiration from his companion's face using a cloth soaked in filthy water. He watched as the crimson fluid dripped from the material as he wrung it out into a bucket. He then wet the cloth once again and laid it across the back of Charvet's neck.

If the atmosphere in the main deck of *L'Esperance* had been appalling earlier in the day, the night had brought fresh discomfort. There were more than a hundred men, dragoons, sailors and marines all crowded into an area little more than ten yards square at the bow of the deck. It was a little better lit than usual, lamps having been ignited to give those watching – and those participating – a better chance to see. Most of the men had discarded their shirts and tunics and stood around, sweat pouring from them, watching this latest and riveting diversion from the rigours of the voyage.

Charvet dabbed at a cut on his bottom lip and spat blood into the makeshift fighting area – a portion of deck, now spattered with water and blood, and surrounded by men anxious to watch the bouts and even more anxious to bet on the outcome. Lausard had already won a purse full of gold coins from a disgruntled marine, who had handed over the money reluctantly as the sailor involved in the first bout was helped away, his face a bloody ruin from the pummelling Charvet had given it. The sailor had been game, perhaps even a little stupid, Lausard thought, refusing to admit defeat until Charvet had broken his jaw with a piledriver of a right hand that had also sent two teeth flying from his mouth.

The second sailor had fared no better. A lucky swing had cut Charvet's bottom lip, but other than that his blows had landed only on the dragoon's powerful arms or shoulders, and he had finally resorted to grabbing and holding on to Charvet as best he could to prevent himself being struck. He hadn't managed it for very long before a series of powerful blows had split his lip, his cheek and finally broken his nose.

The second casualty was being doused with water as the dragoons, gathered on one side of the designated fighting area, clapped and cheered happily, inspecting their winnings. So far the noise had not attracted the attention of any officers who, Lausard reasoned, were probably more content to stay in the comfort of their cabins than to investigate its source.

The stench of sweat and unwashed bodies, so prevalent throughout the journey, seemed to have intensified a hundred-fold and it was tainted now by the coppery odour of blood.

Marek stepped into the centre of the fighting area, oblivious to the puddle of blood he was standing in. He looked irritably towards the dragoons, then back at his own men and at the newest challenger to Charvet. The sailor was already stripped to the waist, and as he stepped forward Lausard noticed a number of scars on his torso. He was also heavily tattooed. Like most of the sailors he was a squat, powerfully built man with an abundance of muscles in his shoulders and upper body.

Charvet eyed his latest opponent with indifference and flexed his considerable muscles, punching the air three or four times as if warning the seaman what was to come. Cheers rose from the watching sailors and marines, matched by shouts of encouragement from the dragoons as Charvet stepped forward.

Marek raised his arms to silence both sides. He waited until the sound had died down, then pointed at the sailor.

'Leonardo,' he shouted, watching as the seaman raised both arms, fists clenched, accepting the adulation of his colleagues.

Charvet hawked and spat, a glob of mucus landing close to the sailor's foot. The man glared at the dragoon but Charvet was undaunted.

Men fumbled for their money or whatever else they were going to bet with, and Marek passed among the sailors, and Rocheteau amongst the dragoons to collect their stake. After the first bout, it had been agreed that the stake wagered on the winner would be divided amongst those who had selected him. It had taken too long for individual bets to be settled at the beginning and both sides were agreeable to this fairer and quicker alternative.

The fighters eyed each other malevolently, standing only a foot or so apart, waiting for Marek to give the signal. Leonardo sneered at the dragoon but Charvet took the gesture as one of bravado rather than confidence.

Marek looked at the two fighters then, taking a step back, called out, 'Fight!'

Charvet struck immediately: a thunderous right-hand punch that slammed into Leonardo's face and sent him reeling. Stepping forward, the dragoon followed up his advantage, catching the sailor with a left cross that snapped his opponent's head to one side and opened a cut over his left eye. Leonardo shook his head, then suddenly he launched himself at the dragoon, managing to avoid another punch and locking Charvet's head in a vice-like grip. He bit deeply into the dragoon's left ear and clung on like a terrier to a rat. Charvet howled in pain and tried to shake the seaman free, but he clung on, blood spilling down the side of Charvet's face. A great cheer erupted from the audience as Leonardo began raining blows into Charvet's face, his teeth still embedded in the dragoon's ear.

Charvet, trying to reason through the wave of excruciating pain, could think of only one course of action. He reached behind him and closed his huge hand on Leonardo's testicles, gripping them, then squeezing with as much power as he could muster.

The sailor opened his mouth to scream his pain, releasing his grip on Charvet's ear.

Taking the advantage, the dragoon spun round, his hand still crushing the sailor's testicles. Finally, he relinquished his hold and watched as Leonardo sank to his knees in agony. Charvet took a step forward and drove one foot into the sailor's face, then before Leonardo could recover, Charvet slammed his right fist into his opponent's face three times. The sound of cracking bone was audible as the sailor's nose splintered, fresh blood spurting on to Charvet and inflaming him further. He struck again. And again. Finally, a powerful left hander sent Leonardo crashing to the floor, where he lay burbling incoherently on the reeking wood of the deck. Charvet raised his arms in triumph and walked back towards the cheering dragoons, touching his savaged ear with the tips of his fingers, and wincing when he realized that a chunk was missing.

'Look what that animal did to me,' he snarled at Rocheteau, who was already wiping blood from the bitten ear.

'Is that the best you've got to offer, Marek,' Lausard taunted. 'A little dog?'

'If you don't like the way my men fight then you are free to withdraw – if you haven't the courage to face them.'

'That wasn't courage. He was too frightened to fight fairly.'

'Fighting does not always follow the same rules. Weren't

you taught to be prepared for anything?' Marek looked at Charvet who was standing with one hand clapped to his torn ear, blood pouring through his fingers. 'It looks like your boy cannot carry on. Perhaps he should forfeit the next contest.'

'I will fight in his place,' Lausard snapped, stepping forward.

'No, Alain, I am fine,' Charvet insisted, shooting out a hand to restrain his companion.

'You need to rest,' Lausard told him. 'Let Rocheteau work on that ear. I know what I'm doing.'

Lausard stepped into the fighting area and strode towards Marek.

'*You* fight me, *now*,' he hissed, pushing the gunnery sergeant.

Marek almost overbalanced and another sailor watching in the front row leaped to his feet and ran at Lausard, who easily side-stepped the clumsy charge and tripped the man as he passed. The sailor went sprawling, but rolled over and came at Lausard again.

Men on both sides were shouting their encouragement as the fighters clashed again.

Lausard drove a fist into his attacker's stomach, winding him. The sailor dropped to his knees but lunged at Lausard, closing his arms around the dragoon's legs and knocking him off balance.

The two men fell to the ground, the sailor trying to strike at Lausard's face. But the dragoon brought his knee up into the other man's side, knocking the breath from him. As the sailor scrambled back, Lausard jumped to his feet and punched him hard in the face. Another blow landed against the side of the sailor's face and sent him crashing to the ground. He struggled upright in time to be met by a blow that sent him back to the deck, his head lolling limply on one side, blood dribbling from his mouth.

Lausard watched as his unconscious opponent was dragged away.

'Now you,' he snarled at Marek.

'Meet your next opponent,' the gunnery sergeant said, grinning, and motioned to the watching sailors, whose cheers seemed to grow in volume. A mountain of a man emerged from their midst. Lausard recognized the thick beard and moustache of the man who now glared at him with a murderous look in his hooded eyes.

'Meet Legros.' Marek smiled.

Lausard felt hands tugging at him and turned to see Charvet standing there, a dirty bandage fashioned from a strip of muslin wrapped around his ear to protect it. Blood was already seeping through the thin covering.

'Let me fight him, Alain.'

Lausard hesitated, glancing at the blood dribbling down his companion's face. 'He knows you're at a disadvantage.'

'He *thinks* I am,' Charvet said, grinning.

Still Lausard would not step aside.

'Hurry up and decide which of you land babies is going to be the first to fall, will you?' Marek goaded.

'Let me fight him,' Charvet repeated.

Reluctantly, Lausard stepped aside and Charvet faced his newest, and largest, opponent.

'I have been waiting,' Legros snarled.

'Then your wait is over at last,' Charvet told him, leaning closer.

Marek raised his hands for silence.

'Officer!' The shout came from the other end of the deck and all the men froze.

'One of ours or one of theirs,' Lausard murmured quietly.

'We'll all be hanged now,' Sonnier said.

Lausard squinted through the gloom and finally caught sight of a familiar figure.

Captain Milliere made his way along the reeking, black-shrouded lower deck to where the throng of sailors and dragoons waited.

'What's going on here?' he demanded, looking around at the men then down at the blood-flecked floor.

'A little diversion from the journey, sir,' Lausard told him. 'A contest between ourselves and the navy.'

Milliere smiled. 'Boxing, eh? A fine sport.' He looked at the sailors. 'I'm not sure your captain would approve though.' He glanced at Charvet and saw the bloody bandage and the slicks of crimson on his face. 'You realize that all sport is more interesting when there is a wager behind it?' Silence greeted his remark. 'Are *you* gambling men?'

Still no one answered.

'Is this bout due to begin?' Milliere asked, inspecting Legros and Charvet.

The dragoon nodded.

Milliere fumbled in the pocket of his breeches and pulled out three gold coins. He held them in his fist for a moment then looked at Lausard.

'Who else will bet with me?' the officer asked, looking around. His gaze was met by men who thought they were being tricked into revealing the purpose of the fights. They all knew that gambling could carry a stiff penalty. Lausard looked at Rocheteau who nodded curtly.

'Where would you place your money, Captain?' Rocheteau asked.

'On my own man, of course,' he said, slapping Charvet jovially on the shoulder. 'I'd back one of my dragoons to beat one of Captain Verdoux's men any time.'

A great cheer went up from the dragoons.

'Will no one else join me in wagering on this contest?' Milliere persisted. He looked at the sailors. 'Have you so little faith in your man that you will not support him with a few francs?'

Marek stepped forward. 'I will bet against you.'

Milliere smiled. 'At last.'

It was as if a switch had been thrown. The lower deck suddenly erupted in a frenzy of shouts and cheers. Bets were placed and collected and Milliere took up position between Carbonne and Delacor so that he had a clear view of the fight.

At a signal from Marek, it began.

The fighters swayed from one foot to the other, moving around in a circle, looking for the best opening. It was Legros who struck first, aiming a blow at Charvet's face, but the dragoon blocked it and struck back, catching his opponent in the side of the face. Despite the power of the blow, Legros never wavered. Instead he struck low at Charvet, driving his fist up into the dragoon's stomach, trying to wind him. Luckily, Charvet had anticipated the blow and tensed his muscles. He hit back and opened a cut on the sailor's cheek. Immediately Legros struck at his ribs, ducking his head and buffeting the dragoon. The two men crashed into one another like bull buffalo, slamming countless punches into each other's bodies with seemingly little effect. Sweat poured from them as they increased their efforts and the men watching realized that this contest was to be unlike those they had previously witnessed. Each punch sounded like the thump of wood on wood, a dull slapping sound followed by the occasional grunt from either fighter. Toe to toe they traded punches, displaying incredible strength and resilience.

Then Legros struck low, smashing his fist into Charvet's genitals, the sudden agonizing pain causing the dragoon to drop his guard. Legros took advantage and smashed two blows into Charvet's face. The dragoon backed off in pain, and he was off balance when Legros advanced upon him, striking him in the face once again.

The seamen shouted their approval as Charvet almost lost his footing on the slippery deck. He ducked beneath another blow and caught Legros with an uppercut, a punch of such terrific force it staggered the sailor. Now it was the turn of the dragoons to cheer, Milliere amongst them.

Charvet caught him again with a left cross, shattering two front teeth and cutting a lip. Blood ran into Legros' thick beard, spraying outwards in a wide arc as Charvet hit him again, driving him backwards until he was almost among the sailors cheering him on. Those nearest pushed the big man back towards the dragoon. But even as Charvet scented victory, Legros managed to summon up some reserves of strength, and as Charvet came at him again, he blocked one blow with his forearm and smashed his other fist into the dragoon's face, roaring his defiance. Charvet reeled back from the impact but then, shaking his head to clear his senses, he stood ready as Legros advanced. The men faced each other, hands raised, preparing to either block or deliver the next blow. Spattered with blood, they were both breathing heavily, trying to suck in lungsful of the stale air. Gazes locked, they watched for the slightest sign of attack from their opponent. Charvet could see that Legros' breathing was becoming more laboured, and he winced with each intake of breath. He guessed that the sailor was injured around the ribs, possibly even internally. Bruises were already beginning to darken around Legros' sides and chest and several large swellings had risen above and around his eyes and cheeks.

Charvet himself was still feeling pain from the blow he'd sustained in his groin and he could taste blood in his mouth. The wild cheering of the men had died down as both seamen and dragoons watched for the first sign of renewed aggression from their chosen man.

Legros blinked hard as sweat ran into his eyes.

It was the split second that Charvet had been waiting for.

He lunged forward and struck twice, catching his opponent in the stomach then the face. Legros' nose seemed to crumble beneath the impact and blood spattered those nearby as well as spraying Charvet. Another powerful left hook opened one of the swellings over the sailor's eye. Charvet moved in to finish the fight, hitting his opponent squarely beneath the chin, a blow that almost lifted the big man off his feet. As he staggered backwards, Charvet caught him with a final blow that smacked into his temple.

Legros went down like a puppet with its strings cut, slamming face first into the deck, his arms motionless at his sides.

The dragoons roared their victory.

Marek kicked at the limp body of Legros. 'Come on, you fool, get up!' he shouted angrily.

One of the other sailors hurled a bucket of bloody

water over the downed fighter, but to no avail; he didn't stir.

'Pay up,' Rocheteau said, grinning. 'It's all over.'

Marek was kneeling beside Legros now and Lausard watched as the gunnery sergeant pressed two fingers to the big man's neck.

'You're right,' Marek said. 'It *is* all over. Legros is dead.' He glared at Charvet. 'You murdered him.'

'He knew the risks,' Lausard said, stepping forward alongside Charvet and Rocheteau.

'They killed Legros,' Marek roared to his watching companions.

A number of the sailors advanced towards the dragoons and Lausard saw more than one of them slide knives from their belts. Lausard himself reached for his sword, pulling it from the scabbard. He was surprised to see Milliere beside him, sword also drawn. The two sets of men stood only a few feet apart, Legros' body lying between them like some kind of bleeding demarcation line. The silence that descended was ominous, as the men glared at each other, each waiting for the other side to move.

The sound that finally galvanized the sailors into action came not from inside the frigate but outside.

Marek raised a hand to his ear. 'Get to your positions now!' he shouted at his men, then he turned to the dragoons. 'We'll settle this later.'

'What's going on?' Lausard demanded as the dull clanging of bells drifted on the still night air.

'Those aren't *our* watch bells,' Marek said. 'They're English. That one-eyed bastard Nelson has found us.'

Ten

The fog was so thick Lausard couldn't see more than ten feet in any direction. It was as though someone had draped the sea and the entire French fleet in a gauze shroud. Coupled with the unearthly silence that had fallen over the armada it was as if the men aboard *L'Esperance* were suddenly the only people alive in the entire world. Only the creaking of the hull and the occasional flapping of a sail in the light breeze broke the overpowering stillness, and every so often the sound of bells drifted across the clouded air. It was difficult to judge how close the English ships actually were. Lausard could not distinguish the difference between French and English bells, but he appreciated Marek's fear meant the enemy must be close.

The fog continued to swirl around the frigate and all the other vessels, masking their occupants' view of both each other *and* their enemy. Sailors waited at their posts in silence, concern etched on their faces, perspiration running down their bodies. Many of them dreaded an attack by the English Navy for fear that *L'Esperance* might be sunk. Lausard didn't even care to contemplate the carnage that might ensue if the English warships actually sighted their prey and opened fire. If indeed it *was* the English who were out there.

'They don't sound very close,' Tabor said quietly, as more bells sounded.

'They might be miles away,' Lausard said. 'Sound carries at night.'

'And if they're not?' Delacor asked.

'This fight is out of our hands,' Lausard told him.

'Well I don't like having to leave my life in the safe-keeping of these sailors,' Delacor snapped. 'I don't trust them. How do we know they'll fight?'

'Because it's their lives too, you idiot,' Rocheteau hissed, looking nervously around him.

'I don't like having to rely on other people,' Giresse said.

'Me neither,' Lausard agreed. 'But this time we've got no choice.'

Moreau closed his eyes and crossed himself.

'God will protect us,' he said softly.

'What's he going to do?' Rocheteau was scornful. 'Steer our ships past the English?'

There were one or two muted chuckles.

'Shut up!' Rocheteau snapped and silence descended once more.

The sound of bells once again drifted through the shrouded night.

On the forecastle of *L'Orient*, Napoleon Bonaparte paced slowly back and forth, occasionally glancing into the thick fog as if he expected it suddenly to part and reveal his enemy.

'Thank God for this fog,' Admiral Brueys said, stroking his chin thoughtfully. 'Let us pray that it remains. While we are hidden from the English we are safe.'

'There are fourteen ships of the line out there,' Bonaparte said angrily. 'We have over four *hundred* ships to oppose them.'

'Most of them overloaded with men and supplies,' Brueys reminded him. 'If the English attack we will have no chance. *Ten* warships would do us untold damage if they manage to find us. All we can do is keep sailing on our present course and pray that we miss them.'

'Can you be sure that the intelligence reports you received are correct?'

'I have no reason to doubt them. The reports said that the squadron was sailing eastward moving at twice the speed we ourselves are. If they *have* got in front of us then they could be waiting when we reach Egypt.'

'How could that be possible?' Bonaparte snapped. 'Nelson doesn't know our destination.'

'I have tried to tell you, General, this man is no fool. He knows which direction we are sailing. He will know that there are only a limited number of destinations we *could* be heading for. Egypt is the most logical.'

Bonaparte waved a hand dismissively in the foggy air. 'I fear you overestimate our English foe.'

Brueys didn't answer. He saw little point in prolonging the conversation when Bonaparte was so set in his own opinion. The General continued his slow pacing back and forth, watched by Junot and Berthier.

'Why not send some ships to the north?' Berthier offered. 'Perhaps Nelson will follow them and we will be able to slip away unnoticed.'

'I will not divide my force,' Brueys said with an air of finality.

'It is not *your* force, Admiral,' Bonaparte reminded him sharply. 'They are your ships but they carry *my* men and *my* equipment.'

'You are reliant on myself and my colleagues to get you to your destination, General,' Brueys retorted angrily. 'If not for the skill of my sailors we would not have come this far.'

'If your sailors and your subordinates are so skilled why are we still being pursued by Nelson?' Bonaparte demanded. 'Why hasn't he been destroyed by now? You run when you would perhaps be better to engage him.'

'War at sea is different to the kind of war you know, General. Kindly allow me to conduct myself in the ways of the sea and to suggest that you reserve your expertise for the land.'

'Should we ever reach it,' Junot offered. 'If you do not avoid or defeat the English then none of us will ever walk on firm ground again.'

'Junot, I'm surprised at your lack of faith. Has luck not smiled upon us so far? Why should we rely on the negative instincts of our admiral here? Better to trust to luck.' There was scorn in Bonaparte's tone that Brueys deigned not to rise to.

'How long before you know whether or not we've outrun them?' Berthier asked.

'They are moving quicker than we are,' the admiral told the chief of staff. 'We cannot outrun them. We can only hope to bypass them. There are four hours until sun-up. If they keep sailing in a northerly direction then we will be safe.'

'And if not?' Berthier pressed.

'Then God help us all,' Brueys murmured.

The unearthly silence continued, every sound cloaked even more densely by the ever-present fog. Lausard remained on the quarterdeck, peering out towards where he imagined the other French ships to be. Finally he turned and headed back down to the main deck. Rocheteau and a number of the other dragoons followed, clambering down the wooden steps into the frigate, to be enveloped immediately by the overpowering stench of sweat, blood, salt water and excrement. The lamps and candles were still burning towards the bow of the ship, and bathed in the lazy light was Legros' body, still in the position they had left it. As Lausard drew closer he saw that the dead sailor's eyes were still open, glazed like those of a fish on a slab. The blood that stained his face and torso had begun to congeal, and looked black in the dismal half-light of the main deck.

'There'll be hell to pay when word of this gets around,' Roussard said nervously. 'Organizing the fights and betting on them was bad enough, but killing one of their men . . .' He allowed the sentence to trail off.

'I didn't *mean* to kill him,' Charvet protested.

'Who cares?' Delacor said. 'At least we got to pick up our winnings before the English arrived.'

'It was an accident,' Lausard said, looking down at the body. 'It might just as easily be Charvet lying there.' He prodded the corpse with the toe of his boot.

'You'll hang for this.' The voice came from the gloom, from a member of a twelve-pounder crew kneeling close by. The sailor was almost invisible in the blackness. 'It was murder.'

'Shut up, fisherman,' Rocheteau ordered. 'No one had

105

better try to hang our friend here or there *will* be trouble.'
He patted Charvet on the shoulder.

'It was a fair fight,' Lausard insisted. 'Legros was just unlucky.'

From the other end of the ship, the dragoons heard the sound of footsteps growing closer. Even through the gloom they could see a group of blue-uniformed marines marching towards them, muskets sloped and bayonets fixed. Marek was with them.

'That's him.' The gunnery sergeant pointed at Charvet and the marine officer stepped forward, pulling his sword.

'What's going on here?' Captain Milliere asked.

'This man is under arrest,' said the marine officer, a slender man with a thick moustache. 'By order of Captain Verdoux.'

'Captain Verdoux has no right to give such an order,' Milliere protested. 'This man is under *my* command, not his.'

'And you are all on Captain Verdoux's ship,' the marine officer persisted, stepping towards Charvet. 'The charge is murder.'

The waiting marines lowered their muskets, swinging them up to their shoulders. Lausard heard the sound of half a dozen hammers being pulled back. He looked at Milliere then at the other dragoons. No one moved.

'Go with them,' the captain said to Charvet finally.

The dragoon stepped forward reluctantly.

'You can't let them take him, Captain,' Carbonne protested, but Milliere raised a hand to silence him and all the men watched as the marines formed up around Charvet. He was marched away towards the stern and into the enveloping blackness.

'You can't let them hang him, Captain,' Lausard insisted.

'I don't intend to,' Milliere said. 'We'll wait until morning, until Verdoux announces his plan.'

Lausard looked on angrily.

'Diplomacy might be called for,' Milliere continued.

'And if diplomacy fails?' Lausard persisted. 'If they condemn Charvet? I for one will not stand idly by while they hang him. I will not let that happen, Captain, and I don't care who I have to kill to prevent it.'

Eleven

The searing early-morning sun seemed to have driven off the English as effectively as it had driven away the sea fog of the previous night. High in the cloudless sky, it bathed the sea and the French fleet in its blistering rays, the temperature rising ever higher as the French continued eastward. It was like sailing into the mouth of hell, Lausard thought, glad to be able, albeit momentarily, to focus on something other than the scene being played out on the quarterdeck of *L'Esperance*.

The dragoons were drawn up in three lines, Milliere and Lieutenant Royere at their head. They were facing two lines of marines who had their Charleville muskets shouldered. Behind them, standing on the forecastle, were Captain Verdoux and his staff. For the first time in weeks, the dragoons were wearing full uniform, and although they had been allowed to remove their brass helmets they were increasingly suffering as the blazing sun burned into the thick wool of their green tunics and leather breeches. Each one of them wore his sword and carried his carbine. Loaded and ready. This was no parade as far as the soldiers were concerned. It was a show of strength. Verdoux knew it too and was grateful for the marines standing before him. The heat in the air was matched only by the tension on the frigate. Tension that he felt may well spill over into something much worse.

For more than thirty minutes the dragoons had remained facing him and his marines. All around them sailors went about their duty, although every now and again one or two of those up in the rigging paused to look down upon the tableau unfolding on the deck below them.

'What do you want?' Verdoux asked finally.

'I want my trooper returned to me,' Milliere said flatly. 'You had him arrested last night on a false charge.'

'I had him arrested on a charge of murder. He killed one of my men.'

'It was an accident.'

'That doesn't alter the fact that one of my men was killed by one of your men,' Verdoux persisted. 'Killed I might add while engaged in an illegal pursuit.'

'You cannot stop men fighting, especially in these conditions,' Royere offered. 'I doubt if this is the only ship on which there have been confrontations.'

'These fights of which you speak were organized for the purpose of gambling. My man was killed because of a petty wager.'

'So what do you propose to do?' Milliere wanted to know.

'I want to see that justice is done.'

'Then release Charvet. He didn't set out to kill your man. I will not have one of my troopers made an example of.'

'And how do you propose to stop me?'

'Present arms,' Milliere shouted and as one man, the dragoons raised their carbines.

The marine officer looked up at Verdoux, waiting for orders.

'You would turn this ship into a slaughterhouse for the sake of one man?' Verdoux said.

'Why not? *You* would assume the role of executioner for the sake of an accident.'

Lausard had his carbine pressed tight to his shoulder, squinting down the barrel at the waiting marines.

'Tell your men to stand at ease,' Verdoux instructed. 'Or you leave me no choice.'

The dragoons did not move.

'Present arms!' Verdoux shouted, and the marines raised their muskets. Both sets of troops now faced each other, weapons primed and ready. One shaky finger, one false move and the quarterdeck of *L'Esperance* would be transformed into a floating battlefield. Lausard felt a bead of sweat trickle down the side of his face. He was standing directly opposite a marine corporal who was blinking nervously, gripping his weapon tightly. Lausard felt surprised at his calm; how at ease with himself he would be to open fire on his own countrymen if the order was given. Obviously the marine corporal did not feel the same. For what seemed like an eternity, the two sets of troops faced each other.

'What is your answer, Captain?' Milliere asked. 'Do I get my man back? Or do I take him?'

Verdoux looked at his staff with something akin to disbelief. 'You would risk so many lives for the sake of one trooper?'

Milliere nodded.

'This is senseless,' Verdoux exclaimed. 'Lower arms,' he called and the marines obeyed.

Still the dragoons remained at the ready.

'My trooper, Captain Verdoux.'

'There must be *some* punishment,' Verdoux said. 'If he is to avoid hanging then he should think himself lucky to escape with a flogging.'

'There will be no flogging,' Milliere insisted.

'That kind of punishment has been banned under army regulations since 'ninety-four,' Royere reminded the naval officer.

'This is not the army,' Verdoux said. 'You are on my vessel, you will abide by my rules. The trooper will be flogged.'

'They're not going to let him go, Alain,' Rocheteau whispered.

'Then a lot of men are going to die,' Lausard said, his aim still fixed on the marine corporal ahead of him.

'You talk about punishment,' Milliere said. 'Don't you think we've suffered enough on this ship since we left Toulon? All of us have been punished by our very presence for the last six weeks.'

'Then blame your General, not my ship,' Verdoux protested. 'None of my men wanted you aboard. The sooner you leave the better and, thank God, that day will soon be here.'

'You know our final destination?'

'We are less than a day's sail from it. Doesn't your General trust you enough to tell you?' Verdoux taunted. 'You will disembark in Egypt.'

A collective sigh escaped the men on deck.

'What are we going to do in Egypt?' Rocheteau murmured.

'That's the other side of the world,' Roussard added.

'We'll never see France again,' Sonnier bemoaned.

If Milliere was surprised by the disclosure, he didn't allow the bemusement to show in his expression. 'Then when we land I will take with me a full complement of troops. All unharmed,' he said. 'Give me my trooper.'

Verdoux smiled wanly. 'Very well. Have him back. Any punishment I could inflict upon him will be nothing to the agonies he will suffer once you land.'

Milliere waved a hand for the dragoons to lower their carbines. They did so almost reluctantly and stood to attention on the quarterdeck, watching as two marines disappeared below. They returned a few minutes later with Charvet between them, and as Lausard watched one of them untied the rope around the dragoon's wrists. He immediately marched across to his companions and took up position between Lausard and Bonet.

'Be grateful,' Lausard said quietly. 'All this is for you.'

Charvet smiled and stood to attention.

Up on the forecastle one of Verdoux's staff was trying to attract his captain's attention, gesturing over the side of the ship towards something. Verdoux finally looked and saw a rowing boat containing six sailors and two blue-uniformed men, who were clinging to the side of the rowing boat, troubled by the buffeting it was taking from the waves. As the captain looked he could see dozens of similar craft being rowed throughout the length and breadth of the fleet. Some were already mooring precariously next to the frigates, brigs and ships of the line and he watched as rope ladders were lowered into the waiting rowing boats. Even as he looked on, such an operation was being performed aboard *L'Esperance*, and a sallow-looking messenger, his uniform stained with salt water, clambered over the side and almost fell on to the quarterdeck. Sailors and dragoons looked on quizzically as the messenger made his way towards the forecastle and Verdoux.

Lausard watched the two men chatting animatedly for a moment, then he saw Verdoux snap an order to a subordinate, who hurried off towards the bow of the frigate. Moments later a stream of different coloured flags and pennants was raised into the rigging of the ship and displayed. It was followed by another line, then another. Lausard had no idea what the flags signified but he guessed they formed some kind of communication, and as he looked around, he saw that other ships in the armada were now also showing pennants. Whatever the message *was* fluttering from the rigging of the ships, it was being passed on with speed and efficiency throughout the entire fleet.

The messenger who had come aboard was dressed in the uniform of Bonaparte's personal guides and, Lausard noticed, he was carrying a rolled parchment in his hand. He took up position on the forecastle and surveyed the men on the quarterdeck, his own gaze met by the puzzled glances of troops and sailors alike as they moved closer to hear what he had to say. He unfurled the parchment and cleared his throat.

'I have a proclamation from General Bonaparte.' He looked around at the men, who seemed largely unimpressed by his announcement.

Lausard looked on indifferently, noticing how pale the messenger looked. He wondered if the man was going to be able to read the proclamation before he succumbed to seasickness. The boat rocked violently as a wave struck it and a number of men, including the watching dragoons, felt their stomachs contract. It was a feeling they had come to know with unpleasant, monotonous familiarity. However, the messenger recovered his composure and began to read.

'"Soldiers, you are about to undertake a conquest whose effects on the world's civilization and trade are incalculable. You will inflict upon England a blow that is certain to wound her in her most sensitive spot, while waiting for the day when you can deal her the death blow."'

He looked around, as if for approval of the words.

'England,' Tabor whispered in confusion. 'I thought we were going to Egypt.'

'We are, you half-wit, now shut up and listen,' snapped Delacor.

'"We shall make some wearisome marches,"' the messenger's voice rang out. '"We shall fight a few battles; we shall succeed in all our enterprises; destiny is for us . . ."'

'Death is for us more likely,' Roussard whispered.

'"The Mameluke beys, who exclusively favour English trade, who have oppressed our merchants with vexations and who are tyrannizing over the unhappy people of the Nile Valley, will cease to exist a few days after our landing,"' the messenger continued, his words ringing with a pride as deep as if he had composed them himself. '"The people with whom we shall live are Mohammedans. Their chief creed is this: 'There is no God but God and Mohammed is His prophet' . . ."'

'That's blasphemy!' Moreau declared. 'There is only one God.'

'Is God a Frenchman?' Rocheteau murmured to his companion.

'I sometimes think the devil is a Frenchman,' Rostov offered.

'"Do not contradict them,"' the Messenger read, swaying slightly as the frigate passed through some particularly venomous surf. '"Act towards them as in the past you have acted towards the Jews and the Italians."'

'What does he mean by that?' Bonet queried. 'That we should slaughter them?'

The messenger paused, looked at the watching men, then went on.

'"Show the same tolerance towards the ceremonies prescribed by the Koran and towards the mosques as you have shown towards convents and synagogues, towards the religions of Moses and of Jesus Christ. The Roman legions used to protect all religions. You will find here customs quite different from those of Europe; you must become used to them. The people of the countries where we are going treat their women differently from the way we do . . ."'

'I am sure that with the correct treatment they will blossom as surely as any European woman,' Giresse sighed wistfully. 'How fortunate for them to experience *my* expertise.'

'"But",' the Messenger's voice was more stern, '"in all countries, the man who rapes is a monster . . ."'

Lausard looked at Delacor who shuffled uncomfortably, aware of other eyes upon him.

'"Looting enriches but a few . . ."'

'Yes, me, hopefully,' Rocheteau said and the men around him were forced to suppress chuckles.

'"It dishonours us, it destroys our resources, and it turns the people whom we want to befriend into our enemies. The first city we shall see was built by Alexander.

At every step we shall find traces of deeds worthy of being emulated by the French."' The messenger studied his audience a moment longer then took off his shako and raised it into the air. '*Vive La Republique, Vive Bonaparte!*'

The troops and sailors matched the shout with a somewhat half-hearted reply.

'A plea to the godless, eh?' Milliere mused. 'For tolerance towards believers. A plea I fear that will fall on deaf ears.'

'Some men choose to be deaf when it suits them, Captain,' Lausard said. 'As for emulating the feats of Alexander, I think that seasick and starving men have little concern for the feats of ancient heroes.'

Milliere could only nod in agreement, watching as the guide hurriedly nailed the proclamation to the main mast of *L'Esperance* then clambered back over the side, easing himself down the rope ladder towards the waiting rowing boat.

Lausard crossed to the starboard side of the ship and looked out across the water. 'Egypt,' he said softly, gazing eastward. 'In one day we at last set foot on dry land.'

'The land of the pharoahs,' Bonet mused.

'And the Mamelukes,' Rostov added.

'Do you think they will see us as liberators?' Lieutenant Royere asked. 'This is part of our duty as Republicans, isn't it? To free those who are held captive. The Egyptian peasants are held captive by the Mamelukes. Perhaps they at least will welcome our arrival.'

'With respect, Lieutenant,' said Lausard. 'I doubt if the Egyptians *or* those who rule them will see us as anything other than what we truly are. We come to this country not as liberators but as invaders.'

'Allow me at least a little of my idealism, Lausard. You and I fight for different reasons.'

'We all fight because we are ordered to.'

'Perhaps,' Royere said. 'One more day at sea. Thank God. May it pass quickly.'

Lausard gave a curt nod. 'I agree. However, we *know* what miseries we are expected to endure aboard ship. None of us can even guess at what awaits us when we land.'

Twelve

'How can you argue with these reports, General?' Admiral Brueys said agitatedly. 'You ordered the reconnoitre of Alexandria's defences yourself.'

'I am not arguing with the reports, Admiral,' Bonaparte said, still gazing at the maps laid out on the table before him. 'I argue about the hysteria surrounding Nelson. Am I never to be free of others' fears about this cursed Englishman?'

'The reports say that the English fleet left Alexandria less than twenty-four hours ago,' Brueys persisted. 'That means there is every chance Nelson is still close by.'

Bonaparte appeared unmoved by this revelation. 'I am well aware of what the reports mean. I know that this means the landing of the troops must take place perhaps a little sooner than I had planned. The weather changing has not helped matters either.'

As if to reinforce his statement, *L'Orient* was suddenly rocked by the choppy sea and the powerful wind that had sprung up during the past few hours. What had been calm, perfect weather for a landing, had rapidly degenerated into something approaching a full-scale storm.

'The problem of *where* to land them remains also,' Bonaparte mused. 'A landing in Alexandria itself is out of the question. The fortifications may be ancient but our enemies will be waiting. We cannot land there without a battle.'

'Also, the approaches to the harbours are narrow, and in this heavy weather there is a danger the battleships might run aground. You would be better off landing here.' Brueys jabbed a finger at the map. 'Aboukir Bay. The water is deeper, it would be safer for my ships.'

Bonaparte shook his head. 'It would waste time,' he said dismissively. 'Aboukir is fifteen miles east. I would have thought, with your terror of Nelson, Admiral, that you would be anxious to allow my troops to disembark as quickly as possible, not to loiter in these waters waiting for him to turn up. No, Aboukir Bay is out of the question.'

'I fear the enemy would expect us to land there too,' Berthier added.

'Precisely,' Bonaparte agreed. 'This fishing village here at Marabout, only eight miles to the west – it would seem to be a good spot.'

'The coast and coastal waters around there are uncharted,' Brueys protested. 'The sea is ugly enough without the extra risk. Why not wait until the weather changes? It would make the landing much easier. There are better spots along the coast that—'

'You speak to me incessantly about the need to avoid Nelson and now you tell me to wait for a change in the weather,' Bonaparte snapped. 'Admiral, we have no time to waste. Luck grants me three days, no more. If I don't take advantage of them, we're lost.' He continued staring at the maps. 'This decision has been forced upon me.'

'Also, the longer we wait, the more time the enemy has to amass his forces against us,' Berthier offered.

'Quite so,' Bonaparte said. 'I will issue orders that the landing is to begin at noon. The troops commanded by Desaix, Menou and Reynier are less than three miles from shore. They will go ashore first. Then those of Kléber and Bon.'

'I still say you are taking a chance landing your men at such a point,' Brueys persisted. 'In calm seas it would be hazardous enough but in weather such as this it is even more of a problem.'

'Not to you, Admiral,' Bonaparte snapped. 'As you told me once before, the army is my concern. Let *me* worry about this landing. I am not plagued by your indecision and caution. If all goes well, I should have two divisions ashore by nightfall.'

'That may be an optimistic estimate,' Berthier interjected.

'Not you too,' Bonaparte said, waving a hand in the air dismissively. 'Is this fear and uncertainty like some kind of plague? Does it spread from man to man?' He looked at Brueys. 'I fear you have infected my chief of staff with your malaise, Admiral. The sea could not stop us. Nelson could not stop us. We have reached our first objective. It is going well for us.'

It felt as if the rowing boat had been lifted into the air by some huge invisible hand. It rose on a wave, seemed to hover in space for a moment, then slammed back down into the choppy sea. The dragoons gripped on to the sides of the rowing boat, on to the wooden seats, some even lay in the bottom of the small craft – anything to prevent them being tossed overboard by the increasingly violent swell of surf. Lausard gripped his seat with one hand and held on to Rocheteau's belt with the other while the corporal retched over the side of the vessel. Spray exploded over the boat in a stinging white curtain, showering the men, drenching uniforms that were already heavy with sweat.

Three rowing boats had left *L'Esperance* carrying the dragoon unit and Lausard could see similar movement from other ships anchored nearby. More green-coated dragoons belonging to their regiment were being ferried ashore from their own transport about five hundred yards to the left. Dozens of small vessels carrying blue-coated infantrymen were heading for shore, streaming away from the ships with as much speed as those sailors rowing could muster. Lausard also noticed that some of the vessels had overturned in the furious surf. A group of infantrymen and sailors were clinging to the overturned boat not that far from them, trying to keep their heads above water, occasionally screaming for help. Equipment was floating on the choppy water. Packs, shoes, gaiters, headgear. Lausard even saw a pair of trousers bobbing about in the surf.

The cavalrymen had the extra disadvantage of having to carry with them their saddles and the shabraques that lay beneath – or at least it would become a major disadvantage once they reached the shore. Lausard could see the dirty sand that awaited them, sloping sharply down towards the sea. A hastily abandoned fishing boat had been left close to the beach and it was being buffeted with each fresh flood of surf on to the beach. How he longed to reach that sand, to be free of the grip of the sea once and for all but, at the moment, it looked a thousand miles away.

They were rowed past the towering edifice of *L'Orient*, some of the men gazing up in awe at the huge battleship. Dozens of rowing boats crammed with men were being guided away from the flagship. Lausard wondered when Bonaparte himself would go ashore. He was still pondering this when a huge wave struck the rowing boat and caused it to list violently to one side. He heard a yell from behind him and saw that Carbonne had toppled into the churning water. Lausard spun round and noticed the former executioner's bald head disappearing beneath the water. But before Lausard could act, Tabor shot out a huge hand and grabbed his companion by the collar, hauling him back into the boat with relative ease. Carbonne coughed and spluttered, emptying his lungs and his stomach of salt water while Tabor looked on indifferently. Lausard smiled at the big man, steadying himself as another large wave lifted the boat then sent it hurtling back down with such force that it seemed everyone aboard would end up in the water. But the craft held and the sailors dug the oars deep into the surf, powering the vessel along as best they could, sweating and cursing from the exertion.

Lausard wiped the stinging water from his eyes. He blinked in an effort to clear his vision, his stomach contracting with appalling regularity. Gaston was huddled in the bottom of the boat, curled into a foetal position, his arms clasped over his head, his eyes tightly shut. The red dye from his trumpeter's tunic had run in one or two places and stained the top of his breeches, and to Lausard looked uncomfortably like blood.

Away to the left there was an enormous crash,

accompanied by the sound of splintering wood and screams of panic that managed even to eclipse the pounding waves. A boat carrying some infantrymen had struck a rock, a hole like some terrible wound having been torn in the hull of the vessel. The craft was sinking rapidly, its occupants either tipped or jumping into the water to escape the stricken boat. Oars and other pieces of timber were quickly tossed skyward by the erupting sea and the air was once more filled with the terrified shricks of men.

Most of the sailors struck out for shore, swimming as best they could in the strong current and savage surf, but the infantry were helpless, a number of them trying to cling to the sinking craft. Two men clung together but Lausard and the others watched as they simply sank together, arms aloft in the vain hope of rescue.

'Can't we do something?' Bonet grabbed at a sailor close to him. 'Row towards them, help them.'

The sailor shook loose and glared at him.

'They're our own men, we can't leave them to drown,' the ex-schoolmaster continued frantically.

'If we try to help them, we'll end up the same way,' Lausard reasoned.

One of the desperate men had managed, somehow, to paddle his way towards the boat and he was shouting for help, water filling his mouth each time.

'We've got to help him,' Bonet persisted.

'His extra weight will unbalance us,' a sailor snapped. 'He's lost.'

'Do you think he'd help *you*?' Lausard grabbed his companion by the arm and stared into his eyes. 'Worry about your own life.'

Reluctantly Bonet took his seat on the wooden bench next to Lausard. When he looked across at the stricken infantryman again, all he saw was a hand disappearing beneath the waves.

'There's some more of our men.' Tabor gestured towards another rowing boat a little further back, as he spotted the green tunics of dragoons.

'I can see that bastard Delpierre,' Rocheteau said. 'It's a pity *he* doesn't fall in. I'd personally hold him under until he drowned.'

Lausard glanced around and caught sight of the ser-geant Rocheteau referred to. 'Never mind him. We've got other problems to think about.' He nodded ahead.

As the surf dipped, the men caught sight of a long line of jagged rocks about fifty yards in front of them. The points were jutting menacingly above the water like filthy teeth. However, there was no other way for the boat to go and the sailors continued to row manfully against the crashing waves. An oar snapped against an underwater rock. The hull of the boat scraped noisily against another protrusion, and Lausard looked down with concern as if expecting the jagged stone to rip its way through the hull at any moment. Fortunately for the dragoons, a powerful wave caught the boat and lifted it clear of the jutting rocks, slamming it down again fifteen feet further on, the impact again spilling the troops into the bottom of the vessel. As the men struggled to regain their seats they were soaked as another wave washed over the boat, threatening to pitch them into the sea. Blinded by spray, racked by seasickness, soaked to the skin and baking beneath the blistering sun, the dragoons held on desperately as the shore approached.

A number of other boats were already unloading their human cargo, men falling gratefully on to the sand, ignoring the incoming tide that swept over them. Their relief at being ashore knew no bounds. The rowing boats immediately turned around and headed back to the waiting ships, ready to ferry more troops ashore. Lausard could only guess at how long the entire landing was going to take. But for the moment his only concern was that he and his companions were about to reach dry land.

The sailors raised their oars and the boat glided the final few yards. Unable to stand another second in the vessel Rostov leaped free and waded through the surf. Charvet joined him, both men holding their carbines above their heads with one hand, dragging their saddles through the water. As the boat touched land, Joubert scrambled out, losing his footing and falling face down in the water. Delacor hauled him up then strode on himself, feeling his own knees begin to sag. The other dragoons were suffering similarly: so long at sea had affected their balance. Sonnier felt drunk and dropped to his knees, his head spinning. Moreau was also on his knees, his head bowed. Roussard fought his way clear of the pounding surf and staggered several yards up the beach before falling on to the sand, a look of relief etched on his haggard features.

Lausard, his arm around Rocheteau's shoulder to steady the corporal, also advanced several yards up the sharply sloping beach, immediately aware of the newest intrusion.

Flies.

There were hundreds of them. Like living cinders they filled the baking air, landing on the men, crawling over their skin and their uniforms, driven away only momentarily by flailing hands. Their buzzing was incessant and loud. The air was also filled with a rancid, vile odour, which Lausard recognized as rotting fish. A number of abandoned half-full nets littered the beach, the catch now at the mercy of the flies and the scorching sun. The combination of flies, the stench of rotten fish, the all-too-familiar odour of salt water and the increasing heat would at any other time have been unbearable for the incoming troops, but they were so happy to be free of the ships that even these discomforts were endured.

All along the beach, troops were spilling gratefully from their transports and Lausard watched as some kissed the ground. Many of the men didn't appear to be carrying any weapons and Lausard could only assume that they had been lost during the hazardous three-mile trip from ship to shore.

Without weapons, their uniforms incomplete and reeking, the men staggering ashore looked more like an army of scarecrows than a force of invaders. They stood in unsteady groups or flopped helplessly on the sand, surrounded by clouds of black flies, their throats parched, their stomachs longing for food, waiting for their officers to give them orders, wondering how they could find shelter from the scorching sun. Those who had lost their head gear were in even more dire straits and some were already pulling their tunics over their heads in an effort to protect themselves. Even the sand burned beneath their feet.

Lausard reached up and momentarily removed his helmet, feeling how hot the brass had become. His entire body was sheathed in sweat, his head swimming from the journey and lack of food or water. When he moved it was on unsteady legs. A legacy of the six-week voyage. Some of the men were even worse. Joubert could barely take two steps before falling to the sand, his head spinning. He blinked hard to try to cure the double vision he temporarily had to contend with. Roussard took off his helmet and looked up at the cloudless sky.

'Don't do that, you fool,' Milliere snapped, suddenly approaching. 'The sun will blind you if you look directly at it.'

'And keep your helmet on,' Lausard added.

Rocheteau swatted away another fly, aware he was fighting a losing battle. The insects swarmed around all the soldiers like a black cloud, landing on any piece of exposed flesh, and crawling across faces, hands and shirtless bodies. Gaston spat as one crawled into his mouth.

'What about our horses, Captain?' Lausard asked.

Milliere could only shrug.

'Your guess is as good as mine. I have no idea which transport they are on or when they are likely to be brought ashore. Until they arrive, we are infantry.'

'Complaining again, *Private*?'

Lausard recognized the voice immediately.

Sergeant Delpierre was striding towards him, smoothing the moustache that grew beneath his hooked nose.

'Private,' he said, grinning. 'There is such a wonderfully ironic sound to that word when I address *you*, Lausard. You and all this scum like you.' He glanced around at the other dragoons. 'How does it feel to be a mere private again? How humiliating was it to lose your rank?'

'I lost it in a good cause,' Lausard told his fellow dragoon.

'In a good cause, *Sergeant*,' Delpierre reminded him.

Lausard glared at the other man.

'Well don't expect to regain it in a hurry,' Delpierre said. 'You are again what you will always be. A common soldier.'

'Rank means nothing. A man is generally what he feels himself to be.'

'And what do you feel *you* are?' Delpierre sneered. 'What kind of inflated opinion of yourself do you have? Do you think yourself better than me? Better than Sergeant Legier over there.' He motioned to the stockily built NCO with his right ear missing, who was busily forming some newly landed dragoons into line on the sand.

'I have no thoughts about *you*, Sergeant,' Lausard told him. 'What I think of you or any other man is my business.'

Delpierre was about to retaliate when Milliere stepped close to him.

'Get on with rallying the men, Sergeant,' the officer ordered curtly. 'I want all of us prepared before nightfall.'

'I can't make the boats hurry, sir,' the sergeant protested. 'Some of the regiment are still being brought ashore.'

'Then help Sergeant Legier organize those who have already landed,' Milliere told him, and Delpierre stalked off across the sand. The captain turned to Lausard. 'I didn't know you were once a sergeant, Lausard. What happened? How did you lose your rank?'

'I had a disagreement with your predecessor, sir,' Lausard told him and a number of the men nearby chuckled, Royere included.

'Nearly *everyone* had a disagreement with Captain Cezar,' the lieutenant said, smiling.

Milliere nodded. 'If you lost your rank it is up to you to regain it,' the captain offered. 'I'm sure there will be ample opportunity during this campaign.'

'Ample opportunity to get killed,' Roussard murmured, brushing a fly from his cheek.

129

'Steer clear of that bastard Delpierre, Alain,' Rocheteau advised.

'I have nothing to fear from him,' Lausard assured his companion. 'Perhaps it is *he* who should fear *me*.' He looked at the sergeant's broad back, watching as he shouted orders to another group of dragoons still struggling to find their land feet.

Stretching in both directions along the beach, infantry, artillery and cavalry were beginning to form into units, the latter two arms of the service being somewhat at a disadvantage as they were without their equipment. The artillery in particular seemed disconsolate about having no guns. The gunners carried a pistol each but other than that their only weapons for the time being were the short swords they possessed. Many of them sat around on the sun-baked sand merely watching as other troops formed up, and the sound of bellowing officers and NCOs began to fill the air as surely as the clouds of flies. Out to sea, the small armada of rowing boats continued to ferry men ashore and the number of troops steadily grew. High above them all, like a massive floating furnace, the sun continued to beat down with unceasing ferocity.

Thirteen

Lausard looked up at the night sky, gazing at the moon as if hypnotized by it. He, like his companions and the other French troops who had landed, had hoped that the onset of night would bring a respite from the unbearable heat, but the temperature had dropped only a few degrees. The raw heat of the sun had been replaced by a cloying humidity that made it difficult to draw breath. Men sat huddled around in groups silently cleaning their equipment as best they could. There was no food and no water and, despite the darkness, dozens of flies still flitted through the gloom and surrounded the troops. Those who tried to sleep found that the sand was still uncomfortably warm from its daytime baking, and if they removed their shirts to seek a little comfort, the irritating grains stuck to their skin and made conditions even more insufferable.

An order had been issued that no fires were to be lit, which struck Lausard as a little ridiculous even though he knew the primary reason was so that enemy troops would not discover their position. Firstly, there was no wood with which to build a fire; secondly, who in such sweltering temperatures would want to sit close to flames; above all, they had neither food nor water to heat over a blaze. From the map that Bonet had taken from his pack, Lausard could see that the French were now about two miles inland, away from the beach where he could still hear troops arriving in the darkness. The journey from the ships had been hazardous enough in daylight, what it would be like in the pitch blackness he could only begin to imagine.

'We're about five miles from Alexandria,' Bonet said, pointing at the map. 'Where we are now used to be a lake. We're in the dry lake bed of Mareotis.'

'It's a pity it's dry,' Joubert commented. 'We might be able to get a drink.'

'It seems a question of whether we starve to death or die of thirst,' Sonnier added.

'Perhaps we should eat Joubert,' Rocheteau teased, prodding his portly companion. 'There's enough meat on him to feed us all.'

The other men laughed, the sound echoing through the night.

'This isn't funny,' Delacor rasped. 'We haven't eaten or drunk for two days. It's no laughing matter.'

'We're all in the same position,' Lausard reminded him. 'There's no point in crying about it.'

'I bet the officers have got food and drink,' Delacor persisted. 'Those bastards aren't suffering like we are.'

'Everyone's suffering,' Lausard insisted, pulling his sword free of its scabbard. He took a piece of rag from his portmanteau and began cleaning the straight-bladed, three-foot-long steel, ensuring it wasn't damp. If it was replaced in its scabbard with moisture on the blade, the weapon would rust. When he'd finished he did the same with the fifteen-inch bayonet that could be fitted to his carbine.

Sonnier was busily cleaning his Charleville carbine, using a rag to dry the frizzen and the priming pan. He had already laid a number of his cartridges on the sand to dry the black powder inside. Damp powder was no good to any man.

'I lost some ammunition in that stinking boat,' Rocheteau said, counting the cartridges from his cartouche. 'I'm down to twenty-three and we haven't even *seen* any enemy troops yet.'

'Perhaps they've all run away,' Roussard offered hopefully. 'When they saw our ships, perhaps they decided it would be better to flee.'

'I doubt it.' Lausard ran a hand through his hair. 'They've probably been watching us since we came ashore. They're more than likely waiting to attack *us*.'

Roussard looked around nervously in the moonlight but was met by the sight of only French troops, mostly infantry. There were other dragoons, men from the same regiment, and a few artillerymen, but no sign of any hostile opponents as yet. Just as there was still no sign of any cannon or horses.

'How are we supposed to fight without horses?' Charvet wanted to know. 'We're meant to be cavalry, aren't we?'

'I haven't seen any of the other cavalry yet,' Bonet offered. 'No hussars and only a handful of Bonaparte's guides.'

'This terrain is no good for cavalry.' Rocheteau picked up a handful of sand and let it drain through his fingers.

'Let's hope we get the chance to find out,' Lausard said.

'Our enemies must have cavalry,' Rostov mused.

'The Mamelukes are legendary horsemen,' Bonet told him. 'They are reckoned to be the finest in the world.'

'And we're supposed to face them on foot?' Rostov muttered.

'They'll do no damage against infantry squares,' Charvet insisted.

'But where will *we* be?' Giresse asked.

'Hiding in those squares, if we've got any sense,' Roussard said.

'There'll be no need to hide,' Lausard responded. 'I don't intend to hide from anyone.'

'Always the hero, Lausard,' Delacor chided. 'Why are you always so keen to fight? Always so eager to face death? What are you trying to prove?'

'I have nothing to prove. I am in this army to fight, just like we all are. We are all soldiers, fighting is our business.'

'But you revel in it. You seek it out. Why?'

'That is *my* business,' Lausard said, glaring at his companion. 'If you are too much of a coward to face death then do not condemn me for your own shortcomings.'

Delacor scrambled to his feet. 'I could kill you for that.'

'You could try,' Lausard told him coldly, his eyes unblinking. He allowed one hand to drop to the hilt of his sword.

Delacor hesitated a moment then sat down again on the hot sand, looking across at Lausard. He finally lowered his gaze and began cleaning his carbine.

'Egypt,' Rocheteau sighed. 'What are we doing here?'

'We are spreading the culture of France throughout a desperate world,' Lausard replied and the other men laughed loudly. 'Freeing those who suffer the shackles of tyranny. Bringing to them what we have.'

'And what is that?' asked Rocheteau, a grin consuming his face.

'Empty bellies and a desperate need for water.' Lausard's remark was greeted by another wave of laughter from the men gathered around.

'We have freedom,' Bonet said. 'France has freedom. All those years of bloodshed, of upheaval, they must have given us something.'

'They gave *us* a place in a jail cell,' Lausard reminded him.

'We are not criminals any longer,' Charvet said.

'That's ironic coming from a man who killed someone during a fight and was nearly hanged for it,' Rocheteau chuckled.

'That was a fair fight . . .' Charvet began but allowed the sentence to trail off.

'No, seriously, Alain,' Bonet continued, 'what do *you* think France achieved by destroying the Bourbons?'

'One set of rulers was merely replaced by another. The Directory are as corrupt as any monarchy, probably worse. We do not fight for *them*, we fight for France and for ourselves. Are any of us better off under the Directory than we were under the Bourbons? No.'

'You sound like a Royalist,' Giresse chuckled.

'A realist.' Lausard smiled.

'We should all thank God we are still alive,' Moreau interjected. 'It was He who saved us from the guillotine, He who saved us from the sea and delivered us here safely.'

'I wouldn't thank him for bringing us *here*,' Roussard said.

'I'd thank him for some food,' Joubert said, rubbing his stomach.

'I'd thank him for the company of a woman,' Giresse added.

'You wouldn't have the strength for a woman after what we've been through,' Carbonne tried to convince him.

'I *always* have the strength for a woman,' Giresse assured his companion. 'I wonder what manner of delightful creature awaits my attention here.'

'According to that proclamation, the women here are treated with more reverence than back in France,' Bonet reminded him. 'They are held in high esteem.'

'I hold *all* women in high esteem. And *they* hold *me* in high esteem after they've experienced my touch and kindness.'

The other men laughed.

'As long as their men have something worth taking,' Delacor snapped irritably. 'I don't plan to leave this place empty handed.'

'And what are you going to steal?' Lausard pressed. 'Sand? There seems to be little else on offer at the moment.' He felt his stomach rumble, the cramps tightening a little more. 'Let's hope there's plenty of food in Alexandria; looking at this map there aren't any other cities of any size for miles. It's all desert.'

'When do you think Bonaparte will order the attack?' Rostov asked.

Lausard could only shrug. 'My guess would be as soon as possible. The quicker the city is taken, the less time there is for the Egyptians to reinforce it.'

'Attacking a fortified city after two days with no food, what does he think we are?' Delacor groaned. 'I bet he's enjoying a meal now. Chicken, bread, cheese, wine.'

'Shut up!' Rocheteau said, hurling some sand at his companion.

'It looks like we've got company,' Rostov said, looking out over the dry lake bed.

The men turned to see a group of officers trudging slowly across the sand, each unit they approached getting to its feet and drawing itself stiffly to attention. Shouted orders began to fill the night and the dragoons also raised themselves from the hot sand, eyes still fixed to the small group of men who moved in and out of the rapidly formed units of infantry. Under the white glow of the moon, they were able to make out at least one of the figures.

'It's Bonaparte,' Lausard said. 'It looks as if he's making an inspection.'

'Isn't that Kléber with him?' Rocheteau was pointing to the tall grey-haired general who strode alongside the Corsican.

As the officers drew nearer, they could also make out the features of Generals Bon and Menou, both sweating in their blue uniforms, Menou carrying his bicorn, the feather dangling from the cockade unmoved in the stillness of the air. Bonaparte himself was dressed in a Grenadier uniform. The top button of his tunic was undone but, unlike those around him, he seemed unaffected by the heat and strode along briskly through the shifting sand, glancing at each soldier, trooper and gunner he came to, running swiftly appraising eyes over them all. The dragoons drew themselves to attention as he reached them, saluting as one man when their commander raised his hand in their direction. He passed by rapidly, on to the next unit, and Lausard looked round to see that Captain Milliere had slipped away from the group of officers and rejoined his regiment.

'We march on Alexandria in one hour,' Milliere informed them.

'Is there still no sign of our horses, sir?' Lausard pressed.

'General Bonaparte will not wait for them to arrive, he says we are well equipped without them, that it would waste time to wait,' Milliere told him. 'We also have no artillery pieces. And yet the plan is to take a walled, fortified city.' The captain raised his eyebrows.

'How many men have we?' Lausard asked.

'Fewer than five thousand,' the officer informed him. 'All starving, all thirsty and all exhausted.' He turned to Rocheteau. 'What odds would you give me on a victory, Corporal?'

'Even money, sir,' Rocheteau said, smiling.

'If I told you there was food and water inside Alexandria would you change those odds?' Milliere grinned.

'I would say that the outcome is not even worth betting on, sir,' Rocheteau continued. 'I would say that the city is as good as ours.'

'That is what General Bonaparte thinks. Let's all hope he's right.'

'These men are in good enough condition,' Bonaparte observed as he continued with his inspection, his fellow officers struggling to keep up with him.

'The promise of food and water should be enough for them,' Berthier commented. 'A full belly is a bigger incentive sometimes than glory.'

Bonaparte laughed. 'There is *no* bigger incentive than glory, my friend.'

They passed more men, all drawn up in lines, standing to attention.

'How many of Desaix's and Reynier's men are ashore?' Bonaparte demanded.

'No more than three or four hundred of Reynier's troops have landed, General,' Berthier informed him. 'They did have further to come than the others, their transport was moored almost six miles from shore.'

'They've had enough time. I want the landing area well protected before we set off to attack Alexandria.' Bonaparte waved a hand in front of his face to drive away an irritatingly persistent fly. 'The artillery should have been in the forward transports too, as well as some horses. If we had just *one* squadron of cavalry able to function properly they could act as a screen for our advance.'

'I would have thought our intentions were fairly obvious to our enemies by now,' Dumas commented haughtily. 'And if you are so worried about a lack of cavalry then wait for the horses to arrive.' The huge mulatto cavalry commander wiped sweat from his face. 'I for one did not come to this infernal country to walk.'

'You have little choice, Dumas,' Bonaparte told him. 'I will not delay the advance any longer. There is no way of knowing how long it will be before the horses are brought ashore. We can always take mounts from the locals.'

'I thought we came as liberators and already you talk of stealing from these people.'

'They will be reimbursed,' Bonaparte snapped. 'We are bringing them freedom. What greater payment is there than that?'

'I don't care one way or the other where my men get their mounts,' Dumas persisted, 'only that they do.'

Bonaparte chose to ignore the comment and continued walking, passing more troops, casting an almost cursory glance over them. Bedraggled was the best word he could think of to describe them. Over two years ago, when he had taken command of the Army of Italy, he had seen men in a similar condition: shoeless, without weapons, many without uniforms; starving, penniless and resigned to the fact that defeat and possibly death was all they had to look forward to. Morale at rock bottom. He had taken command of an army of scarecrows and turned them into an invincible fighting machine. The bulk of that fighting machine was with him here in Egypt but, as he walked briskly among them, he could not help but feel that they had left that air of invincibility behind them on the rough seas between here and their homeland. The rigours of exhaustion, hunger and thirst were etched deeply into the features of nearly every soldier he surveyed as they stood obediently beneath the moonlight awaiting his order to begin their advance on Alexandria.

Standing on a ridge looking out over the dry lake bed of Mareotis, Bonaparte knew that the rest of his army was still coming ashore at Marabout but it was towards the north-east that his gaze was drawn, towards Alexandria. He felt as though some kind of invisible magnetic force was pulling him towards its spires and minarets, towards the city named after and founded by the conqueror he sought so desperately to emulate and eventually eclipse. He wondered if all those many hundreds of years ago Alexander had stood here in this same spot, anticipating his own coming conquests, aware of his own destiny and so eager to fulfil it. He was aware of the questioning gazes of his companions, of a certain restlessness among them, but even that could not disturb his meditative attitude and an unshakeable belief that what he had already embarked upon would bring him even greater glory.

It was another ten minutes before he spoke and gave the order for the advance to begin, watching as the commanders dispersed. Despite the cloying heat, Bonaparte felt a shiver at the back of his neck. The troops were beginning to form into a large column, ready for the journey. He smiled to himself. The time had come.

Fourteen

As he marched, Lausard was surprised at the varying consistency of the sand. In places it was soft and he sank as deep as his ankles whereas in others it was firmer and much easier to walk on. Unfortunately the majority was soft, making the troops' passage even more strength sapping. There was no road leading to the city, only an endless sea of sand, featureless and barren. No trees, no grass – and certainly no water.

Lausard looked up at the sky and saw that the moon had sunk almost out of sight; he guessed that dawn could not be more than thirty minutes away. The air was already warm and the day threatened increased temperatures. He, like the other dragoons, marched as best he could; all were weighed down by saddles and shabraques, their swords trailing in the sand or bumping against their dust-covered boots, their carbines held in their free hand. Lausard could already feel sweat pouring down his face, soaking through his woollen tunic and covering his legs, encased, as they were, in leather breeches. In contrast, up ahead the infantry marched with just their packs, bulging with what few personal belongings they had brought from the ships, and muskets sloped.

Lausard could see Bonaparte at the head of the column, striding determinedly through the sand. He was surrounded by a collection of officers, including Caffarelli, who seemed to be having the most difficulty negotiating the landscape. His wooden leg sank into the soft sand, and more than once Lausard saw the huge figure of Dumas physically lift the engineer clear. Dommartin also trudged along disconsolately, glancing up at the sky as if dreading the arrival of dawn and the onslaught of heat it would bring. The generals looked curiously out of place, the commander of cavalry having no horses at his disposal, while Dommartin, the artillery general, was equally lacking cannon. Berthier and Junot trailed along in the wake of Bonaparte, both trying to keep pace with him.

The endless dunes sloped up and down, the incline sometimes gentle, sometimes precipitous, and the men had trouble retaining their footing as they descended some of the sharper ones. Joubert overbalanced but a hand hauled him upright.

'God, I'd give my soul for a drink,' the big man said, wiping sweat from his face.

'Do not take our Lord's name in vain,' Moreau ordered irritably.

'Why can't God make it rain?' Joubert continued.

'God has no control over *this* country,' Bonet offered. 'It is a law unto itself.'

'It's a hell-hole,' Delacor added, glancing up at the sky.

The clouds were tinged with a bright orange hue, signalling the imminent arrival of dawn. And with dawn would come the unforgiving heat. Rocheteau checked his timepiece as the sun began to rise higher into the cloudless heavens. As it beat down on the marching men, Lausard wondered if he was the only one to notice the pace of the march change. It slowed to a walk as the men were blanketed in a heatwave unlike anything they had ever experienced before. Yet still they pressed on, aware now of a hot wind that had sprung up from the south, which sent particles whipping into their faces, adding to their misery. Sand stuck to their sweat-stained faces and hands. Those who opened their mouths to speak found their tongues were immediately covered by sand and they were forced to spit to clear it. But with no saliva this was a difficult task. Thirst that had seemed unbearable even as the march began was now growing intolerable. Lausard reached into his pocket, pulled out a handkerchief and tied it swiftly and expertly around his mouth and nose, giving himself at least some respite from the stinging grains. He wondered how long it would be before weapons were clogged by the fine clouds.

Up ahead two infantrymen toppled over, one of them rolling on to his back. Companions tried to haul them to their feet but neither of the men could move. The column continued.

Lausard felt his own legs trembling, the breath catching in his throat, but he drove himself on, putting out a hand to steady Giresse when he threatened to fall.

'How much further?' Sonnier gasped, feeling the heat from the sand even through the soles of his boots.

No one could tell him.

Lausard saw men pulling off their tunics in an effort to relieve some of the incredible discomfort caused by the heat. One or two even hurled the garments aside to lighten their load. He and the men around him were faced with a difficult decision: they could either remove their brass helmets and risk sunstroke or retain them and suffer even more acutely from the ravages of the sun. The metal itself was heating up. Lausard could feel his hair plastered to his head and neck, and when he blinked salty sweat ran into his eyes; however, at least it helped to keep his vision clear as it washed away the grains of sand. And through it all there were the flies. Black clouds of them swarmed around the troops and crawled over them in such numbers that, after a time, the men didn't even bother to swat them away.

It was Rocheteau who spotted the four figures on the crest of the ridge to the north. He tugged at Lausard's sleeve and pointed in the direction of the horsemen.

Through the swirling sand and the shimmering heat it was difficult to make out their features or even if they wore uniforms. They sat motionless on small white ponies and Lausard squinted in an effort to pick them out. He could see that two of them were carrying long spears, their bodies wrapped in white robes.

'Give me your telescope,' he said to Rocheteau, who handed him the implement. Lausard put it to his eyes and adjusted the focus, gazing at the watching horsemen, who were pointing at the column of French troops.

'What do you make of that, Bonet?' Lausard said, handing the telescope to the former schoolmaster.

'Bedouins,' Bonet said without hesitation, studying the horsemen. 'Local tribesmen.'

'Hostile?' Rocheteau asked.

'I should think so,' Bonet murmured.

As Lausard watched, the four horsemen disappeared

behind the sand dune as if they had melted into the desert itself. Others in the column had spotted them too and many men were pointing in the direction in which the tribesmen had disappeared. But the march continued, fairly large gaps now opening up between the units despite the efforts of officers to retain the closeness of the marching men. Lausard trudged on, glancing up at the hills every so often as if expecting to see the watching Bedouins again. Nothing moved on the ridge.

The shouts that came from the front of the column suddenly dragged his attention away from any thoughts of Arab horsemen. He looked round to see dozens of men racing from their formation towards a deep cleft in the sand that was surrounded by coarse grass.

'My God, it's a waterhole,' Bonet declared, suddenly pulling away from the rest of his companions and joining the headlong race for the source of water.

Officers and NCOs made no attempt to stop the men's frantic dash towards the waterhole; most had joined the charge, troops crashing into one another in their eagerness to get at the precious fluid. Delacor was the next dragoon to run off, then Joubert and a dozen more of the green-coated troopers. It took Lausard only a moment or two to follow them, he and Rocheteau wandering across to join the rapidly growing throng. They pushed their way through the heaving mass to see that the waterhole was in fact a makeshift well. At least it had *once* been a well. The source of possible moisture was filled with sand and rocks almost to the top.

'Those bastards!' Delacor stared at the polluted, useless well.

Other men were turning miserably to rejoin their units, realizing that the promise of water was now as remote as any chance of respite from the blistering heat and the swarms of flies.

'There'll be food and water in Alexandria,' Lausard said.

'If any of us get there alive.' With this, Delacor turned and followed his colleagues back into their formation.

Many of the men had sat down on the burning sand when the dash towards the well had begun, too exhausted to join the rush. Some now rose and began marching again; others could not drag themselves upright and simply sat watching, seemingly unconcerned, as the column moved on. Indeed, several men lay stretched out in the sun, ignoring the rays burning their flesh. Infantrymen, even a few of the dragoons, could march no longer. They would catch up later, they told themselves, when they had time to regain their strength. They would not, *could* not move another step and few of their NCOs made any attempt to force them. Even Delpierre stalked past two dragoons lying spreadeagled on the sand, making no effort to rouse the men. He marched on as efficiently as he could, his own throat parched, his own belly rumbling and crying out for water. Sand grains stung his eyes and made them tear, the moisture rolling down his already reddened cheeks. He licked at the salty droplets when they trickled to his mouth.

Lausard's helmet was like a small oven on his head, the brass absorbing the incredible heat. He removed it, but as soon as he felt the searing heat on his scalp, he quickly replaced it. He felt light headed; the heat, lack of food and water, combined with exhaustion, gradually wearing him down, as it was every man in the column. He looked back and saw dozens of men lying or sitting on the hot sand. Most had taken off their uniforms, some had even stripped as they tried to counter the sweltering effects of the sun. Close to Lausard Gaston stumbled, dropping to his knees momentarily. Lausard picked up the young trumpeter, hoisting him back on to his feet.

'Keep moving,' he told the boy. 'You must keep moving.'

At the head of the dragoons Captain Milliere and Lieutenant Royere were stumbling through the sand. Royere looked particularly badly affected by the heat and was dragging his saddle, the leather now coated by a thin film of sand and dust. He seemed to be moving as if in a trance, each step an effort, every yard a battle.

Rostov walked with his head bowed, staring down at the sand, cursing it and the heat.

'Alain, look.' Again Rocheteau was gesturing towards the hills, towards the figures silhouetted against the clear blue sky.

Bedouins.

Lausard counted twelve this time. They were still watching the column, perhaps counting its numbers, calculating its condition, satisfied that their sabotage of the well had deprived these invaders of some much needed water. As Lausard watched, another dozen joined the band of onlookers. Then even more. Their number had swelled to almost fifty now, many of them carrying long spears, clearly visible as they sat astride their sleek ponies.

To the south, Lausard counted another thirty of the Arabs, and even as he watched their numbers swelled alarmingly.

'Do you think they'll attack?' Rocheteau asked.

Lausard didn't answer, and simply watched as yet more

of the tribesmen came into view on both sides of the dunes. He guessed that they must be about five or six hundred yards away. Waiting.

'How many do you think there are?' Roussard was unable to keep the anxiety out of his voice.

'Well over a hundred,' Lausard replied. 'And that's only what we can *see*.'

The Bedouins remained motionless, seemingly content with watching the bedraggled French troops.

Then, suddenly, they began to move. The leading horsemen turned their mounts and began riding parallel with the column.

'They're tracking us,' Lausard said, aware that the number of tribesmen continued to grow. He looked to his right and left and guessed that there must be over two hundred Arab horsemen by now. They were moving at the same pace as the column, and as awareness of their presence spread through the French, so too did fear. Was there to be an attack? If so, when?

Even more tribesmen joined the slowly moving sentinels, and it seemed to Lausard as if they were emerging from the sand itself. Still the steady procession continued, the Bedouin guiding their horses along patiently, level with the increasingly nervous troops. Some of the men who had stayed behind on the scorching sand scrambled to their feet and attempted to catch up with their comrades, eager not to be left to the mercy of these desert dwellers. But many found their strength had left them, and they could only crawl in vain pursuit of the safety offered by their respective unit.

With each torturous yard the French marched, more Arabs appeared, and Lausard was now convinced that well over three hundred Bedouin flanked them.

'Perhaps they're some kind of escort,' Tabor offered, looking at the Bedouin.

'They're not an escort, idiot.' The nervousness was apparent in Delacor's voice. 'Why don't they attack?'

'They're trying to frighten us,' Charvet surmised.

'Well they're doing a good job,' Sonnier assured him. 'Delacor's right, why don't they attack and get it over with?'

Lausard looked to his right and left and saw that both groups of Bedouin had brought their horses to a halt and were forming up in untidy groups. 'It looks as if you're about to get your wish.'

Up on the hills, the groups of Bedouin to the north and south were now still, gathered together in large groups about one hundred and fifty strong on each flank. They sat motionless for agonizing seconds, watching the marching Frenchmen impassively.

Lausard was looking from right to left constantly, watching for some sign of movement from the tribesmen, waiting for both groups to come hurtling at the column. Then he heard a high-pitched shriek, followed quickly by another then another until both ridges echoed with the screams of the Bedouin. He watched as the long spears were raised into the air and felt his heart beat faster.

The first of the horses from the group on the northern ridge suddenly lurched forward, its rider holding his spear in his left hand, screaming something in Arabic as he hurtled towards the startled French.

Another horse burst from the group on the opposite ridge and also began galloping across the sand.

But that was it. Two men. No more.

From either side of the stunned Frenchmen, they raced forward.

'Hold your fire!' shouted an infantry officer whose men had formed two lines about fifty yards from the dragoons. Totally puzzled, they watched as the Bedouin warriors drew closer, waving their spears madly in the air while their tribesmen sat in silence again on either ridge.

Lausard's hand slipped to the hilt of his sword as the tribesmen drew closer. Rocheteau had raised his carbine to his shoulder. They could now see the faces of the Bedouin, contorted as they screamed their defiance and hurtled on towards the French column or, Lausard noted, the gaps in it.

The tribesmen hurtled through a gap between units of about twenty yards, passing within touching distance of the French and of one another. Then they swept on up the respective slopes and rejoined their fellow tribesmen. Almost immediately, more of the Bedouin sped their mounts forward and Lausard counted six from each group gathering this time, all shrieking madly and waving their spears.

Fifty yards from the French column, they split up, three or four sweeping through one gap in the bemused Frenchmen, half a dozen others riding into and beyond another breech in the lines. As with their predecessors they galloped up the hills to join their waiting companions.

'What kind of game is this?' Rocheteau snarled. 'Do they mean to attack us or not?'

'I would imagine they realize we cannot chase them with no cavalry,' Lausard said. 'They are trying to see what we do next.'

More horsemen detached themselves from the Bedouin hordes and followed the same routine as their companions, sweeping through the gaps with blood-curdling screams and little else. One of them spat at Milliere as he passed but that was the extent of the aggressive activity. The French infantry had lowered its weapons and were watching warily as yet another group of Bedouin came charging down the slopes, shrieking madly. This time some rode off towards the rear of the column, towards the stragglers. Lausard watched as an infantryman, dressed only in a pair of ripped pantaloons, was grabbed by one of the larger Bedouin and hauled up across the saddle, carried off like some kind of trophy. This happened three or four more times, the starving, exhausted Frenchmen powerless to fight back.

More Bedouin swept down towards the French, who now watched them more carefully. One of them slowed his horse as he drew near, adjusted the position of his spear and, as he rode through, drove the long weapon towards a watching infantryman.

The sharp point caught the man in the throat and he keeled over, blood spurting from the wound, staining the sand.

Angry shouts now rose from the French ranks.

Sonnier swung his carbine up to his shoulder and fired at the fleeing Bedouin, watching with satisfaction as the man toppled from his horse and lay still in the sand.

With the sound of the single shot still reverberating over the dunes, a number of the tribesmen turned and rode away, taking their captives with them. A dozen others, however, made one last charge towards the French.

Lausard drew his sword, ducked beneath the jabbing spear of a tribesman, and struck out with a powerful back-hand slash that caught the Arab across the chest, tearing through his flimsy garments and scything into his chest. The tribesman toppled backwards from his horse and fell at Lausard's feet. Rocheteau used his pistol on the Bedouin nearest to him, waiting until the man was no more than two yards away before firing at his attacker's face.

Tabor grabbed his assailant by the arm and, using his massive strength, pulled both him and his horse to the ground. The horse scrabbled wildly to regain its footing, one hoof slamming into the cheekbone of its rider, effortlessly shattering the bone. The Bedouin staggered to his feet as the horse galloped away, but before he could turn and run, Delacor had finished him with his sword. The other Bedouin turned their mounts and rode off, disappearing over the hills as quickly as they had come. By the time Lausard looked up, the ridges were empty again. The Arabs had vanished like ghosts. All that remained of their presence were the pony tracks in the sand and half a dozen bodies over which flies were already swarming.

'If that's the stiffest resistance we come up against we should conquer this country in a week,' Rocheteau said, smiling.

Lausard didn't answer. He wiped his bloodied sword blade with a piece of cloth then slid it back into the scabbard.

'What horsemen,' Bonet enthused. 'They didn't have any saddles. The horses didn't even have proper bridles, just reins in their mouths.'

'We should have tried to capture some of the horses, it would have saved us walking,' Delacor observed.

'They weren't shod either,' Bonet added. 'I suppose that's so they get a better grip in the sand.'

'Why did they take those men prisoner?' Tabor wanted to know.

'God knows,' Lausard murmured. 'I don't even want to think about what they might do to them.'

'It will discourage stragglers from now on,' Rocheteau chuckled, looking up at the dunes once more, his tone turning reflective. 'What kind of men fight like that?'

'Or ride like that? I'd back one of them against any one of us in a race,' Charvet said.

'Do you think they'll be back, Alain?' Rocheteau asked.

Lausard wiped sweat from his face, his eyes still scanning the dunes. 'It isn't a matter of if, it's a matter of *when* and how many.'

Ahead of the column was a steep slope. Men toiled up it in the blistering heat, scarcely able to force their shattered bodies along in the sucking sand. Lausard watched as many of them paused as they reached the top; he assumed it was from exhaustion, but as the dragoons crested the ridge he saw why so many had slowed their pace. It was the sight before them that caused them to pause. The bleached stone walls swarming with frantic defenders, the ancient cannon barrels protruding through the embrasures and, beyond these outer walls, a number of minarets and spires.

'Alexandria,' Lausard murmured.

Fifteen

Lausard guessed that the stone monument about five hundred yards away, poking upwards into the cloudless sky like an accusatory finger, was close to seventy feet tall. It was towards this monument that he saw Bonaparte and his generals moving, the Corsican gesturing all about him as he walked.

The shouts of officers and NCOs filled the air and Lausard saw that the troops were moving into position in preparation for attack. Exhausted, starving and racked by thirst as they were, the French troops were to be given no rest before the city was assaulted. The bulk of the infantry was marching to the north, in the direction of a smaller, triangular fort that guarded the approaches to the city. Lausard's weary unit formed up behind a demi-brigade and marched towards one of the main gates to the north of the fort. Lausard could see the tall, grey-haired figure of General Kléber issuing orders to his subordinates, who scurried off to complete them.

'What time is it?' Lausard asked Rocheteau, his eyes never leaving the silhouette of the city.

'Eight.'

'I don't think I can take another step without food,' Joubert insisted.

Lausard was about to answer him when the early-morning air was suddenly filled with an unearthly screeching.

'What the hell is that?' Delacor demanded, looking towards the city.

It took the men just a few seconds to realize that the defenders lining the walls were shrieking uncontrollably, either in fear or in an attempt to frighten off their attackers.

A moment later there was a thunderous roar of cannon fire as the guns on the walls of the fort opened up and the projectiles could be heard whistling through the scorching air. They landed in the soft sand about twenty yards ahead of the waiting French troops, sending up geysers of dust and sand.

'Forward!'

No one was quite sure where the order had come from but, as one man, the French advanced, carbines sloped uniformly. Lausard looked across and saw that the troops commanded by Menou and Bon were also moving forward. The shrieking that had greeted their initial arrival seemed to double in volume but it served only to aggravate rather than deter the attackers.

As they drew nearer to the cracked walls the first popping of muskets began to fill the air, but there was no uniformity to the fire. Lausard could see men leaning over the walls firing down on him and his companions.

The infantry, carrying ladders to scale the walls, had already reached the fortifications and were beginning to climb.

Sonnier raised his carbine and aimed at one of the defenders on the parapet, smiling as he saw his quarry struck by the ball. The Arab tottered uncertainly for a second then toppled over the battlements, his scream cut short as he struck the sand below. Sonnier was reloading when he was struck on the shoulder by something heavy, something that had been hurled from above. He went down clutching at his arm and Lausard saw that a sharp rock the size of a man's fist had caught his companion, causing him to drop his weapon. Another smaller projectile slammed against Lausard's helmet, the impact staggering him momentarily. Suddenly the air seemed to be filled with stones, all hurled with great power and desperation from the battlements. The hail of rocks struck the attacking French and more than a dozen infantrymen toppled from the scaling ladders, one with his forehead laid open practically to the bone. Men at the foot of the walls were now firing up at the defenders and the air began to fill with the stench of acrid smoke that was rolling across the sand like man-made fog, adding to the already foul quality of the air. As the firing intensified, the morning air seemed to turn red hot. It was like taking lungsful of air directly from a furnace.

Roussard was hit by a rock that cracked one of his fingers.

Tabor staggered as another thudded into his chest.

Only the occasional musket was fired from above and Lausard heard a bullet whistle past his ear and bury itself in the sand. Ahead of him several infantrymen had succeeded in clambering to the top of a ladder and were swinging themselves over on to the parapet. More swarmed up after them and the dragoons followed.

As he pulled himself over the battlements, Lausard

drew his sword in time to meet the charge of an Arab, who swung what looked like an axe at him. Lausard ducked beneath the clumsy attack and drove his sword into the man's stomach, pulling him on to the blade then wrenching it free. There were nearly two dozen Frenchmen on the ramparts now and the numbers were growing by the second as more and more climbed the ladders. Many of the defenders jumped down into the fort, anxious to escape the battle, but others fought on. Lausard was struck in the face by a rock. He tasted blood on his lip and lurched towards his attacker, catching him by the throat and hurling him off the parapet.

Further along, Rocheteau had flattened one attacker by slamming the butt of his carbine into the Arab's face and was about to bayonet another of the terrified men but before he could strike the Arab leaped from the rampart, crashing through the roof of a stable below as he fell.

Lausard saw Captain Milliere and Lieutenant Royere both using their swords against the hapless defenders. Royere was suddenly struck by a rock and went down heavily, bleeding from a cut behind one ear. Milliere turned on his companion's assailant and drove his sword into the Arab's chest. However, the blade stuck between the man's ribs and, as he fell back, the sword was pulled from Milliere's grasp, leaving him momentarily defence-less against another, much larger assailant, armed with a wickedly curved sword.

The officer ducked under the first vicious swing but Lausard could see that the crush of men fighting left little room for manoeuvre on the ramparts. He pushed his way through the mêlée and stepped in front of Milliere's attacker, blocking the devastating downward stroke, then driving his fist into the Arab's face. The impact drove the man back and Lausard struck out with his sword, driving the blade through the Arab's throat, ignoring the blood that spattered him.

Milliere pulled his weapon from the body of the man he had killed and slapped Lausard on the shoulder in a gesture of thanks.

They both helped Royere to his feet, the lieutenant wincing as he touched the cut behind his ear, but he nodded that he was all right and the three men pressed on, aware that the ramparts were now almost exclusively occupied by blue- and green-jacketed troops. The defenders who weren't already dead were fleeing. Rostov shot one down as he tried to climb down a ladder, watching with satisfaction as the body hurtled to the ground.

Lausard looked down over the battlements and saw that hundreds of French troops were advancing towards the outer walls of Alexandria, tricolours flying high above them. These men, like himself, were, he thought, not fighting for pride or honour; they were attacking with such fury because they were all too aware of the provisions that awaited them within the walls of the ancient city. Food and water. Men ran at the walls with little regard for their lives, propping the ladders and scrambling up like monkeys, roaring oaths, seemingly oblivious to the shower of rocks and the desultory volleys of musket fire that greeted their assault.

The triangular fort was empty now, home to only the dead and wounded of both sides. French troops ran through the buildings looking for any scraps of food or traces of water; when they found none, they rejoined their comrades in the assault on the outer walls of Alexandria.

Lausard scrambled down a ladder and joined the rest of his unit, many of whom were firing upwards at the walls. Smoke was drifting across the battlefield making it difficult to see more than ten yards in front, the noxious clouds swirling around the men like reeking fog. Lausard heard cheers, screams, curses. He heard voices bellowing in Arabic, many of those screaming.

Carbonne lurched towards him out of the smoke, his face bleeding, his cheeks smeared with powder. He was gasping for breath, finding it difficult to draw in air that was red hot and seared the lungs.

'The main gates have given way,' he declared triumphantly. 'The infantry have broken through.'

The exhaustion the men had felt an hour earlier was forgotten, all other considerations replaced by the desire for victory, the desire to storm the city and get at its supplies. Lausard heard bugles sounding the advance, heard officers bellowing orders and, above it all, the constant crack of musket fire.

He followed Carbonne through the thick smoke, a light wind suddenly blowing away the black pall to reveal the open gates, now battered by the ferocious attacks on it. French troops were flooding in, waving their swords and muskets above their heads, firing on anything that came within range.

Rocheteau appeared at Lausard's side, his face blackened by the smoke but his expression cheerful. 'We have them. And we have their city.'

As Lausard followed his companion he glanced to his left and saw several soldiers gathered around a grey-haired officer, whom he recognized immediately as Kléber. The general was bleeding heavily from a wound above his eye, blood soaking through the bandages as quickly as the surgeon could tie them.

Lausard ran on, into the city itself. Immediately, several

musket balls hit the ground close to his feet, and he and Rocheteau dived for cover behind some barrels. The shots had come from a nearby house, and infantry were retaliating, pouring fire back into the buildings. The narrow streets were awash with choking fumes that stung Lausard's eyes and scorched his throat. He coughed and spat, then reached for a cartridge from his cartouche; he bit off the ball and, holding it in his mouth and tasting the black powder as he did so, he poured powder down the barrel, pulled the ramrod free and spat the ball down the carbine, ramming the remains of the cartridge down after it. He tapped the weapon gently against the ground to allow more powder to spill out into the priming pan, then he swung the weapon up.

Rocheteau, like most of the infantry and the dismounted dragoons, had fixed his bayonet, the fifteen inches of needle-sharp steel gleaming on the end of the weapon.

The two men moved off down a street, finding it difficult to walk side by side as the thoroughfare was so narrow. From all around them they heard screams, the constant crackling of fire, orders shouted in French, and oaths roared in many languages. Lausard heard a child crying and a woman weeping, but he could not tell where these sounds came from or how close they were. The interior of the city was bedlam. Men, women and children ran back and forth in the smoke and flames, some fighting, some trying to escape, some trying to hide and, through it all, the French forged on through the labyrinthine streets shooting, bayoneting or sabring anyone who crossed their path.

The coppery smell of blood began to mingle with the cloying gunpowder.

A loud bang sounded to Lausard's left, which he recognized instantly as the discharge of a pistol and he heard a ball whistle past his ear. Spinning round he swung his carbine up to his shoulder and, in one fluid movement, sighted and fired at the Arab who had shot at them from a doorway. The carbine spat out its deadly load, the bullet finding its target. The Arab went down like a rock, blood spewing from the wound in his chest. Rocheteau crossed to the body and ran his bayonet into the man's face angrily.

'Bastard!' he hissed under his breath and, for the first time, Lausard saw that his companion had been struck by the pistol shot. A piece of flesh the size of a thumbnail had been blown from Rocheteau's left ear, and blood was coursing down the side of his face, mingling with powder stains.

The two men moved on, finding that they'd been joined in the narrow street by half a dozen infantrymen, who were moving in and out of the houses looking for any of the enemy who might be hiding, and also for any food or water they could find. They emerged empty handed, the discovery only serving to galvanize them further.

Lausard and Rocheteau emerged into a large square already filled with troops, some gathered around a trough in the centre. Any water in it had been drunk by the time the dragoons reached it and several men lay around on the bleached cobblestones burbling incoherently, as intoxicated as if they had drunk a gallon of wine. A large building filled the skyline directly opposite, and from its shining dome Lausard guessed it was a mosque. A dozen or more infantry were approaching the main doors, muskets lowered, more than one of them admiring the jewels that festooned the heavy wooden partitions.

Several dead bodies, most of them Arabs', their robes torn and bloodied, littered the square. Some had already been stripped, their silken garments taken as souvenirs by the French. Lausard saw several men from his own unit wandering about the square. He recognized Charnier, a corporal from the third squadron, busily ripping gold earrings from a couple of dead natives before slipping them into his cartouche. He waved amiably at Lausard, ignoring the occasional bangs and cracks of pistols and muskets still exploding periodically from the houses that overlooked the square. But only a handful of the city's residents had chosen to fight on and the firing was sporadic; most had surrendered or fled.

Like Lausard and Rocheteau, a number of infantry-men were heading towards the mosque, admiring its bejewelled doors.

'Easy pickings.' Rocheteau smiled.

Suddenly the doors of the mosque burst open and the men froze. Standing inside the holy building were more than twenty Arabs, men and women, all armed with muskets and pistols.

For what seemed like an eternity no one moved, then the Arabs opened fire.

A savage volley of bullets raked the advancing French and a number went down in the hail of lead, one man clutching his face, another screaming madly as he held up a hand that had been holed by a ball. A sergeant grunted as his knee was shattered by a shot.

A rolling bank of smoke filled the doorway to the mosque and screams immediately replaced the roar of fire as the enraged troops rushed towards the building, crashing into the doors and forcing them open, driving the defenders back inside. Lausard saw an officer raise his sword above his head and charge in with the infantry. 'Kill them all!' he roared, his face contorted with rage.

Rocheteau drew his sword and dashed in after the infantry, closely followed by Lausard. Inside the mosque every sound was amplified; every shot was deafening, every scream of pain or desperation magnified, every curse or prayer intensified.

Those who carried weapons were cut down first, their bodies trampled as the soldiers sought to reach those beyond.

A child of no more than five clung to its mother, and Lausard watched as one infantryman shot the woman while another drove his bayonet through the child, lifting it into the air like some kind of obscene trophy.

An old man raised a hand to surrender, only to have it hacked off by a sword blade.

A woman threw herself to the floor, prostrate before a large sergeant, who merely brought his foot down on the back of her head with all the power he could muster. He repeated the action a number of times before finally running his bayonet into the motionless body, then charging on to skewer a man who was on his knees praying.

Rocheteau struck an Arab across the face, laying the flesh open to the bone with his sword. The man dropped to his knees, head bowed as if seeking mercy. Rocheteau had none to spare and struck again, a powerful blow that practically severed the man's head. He toppled sideways on to a dead child.

Most of the Arabs who remained alive had retreated to the rear of the mosque where, without exception, they prayed, their voices amplified by the hollow interior. The floor was awash with blood, and Lausard strode through it towards the officer who had ordered the attack, who was aiming his pistol at the head of a terrified child, clinging desperately to its mother.

'Enough!' Lausard shouted, grabbing the officer's arm.

The man shook loose of the dragoon's grip and glared at him with blank eyes. It was an expression Lausard had witnessed before; a trance-like stare that consumed men who had killed to excess. The air reeked of blood and excrement, the cries of the Arabs echoed loudly around the confined space.

'They fired upon us, they deserve to die,' the officer said, his pistol still pointed at the child.

'Look how many have,' Lausard said, motioning around him at the carpet of bloodied corpses covering the floor of the mosque. 'It is time to stop.'

Something flickered behind the officer's eyes; Lausard couldn't be sure what. Realization? Pity? Humanity? He blinked hard and nodded, as if emerging from his hypnotic state.

'They fired on us.' His voice was barely above a whisper.

'I know,' Lausard told him.

The officer turned and ordered his men from the mosque, the infantry wandering out back into the blistering heat of the noon sunshine. Lausard watched them go, then he turned to look at the Arabs still gathered in prayer at the rear of the mosque. Their heads were bowed, all apart from an old man with a long grey beard who got to his feet, walked across to the dragoon and kissed his hand. He babbled something in Arabic and dropped to his knees at Lausard's feet.

'Why did you stop them, Alain?' Rocheteau asked. 'You once said that there were no innocents in war. Besides, they *did* fire on us, that officer was right.'

Lausard drew his sword suddenly and held the hilt towards his companion.

'Take it,' he said angrily. 'Finish what you started. Is that what you want, Rocheteau? They are all helpless now. It shouldn't take more than a few minutes to slaughter the rest of them.'

Rocheteau looked at him warily, the sword only inches away from him.

'We've killed civilians before,' the corporal reminded him. 'What's the difference now?'

'Perhaps you're right,' said Lausard, and he turned his sword, gripping the hilt, drawing it back so that the point was pressing against the throat of the old man. 'Let's kill them all.'

The old man shrieked something unintelligible and tried to back away but Lausard held him by the shoulder.

Rocheteau jumped to his feet and grabbed Lausard's sword arm. 'All right, Alain,' he said. 'You've made your point. They live.'

Lausard slowly withdrew his sword and sheathed it. 'We might be killers, but we aren't yet murderers.'

The two dragoons turned and headed out of the mosque, the prayers and cries of the surviving Arabs echoing inside their heads.

Sixteen

'It isn't how I'd imagined it,' Bonet said, looking around. 'I'd been expecting something more imposing. Something magnificent. Not this.'

The former schoolmaster stood in the centre of one of Alexandria's main squares gazing around him sadly. Lausard, too, was less than impressed by the city founded by Alexander so many centuries earlier. The tall stone monument he'd seen prior to the attack on the city was, Bonet had informed him, named Pompey's Pillar, but other than that there was little to suggest a place of awe and splendour – only one of filth and squalor. The streets were unpaved and filthy, the buildings a jumble of hovels constructed from unbaked clay bricks, wood and dirt – the only buildings that looked even remotely impressive were the mosques, of which there were many. And what struck Lausard particularly was the absence of trees: other than a few date palms, there were none.

'I don't care what it looks like now I've eaten.' Joubert was munching on a flat cake he'd purchased at one of the bazaar stalls moments earlier.

The bazaar itself was a kaleidoscopic collection of soldiers, Arabs and traders, some of whom had come from the desert to sell their wares. Lausard noticed stalls selling pigeons, sheep, lentils, watermelons and tobacco. The men had eaten and drunk their fill within hours of the capture of the city, and ever since had been anxious to stock up with food in case of another shortage. Most of the infantrymen wandering about had their packs stuffed with all kinds of provisions. Water was the most expensive commodity as, even in the city itself, it seemed to be in relatively short supply. However, a number of Bedouin groups had been sent out into the desert to lead Caffarelli's engineers to nearby wells, and water was being ferried back to the city for the benefit of both the French and their new-found allies.

'I don't think much to their women,' Giresse commented as a girl in her early twenties passed by. She was wearing a dirty blue shirt and nothing else. He looked down at her filthy bare feet and noticed that her toenails were painted red. She was followed by two young children, both naked, who were jabbering in Arabic to each other and looking curiously at the French as they passed them.

'What's so different about here to Paris?' Rostov said. 'The streets there are filthy; we were no better than these people, living in filth.'

'At least we had some dignity and didn't walk around in rags or allow our children to roam the streets naked,' Delacor protested indignantly.

'And what fine suit of clothes were *you* wearing when you were arrested?' Lausard asked.

The other men laughed.

'I was dirty for a reason. I couldn't help it.'

'Perhaps it is the same with these people,' Lausard responded.

'Five hundred years of slavery has crushed their spirits,' Bonet offered.

'And what were we but slaves to the Bourbons?' Delacor retaliated. 'Now slaves to Bonaparte and the Directory instead.'

'Better slaves than dead men,' Roussard interjected.

'We are not slaves, we are soldiers,' Lausard said sternly.

'What's the difference?' Delacor demanded.

'You used the word dignity,' Lausard reminded him. 'Perhaps we still have some of that left. As long as we retain it we will also retain our humanity.'

Rocheteau raised one eyebrow as he looked at Lausard.

Something unspoken passed between the two men. Rocheteau remembered how Lausard had acted in the mosque and wondered if that was the humanity his colleague spoke of.

Up ahead a small crowd had gathered, comprised almost entirely of French troops, among them many green-jacketed dragoons. Lausard and the others pushed their way to the front of the throng, anxious to see the object of interest. On the cobbles of the square Charnier, from the third squadron, sat cross-legged and behind him a huge Arab, stripped to the waist, was sharpening a razor against a flat stone.

'I thought I needed a shave,' Charnier said, smiling. 'I don't know why everyone wants to watch.'

Lausard looked down at his companion then up at the Arab barber, and a slight grin creased his features. 'You have more faith than I, my friend.'

'He's only a barber,' Charnier said dismissively. 'What harm can he do to me?'

Richard Howard

Lausard saw the barber being guided into position by an assistant and the grin broadened on his face.

'*I* wouldn't trust a blind man with a razor,' Lausard told him, laughing aloud as the smile faded rapidly from Charnier's face. As it did the big Arab suddenly clamped both knees around the Frenchman's head, one against each ear, tilting the dragoon's chin upwards. He then set to work, moving the razor with devastating speed and skill, shaving off the thick growth of bristles that covered the Frenchman's cheeks, chin and neck.

'Blind?' Charnier shrieked, unable to move as the barber continued his work.

The watching men were convulsed with laughter.

'If you want to keep your nose, I'd keep still.' Rocheteau chuckled.

Lausard watched as the steel was wielded with such skill and precision that Charnier barely felt it against his flesh. The barber finished with a flourish and released Charnier from his grip to a loud chorus of applause from those watching.

'I don't think you'll ever be called upon to show your courage in any other way, my friend,' Lausard called, laughing, but Charnier was unable to reply. He simply pushed a couple of coins into the barber's sweaty hand, staring at the milky cataracts that discoloured the man's eyes.

'Blind,' he mumbled as two of his colleagues helped him to his feet, the laughter of the other troopers echoing in his ears.

'I wouldn't have trusted that bastard to shave *me*,' Delacor said. 'I don't trust any of these pigs.' He looked disdainfully at a group of Arabs sitting close by.

'They probably don't trust us either,' Bonet reminded him. 'After all, we have invaded their country.'

'Not *invaded*, Bonet,' Lausard corrected him sardonically. 'Liberated. Isn't that our mission as soldiers of the Republic? Some of the idealists in the army think so and doesn't it say so in this proclamation from Bonaparte himself?' He reached across and pulled a large piece of paper from a nearby wall, surveying carefully the words printed on it. Hundreds of them had been read aloud to the inhabitants of the city and also posted throughout Alexandria the previous day. Lausard read aloud. '"In the name of the French Republic, founded on liberty and equality, the commander in chief of the French armies, Bonaparte, lets it be known to the whole population of Egypt that the beys who govern Egypt have insulted the French nation and oppressed French merchants long enough: the hour of their punishment has come. For too many years that gang of slaves, purchased in Georgia and the Caucasus, has tyrannized the most beautiful region of the world. But Almighty God, who rules the universe, has decreed that their reign shall come to an end."'

'God has decreed nothing concerning this country,' Moreau interjected. 'This invasion was decreed by civilians, by men, not by God.' He crossed himself.

'I agree,' Delacor added. 'His holiness here is right. This entire expedition was dreamed up by the Directory.'

'What makes you think that?' Rocheteau wanted to know. 'Since when did you become a politician?'

Some of the other men laughed.

Deep in thought, Lausard stroked his chin. 'You could have a point, Delacor,' he mused. 'A strong army is a threat to the Directory, especially when it has a leader as powerful as Bonaparte.'

'Perhaps that's why there are so many civilians on the expedition,' Roussard offered. 'They're probably spies, sent by the Directory.'

'That's ridiculous,' Bonet told him. 'They are learned men. Historians, architects, artists and writers. They are here to chronicle the culture of this country, not to spy on *us*.'

'How do you know that?' Roussard persisted. 'Those preening "pekinese", I don't trust any of them. All they do is complain about their conditions.'

'Like some others I could mention?' Lausard quipped and the men laughed.

'I heard from someone in the second squadron that all of them had been put on privates' rations and in quarters fit for privates,' Joubert said.

'Good. Let them suffer as we suffer. What use are they to us anyway? They are only any good if they can use one of these.' Delacor patted the hilt of his sword.

'There is always a need for brains as well as brute force,' Bonet said.

'And what was it that took this city?' Delacor challenged. 'I didn't see too many of your thinkers and painters up to their ankles in blood yesterday. They were probably busy hiding or they didn't want to dirty their precious hands with Arab blood.'

'What else does the proclamation say, Alain?' Rocheteau asked.

Lausard scanned the paper, his lips moving silently for a moment, then he began to read again, loud enough for all the men to hear.

'"Once you had great cities, large canals, a prosperous trade. What has destroyed all this if not the greed, the iniquity and the tyranny of the Mamelukes?"' He glanced over another portion of the proclamation. '"Tell the people that the French are also true Moslems,"' Lausard read.

'I don't wish to be classed with these heathen.' Moreau was indignant.

Lausard ignored him and read on. '"The proof is that they have been to Rome the great and have destroyed the throne of the Pope who always incited the Christians to make war on the Moslems, and that they went to the island of Malta and expelled the knights, who fancied that God wanted them to make war on the Moslems."'

'This is heresy,' said Moreau, trying to snatch the proclamation from Lausard.

'No it isn't,' Lausard told him. 'It's propaganda. Bonaparte is trying to convince the Arabs we're their friends, not their conquerors.'

'I hope it works,' Rostov added.

'"All villages that take up arms against the army will be burned to the ground,"' Lausard read on.

'So, we are to kill more civilians if we are ordered,' Rocheteau observed.

Lausard nodded.

'Bonaparte calls the Mamelukes tyrants and then tells us we will have to kill women and children,' Bonet commented.

'It wouldn't be the first time, would it?' Lausard said quietly.

'To hell with them,' Delacor rasped. 'I don't care *who* I have to kill.'

'"May God curse the Mamelukes and bestow happiness on the Egyptian nation,"' Lausard read mockingly.

'There you have it. We are now bringers of happiness as well as liberators.' He balled up the proclamation and threw it into the gutter.

The men made their way back through the narrow streets and crowded bazaars and it seemed as if every house and building inside Alexandria had been used to billet French troops. Even the houses of the rich had been used by officers. Some of these dwellings had gardens, but other than that and gold ornamentation adorning some doors and windows there was little to distinguish them from the hovels inhabited by other residents of the city. Rumours about bubonic plague were circulating, of how the yearly epidemic had only just run its course, and it struck fear into the French.

'Perhaps Delacor is right, perhaps the Directory really *are* trying to get rid of us,' Rocheteau observed as they neared their billets close to the Rosetta Gate. 'First they nearly starve us to death during the sea voyage, we arrive in a country that doesn't want us and then we find out we could all catch the plague.'

'A man could be forgiven for thinking the odds were against him,' Giresse added.

'It's all a gamble, isn't it?' Lausard said. '*Life* is a gamble. It seems that *our* odds are shortening though.'

The conversation died as they saw Captain Milliere advancing towards them, forage cap protecting his head from the blistering sunshine. Like his men he was dressed in the single-breasted *surtout* and grey overalls the dragoons wore on campaign.

'You are cavalry again,' he informed them, smiling. 'The horses arrived from the landing site an hour ago. They are being inspected by the farriers now, but I warn you – they are in a bad way.'

'How bad, sir?' Lausard asked.

'Like us, they were hungry, thirsty and sick,' Milliere told him. 'At least forty from this regiment alone died during the journey. I'm surprised it wasn't more.'

The dragoons hurried off in the direction indicated by Milliere, who held up a hand to halt Lausard.

'A word,' he said quietly, snaking one arm around Lausard's shoulder. 'I have already received orders from General Bonaparte himself that the first columns of infantry are to leave here tomorrow. He does not want them advancing into terrain that has not been scouted. Now that our horses have arrived I can send out patrols. I want you in one of those patrols. Lieutenant Royere will command and he will need good NCOs to back him up. I know that you lost your rank in Italy.'

'General Bonaparte himself took it from me, sir,' Lausard said, a wan smile on his lips.

'Well, *I* am returning it. I have watched you, Lausard. During the voyage here and during the fighting you conducted yourself with honour. That honour should be rewarded. As from now, you are a sergeant again. General Bonaparte has approved the promotion.'

Lausard smiled.

'Go and find your horse, *Sergeant*,' said Milliere. 'Tell your companions.'

'I'm sure some of them will be delighted, sir,' said Lausard, saluting sharply. 'Thank you.'

'Perhaps you shouldn't thank me for sending you out into the desert,' the officer mused. 'God knows what you'll find.'

'I doubt if even God knows what we'll find out there, sir, and I still thank you.'

'And if you find death?'

Lausard didn't answer. He simply headed off to look for his horse.

Napoleon Bonaparte pointed at one of the many maps spread out on the table in the room then looked around at the officers who stood with him.

'Cairo,' the Corsican said. 'By marching upon it we will force the Mamelukes into a battle and that, gentlemen, is precisely what we must do. They would be content to avoid us until the conditions favour them. They would fight us on ground of their own choosing if we let them. We must force their hand. Marching on Cairo will do this. It will ensure that they confront us and, when they do, we will destroy them.'

'You seem very certain they will oppose us so quickly,' General Kléber said, his head still heavily bandaged from the wound he'd received the previous day.

'They will not allow us to take their capital city without a fight,' Bonaparte said assuredly. 'But that fight must come sooner rather than later. If we delay too long the Nile will flood, it will make troop movement difficult.'

'This desert makes most things difficult,' Dumas declared, brushing a fly from his cheek. Even in the relative stillness of the night the insects continued to fill the air in unwanted abundance.

'You shouldn't complain, Dumas.' Bonaparte smiled. 'At least you and your cavalry have horses now.'

'Most of them. Some will still have to fight on foot. The supply trains and the horse-drawn artillery are still without animals.'

'That is the concern of Caffarelli and Dommartin, not you,' Bonaparte reminded him. 'Just ensure that *your* men perform the tasks I assign them. They will be used mainly in a scouting role until other mounts can be acquired.'

'And how do you propose to *acquire* these additional mounts?' the cavalry general asked, a note of doubt in his tone. 'I have seen few horses of any quality here since we landed.'

'I have already met with thirteen Bedouin sheiks,' Bonaparte told him. 'For a cash payment they will supply us with three hundred horses and five hundred camels. In addition, they have also agreed to supply us with a further one thousand camels and camel drivers who we may hire for a negotiated price.'

'Camels?' Dumas said incredulously. 'You would use camels to draw artillery and supply trains?'

'I would use oxen if I thought it would help our cause here. Besides, camels are perfect. They are stronger and they will cope with the terrain better than our own horses.'

'Do you trust these Arabs enough to trade with them?' Dumas wanted to know.

'It isn't a matter of trust, it's a matter of necessity,' Bonaparte informed the mulatto. 'I need troops on the move as soon as possible. This entire campaign, as in Italy, relies on speed and on the concentration of our troops against the Mamelukes as quickly as possible.'

'What is your plan?' Kléber moved closer to the profusion of maps as he spoke.

'You, Kléber, will remain here with two thousand men to garrison the city,' Bonaparte instructed, his words spoken with enthusiasm. 'Desaix's division will march out tonight; they will be followed tomorrow by Bon's division, then by Reynier and Vial. Murat and Dugua will march on Rosetta in the north; they will then be supported on their march south by a flotilla that will patrol the Nile itself. The entire army will rendezvous at El Rahmaniya.'

'A march across open desert,' Dumas commented, looking at the maps.

'The distances are minimal,' Bonaparte protested. 'Desaix, Bon, Reynier and Vial's divisions will pass by way of Damanhur, just forty-five miles from here. It is another fifteen miles from Damanhur to El Rahmaniya. Three days' march at most.'

'I must confess, I share Dumas' concern about the terrain and the conditions,' Berthier offered. 'A three-day march across such hostile country is not an enticing prospect.'

'There are many places where the troops can stop en route,' Bonaparte said sternly. 'Such as Beydah or El Karioun. They can stock up on provisions and water there, I'm sure the locals will be only too happy to co-operate. They will see us as their saviours, why should they make our progress difficult? Furthermore, I do not want the local population antagonized during these marches. All supplies purchased and any labour performed will be paid for by cash, in local currency. Some of the gold and silver we brought from Malta has already been exchanged to facilitate this.'

'At a greatly disadvantageous rate, I might remind you,' Berthier said.

'What else were we to do? There was no mint in Alexandria and the loans we raised were insufficient for our needs. These people we go amongst are hostile, fanatical, distrustful and excitable. I want them to know that we French come as friends and liberators and as respectors of their culture and their country. Not as thieves and murderers like the Mamelukes who have oppressed them for so long. I swore to free them and that is what I shall do. The *fellahin* will be grateful to me. They will welcome us all with open arms once we have destroyed the Mamelukes.'

'Since when do invaded nations welcome their would-be conquerors?' Dumas demanded. 'They see through our intentions.'

'What they see is not important,' Bonaparte said. 'Perhaps they *do* fear us as conquerors but that fear is nothing compared to what we offer them. We offer them freedom from a yoke of tyranny they have worn for hundreds of years. If they distrust us now they will grow to respect us once the beys are removed from power. As I said, this must be done with utmost speed. The Mamelukes must be destroyed and Cairo must be taken within four weeks.'

'And what if that is impossible?' Kléber pressed.

The Corsican smiled. 'The word impossible has no place in my vocabulary. Nor should it have in yours. We have already pushed back the limits of human capability and this campaign has yet to begin in earnest. Glory awaits us. I suggest we do not keep it waiting.'

Seventeen

Lausard reined in his horse and patted its neck. Although the animal had been ridden for less than twenty minutes, a combination of the almost intolerable heat and the horse's poor condition meant that it was already well lathered. Lausard looked down and saw that the animal's tongue was lolling from its mouth and it was panting heavily, as desperate for water and food as were most of the men. Before leaving the outskirts of Alexandria at dawn the horse had eaten half a bag of oats and drunk a little, but none of the French mounts were on anything like normal rations and hadn't been since they'd first left Toulon.

Lausard tried to think back to the voyage, the storming of Malta and the constant fear of attack by Nelson's warships, but the entire episode seemed to have blurred in his mind. It felt like centuries since he had left his homeland. It crossed his mind that it must feel the same way for his horse. Struggling under the weight of its rider and his saddle and shabraque and equipment, thirsty and woefully short of sustenance, it was a miracle the animal could even walk let alone break into a trot, something he had urged it to do frequently during the journey from Alexandria. Lieutenant Royere, who was commanding the patrol, had given orders that the horses were not to be worked too hard because of their condition, an order the other eleven men in the patrol had been only too happy to comply with. Their mounts were in a similar, sometimes worse state. The animals ridden by Charvet and a tall Gascon named Tigana had suffered so badly that their ribs were showing, pushing against their normally sleek coats. But, like their riders, they fought their way through the sand and the heat, able to do nothing other than endure the discomfort.

It was Tigana who now drew his mount to a halt alongside Lausard, removing his helmet briefly to wipe sweat from his already sodden face. He was a thin-faced individual with sad eyes but his horsemanship was almost legendary within the regiment. He'd been raised on a farm on the outskirts of Paris, his parents having died in an outbreak of typhus in Gascony. Taken in by an older brother he had worked with horses on the farm for most of his life until they were seized by the Republican army, so desperately in need of remounts and food. Tigana had refused to let any horses be slaughtered for meat and had ended up in prison for 'wilfully obstructing the aims of the Republic'. When the army found itself in need of troops two years later, he had been taken from his cell in Bicetre and forced to fight, just as Lausard and most of the remainder of the regiment had been.

Lausard nodded a greeting to the trooper then looked out over the forbidding terrain.

The plains of Beheira formed an unending carpet of inhospitality to all who crossed them. Lausard failed to

see how even the Bedouin warriors who called them
home could exist in such an arid and desolate environment. All he could see was sand, great shifting expanses
that seemed to shimmer in the haze. There were no
roads, no recognized routes across this wilderness. He
had no doubt that the Bedouin used trails, but how,
he could only imagine. With the constant hot wind the
sand covered anything stationary within hours, blowing
around like stinging grains of hot shrapnel. Lausard
brushed some from his nose and the corners of his mouth
just as his horse snorted to clear its own nostrils of
both sand and flies. The sergeant could feel the sweat
soaking through his tunic, staining the material in a
huge dark smear all across his shoulders and down to
his kidneys. He had a little water left in his canteen
but decided to wait a while before drinking it. He knew
that a sip would not suffice; he would have to drain
the entire contents to even come close to slaking his
raging thirst.

'Have you found anything?' Lausard asked finally.

'Some camel droppings, a few tracks,' Tigana told him.
'But if you mean water . . .' He shook his head.

'Any sign of Bedouin?'

Again Tigana shook his head. 'Just the tracks. They
were probably around but I didn't see them, though God
knows where they could hide in the middle of this.' He
waved a hand in the direction of the featureless sand.
'What about you, Sergeant, any luck?'

'There's supposed to be a village about a mile or two
ahead,' Lausard informed him, pulling a map from his
pocket and unfolding it a little. 'El Tantara. Perhaps
there'll be food there for us *and* our horses.' Again he
patted the neck of his mount. 'If there is, Desaix will

want it for his men so we'd better get what we need first.' He folded up the map once more and flicked his reins, coaxing his horse forward.

The patrol was spread out across a frontage of about three to four miles, some thirty minutes' ride from General Desaix's marching troops, who were making their way even more slowly and tortuously across the burning sand. Other patrols of varying size had been sent further south, and some north towards Lake Idku and Aboukir, while the bulk of the dragoon regiment crossed the desert as part of Desaix's division. If anyone in Lieutenant Royere's patrol found provisions, water or caught sight of the enemy, they were to ride back to the column immediately with the information. But, Lausard thought, while the possibility of finding food and water in this barren wilderness was remote enough, the chance of finding any Mamelukes was even slimmer. They had no reason to attack when they could simply lure the French deeper and deeper into the desert. Indeed, the sergeant wondered if this campaign might even be settled *without* a battle. The sun and sand were probably as capable of destroying any army as were the Mamelukes. Why should they risk their lives in combat when the elements would do their work for them?

The sand dunes rose steeply and the two dragoons found their mounts were having difficulty making the climb. Lausard resisted the temptation to put spurs to his horse and the animal finally reached the top of the ridge, panting even more heavily. He wiped sweat from his eyes and looked down, shaking his head as he gazed at what lay before him.

'What's that?' asked Tigana, similarly perplexed by the sight.

'The village of El Tantara,' Lausard replied, his voice low.

There were fewer than a dozen small huts constructed of mud and straw, all deserted. Abandoned. Two or three palm trees grew close to one of them and there was what appeared to be a well, but not by any stretch of the imagination could this be called a village. Lausard and Tigana rode forward slowly, their eyes focusing on the well. When they reached it they both dismounted.

The wind seemed to have dropped a little and it was replaced instead by the loud, insistent buzzing of flies. Great, corpulent black ones that swarmed around the lip of the well as if it were an open wound. Lausard crossed to it as Tigana wandered into the nearest of the hovels. As Lausard drew nearer he recoiled from a particularly foul smell. A putrid odour that clogged in his nostrils and forced him to raise a hand to his face. He peered down into the well.

It was half filled with rocks and dirt but it also housed the remains of a camel. Lumps of rancid meat had been tossed down into the water with the other debris, ensuring that even if some fluid was extracted from the dirt it would be tainted and undrinkable.

Lausard stepped away from the poisoned well and glanced over to see Tigana walking from hut to hut. His inspection didn't take long. As he walked back towards Lausard he paused beside several piles of horse droppings, picking up one of the dung balls in his hand. He broke it open and glanced at the inside.

'Still moist. Whoever was here couldn't have left more than thirty minutes ago. This stuff dries quickly in the sun.'

'Bedouin,' Lausard murmured, noticing some camel

tracks nearby. 'I would ask you if you're sure but I usually make it a point of honour never to argue with a man about horseshit.'

Tigana chuckled.

Lausard pulled the map from his pocket once again and studied it.

'There are dozens of places marked on here between Alexandria and Beydah,' he mused. 'Towns and villages. But who's to say they're any bigger than this?' He glanced around at the crumbling mud huts.

'And there's the Bedouin to worry about,' Tigana said, his colour draining slightly. 'I heard what they did to some of those they took prisoner. They raped them, as men would rape women.'

'Who knows what goes through the minds of men who live on camels' milk all year round?' Lausard said, wandering back towards his horse. 'Come on, we'd better move. We're supposed to rendezvous in an hour with the rest of the patrol at Barada.'

'Let's hope they've had more luck than we have,' Tigana said, swinging himself into the saddle.

'I wouldn't bet on it,' Lausard said quietly. 'I really wouldn't.'

The village of Barada lay in a hollow, although, Lausard thought, it looked more like a collection of hovels. Even though the dunes on all four sides sheltered the dwellings from the hot wind, they also acted as a heat trap, snaring the rays of the blistering sun, reflecting them off the steep slopes of the dunes. It was difficult to breathe the air was so warm, and as Lausard and Tigana guided their horses down the steep slope towards the village, they both felt the air temperature increase. Tigana removed his helmet but the ferocity of the sun soon persuaded him to replace it. His exposed skin was already seared red – he didn't want to risk sunstroke as well.

Lausard heard voices, one of which he recognized as Rocheteau's. A second later he saw the corporal's horse tethered to a nearby palm tree, the animal pawing the sand with its hoof, shaking its head as the flies constantly buzzed around it.

The other voices, he soon saw, belonged to Delacor, Moreau and Fornac. They were gathered around one of the huts and, as he and Tigana drew nearer, he saw that they were standing before a wiry-looking Arab, who seemed relatively undisturbed by their threatening gestures and tone. He merely looked at each of their faces in turn as if trying to memorize some detail of their features.

'What's going on?' Lausard called and Rocheteau spun round, a smile flickering on his face.

'Alain, did you get lost?' he said. 'Come and see what we found here.' He nodded towards the Arab, who observed Lausard with the same cool indifference with which he regarded the other dragoons.

Lausard dismounted and wandered across to the little group.

'He saw us coming,' Rocheteau said, motioning towards the Arab. 'But he never attempted to run.'

'He's up to something,' Delacor hissed.

'Have you searched the village?' Lausard asked, glancing away from their captive for a second to run appraising eyes over Barada itself: fifteen or sixteen huts, clumps of palm trees and a well. It could have been any village anywhere in Egypt. There was nothing to distinguish it from any other.

'There's a little grain,' Rocheteau told him. 'That's it.'

'What about water?' Lausard pressed.

'The Bedouin have filled the well with camel shit and sand,' Rocheteau told his companion. 'We'll get nothing out of that.'

Delacor took a step towards the Arab and raised his hand as if to strike him, but the man remained defiant, standing motionless.

'Every well or cistern we found has been contaminated,' Delacor rasped. 'There's no water.'

'All the other villages we found were deserted too.' Fornac brushed a fly from his face as he spoke. 'They've all run off into the desert to hide.'

'Or prepare themselves,' Lausard murmured, looking once again at the captive Arab. 'So why didn't this one run?'

'Riders coming in,' Moreau called, pointing to the south of the village, and the dragoons turned to see six more horsemen, led by Lieutenant Royere, making their way towards Barada.

'A prisoner?' Royere mused, dismounting.

'We should shoot him here and now,' Delacor suggested.

'We have no reason to kill him,' the officer said. 'Besides, he may be of use to us. We found tracks to the south-west, camels and horses. Hundreds of them. It's a Bedouin raiding party but much larger than any of us could have expected, and they've got between us and the main column. We're cut off.'

'What do we do?' Sonnier said worriedly. 'They'll destroy us.'

'We could try to make it back to the column, but if they catch us out in the open they will destroy us.'

'Which direction were they moving?' Lausard wanted to know. 'They might have been moving *towards* the army, away from us.'

'They were heading straight for here,' Charvet told the sergeant.

'So do we try to outrun them, stand and fight, or surrender? Perhaps our friend here could act as a go-between.' Royere motioned towards the Arab.

'I'm not giving myself up to those animals,' Tigana said. 'I'd rather die fighting.'

'We should take a chance and try to rejoin the column,' Sonnier offered. 'Some of us will make it.'

'If we surrender they might spare us,' Chatillo said. 'Prisoners have already been traded. Some of the other men who were captured were returned for ransom.'

'And what if the army won't pay a ransom?' Delacor snapped. 'What then? I say we fight the bastards.'

'I'll kill myself rather than be taken prisoner,' Tigana added.

'We haven't got a chance, we don't even know how many of them there are,' Chatillo persisted.

'We have to make a run for it, they won't get us all,' Sonnier persisted.

'I will not be responsible for the deaths of these men if I can avoid it,' Royere said. 'Running across the desert on tired horses is a sure enough way of getting us all killed. What do you say, Lausard?'

'Stand and fight them, Lieutenant. I for one would rather die with a sword in my hand than running from men such as this.'

'And I,' Rocheteau echoed.

'If only we knew their strength,' Royere mused.

'There are about two hundred of them.'

The men looked round in bewilderment at the source of the words. The Arab stood unflinchingly before them, amused at their reaction.

'They passed close to here about an hour ago,' he continued.

'You speak our language,' Royere exclaimed.

'I speak many languages. Yours, English, Arabic and my own.'

'What is your name?' Royere pressed.

'Karim.'

'Why are you not with your people?'

'I *have* no people any more. I am not a true Egyptian. I am Circassian, brought to this country by the Mamelukes when I was ten. Taught to ride and to fight by them, educated by them but enslaved by them until I escaped when I was eighteen. I have lived in the desert for the past four years, an outcast among people who think of me as one of their own. But I do not belong among them; I will not be a slave to any man.'

'Whom do you owe your loyalty to?' Lausard wanted to know.

'To myself and my beliefs. I owe no loyalty to *any* man.'

'He's dangerous,' Delacor said sharply. 'I say we should kill him. How do we know any of what he's saying is true?'

'If it were lies what would it matter?' Karim said. 'There was no need for me to speak at all and yet I chose to tell you the strength of the Bedouin who will come to attack you. I don't ask you to trust me, simply to listen to me.'

'What makes you think the Bedouin will attack us?' Royere asked.

'If you found *their* tracks then you can be sure they will

have found *yours*. They will destroy you because you are trespassers on their lands and because they have been commanded to fight you.'

'Commanded by whom?' Royere pressed. 'I heard that many tribes were to help us. They were supposed to be our allies.'

'The ulemas and sheiks of Cairo have sent word to the tribes to fight you. They have been called to wage a holy war against you invaders and they will,' Karim informed the men. 'If they can destroy you in ones or twos, twenties or thirties, in hundreds or thousands, they will.'

'And when the time comes, who will you fight with?' Lausard asked.

'You and your leader came to liberate Egypt, to free it from the rule of the Mamelukes. I have nothing but hatred for the Mamelukes and I feel no allegiance to the Bedouin. I will fight with you against whoever opposes you.'

'You can't trust this bastard, Lieutenant,' Delacor persisted. 'As soon as our backs are turned he'll either run or stick a knife in us.'

Royere regarded Karim evenly then looked at Lausard.

'I think we need all the help we can get,' said the sergeant.

'I agree. Arm yourself, Karim. You fight with us now.'

Eighteen

In the burning heat of the afternoon sun the dragoons worked furiously, pausing every thirty minutes to sip at water that had been carefully rationed to one cup per man. The desire to gulp down the precious fluid was overwhelming but they knew that they must try to control the raging thirst that tormented them, to concentrate on their labours in the hope that they might forget their discomfort. It did little to help. Toiling in just their breeches they felt the sun scorching their flesh, burning them with its fiercesome heat and sucking the very breath from their lungs.

Karim had found a few tools: an axe, a couple of large knives, a scythe and some rudimentary chisels. Tabor had been given the axe, his prodigious strength having been employed to chop down several of the palm trees growing around the village. As he brought each one crashing down, Tigana and Carbonne dragged it to its appointed place where it was split several more times into long shafts; both ends were sharpened and driven into the sand with about three or four feet of wickedly pointed wood sticking menacingly out.

Lengths of rope were tied around other palm trees, the ends loose and trailing back into the collection of hovels.

Fornac was carefully loading carbines and sharing out ammunition, the prepared weapons laid upon a shabraque to prevent them clogging with sand.

Moreau was minding the horses, ensuring that they were tethered in the centre of the village. He fed them what little grain had been found in Barada then, that done, he helped Sonnier, who was busy sharpening swords and bayonets against a stone.

Rocheteau and Lausard dragged a wagon into position and, with Chatillo's help, overturned it, placing bags of sand behind it to act as a firing platform.

Charvet was sharpening smaller, thinner lengths of wood to be used as additional weapons if the fighting became too desperate or if the dragoons' bayonets weren't up to the task. Made from easily malleable metal, Charvet had seen them bent easily by strong men. As he whittled points he tried not to think about the possibility of hand-to-hand fighting, although if it came to if he would be ready. Karim joined him and began sharpening pieces of wood using a short knife he took from his belt. Also attached to the thin strip of leather was a curved scabbard containing, Charvet assumed, a matching sword, the angle of the blade from hilt to tip even more pronounced than that of a light cavalryman. Karim finally noticed the Frenchman's interest and drew the weapon.

The blade was wafer thin and looked as if it would break at the slightest contact with anything solid. Karim offered it to Charvet, who was surprised at its lightness.

'How do you cut anything with this?' he asked, hefting the blade.

'It is the sharpness of the blade that matters, not its weight. A sharp sword will cut in any hands.'

'Is that the kind of sword the Bedouin use?'

The question came from Lieutenant Royere, who was strolling towards the two men accompanied by Lausard and Rocheteau.

'They are not skilled fighters,' Karim told him. 'This weapon is the weapon of the Mamelukes. One of their leaders is said to be able to decapitate an ox with one blow of a sword like this.'

Lausard took the weapon from Charvet and inspected it, touching his fingertip to the blade. He applied no pressure and yet the skin on the pad of his middle finger still split, although not deeply enough to draw blood.

'And you know how to use this?' he asked, returning the blade to Karim.

'I was taught from the age of ten. The men who taught me were masters of the sword.'

'Your admiration for them is commendable,' Royere noted. 'I trust it will not interfere with your ability to fight them.'

'The men who are coming here to destroy us now are not the men who taught me,' Karim reminded him. 'Those who will come here are the true people of this country who despise the Mamelukes as surely as I do, but they would destroy me as well as you. Do not fear for my loyalty.'

'Why will they want to kill you when you're one of them?' Lausard queried.

'*Like* them, but not one of them,' Karim corrected him. 'Now, do you wish to continue arguing with me or would you perhaps be better employed readying yourselves for the Bedouin attack?'

Lausard smiled and slapped the Circassian's shoulder.

'The traps are set at the approaches to the village,' said Rocheteau, turning to look at Royere. 'And all the weapons are ready.'

'How will the Bedouin come at us?' Royere addressed Karim.

'They will try to ride you down. It is all they know.' Karim looked around at the dunes that rose on all four sides of Barada. 'They may come from just one direction, they may attack from all four sides at once. It is impossible to say what they will do.'

'The stakes and ropes will slow them down,' Lausard mused. 'We need concentrated fire against them on those parts of the village that are not protected.'

'Concentrated fire,' murmured Fornac, who had joined them. 'From twelve men? We haven't got a chance.'

'Enough of that talk,' snapped Royere. 'We don't know how far away the rest of the army is. General Desaix and his men might even reach us before we are attacked.'

Lausard caught the officer's eye and saw the lack of conviction in his expression.

'What's that?' Rocheteau murmured.

It sounded like the sea breaking on the beach. A low rolling rumble growing steadily in volume. It was coming from the north.

'Can you feel it?' the corporal continued. 'The ground is shaking.'

'Take your positions,' shouted Royere and the dragoons rushed to retrieve their weapons, five or six of them scurrying to the firing platform behind the overturned wagon. Sonnier took up position on the roof of one of the mud huts, his carbine trained in the direction of the steadily growing noise.

Lausard and Rocheteau were close to the wagon, sheltering behind more sandbags. Nearby, Tabor held one end of the thick rope strung between two palm trees about fifty yards from the makeshift rampart. In his other hand he held his sword.

Royere checked his pistols, jamming both into his belt.

The rumbling grew louder and now the men could also hear yelling, the snorting of camels and the neighing of horses. All eyes turned towards the crest of the northern dunes.

Moreau crossed himself.

Lausard felt his heart thudding heavily against his ribs.

Rocheteau swallowed hard, a bead of perspiration trickling down the side of his face.

Tigana gripped his carbine more tightly, whispering softly to himself as he squinted down the sight.

Carbonne pressed one palm to the sand, feeling the heat but also the incredible vibrations that shuddered all the way up his arm. He closed his eyes tightly for a second, trying to control his breathing, although it was difficult to suck any air from the scorching heat that surrounded him.

Lausard watched the crest, saw dust clouds rising, heard the thundering of hooves growing ever louder, then, finally, he saw them. The full mass of the Bedouin seemed to reach the crest at once. A great seething swarm of men and animals, the leading riders roaring at the tops of their voices, both to urge on their mounts and also to frighten their enemies. The Bedouin were an impressive sight, pouring up and over the crest like a tide, some of them waving spears, others brandishing swords and even pistols. He pulled his carbine more tightly into his shoulder and waited for the order.

Royere was pacing slowly back and forth, watching as the Arabs flooded down the reverse slope and galloped towards the collection of hovels that formed Barada. They were five hundred yards away and closing rapidly, spear points gleaming in the sun, their tightly packed group spreading out into several ragged lines. But there was no order to the charge and Royere wondered if the horses and camels might even be blown by the time they reached the French.

Four hundred yards. And they came with the same frenzied speed.

One group had veered off to the left slightly and Lausard wondered if they were going to try to hit the French in the flank. He nudged Rocheteau and Tigana and they joined him as he scuttled to a position about twenty yards to the right of a clump of palm trees. It was then that he realized the riders were heading for the rope strung between the trees, at present hidden from their view as they charged.

'Tabor,' the sergeant called out. 'The rope. Tie it off. Now.'

The big man obeyed, hurrying to wind the thick hemp around a tree near him to secure it.

With the Arabs dashing towards the palm trees the now-tightened rope suddenly sprung up, only feet from their speeding horses. Unable to stop, they went crashing into it, the rope taking the animals around the forelock. It was enough to bring a dozen of them down in a flailing heap, and Lausard looked on in satisfaction as two of the Arabs were crushed beneath their mounts and another smashed in the face by a wildly kicking horse's hooves.

'Fire!' Lausard shouted, and he and his two comrades brought down another horse and two Arabs.

The rest jumped to their feet and ran.

The blast of muskets caused both Frenchmen and Arabs alike to glance in the direction of the first contact, but the howling Bedouin continued charging towards the rest of the dragoons.

From his perch up on the roof of one of the houses, Sonnier took aim and fixed a tall Arab riding a camel in his sights. The man was still two hundred yards away but he would make a good target once in range.

Lausard pulled another cartridge from his cartouche, bit off the end, held the ball in his mouth, dropped powder in, spat the ball after it then rammed down wadding. The taste of powder filled his mouth as he swung the carbine up to his shoulder and waited as the enemy came within one hundred yards.

They were nearing the wooden stakes. Covered carefully with palm leaves, the vicious spikes were invisible to the onrushing riders as they hurtled closer and closer.

'Ready!' Royere shouted, raising his voice above the rampaging Arabs.

Those at the front had reached the spikes.

Too late, they realized what lay beneath the concealing leaves.

The razor-sharp points seemed to erupt upwards from the sand, as if pushed from beneath by invisible hands.

The leading riders tried to turn their mounts to avoid the trap but the sheer momentum of those behind pushed them forward on to the deadly spears.

Lausard watched as the leading horses were impaled on the wooden stakes and their agonized shrieks began to fill the air. Men, unhorsed as their mounts were skewered, fell beneath the churning hooves of those following. One man tried to pull his mount around, away from the points, but the animal pulled up sharply and sent the rider spinning from its back. He screamed loudly as the stake pierced his body. Others shared the same fate, catapulted over their horses' necks to be impaled on the stakes. The sand all around began to turn red and those Arabs behind were held up by the crush of dying men and horses, frozen in one place, unable to either attack or retreat.

'Fire!' Royere bellowed and the dragoons opened up.

A loud explosion of musket fire rolled over the scene, the pan-flashes and muzzle bursts followed immediately by choking clouds of sulphurous smoke.

More Arabs went down, struck by the lead balls and the dragoons frantically began to re-load, spitting bullets down barrels, ramming them home with wadding, then preparing to fire again, choking on the stench of their own gunpowder, spitting the black grains as they tasted charcoal and saltpetre. By now, some of the Bedouin had managed to either bypass the confusion or extricate themselves from the bloodied mess, and they were now hurtling towards the hovels where the French sheltered. Another volley of fire brought more crashing down, horses rolling on riders, wounded men trying to crawl away bleeding their life into the scorching sand.

Then the first riders reached the French. Lausard swung his carbine like a club, slamming it into an Arab and knocking him from his horse. As the man struggled to his feet, Lausard drove his bayonet into the man's chest twice, then turned to face another Bedouin, who was coming at him with a large, flat-bladed sword. Lausard pulled free his own sword and blocked the Bedouin's first strike, then he shot out a hand and pulled at the horse's bridle, the sudden shock causing the animal to rear. It flung its rider to the sand, and as he tried to get up, Lausard thrust his sword into the man's throat.

Royere fired both his pistols simultaneously at an attacking Arab, both balls striking the man in the chest. He toppled from his horse, the terrified animal sweeping past.

Fornac turned to deal with one Bedouin, exposing his back to another. The Frenchman shrieked as the second Arab drove a long spear into his kidney, forcing the weapon on with such force that it erupted from the Frenchman's stomach. He dropped to his knees clutching at the bloodied point. Lausard saw that the Arab was now defenceless and stabbed him in the side, hauling him from his horse, then driving the blade into his face to finish the job.

Karim stood firm as a Bedouin bore down on him. He ducked under the Arab's swipe then spun round and, with one savage blow, hacked off the Bedouin's hand. The appendage spun into the air, spurting blood, and the Arab rode off shrieking. Sonnier shot him as he swept past, the body landing with a thud on the sand.

Lausard ducked as he heard a bullet whistle past his ear. It struck the wagon close to him.

He turned to see three Arabs firing at him from horseback.

'Those are Charlevilles.' Rocheteau was beside him. 'They're shooting at us with our own guns.'

'They must have taken them from prisoners,' Lausard observed, keeping low as another shot smacked into the wood close to him.

Royere was reloading his pistols when he shouted in pain and went down in an untidy heap, clutching his leg.

Lausard and Karim rushed across to him, seeing immediately that the officer was bleeding from a wound just above his knee. Lausard checked the entry wound and was relieved to see a larger, more ragged hole at the back of Royere's thigh.

'You're lucky, it went straight through.' The sergeant began ripping at the officer's breeches, exposing the wound more fully, pulling small pieces of material from the ragged edges with his fingers, waving away the flies that buzzed round the bloodied hole. Karim saw that one of the Bedouin had dismounted from his limping horse and was running straight at Lausard and the wounded officer, sword brandished above his head, yelling insanely. The Circassian stepped into the Bedouin's path, swinging his scimitar up to parry the blow. As the Arab prepared to strike, Karim lashed out. With a blow combining devastating power and effortless expertise, he caught the attacker just below the chin. The razor-sharp steel of the scimitar sheared through bone and flesh with ease and the Arab's severed head spun into the air, propelled by a geyser of blood. The body remained upright for a moment then hit the ground with a thud.

Royere began crawling towards one of the hovels, leaving a trail of blood behind him. Lausard snatched up one of his pistols, handing the other one to the officer, who was gesturing towards three Bedouin riding towards the village at break-neck speed.

'Rocheteau!' Lausard shouted, drawing the corporal's attention to the onrushing horsemen.

The corporal tore the end off his cartridge, poured in powder, spat the ball in, rammed the wadding and raised his carbine, desperate to get a shot off in time. So eager that he realized he'd forgotten to remove his ramrod from the barrel. As he fired, the metal stave was shot out of the barrel like a spear. It embedded itself in the leading Arab's chest and he screamed, clutching at the metal rod as he toppled from his horse. The other two wheeled their horses and turned away, one of them struck in the back by a bullet.

The men saw that all the Bedouin were turning, fleeing, riding back over the bodies of their own dead and wounded, leaving their comrades impaled on the wooden spikes, on the blood-drenched sand or slumped beneath the bodies of their dead mounts.

Lausard helped Royere to the shade offered by one of the mud hovels.

'You take command,' Royere said breathlessly, hastily wrapping a piece of cloth around his injured leg.

'You're going to be fine, you've just lost some blood,' Lausard assured him.

Royere smiled and raised hands covered by the crimson fluid. 'I can see that,' he said quietly. 'I'm giving you an order, Lausard. Take command. Do whatever you have to do to save these men and, if you have to get out of here and leave the wounded behind, then do it.' He gripped the sergeant's arm tightly. 'And I mean *all* the wounded.'

Lausard looked down at the officer's bullet-torn leg.

'Alain, they've gone,' Rocheteau shouted. 'All of them.'

'But they'll be back, won't they?' Lausard looked at Karim.

The Circassian nodded slowly.

'One dead, five wounded including the lieutenant,' Rocheteau reported. 'I've told Sonnier and Tigana to bury Fornac.'

'How bad are the wounded?' Lausard asked, glancing

across to where Sonnier and Tigana were scrabbling in the sand, creating a makeshift grave for their dead companion.

Rocheteau shrugged. 'Moreau was kicked by a horse. Charvet has a cut across the arm, Chatillo has a bullet wound in the side and Carbonne lost the top of a finger. They'll live. They can fight on. What about Lieutenant Royere?'

'We have to get him out of here before infection sets in,' Lausard said, walking slowly across the sand. 'Karim stopped the bleeding and patched him up well enough, but he won't last too long without proper attention and food and water.'

'That goes for all of us, Alain,' the corporal reminded him. 'None of us have drunk anything for over fifteen hours.' He looked up at the sky. 'This stinking weather. This stinking desert.'

'The Bedouin know our strength now, they'll attack again. Karim is sure of it.'

'Do you trust him, Alain?'

'Why shouldn't I?'

'He's one of them.'

'He's no more one of them than any of us, besides, you saw the way he fought. He knows this desert and its ways, Rocheteau. He may yet be our saviour.'

Rocheteau looked puzzled.

'If we sit and wait for the Bedouin to attack again we could all die of heatstroke, hunger or thirst,' Lausard explained. 'We can't outrun them in open desert, they'll cut us to pieces. There'll be no relief from Desaix's column because no one even knows we're here. As far as Desaix is concerned we're still scouting, or perhaps he thinks we've run off to find water or food for ourselves, or just been killed by the Arabs. Who knows? What I'm trying to tell you is we have to reach the column. Someone has to ride back to Desaix and bring help here, to relieve us. Someone has to ride across the desert and return with reinforcements. I'm going to send Karim and two other men. The column can't be more than half a day's ride from here.'

'That Arab bastard will run off and join the Bedouin,' Delacor said, who had overheard part of the conversation.

'No he won't,' Lausard said. 'You'll be there to make sure he doesn't. I'm sending you with him. You and Tigana.'

'And what do *we* do?' Rocheteau wanted to know.

'We hold the Bedouin here until they return with extra men; I doubt if they'll attack at night. As soon as the sun goes down, Delacor, you, Karim and Tigana will ride for the column. Understood?'

Delacor nodded slowly.

Lausard and Rocheteau continued walking.

'Do you think they'll make it?' the corporal said.

'Bonaparte promised us all six acres of land, didn't he?' Lausard mused. 'Well, if they don't bring help then you and I won't get six acres, we'll get six *feet* of Egyptian sand.'

Nineteen

The night was pitch black and other than one small fire in the centre of Barada, the dragoons were without light. Hemmed in on all sides by a sea of gloom they surrounded the dull yellow light of the fire as if seeking refuge in its dancing flames. They certainly didn't need the heat; the raging temperatures of the daylight hours scarcely dropped with the onset of night and the air was still humid and stifling.

Lausard walked to the rim of the dunes and peered out into the desert. Beyond he saw what at first looked like hundreds of fireflies but which he then realized were the fires of the Bedouin tribesmen, waiting until morning to relaunch their attack. Lausard had no idea how many of them there were but every so often, when the wind was blowing in the right direction, he could hear excited chatter and the guttural sounds of camels.

Judging by the number of fires it appeared that more tribesmen had joined those who had attacked. Lausard wondered how many of the desert warriors would come at them the following day.

'How will you get through?' he asked Karim, as he approached the Circassian. 'It looks as if they're everywhere.'

Karim nodded gently and swung himself on to his horse's back, Delacor and Tigana following his example.

'Give me one of your bullets.' Karim held out his hand to Lausard.

The sergeant looked puzzled but reached into his cartouche and did as he was asked, watching as Karim bit off the ball and threw away the remains.

'Do as I do,' Karim said, showing that he still had the ball in his mouth. 'Chew it. This will stimulate saliva, it will help your thirst a little.'

'You have six hours before first light,' Lausard told them.

'Then so have you,' Karim echoed. 'The Bedouin will not attack before dawn.'

The three horsemen led their mounts down the reverse slope of the dunes and within seconds they were lost in the almost palpable blackness of the night. Lausard turned and headed back towards Barada, walking past the corpses of dead Arabs that had already swelled like overripe melons in the blistering heat. The stench of death hung heavy in the air and, all around, the flies swarmed over the banquet: men, horses, puddles of dried blood. Come first light, Lausard knew that there would be much more for them to feast on.

Six hours. Would it be enough?

'We'll never make it to Desaix's column if we have to walk the horses the whole way,' Delacor said irritably.

'Keep your voice down,' Tigana ordered, looking around him in the darkness.

Karim remained silent, guiding his horse across the sand, occasionally glancing at the myriad camp fires of the Bedouin. In places they seemed only a few hundred yards away, in others it appeared as if they were way off in the distance, thousands of miles across the black desert like grounded stars.

'When do we start to ride?' Delacor persisted.

'When I say it is safe,' Karim told him. 'Are you so eager to die? If we begin hurrying the horses now the Bedouin will hear their harnesses, they will be upon us in seconds.'

'How do we know you're not leading us into a trap, anyway? You're just like them.'

'I am nothing like them, do you find it so hard to understand?' Karim snapped at Delacor. 'I told you, I am Circassian. My home is in the Caucasus. I was brought here, like many of my countrymen, by the Mamelukes. Every Mameluke has two man-servants, *serradji*, and I was to be raised as one. I was educated, instructed in the fighting arts, taught to ride but I was still a slave. I ran away when I was sixteen and I've been living in the desert ever since.'

'Why don't the Mamelukes just train the Egyptians to be their slaves?' Tigana wanted to know.

'They use the *fellahin*, the local peasants, as infantry but they afford them none of the honour that goes with their own caste,' Karim explained. 'They have harems full of Egyptian, Nubian, Abyssinian, Georgian, Armenian or Circassian women but they rarely have children by them and marry only their own kind. Mameluke wives often cause themselves to abort to preserve their youthful looks and keep their hold over their husbands, so the Mamelukes buy boys from the Caucasus and train them as warriors and *serradji*. I would not be a slave to those men.'

'Very noble,' Delacor said acidly. 'These Mamelukes, do they fight alongside the Bedouin?'

'The Mamelukes look down on all except their own,' Karim said. 'The Bedouin are ungovernable, their fighting abilities are limited and of little use to the Mamelukes.'

'If these Mamelukes are such great fighters, why don't they confront us?' Delacor asked. 'Why are they still running from us? Why haven't we even *seen* one of them yet?'

'They are waiting for the right moment,' Karim said. 'They know that the longer your army is in Egypt, the greater the likelihood it will crumble to thirst, hunger and disease. Three useful allies. When you and the rest of your army are on your knees, they will attack then.'

Tigana was still chewing the bullet as he'd been ordered, the taste of lead strong in his mouth. However, it seemed to be having the desired effect and for the first time in more than a day his mouth wasn't intolerably dry.

'Don't you know of any water holes around here, Karim?' he asked. 'You've lived here long enough.'

'There are usually one or two wells or cisterns to each village. The Bedouin have poisoned most of them, as you know. The closest are at Beydah and El Karioun, in the opposite direction to that in which we travel.'

'There must be some nearby,' Delacor pressed. 'We can't—'

Karim raised a hand to silence him.

Immediately, all three men halted their horses.

About twenty yards to their left they heard voices babbling excitedly in Arabic.

212

The men remained motionless in the saddle. Delacor stroked his horse's neck gently as the animal tossed its head from side to side, worried the sound of the bridle buckles would be heard in the stillness.

The voices seemed to be growing closer. Then, suddenly, they were gone.

Karim sat motionless for a moment longer then dug his heels into his pony and the animal began moving across the sand once again, followed by the two dragoons. Even though they could barely see where they were going, the men were aware they were descending a slope, the dunes closing around them.

'We follow this dry river bed for another two miles,' Karim informed them. 'Then we ride like the devil to find your general.'

The four Bedouin suddenly loomed up towards the trio of men as if they'd risen from the sand itself. Large men armed with swords and spears, they flung themselves at the dragoons and their escort, one of them knocking Delacor from his saddle. As Delacor hit the sand he saw more of the tribesmen emerging from the blackness, then suddenly he felt a crashing impact against the back of his head and he slipped into unconsciousness.

Karim and Tigana were also taken by surprise, neither man having the chance to draw his sword before the Bedouin overran them. As Karim was pulled from his horse, fists and feet raining down on him, he had one brief, terrifying thought: the Bedouin wanted them alive. He could see Delacor's unconscious form being dragged by three of the tribesmen and Tigana trying to fend off blows until his resistance was ended by a blow across the forehead. Karim watched as one of the Bedouin lifted the dragoon's discarded brass helmet like a trophy and tried to put it on over his own headdress, but another Arab snatched it off and ran away into the desert pursued by the first man. Some of the tribesmen were already pulling at the buttons on the dragoons' tunics, cutting them free with knives when they couldn't tear them off. Two more were trying to pull off Delacor's boots, squabbling as they wrenched at the leather, one of them eventually freeing the right boot and whooping triumphantly as he held it aloft.

Karim saw faces close to his own, smelled rancid breath and heard curses. He felt hands against his skin as the Bedouin inspected its roughness compared to that of the captured Frenchmen. Threats were shouted at him in Arabic and a globule of mucus hit him just below the left eye, running down his cheek like a sticky tear. He felt the point of a dagger being pressed against his side, another slashing open his silk robe.

Karim was dragged along and soon he noticed the night was illuminated by the glow of dozens of camp fires. He saw dozens of Bedouin rising from their positions around these fires, all eager to inspect the captives as they were dragged towards a large tent in the centre of the camp.

Both of Tigana's boots had been taken by now, as had his tunic, the buttons from his shirt and his helmet. Delacor was naked but for his torn breeches, and even these were being tugged from him as the Bedouin hurled him, unconscious, into the tent. Karim watched as three or four of their captors rolled the dragoon on to his stomach, one laughing as he caressed his buttocks. The Arabs nearby were beginning to pull their robes open to reveal their nakedness beneath.

Karim had known what was to happen from the moment they were captured but only now did he attempt

214

to fight, suddenly wriggling free of the three men who held him. He struck one hard in the face, splitting his lip, a final act of defiance. The stock of a musket was slammed into his temple and he went down heavily, enveloped by the merciful oblivion of unconsciousness.

All three men were naked when they awoke. Arms bound behind their backs they lay on the hot sand inside the tent, emerging one by one from their own private darkness.

Delacor was the first to awake, the throbbing in his head matched only by an even more excruciating pain around his groin and anus. He winced as he tried to roll over, looking across at the lifeless forms of Karim and Tigana. He gritted his teeth and tried to twist his hands free of the rope that had been bound so tightly around his wrists that it shaved away skin at every movement. He cursed under his breath, aware not only of his pain but of the musky, sickly stench inside the tent. He managed to shuffle, worm-like, towards Karim and butted the Circassian's shoulder in an attempt to rouse him. After a second or two Karim slowly opened his eyes and glanced across at the Frenchman. Delacor grunted in pain again as he moved.

Tigana was beginning to stir and he too felt the same searing pain around his groin and buttocks. He moaned as he tried to sit up, his stomach contracting. For a second he thought he was going to be sick, but the feeling passed.

It was still dark outside the tent, the interior lit only by a battered oil lamp. Tigana could see what remained of their uniforms lying in an untidy heap near the exit. All the buttons had been ripped off, the collars torn away. They were little more than rags.

'They're going to kill us, aren't they?' he said, his voice a low guttural rasp.

'Eventually,' Karim told him. 'We have to get away.'

'And how do you propose we do that?' Delacor said. 'We're miles from help, they'd ride us down even if we managed to get out of this stinking tent. And if we did get away, where do we go? Further into the desert? Back to Barada to be slaughtered?'

'Sergeant Lausard sent us out to find the main army,' Tigana reminded his colleague.

'I know that, you idiot, but would you mind telling me how we're going to do that trussed up here like turkeys. And I bet those bastards haven't finished with us yet, have they?'

Karim shook his head. 'That might be our chance,' he said, looking towards the flap of the tent. 'If we can be ready for them when they come back we might be able to get away.'

'If we can get free of these ropes,' Delacor reminded him. 'But even then we have no weapons, no horses. It's impossible.'

Karim ignored him, concentrating instead on flexing his wrists within the tight bonds. He winced as the rope chafed his skin, drawing blood in several places. Tigana offered his bound wrists to Delacor, who shuffled closer and clamped his teeth around the rope, chewing frenziedly. His mouth, already parched, grew even drier as he chewed at the rope and he made little headway. But then he spotted a loose length of the knot and began pulling at it frenziedly, ignoring the blood that streamed from his gums, almost grateful for the lubrication it allowed him. Grunting, he tugged harder and the rope began to give. Tigana twisted his wrists and the tightly fastened bonds gave way slightly. The gap grew wider until, finally, he could slip one hand free. He held it up triumphantly, blood staining his wrist.

'Untie me.' Delacor rolled on to his stomach.

Tigana undid the rope with relative ease.

Karim had also freed himself.

'Come on, let's get out of here,' Delacor urged.

'No, we must wait for the Bedouin to return,' Karim instructed.

'Return and do what? Kill us? Or even worse? I have learned that there are some things worse than death.'

Karim heard the sound of excited chattering outside the tent and he signalled to his companions to be silent. All three men slid their hands back into their bonds, ensuring that they could free themselves easily when the time came. They sat up, watching as three Bedouin entered the tent, led by a large man with a bushy beard who walked straight across to Karim and spat in his face, snarling something at him. The Circassian looked on impassively as the Arab drew a long jewelled dagger from his belt and held it beneath his chin, the point digging into the soft flesh there. He rasped something in Arabic and gestured towards the two Frenchmen.

'What did he say?' Tigana demanded.

'He asked me why I ride with Infidels,' Karim answered, never taking his eyes from the bearded Arab. He spoke quickly in Arabic, his expression never changing. The Bedouin all looked at him angrily, another of them taking a step towards him, also drawing a dagger. Delacor and Tigana looked on in horror and Tigana slid one hand from his loosened restraints.

Karim and the Bedouin were still speaking to each

other, their voices occasionally rising in volume and the two Frenchmen could only guess at what was being said. The bearded Arab was gesturing towards them now even though his fiercesome gaze was fixed on Karim. Another Bedouin moved towards the Frenchmen, kicking out at Delacor with his foot, rolling him over so that his face was in the sand. He ran a hand over Delacor's buttocks and shouted something at Karim.

'What are you saying to them?' Delacor shouted as he felt the Arab's hands on him. 'I won't let these bastards touch me again.'

Delacor smelled fetid breath close to his face. 'Karim!' he bellowed.

'Strike now,' the Circassian ordered.

Delacor slipped his hands free and grabbed the Arab by the throat, forcing him down on to the sand, the sheer speed of the attack taking the Bedouin by surprise. Delacor grabbed the back of his enemy's head with one hand and his chin with the other and, with one expert movement, wrenched the Arab's head hard to one side, the sound of his breaking neck reverberating inside the tent. He immediately pulled a dagger from the dead man's belt and turned on the next Arab, catching him by the hair and sliding the blade into his neck just below his ear.

Karim brought his foot up into the groin of the bearded Arab, the impact forcing the breath from the Bedouin. He fell forward and Karim slipped the rope around his neck, tugging on both ends with all his strength. He straddled the Arab, feeling his body shudder as the life was throttled from him.

Meanwhile, Tigana caught the other Bedouin by the arm and wrestled him to the ground, his hand closing around a sharp stone just beneath the surface of the sand. The Gascon gripped it in his fist, held the Bedouin's head down and rained blows into his face, pounding away with the stone until the Arab's visage was reduced to a bloody pulp. Tigana finally fell forward, exhausted, lying on the sand next to his dead foe, the rock still in his now crimson fist.

'Put on their clothes,' Karim instructed, already tugging the dead Arabs' garments from them.

Delacor seemed not to hear, kicking frenziedly at the body of one of the dead Bedouin, snarling incoherently with each savage impact. Karim watched him for a second or two then gently touched his arm.

'We have to get out of here before others come.'

Delacor turned to him with blank eyes.

'Now,' Karim persisted. 'There isn't much time.'

Delacor drove one last angry kick into the face of one of the dead Bedouin. Breathing heavily from the exertion, he tore off the Arab's clothes and wrapped them around himself as Karim instructed.

'We'll never get out of here alive, they'll see our faces,' Tigana said, pulling a sash around his waist.

'You saw how dark it is. They won't be expecting us to have escaped, they're not going to question us. They won't even see our faces in the night,' Karim said with more assurance than the Frenchmen enjoyed.

'What were you saying to them to make them so angry?' Delacor wanted to know. 'Were you trying to get us killed?'

'They were going to kill us anyway,' Karim told him. 'I told them they were all cowards and sons of camels who would be blown to the four winds like the sand in a storm.'

'What about these bastards?' Delacor pointed to the bodies.

'Leave them. We have to go now,' Karim said, watching as Tigana gathered up their ravaged uniforms and what remained of their equipment. Karim was surprised to see his scimitar on the sand beneath the green jackets. Tigana passed it to him and he hefted it before him proudly.

'Why did they take our swords but leave yours?' the Gascon asked.

'They have seen weapons like mine before, your swords are unusual to them. Now let's get out of here before it's too late. And when we get outside both of you keep quiet, no matter what. I will speak for all of us.'

Delacor gripped his arm. 'I'm still not sure we can trust you.'

'You had better hope you can,' Karim stated simply and stepped out into the night.

A camp fire was burning about thirty yards from the tent, the Bedouin around it sleeping, one propped against the side of his camel. The animal snorted in the direction of the three men but few of the Arabs themselves even glanced at the figures emerging from the tent. They made their way to where twenty or thirty horses were tied together by their bridles. Karim walked calmly but the two Frenchmen found the urge to run to the horses, leap on to one and ride away as fast as possible almost overwhelming. When they finally reached them they found two tribesmen standing talking. Karim greeted the men in perfect Arabic and one even laughed, slapping him on the shoulder and gesturing towards the horses. The Circassian signalled for Delacor and Tigana to mount up, which they did with difficulty, struggling with the unsaddled ponies. Both teetered precariously on their mounts' backs momentarily, Tigana silently praying that his horse wouldn't rear up and throw him, then they steadied themselves and gripped the thin leather reins favoured by the Bedouin.

Karim was still standing talking to the two guards, not wanting to make their exit seem overly hurried, but the combined effect of not knowing what was being said and the feeling that the Arabs somehow knew that the men beneath these clothes were not like themselves was driving Delacor insane with worry. Worry that was seconds from becoming full-scale panic. He knew he had no choice. He would have to dig his heels into the pony and run for it. He looked down at Karim then straight ahead. Still the Circassian was talking, patting the neck of one animal as he did so. Delacor gripped his reins more tightly, preparing himself. Tigana also felt the growing sense of terror, the unshakeable belief that they were about to be discovered or that someone was going to stumble on the dead bodies in the tent and raise the alarm.

Karim finally swung himself on to the back of a pony and flicked the reins, urging the animal on. It set off across the sand followed by the two relieved Frenchmen.

Tigana could not resist a look behind him but the two Bedouin were already invisible in the darkness.

'Now we must reach the column,' Karim said. 'It'll be dawn in less than two hours. When the Bedouin attack again they will not give up until they have destroyed Barada and all the men in it.'

The horses and their riders sped across the sand aware that even the speed of the sleek Arab ponies might not be enough.

All three had the unshakeable feeling that they would

return to the village to find only the corpses of their comrades.

Two hours.

They rode on.

Twenty

'We're all going to die, aren't we?' said Charvet, glancing up from cleaning his carbine, his eyes peering in the direction of the dunes that surrounded Barada. 'Delacor and the others aren't going to reach Desaix's column in time. We haven't got a chance.'

Lausard was sharpening his sword against a stone, testing the edge with the pad of his thumb every so often.

'Does it really matter that much to you where you die, Charvet?' the sergeant asked. 'Here, Italy, France, Prussia, Austria. What's the difference? Bullet, sword or guillotine. Death is death however it comes.'

'Aren't you afraid of dying, Alain?' Rocheteau said.

'Men who have nothing to live for usually don't fear death,' Lausard told him. 'Sometimes death becomes the most attractive option when compared to a life that offers so little.'

'Well, I'd rather have any kind of life than die here today.' Rocheteau was defiant.

'A life lived in gutters and sewers, starving, fighting

for the next sous, the next piece of bread. Is that kind of existence so difficult to leave behind?'

'I don't fear death because I know that it will unite me with God,' Moreau offered.

'Death will unite you with six feet of earth, nothing more,' Lausard said dismissively. 'Do you think any God of yours would have put you in this position? What kind of God do you worship, Moreau? One who throws away the lives of men the way fools throw away fortunes?'

'There are no fortunes in France any more,' said Charvet. 'All those who had them are dead.' He chuckled.

'Do you honestly believe that?' Lausard said. 'Do you think there are no rich men in France? What about the Directory? What about our own generals? They made fortunes during the Italian campaign. I thought the Republic was created to make men equal. What was all the misery for if it failed?'

'It didn't fail,' said Lieutenant Royere, hobbling out of the darkness, using a carbine as a makeshift crutch. His injured leg was heavily bandaged with pieces of cloth torn from garments found in the abandoned hovels of the village. 'The Bourbons were destroyed. The rich were removed from power and their wealth redistributed.'

'Your idealism is showing again, Lieutenant,' Lausard said, smiling.

The officer sat down next to him.

'As is your cynicism, Sergeant,' he said, patting Lausard on the shoulder. 'But I must say I agree that the wealth wasn't redistributed with quite the fairness embodied by Republican ethics.'

'We've had none of it,' Charvet said. 'When was the last time we were paid?'

'There isn't anything to spend your money on out here,' Tabor offered.

'That's not the point,' Charvet told him. 'We never get what we're promised.'

'Bonaparte promised us nothing but hardship and he's given us that,' Rocheteau said. 'Perhaps he *has* kept his word.'

'A man's word should be as valuable as gold,' Lausard murmured. 'Any man who gives his word and then breaks it has no honour.'

'It isn't what he says that matters, it's who he says it *to*,' Rocheteau added. 'It's the same as responsibility. Mine is to this unit; not to the whole army or even to France but to men who fight alongside me.'

'So, you are not a patriot then, Corporal?' said Royere.

'I love France but I don't want to die for her,' Rocheteau told the officer.

'So what beliefs are worth dying for?' Royere continued.

'No belief is worth dying for,' Lausard interjected. 'A belief is something worth *killing* for, not dying for. If I die for a belief, who does it benefit? Others perhaps less worthy than myself?'

'For a thief, Lausard, you have a remarkable faith in your own worth.' Royere smiled. 'I respect that.'

'There is nothing in *me* to respect, Lieutenant, believe me,' Lausard told him, getting to his feet.

'Where are you going, Alain?' Rocheteau wanted to know.

'To check on Sonnier,' the sergeant replied, disappearing off into the gloom, heading towards the dragoon who stood sentry about a hundred yards away. Royere scrambled to his feet and hobbled away after the sergeant. He caught him after a few strides.

'What did you mean when you said others less worthy than yourself?' the officer enquired.

Lausard glanced at him warily. 'Does it matter, Lieutenant?'

'I was curious. You are full of contradictions, my friend. You claim not to value your own life and yet you fight like the devil to preserve it. You say you belong in the gutter and yet you have a nobility about you most men would kill for. You care nothing for the Republic and yet you are one of its finest products. The embodiment of what that struggle was about. You claim to be as ignorant as some of the men you fight alongside and yet it is clear to anyone that you have an intellect far superior to any of them. As I said, contradictions.'

'What is *your* background, Lieutenant? Are you a product of the Republic too? Did years of hardship shape your resentment for the upper classes and the rich? Did you despise them enough to see them slaughtered? Did *you* stand in the Place de la Revolution and cheer each Aristocrat's death?'

'I was too busy enjoying the sun in Navarre, helping my father with his mill,' Royere said, smiling. 'I didn't suffer any undue hardship and I never despised the upper classes. But I could see that what was happening in France then was wrong. Whether the slaughter of the privileged was a way to right that wrong, to this day I don't know.'

'What does it matter now?' Lausard said dismissively, slowing his pace to allow the wounded officer to keep up with him. 'All those bodies in unmarked graves. Rich *and* poor. And for what? So that we could follow Bonaparte halfway around the world to die in some hellhole like Barada? Is that our legacy from your Republic, Lieutenant? Ten unmarked graves in the desert?'

'It needn't be. The sun will rise in less than thirty minutes. If you leave now, you have a chance of reaching the column. Leave me behind, I can't ride like this.' He motioned to his injured leg. 'I told you to get out if you could. I and the rest of the wounded will stay. We will not hold you back. Not all lives here need be wasted.'

Lausard shook his head.

'I will order you to leave if I have to,' Royere insisted.

'And if I choose to ignore that order, Lieutenant? What will you do? Have me shot? No. We *all* stay. One way or another we remain together. Even if that unity brings death. Unity, Lieutenant. Wasn't that one of the doctrines of your Republic? It is the one lesson worth learning. When the sun rises we will see that lesson put into practice. How many of us live to praise it remains to be seen.'

It was a long time since Lausard had watched the sun rise. He wiped sweat from his forehead and squinted as the shimmering perimeter of the blood red orb poked its way over the horizon, splitting the thick blanket of night and sending scarlet gashes tearing across it. With the coming of light, the heat grew in intensity until it sucked the breath from the men's lungs and scorched the air itself. Rising higher in the sky, the sun drove back the vestiges of night and began to claim the land for itself, spreading its pall of blistering heat across the sand as it took command of the heavens. It glinted on the weapons of the waiting dragoons, who stood in position watching the dunes, waiting for the inevitable onslaught.

Lausard walked back and forth, his sword bumping against his boot, his carbine slung over his shoulder by its strap. Both his pistols were jammed into his belt, loaded and ready. He glanced at each of his companions in turn.

At Lieutenant Royere, his leg heavily bandaged, propped against one side of the overturned wagon watching the crest patiently.

Charvet kept lifting his carbine to his shoulder, lowering it then raising it again. When he tired of that he tapped the hilt of his sword agitatedly.

Tabor stood motionless, occasionally looking up at the cloudless sky, his huge frame dwarfing that of Chatillo who was kneeling on the hot sand, his jacket removed to reveal the bandages wrapped around his torso. There was blood on the makeshift dressing from the wound in his side and Lausard noticed how pale the dragoon's face was despite the heat.

Moreau had his head slightly bowed and his lips were moving silently.

A few yards further back, Sonnier had again taken up a position on top of one of Barada's mud huts, his pistols and carbine close at hand.

In the hovel across from him, Carbonne stood in the doorway, either inspecting the stump where the top of his little finger used to be or kicking impatiently at the sand.

Rocheteau was crouched behind two fallen palm trees, cartridges laid out on a piece of rag beside him for easy access. As Lausard approached he turned and shrugged his shoulders in the sergeant's direction.

'Alain, why us?' he said wearily. 'Out of all the men in the French army who could have been here, why did it have to be us? Stinking luck, eh?'

Lausard nodded and joined him. 'You should be used to it by now, you've had bad luck all your life.' He smiled.

'I suppose you're right. Moreau would probably say it was the will of God.'

'It was no God who put us where we are now.'

'No. It was a Corsican.' Rocheteau chuckled at his own wit.

'I wouldn't change places with any man,' Lausard stated flatly. 'What do you want? To be sitting back in Paris in some prison cell waiting for them to carry you to the guillotine? At least here we're free.'

'Free to do what? Die? What *are* we doing here, Alain?'

Lausard smiled crookedly. 'We are spreading the Revolutionary culture, throughout a desperate world. Don't you feel honoured?'

Beneath them, the ground began to shake.

The initial shudder grew steadily into a wave that seemed to roll across the entire desert.

'This is it,' said Lausard, running back across the village, checking on the men once more, his heart thudding hard against his ribs, the heat momentarily forgotten. He was surprised at how focused he was, his vision, his mind all clear and prepared for what may come. And if it was death that came then he was ready for that too.

The shaking of the ground was now accompanied by a steadily rising rumble of sound. Horses' hooves ploughing through sand, the distant neighing of animals being urged on by their riders. A dust cloud rose above the northern dunes, signalling the approach of many horsemen and the dragoons looked in that direction, filled with either fear, desperation or resignation. Lausard felt a curious exhilaration, as if fire was running through his veins. It was a feeling akin to semi-drunkenness, a raising of his spirit. He felt sweat trickle down his face and he looked up into the clear blue sky, marvelling at the purity of the heavens. It was as though all his senses had been heightened. As he pulled his carbine into his shoulder the smell of the black powder seemed even more pungent than usual, the feel of the metal trimmings on the barrel caused his skin to tingle.

Now he turned his attention to that growing dust cloud, to the increasing volume of the horses' hooves. Again he looked around at his companions and, whatever emotions possessed them, there was a grim determination etched on each of their features. If they were to meet their deaths this blistering morning then it would be with passion and courage, battling to their last breath, taking as many of their enemies with them as they could. Lausard swore an oath to himself that if he was to die he would leave the sand around him piled high with the bodies of Bedouin, thick with their blood.

From the sound of the approaching horde the men realized that the onrushing horses on the other side of the dunes were no more than two hundred yards away by now. The bodies of dead animals from the previous day's fighting still littered the approaches to Barada. Like their riders they had been ravaged by the heat and by flies and ants, their stench filling the air like a noxious cloud. Many more would soon join them today, Lausard thought.

He moved closer towards Lieutenant Royere as the riders prepared to crest the ridge.

'You should have run while you had the chance,' Royere said, thumbing back the hammers on both his pistols.

'We started together, we'll end it together,' Lausard murmured.

'Do you think they will call us heroes?'

'I will be content for them to call us soldiers.'

The first line of horsemen was about to sweep over the dunes.

'Ready!' shouted Royere.

'What do you think heaven is like?' Tabor asked, his eyes never leaving the ridge.

'You'll know in a few minutes,' Charvet told him.

'Let us hope that God will judge us kindly,' Moreau commented. 'After some of the things we have done He would be entitled to turn his back on us.'

'He already has,' Charvet retorted.

'You put your trust in God, I'll put mine in this,' said Lausard, tapping the barrel of the Charleville.

The horsemen swept over the ridge and hurtled down the slope towards Barada.

'My God!' murmured Royere.

Lausard didn't speak, lowering his carbine slightly.

'Tell me I'm not dreaming,' Charvet said.

'It's a miracle,' Moreau whispered. 'A miracle sent by God.'

The horsemen riding towards them were dressed in the green jackets of dragoons. The horsehair manes on their helmets streamed out behind them as they cantered towards Barada, towards the incredulous troops who looked on in disbelief.

It was Lausard who recognized Captain Milliere riding

at the head of the men, flanked by Delacor, Tigana and Karim. He also spotted Bonet, Rostov and Joubert amongst the leading riders.

'They got through,' Rocheteau said, appearing at his side. 'They actually got through.'

'Did you think they wouldn't?' Lausard managed a smile.

Rocheteau patted his companion on the shoulder and sighed in relief.

Lausard saluted as Milliere reined in his mount before him.

Behind him there must have been close to one hundred men; it looked as if an entire company was present. Sweating men on lathered horses looking uncomfortable beneath the now blazing sun, but Lausard welcomed the stench of unwashed bodies. Gaston smiled at the sergeant and waved his trumpet in triumph. A number of the dragoons, including Milliere, dismounted, glancing at the corpses of the Bedouin that littered the area around Barada.

Delacor, Karim and Tigana were crossing the sand behind Milliere, and Lausard saw that the Circassian was wearing the green jacket of a dragoon. He was walking a little uncertainly in the boots but apart from that he looked comfortable in his new attire. He reached the sergeant and extended his right hand, which Lausard shook warmly.

'It seems I am one of you now.'

'God help you,' Rocheteau chuckled.

Lausard noticed that the Circassian still wore his scimitar, the curved blade attached to his belt by two straps. 'You did well,' he said. 'All of you.' He shook hands with Delacor and Tigana too.

'It seems you had some trouble here,' Milliere observed, nodding towards the Bedouin corpses.

'A little. We weren't expecting you, Captain. How close is the main column?'

'Two or three miles behind,' the officer told Lausard. 'We are to push on to Damanhur. Some say there is water there and God knows we need it.'

'What about the Bedouin?'

'They have fled,' Karim announced. 'They would not stand against other horsemen. We passed through what was left of their camp about an hour ago.'

'What now, Captain?' Lausard asked.

'We rejoin the main army. We continue across the desert as General Bonaparte ordered. Cavalry units will continue to act as scouts and intelligence. The General is still eager to find the Mamelukes.' Milliere looked up at the cloudless sky. 'I would be just as grateful to find some water and some food, for ourselves *and* the horses.'

Lausard nodded his agreement, glancing around at the dead bodies scattered across the sand.

'God was with us,' said Moreau, wandering past him. 'We have Him to thank for our lives.'

'You've got *us* to thank for your lives, your holiness,' snapped Delacor, pointing first at his own chest then at Karim and Tigana. 'We brought the help and you should pray to your God that you never have to go through what we went through to save your miserable skin.'

'We were lucky, Alain,' Rocheteau added, wiping sweat from his face.

'Luck had nothing to do with it,' the sergeant said, watching as Lieutenant Royere was helped on to his horse. The officer looked across and waved at Lausard, who returned the gesture.

'I say it was a miracle,' Rocheteau insisted.

Lausard held up his carbine. 'A miracle of men and weapons. Bravery and honour. We owe our lives to our own abilities. It is as simple as that.' He walked off to find his horse.

The man was in his late twenties, Lausard guessed, although it was difficult to tell because of his haggard appearance. Also virtually impossible to distinguish was his unit. Cavalry, infantry or artillery? The dragoon sergeant had no idea. The man was sitting on the burning sand dressed in nothing more than a pair of filthy undershorts. The skin on his back and chest was blistered and red from the sun, the soles of his bare feet raw and bloody from the march across hot sand. He sat cross-legged, the pistol pressed to his temple, his lips moving soundlessly. As he pulled the trigger, Lausard looked away, the sound reverberating over the dunes.

When Lausard looked back, the man was lying on his back, blank eyes staring at the sky, a spreading pool of blood seeping into the sand around his head. There were bodies on either side of the slowly moving column, most of them almost naked. Soldiers who still marched had discarded their packs, their tunics and in some cases even their weapons. Officers and NCOs made little or no attempt to stop them. Indeed, a number of the higher ranks had done the same. Anything to bring temporary relief on a march that was killing them.

Lausard had no idea how long he and his companions had been in the saddle. He thought perhaps twelve hours. Since rejoining the main column they had been moving steadily across the endless sand with little idea of where they were going. Men and horses had been falling with appalling regularity throughout the march. Some men had staggered away from the column screaming for water and Lausard had lost count how many had taken their own lives. Many others had simply collapsed on to the hot sand and waited for death to take them, unable or unwilling to take another step in this living hell. No trees, no shade, no food, no water, no respite from the sun. Lausard himself rode with his head down, his horse stumbling a number of times, its own strength pushed to the limit. Like most of his regiment he rode a large, powerful animal bred in Normandy; renowned for their strength, even these magnificent creatures were helpless beneath the intolerable heat. Somewhere behind him he heard a plaintive whinny and one of the animals crashed to the ground. Neither it nor its rider rose again, preferring death to the misery of the march.

Large numbers of troops staggered along with bandages wrapped around their eyes, blinded by the rays of the sun, the damage done to their sight further exacerbated by the burning dust of the khamsin, the red hot southerly wind that swept across the dunes like airbound fire. Lausard and a number of others had tried tying cloths around their faces and the muzzles of their horses to prevent their and their animals' nostrils clogging with the foul dust, but it did little to help. The route of Desaix's men could easily be followed by the trail of bodies, discarded uniforms and weapons, and dying horses.

Every now and then half a dozen Bedouin would appear on the dunes, watching the painfully slow progress of the French, but the troops paid them little heed. It was as if they *wanted* the tribesmen to attack. At least a fight would take their minds off their terrible predicament and, if they were lucky, it might bring a quick death rather than the long, lingering death from thirst, hunger and exhaustion that seemed to be their fate.

Lausard looked across at Rocheteau who had his head bowed and his eyes closed. Lausard reached out and tugged on the corporal's arm, rousing him from his stupor. Rocheteau looked blankly to the left and right, his eyes wide and staring, then he came to his senses, shook himself from his lethargy, nodded at Lausard and shifted slightly in his saddle.

Joubert had slumped forward virtually on to his horse's neck. Rostov rode with his eyes closed, protecting them from the sun and the dust. Roussard was whispering silently to himself as his horse struggled along, barely able to find the strength to transport itself never mind its rider through the shifting sand.

Bonet and Giresse had dismounted and were stumbling ahead of their exhausted mounts, tugging the animals along by the reins, the temporary removal of their extra weight giving the stricken horses something of a respite. But the men could barely drag one foot in front of the other and after another thirty minutes they both climbed wearily back into the saddle. Lieutenant Royere appeared to be riding with less difficulty than his men, despite his wound. Like so many men in the column, he was more concerned with the horrendous heat and his raging thirst than with his injured knee.

The only man who seemed in control of the situation was Karim. His pony stepped enthusiastically through the sand, the Circassian himself still chewing on a piece of leather to stop his mouth drying up. But despite his outward assurance, Lausard could see in the Circassian's face that he too was suffering, and Lausard reasoned that even one who is used to living in such a hostile environment must still occasionally suffer its torments. For his own part he had never experienced anything like this in his life and doubted, if he survived, if he ever would again. The pure, unadulterated misery and hopelessness of their situation was crushingly reinforced as each new dune was surmounted and all that greeted the men upon reaching its crest was further expanses of unforgiving sand, baked by the constant scorching heat of the sun.

Lausard was beginning to wonder if this would be the first campaign where an entire army was wiped out without ever encountering its enemy. Other than the Bedouin, they had seen nothing of their true opponents. The Mamelukes. He assumed they were massing their forces somewhere, preparing to strike. A quick glance around at the demoralized troops made him fear for their fate should the enemy strike in any reasonable numbers. As well as the suffering, Lausard was aware of a senselessness to this entire episode. He wondered why Bonaparte had sent close to eighteen thousand men into the middle of a waterless wasteland, knowing how inappropriately they were equipped. What was he thinking of?

Lausard was still trying to work it out when he felt a hand tugging at his arm and he turned to see Tabor staring at him. On closer inspection Lausard noticed that the big man wasn't looking *at* him but past him, into the distance. He was pointing fixedly and Lausard now saw what had caught his attention. About five hundred yards to the north was a massive expanse of clear, blue water. Lausard wondered what it was. A lake? The tributary of the Nile? Had their journey taken them that far already?

Whatever it was it shimmered beneath the baking sun, a teasing, tempting oasis amid the oceans of dry sand. Salvation. Life.

Dozens of infantrymen had already broken rank and were running towards the shimmering blue expanse, some screaming joyfully, others already pulling off what remained of their uniforms, ready to throw themselves into the beckoning blueness. Ahead of Lausard, half a dozen dragoons urged strength from their shattered mounts and rode towards the shimmering vision, and despite himself Lausard joined them, eager to taste the water, to feel the liquid on his flesh, to drink until he was full. Perhaps they were to be spared after all.

Karim followed at a leisurely pace, watching as officers and men alike joined the mad rush towards the shimmering expanse.

Delacor leaped from his horse close to the water and ran on, followed by dozens of infantrymen. They ran on towards the water. And into it. Yet there was no cooling moisture, no relieving feel of water on their baked flesh. One of the infantrymen raised a hand to drink and spat as he felt sand in his mouth.

Lausard was by now standing where the shore of the lake had appeared to be. He dropped to his knees and plunged his hands not into cooling water but into hot sand.

'What witchcraft is this?' shrieked Delacor, holding up his hands, watching the sand pour through his clenched fingers. 'Where is the water? I *saw* it. I saw water. We all did, didn't we?'

Two of the infantrymen were crawling around on their bellies licking at the sand, coughing and spluttering. Another was sitting on the sand sobbing.

Lausard dug his hand into the sand and held the burning particles in his fist.

'A mirage,' said Karim, appearing beside him. 'I have seen them myself. There is no water. It is a trick of the eye.'

Lausard got to his feet, staring at what, moments earlier, had looked like a vast blue lake. It was only sand. It had only *ever* been sand. The sergeant was breathing heavily, his eyes screwed tightly together. He could hear the wails of anguish coming from the hundreds of other men gathered around, many crying like children. Others simply turned and trudged back towards the column, which had continued to move on at its slow, faltering pace.

Karim dismounted and took Lausard by the arm, handing him the reins of his horse. Lausard nodded slowly and remounted, looking around at the frantic troops still sifting through the sand for any trace of the water they were certain they had seen. More than a dozen lay on the sand, refusing to move, content to await death in this arid, unforgiving wilderness.

Tabor was stumbling around, arms outstretched, occasionally dropping to his knees.

'Come on,' Lausard said. 'There is nothing for us here.'

'I cannot *see*, Sergeant. I am blind.'

Bonet heard Tabor's words and hurried across to the big man, leading him back towards his horse, helping him on it. He pulled free Tabor's belt and fastened it around the big man's eyes, then he took the reins and led the horse back towards the column. Lausard watched him go.

'Blind or dead, what difference does it make?' Delacor snarled.

'Come on, we're leaving,' Lausard said.

'I can't go any further,' Delacor said wearily, the anger suddenly leaving his voice. 'I've had enough. What's the point in carrying on? We're all going to die. You know that too. Just leave me.'

'Get on your horse, Delacor,' Lausard ordered.

'And what if I don't? Are you going to shoot me? You'd be easing my suffering if you did. Don't threaten me with death when death is the best option I have. Shoot me now. I'm *asking* you to do it.' He extended both arms.

'Get on your horse,' Lausard repeated. 'I won't leave you here to die.'

'Then stay and die with me,' Delacor said quietly.

Lausard dismounted and walked across to the trooper.

'Death is all there is for us now,' Delacor said, resigned to his fate. 'I haven't the strength to fight it any longer.'

Lausard looked at his comrade for a second then, with lightning speed, he drove a powerful punch into the right side of Delacor's jaw. The blow took the dragoon by surprise and he was unconscious before he hit the sand. Lausard dragged the dragoon's body across to his horse and, with Karim's help, lifted him across the saddle, then the two men remounted and headed back towards the column, Lausard leading Delacor's horse.

'He wanted to die, why didn't you let him?' Karim asked.

'Because he's *my* responsibility. He's one of *my* men. As I said before, we started this together, we'll end it together. No matter what.'

'Do you still believe in what your General Bonaparte says? He uses you like pawns in a chess game.'

'Pawns are sometimes sacrificed for the advancement of the king,' Lausard replied. 'Bonaparte still has eighteen thousand pawns left. I fear this game is far from over.'

Twenty-One

Time no longer had any meaning for Lausard. Hours, minutes, seconds, even days and weeks had all become just words. All that he and his companions were aware of were thirst, heat and exhaustion. How long they had been riding through the desert had no relevance; as far as Lausard was concerned, they would be riding for ever, never seeing anything but a few miles of parched, lifeless sand in all directions. More men would die, go blind or kill themselves and their bodies would be covered by the khamsin-driven sand. In time, the entire column would simply cease to exist, buried by the sands of Egypt as surely as a sunken galleon is covered by the raging sea.

Other than the cries of dying men and the pathetic exhortations of those begging for help that could not possibly arrive, the column moved in virtual silence, men dragging themselves through the sand, some on their knees, although most of those gave up after a few hundred yards. Of those men who went down, few got up again, and their comrades could not find the strength to support them. Not that they wanted help; they were resigned to a death from hunger, thirst or heat, and they wanted nothing more than to be left alone to await it. The same was true of many of the horses. Lausard had counted at least two dozen of the stricken beasts crash to the ground, unable to continue, as desperate for water as their riders. They lay still on the sand, just their heads rising occasionally in a useless gesture of anguish. The corpses of man and beast were covered almost instantly by swarms of the black, bloated flies that seemed to appear from nowhere to feast on those who had fallen.

Since the mirage, Lausard had been reluctant to trust even his own eyes. The same false hope had been experienced more than once during the journey and men had still rushed towards those shimmering illusions in the hope that what they saw was real, only to find nothing but sand. After each crushing disappointment, at least one man had ended his own life, tired of the suffering, and Lausard was now sure that the number of suicides must be close to fifty. How many had been claimed by the heat, thirst and hunger he couldn't begin to imagine.

Throughout their horrendous trek, Bedouin tribesmen would appear on the hills, sometimes in ones and twos, sometimes in groups of up to a dozen, seemingly satisfied with picking off the many stragglers. Some they killed there and then, riding past and cutting them down with their swords, running them through with their spears. Those less fortunate were hauled up on to the sleek Arab ponies and carried off into the desert shrieking, collected by these desert warriors as if they were trophies. Hardly any of the men even bothered to shoot at the marauders any more.

Lausard looked around him at the men of his unit.

Their uniforms were covered by a fine sheen of sand, their faces scorched by the sun, their equipment filthy. At least what remained of it. Many had tied their jackets across the backs of their shabraques. Some had even removed the saddle-cloths in an effort to spare their horses some discomfort, but this attempt at kindliness had backfired as the persistent rubbing of the saddle against the horses' backs had produced appalling saddle-sores.

As Lausard looked in to the distance he wondered if the minarets and cupolas, the palm trees and the greenery he saw rising about half a mile before him were figments of his tortured imagination as the phantom expanses of water had been. He decided that they weren't and slapped Rocheteau on the arm. The corporal, who had been dozing in the saddle, looked up, his gaze following Lausard's pointing finger.

'Am I still dreaming?' Rocheteau pleaded.

'If you are then so am I,' Lausard told him. 'And so is the rest of the column.'

All eyes now seemed fixed on the buildings and palm trees ahead and many men began to cheer.

'It is the city of Damanhur,' said Karim. 'The seat of a bey, one of the centres of the cotton trade.'

'To hell with that,' snapped Delacor. 'Will they have food and water there?'

Karim nodded.

'And who will we have to kill to get it?' Lausard murmured.

The entire column moved forward with a haste and organization that had seemed impossible an hour earlier. Officers and NCOs shouted orders and the entire motley crew of troops formed up into their units as they marched with surprising efficiency towards the waiting city. To the starving, thirst-crazed troops of Desaix's division, Damanhur looked like the most beautiful place on earth. Even Lausard managed a smile.

Napoleon Bonaparte paced agitatedly back and forth inside the large barn-like building, stopping occasionally to chew on the plate of wheat cakes standing on the table along with a jug of milk. The small but very welcome meal had been presented to him a few hours earlier upon his arrival in Damanhur. He and his headquarters staff had ridden from Alexandria the previous evening through the darkness of the desert, a journey that had brought them to the city in just ten hours. The troops of Desaix and Reynier, who now occupied Damanhur, had taken four days to cover the same distance.

Bonaparte peered quickly at the pile of papers on the table. He looked at each requisition order, each report, each despatch with the same casual expression, but the two other men present knew that the speed with which he read and digested these pieces of information was not born of indifference but of a burning energy. His chief of staff, Berthier, sat at another table scribbling notes, while the General's aide-de-camp, Sulkowski, looked on, his eyes never leaving his commander.

Sulkowski was dressed in the uniform of a hussar, the red pelisse slung over his left shoulder, the buttons of his dolman jacket undone – his only concession to the heat that filled the room. His right hand was bandaged, the legacy of the French attack on Alexandria more than a week ago now. It felt as if it had been longer. Sulkowski felt as if he had been away from his homeland for an eternity. First the privations of the long sea voyage and now the inhospitality of Egypt had combined to make

Bonaparte's Invaders

him long to see France but, above all, his native Poland. In fact, the surroundings he now found himself in made him want to see *anywhere* other than this endless hell of sand, flies, disease and thirst, and Arab tribesmen. He, like so many other men, officers and private soldiers alike, was already disillusioned with the country, even with the motives their General had for bringing them here. The arrival at Damanhur had done little to alter that feeling. What had been professed to be a city of some size and importance had turned out to be little more than an agglomeration of mud and straw hovels, interspersed by a series of less than impressive mosques. The city had not been the paradise the French had hoped for but, Sulkowski thought, it was better than the desert. *Anything* was better than the desert.

Bonaparte finished reading the last of the papers on the table and turned towards Berthier, regarding his chief of staff silently for a moment. Then he switched his piercing gaze to Sulkowski, who noticed that his commander's brow was furrowed slightly, as if he battled with a troubling thought.

'In every one of these reports there is mention of disquiet within the ranks,' Bonaparte said eventually. '*All* ranks. It seems everyone is infected with the same discontent. I have generals complaining to me that they haven't enough food or drink for their men. Where do they expect me to get it? Do they expect me to pull it from empty air?'

'Your men expect much of you because they are accustomed to you delivering much,' Berthier told him. 'The French army are born grumblers.'

'These are not grumblings, Berthier,' Bonaparte said holding up a handful of the despatches. 'In these I read not just of discontent but of the threat of mutiny from some units.'

'In times of suffering thoughts can become extreme. And it has been hard on them.'

'It has been hard on *all* of us. War is never easy, Berthier. You know that. I expected my men to know it. These men we have here are the men who conquered Italy, the men who destroyed the finest armies Austria could send against them. They were scarecrows when I took command of them. Their officers were timid and unadventurous. I transformed them all. I *made* them what they are and now all I get as thanks is talk of mutiny.' He hurled the papers aside angrily.

'It will pass, General,' said Sulkowski. 'Once the men have eaten their fill and gathered some loot they will be more amenable to their situation.'

'Will they? Food and drink may satisfy private soldiers but they are not the only ones complaining, are they? This spleen has infected those of the highest rank. Despair is an epidemic that must be treated.' Bonaparte nodded towards the main door that led into his room and Sulkowski crossed to it, lifting the locking bar and ushering in those who waited outside.

Bonaparte watched as the men filed into the room, hats in hand: cavalry generals Mireur and Dumas, divisional commanders Desaix and Reynier. They formed a line before him, their expressions as grim as that of their commander.

'I have read your reports,' Bonaparte addressed them, 'and I am disappointed in you. That is one of the reasons I called you here. It seems that not only can you not control your men, you cannot control your own emotions either. These reports have a hint of

248

hysteria about them. Where is your pride? Where is your belief?'

'Back in France where *we* should be,' Mireur said sharply. 'We should never have come to this place to begin with. This entire expedition is a hopeless and irresponsible adventure that can only end in failure.'

'I agree with Mireur.' Dumas spoke. 'Surely not enough thought went into the planning of this invasion or we would not all be suffering as we are now.'

'This is no invasion,' Bonaparte retorted. 'It is a logical and necessary progression in the expansion of the Republic, of great strategic and political importance.'

'My men care nothing for these matters, all they care about is that they have no food,' Desaix said. 'Time and time again during my march across the desert I requested provisions from you and received nothing. No rations have been distributed since we landed nearly two weeks ago. This negligence has cost me fifteen hundred men.'

'My division, too, has suffered,' Reynier added. 'I asked for help and was given none. I have seen men die in agony for want of a mouthful of water. More than forty men were trampled to death at El Beydah so desperate were they for water. I watched comrades fighting over a cupful of dirty water, men suffocating in the rush, others killing themselves when they could not drink.'

'You think I do not realize this?' Bonaparte shouted. 'These are *my* men you speak of. Each one of them like a son to me.'

'You do not see their suffering at such close quarters,' Dumas insisted. 'You do not know them as we do. Your nerves may be of steel but ours are not. To stand by helplessly while the men who we command lose their minds in despair is more than any man can take. We have to experience that every day. You do not. You are above it. Cocooned by your staff and your *savants*, those "pekinese" who would march into the mouth of a lion if you ordered them too. They have no minds of their own. They are fit only to live as puppets with you pulling their strings.'

Sulkowski took an angry step forward but Bonaparte raised a hand to halt him.

'Be careful who you insult, General.' Sulkowski glared at Dumas. 'Or I will show you how puppets fight duels.'

'My remarks were not addressed to you. I know of your bravery.'

'Then know too that these men of science and learning whom you despise so much are also capable of reason,' Bonaparte snapped. 'They have their place here as much as any fighting man. And do not presume to tell me about my own army. I know my men suffer and if there was any way to allay that suffering I would, but sacrifices must be made. If some small parts must be lost for the good of a whole machine then so be it. Eighteen thousand men have crossed the desert to this point, if a few hundred have been lost it is a regrettable but very small price to pay to achieve our ultimate goal.'

'*Your* goal, General,' Dumas corrected. 'The longer this sorry mess continues, the more convinced I am that it is personal glory at stake here, not the advancement of the Republic. It is the advancement of Napoleon Bonaparte that we suffer and die for.'

'You are talking sedition,' Bonaparte said vehemently. 'Be careful or I will do my duty. Your five foot ten inches would not save you from being shot by a firing squad two hours from now.' He ran a furious gaze along all the faces before him. 'Perhaps you have all grown soft. Is this kind of warfare so much harder on you? Do you miss the comforts of the Italian palazzi and casinos so much? You all grew fat on the spoils of *that* war, didn't you? Where is your strength now?'

'It is not just the physical hardship that is causing these problems,' Desaix said evenly. 'It is the sense of isolation that we and the men feel, a loathing for the country and its people. It is impossible to convey in words the disgust, the discontent, the melancholy and the despair of this army. When men would rather take their own lives than march another mile, what does that tell you? Not about the men but about this country, about this entire expedition. Some feel that what they are being put through is inhuman.'

'To make men do what *I* make them do requires a strength of character you cannot begin to imagine. You accuse me of inhumanity. Well, let me tell you, if I had been the least bit more human this entire army, and all of you, would have perished. The worst is over. I know that morale is low and there is but one way to raise it. A victorious battle. And that is what I will give this army.'

'A victory against whom?' Mireur asked the question on all of their lips. 'An enemy we have not even encountered yet? Where *are* the Mamelukes? How are we to defeat them if we cannot even find them? Are we to spend the rest of our lives marching across sand scarching for them?'

'We are less than sixty miles from Cairo,' Bonaparte said. 'The Mamelukes will not allow their capital to be threatened, that was what I said from the beginning of this campaign. All we have to do is continue our march and *they* will come to *us*. Trust me in this.' He turned his back on the other generals. 'This meeting is adjourned. You have spoken, I have listened and I have listened enough. Leave me.'

The generals filed out slowly, Sulkowski closing the door behind them.

Bonaparte returned to the plate of wheat cakes and ate one.

'These are dangerous times,' Berthier commented. 'An enemy massing before us and the threat of mutiny within our own army.'

'There will be no mutiny. If there is I will crush it with the same swiftness and fury with which I will crush the Mamelukes. This expedition cannot be allowed to fail, least of all by the men I brought here to carry it through. I will show no mercy to such men. Even if they *are* my own.'

The market was crowded with soldiers from all units. All, it seemed to Lausard, intent upon one thing: the purchase of as much food as they could possibly carry. None of them knew when they would come across civilization again – or what passed for civilization. Lausard crossed to a stall where wheat cakes were baking on hot ashes. The smell was appealing and he took one, chewing it quickly, ignoring the protestations of the stall owner who babbled at him in Arabic.

'What is he saying?' Lausard asked Karim and the Circassian smiled.

'He says that you are welcome to his wares. He says that you do not look like the demon he expected.'

'Demon?' Lausard chuckled. 'What does he mean?'

'Ibrahim Bey posted notices in every town and city telling the locals that you French, you Infidels, had fingernails a foot long, enormous mouths and ferocious eyes.' Karim grinned. 'He said you were savages possessed of the devil and that you went into battle linked together with chains.'

Lausard smiled then looked across to another of the stalls where Joubert and Roussard were arguing furiously with an Arab trader, pointing at his goods and then at him, while the Arab himself was pulling at their tunics. Lausard and Karim, now joined by Rostov, wandered across towards the mêlée.

'I'm trying to pay him but he won't take the money,' said Joubert, trying to push away the Arab who was still tugging at his jacket. 'One goose, one chicken, one bag of beans and one bag of lentils. Thirty-five paras each for the goose and the chicken, one para each for the lentils and beans. As set out in the orders of the day and *he* won't take the money.' Joubert pointed towards the trader, who was still babbling frantically and indicating Joubert's tunic. Joubert pushed him away. 'What does he want?'

Karim spoke to the Arab in his native language, the dragoons looking on as he pointed at them. Karim nodded as he listened to the trader.

'He wants the buttons for payment. He says for two buttons you can take everything.'

'What does he want with buttons?' Rostov asked. 'Surely the money is of more use to him. Why won't he take coins?'

'Because if the Mamelukes find anyone in possession of foreign currency, they will accuse them of having dealt with the Infidels,' Karim explained. 'At the very least they will confiscate the coins.'

'So he thinks the Mamelukes are going to beat us?' Lausard observed. 'He's no fool, is he?'

'He is being cautious,' Karim continued. 'If he takes your buttons as payment and the Mamelukes *do* win, should they find them on him he can always claim that he acquired them honourably by killing and robbing an Infidel. If *you* win, the buttons will be worth more than the current price of the merchandise.'

'So either way *he* wins,' Lausard murmured.

The Arab said something excitedly and pointed at Lausard.

'He says he will sell you a horse for six buttons.'

'Tell him to go to hell,' Lausard muttered.

'As for the food, he will not sell it to you unless you pay with your buttons. It is as simple as that.'

Without hesitation Joubert tore two of the pewter buttons from his tunic and thrust them into the eager hand of the excited Arab, snatching up his purchases. As the men made their way back towards the houses where they were billeted, they saw many other troops walking around minus a few buttons. One corporal of the Twenty-fifth Demi-Brigade had just two left on his jacket but he was weighed down with provisions. Lausard wondered how long his purchases would last him. He or any of the men who were milling around the streets and squares of Damanhur carrying everything from bags of dried dates to live chickens. A few men had bought water bottles but it seemed a little late for that. If more had been equipped with drinking vessels before leaving Alexandria, thought Lausard, then perhaps that part of the march would have been slightly less tortuous. He wondered how much further they would be forced to march at the whim of their commander. Supposedly, the Nile itself was less than fifteen miles away. Perhaps there they would all be able finally to quench thirsts that had built up to intolerable levels.

As they returned to their billets, they saw Delacor, Tigana and Carbonne sitting outside the huts smoking from a clay pipe they had purchased for a tunic button at another market. The tobacco had cost another two buttons. Some of the other dragoons paused to share the smoke but Lausard headed inside the hovel to where he knew Tabor and Bonet waited.

The big man was lying on the ground, his eyes bandaged. Bonet sat beside him.

'Is he any better?' Lausard asked.

'I took the bandages off for a while earlier on.'

'I could see better, Sergeant,' said Tabor. 'I can't see clearly yet but it doesn't hurt.'

Lausard patted his arm. 'Your sight will return soon,' the sergeant assured him. 'Keep your eyes protected from the sun for the time being.'

'Any news, Alain?' Bonet wanted to know.

'We march out tonight for El Rahmaniya.'

'We've only been here a day,' Bonet protested. 'Bonaparte could have given us longer to rest.'

Lausard shrugged. 'Perhaps he wants to hurry us to our deaths.'

'Do you think we will win, Alain?'

'Yes, I think we will beat the Mamelukes. I think Bonaparte will have his victory, he will probably even conquer this country and subjugate its people in the name of his Republic. Whether or not any of *us* ever survive to tell about it is a different question.'

'I don't want to die here,' Bonet said. 'Not in this godless country.'

'I have seen no evidence of a God in *any* part of the world and that includes France. What kind of God looks on while countrymen slaughter each other? While innocent women and children are dragged to the guillotine just because they are fortunate enough to have money or to possess different political views to those in power? If there ever was a God he turned his back on *our* world a long time ago.' Lausard got to his feet. 'We face another march across the desert, Bonet. How many of us will even manage to survive *that*? If you are looking for a God, don't look for him in the sands here. In fact, save yourself the trouble of looking anywhere. You would have more chance finding water in this dried-up land than of finding a God.'

He turned and headed towards the doorway, out into the blistering heat.

Twenty-Two

The men who refused to march belonged to the Twenty-third Demi-Brigade. As if by some prearranged signal, virtually an entire battalion of the infantry had moved, en masse, away from the slowly moving column. Many had discarded their tunics before they had even sat down on the hot sand; others had hurled away their bicorns, trampling them angrily. One officer had pulled his sword from its scabbard and snapped it across his thigh, hurling the two broken segments away in disgust.

As he looked on, Lausard wiped his face and tried to suck in some air, but it felt like passing through an enormous oven. The heat was incredible, even by the standards they had become all too used to. Lausard counted more than seventy men now sitting on the sand, showing no intention of moving. He wondered how many other men in the column felt the same way, how many in his own unit would join them if they had the chance?

The remainder of the men of the Twenty-third slowed their pace, finally coming to a halt as the shouts of officers echoed back and forth in the searing heat. Some of those who had left the column had stretched out on the sand, looking incapable of further movement no matter what their officers and NCOs bellowed at them.

As the column came to a halt, Lausard and the dragoons found themselves little more than twenty yards from the immobile infantrymen, who continued to ignore the furious shouts of their superiors. Lausard was aware that this was far more than a simple mass expression of exhaustion. The other troops looked on, some with bewilderment and others with admiration, even envy. Five or six men at a time might leave the column – Lausard had seen it happen all the way from Alexandria – but seventy or more at once . . . This was something far more insidious than weariness or discontent.

'What the hell are they doing?' Rocheteau murmured.

'They're doing what we should all do,' Delacor interjected. 'They're giving up. They've had enough. It's called common sense.'

'It's called mutiny,' Lausard responded, watching keenly. 'Look.'

Thirty or forty infantrymen from another battalion were also leaving the column, ignoring the shouts of their officers and NCOs. They trudged away from the column and sat down on the sand, heads bowed.

Captain Milliere rode up and down the length of the dragoon units as if daring any man to follow the actions of the infantry. Sergeant Delpierre rode close to Lausard and paused momentarily.

'Aren't any of your bastards going to leave?' he hissed. 'It seems this is the time for cowards.'

Lausard glared at him, at his ravaged features and

sweat-covered face. 'Why don't *you* leave? No one would miss you anyway, you whore's son.'

Delpierre tugged on his horse's bridle and rode back down the column, snarling at a dragoon who could not keep his mount still.

'What happens now?' Rocheteau asked, his eyes never leaving the large group of infantrymen, who seemed unconcerned that two lines of their comrades were marching towards them with fixed bayonets. From the head of the column, surrounded by half a dozen staff officers and guides, General Desaix was leading his horse towards the scene. He waved a hand in the air to halt the advancing troops, then approached the tall officer who had broken his sword.

Desaix saluted the man. 'What is your name?'

'Captain Noiret, Twenty-third, sir.' The officer returned the salute sharply.

'I gave no orders for a halt. Get back to your positions now. General Bonaparte ordered us to march on El Rahminaya and we can afford to waste no time.'

'I will not march, sir, and neither will my men. Not until we have had the water and provisions we've been promised.'

'I cannot give you something I do not have.'

'Then we will remain here, sir.'

'I cannot allow that, I cannot allow disorder within the ranks.'

'But you have it, General,' Noiret said angrily. 'I would not do this unless I had to. I would not betray my comrades without good reason. I love this army, I would die for General Bonaparte or you, sir – but in battle, not from hunger and thirst. Where is the honour in that?'

'I understand how you feel,' Desaix told him. 'But we all suffer in the same way. If there was anything I could do about your predicament, don't you think I would?'

'I do not *blame* you, sir,' Noiret told him. 'And I realize that we are all in a similar position, but I will not, I cannot, take this any longer, and neither can these men.' He gestured towards the dispirited, lost souls squatting or lying on the burning sand. They seemed oblivious to what was going on around them. 'We will not march on.'

'General Bonaparte has ordered that any mutiny or sedition is to be dealt with summarily,' said Desaix. 'I will not ignore his orders. While I understand your grievance, I cannot support it and I cannot tolerate it. Orders dictate that I must act, so I ask you once again to lead your men on to El Rahminaya.'

'And if I refuse, sir?'

'I will have no choice but to have you shot.' Desaix turned to one of his ADCs. 'Select twenty-four men for a firing squad now.' The ADC nodded and guided his horse towards the nearest infantry unit, relaying Desaix's orders to their officer. The general looked intently at Noiret, who seemed unfazed by this latest development, even as he saw the soldiers sloping towards where he and his exhausted men waited.

'Do not make me do this, Captain,' Desaix said. 'Believe me, I take no pleasure in it.'

'You must do your duty, sir. The prospect of being shot, even by my fellow countrymen, is not something to be feared. At least not in this vile country. Instead of a slow, lingering death from thirst and starvation, you offer me a quick death. I welcome that. If you shoot me you do not punish me, you reward me by ending my suffering. But no matter what you choose to threaten me with, I will not march another foot.'

'Then you leave me no choice. As an example, you and twelve of your men will be shot.'

'Is that the way to restore morale, sir?'

'I am ordering this because I too am following orders,' Desaix snapped, watching as an ADC moved among the rebelling men, pulling them to their feet until twelve stood close to Noiret.

'I thought Desaix was supposed to be a more understanding man,' said Bonet, watching with the other dragoons.

'What do you expect him to do?' Lausard challenged, his gaze never leaving the twenty-four-man firing squad as it readied itself under the watchful eye of a large sergeant. 'This mutiny could spread throughout the entire army if it isn't checked.'

'So you agree with our own men being executed do you, Alain?' Rocheteau pressed him.

'Those men have gone through no more than we have. They have suffered no more than us, they have not been deprived of anything we ourselves have not gone without. Why is their situation worse than ours? They complain of no food and water. So does most of the army, ourselves included. But we march on. We don't give up.'

'Perhaps we are bigger fools than they,' Delacor suggested. 'Perhaps we would be better off seeking death before a firing squad than suffering the torments of the desert and this stinking country.'

'Then join them,' Lausard said. 'If you are so keen to end your life then take your horse and join them. Perhaps I should have left you back in the desert when you wanted me to.'

Delacor did not speak. He was too busy watching the first four of Noiret's men being bundled in front of the firing squad, who already had their Charlevilles shouldered and were taking aim at the hapless men. When the order was given to fire, the sound of two dozen muskets tore through the air, a great choking cloud of smoke rolling towards the dragoons. When it finally cleared, driven away by the hot wind, the dragoons saw the four bodies sprawled on the sand, surrounded by spreading pools of blood. Lausard watched as the next four men were shoved in front of the busily reloading firing squad. Then, when they had been despatched, the last group, led by Noiret, moved into position to await death. Noiret looked defiantly at the hovering gun barrels. A fraction of a second before the order to fire was given he looked at Desaix, then back at the yawning muzzles. As they breathed fire and lead, Moreau lowered his head in prayer. When the smoke cleared again, five more bodies lay on the already drenched sand.

Desaix wheeled his horse and rode back towards the front of the column, not looking back to see how many of the would-be deserters had rejoined the division. Very few wandered back to their comrades as the column moved on, preferring to remain beneath the mighty flare of the sun.

Lausard had been impressed at the fortitude with which the men had faced the firing squad, but their courage, he mused, had been worthless. It had gained them nothing. It had been only a minor diversion. If three hundred men or even a thousand had been shot for refusing to march on, he reasoned, it would have made no difference to Bonaparte. The Corsican obviously intended seeing this campaign through to the bitter end no matter what the toll of misery and suffering. He glanced across at the bullet-blasted bodies as the dragoons rode slowly past.

Delpierre rode past him and spat in their direction. 'Cowardly scum.' He looked directly at Lausard, who ignored him.

'Why does that man hate you?' Karim asked, as Delpierre rode back towards the rear of the dragoons.

Lausard smiled. 'Ask *him*'

'It does not concern you that one of your comrades despises you?'

'He's no comrade of mine. He's in the same regiment that's all. But even if he *was* in this unit, why should I be troubled by his hatred? He means nothing to me. I don't ask *any* man to like me. I appreciate their respect but I care nothing for their feelings towards me.'

'But you would risk your life for them?' Karim persisted.

Lausard nodded. 'As if they were my brothers. Is that so hard to understand, Karim? Perhaps that is why the Mamelukes think we are possessed by demons. Sometimes we don't even understand our own actions, let alone those of others.'

'So you would fight alongside men you hate or who hated you? You would risk your life for those you have nothing in common with?'

'Yes. Because in the end it isn't a matter of belief, it's a matter of honour. And honour is the one thing I have left that I value. And I will take it to my grave. Wherever that may be.'

The column moved on.

Lausard had been expecting a majestic, awe-inspiring

blue and green expanse of water cutting through the sand like a sword through silk. What he saw was a dirty brown ribbon of water meandering between sand dunes. There was very little majesty about the Nile at its lowest level. Nevertheless, it was a sight to cheer any man. Water. No matter how filthy, how polluted by mud.

On both sides of the sloping banks palm trees grew abundantly and, amidst the patches of greenery covering the land around the river, the men found large round objects bigger than cannonballs, which some of them recognized as water melons. Dotted close to the westerly bank were two or three dozen of the mud and straw hovels now so familiar to the French, and a couple of abandoned camels roamed amongst the crumbling buildings.

The town of El Rahmaniya was even less impressive than Damanhur had been, but Lausard, like most of the men in the column, was more interested in the sight of the Nile and the water melons than in the town itself. Even as he watched, men began to break ranks and run towards the river, officers among them. No attempt was made to check the stampede of troops, who seemed to have discovered new strength in their frenzied race to be the first to reach the cooling waters. Several dragoons broke away, urging on their horses at a gallop, such was their eagerness to reach the Nile. They passed the infantrymen who struggled through the sand, desperate to reach the river before it disappeared like one of the all-too-familiar mirages. Lausard saw Captain Milliere raise his hand in an effort to halt some of the dragoons but, realizing the futility of trying to stop the men, he gave up and joined them himself. Even Lausard spurred his mount and joined the headlong rush.

The leading troops crashed through the patches of

water melons, crushing some beneath their feet. Many of the men fell on the fruit as if it was a kind of heaven-sent manna, ripping it open and gorging themselves on the red pulp within. They stuffed chunks of it into their mouths, savouring the moisture, screaming their delight and relief. Some were so ravenous they even ate the skin.

Most, Lausard included, hurtled on towards the banks of the Nile and into the water itself. Even the horses seemed to be seized by the same maniacal joy as their riders and threw themselves full length into the muddy depths, tossing their riders from the saddles. Many of the men didn't bother to remove their uniforms, and plunged into the muddy flow, mouths open, drinking down the soothing liquid with an unbridled ecstasy.

Lausard launched himself from his saddle and landed with a loud splash. He swallowed great gulps of the muddy water, hardly aware of the sand grains it contained. He felt his belly swelling as he continued to drink, noticing that Rocheteau, Moreau, Delacor and even Milliere and Lieutenant Royere had joined him in the muddy river.

On the shore, more men were tearing off their clothes, running naked into the water, their shouts of delight mingling with those of the men already slaking their thirsts. Having satisfied their immediate needs some were contentedly floating on their backs or swimming back and forth slowly, enjoying the coolness of the water on their skin.

As men and horses alike drank until their stomachs were full, Lausard looked up and noticed Karim sipping slowly from a metal cup. The Circassian raised the cup in salute and Lausard smiled.

Charvet, Bonet and Joubert were sitting surrounded

by melons, cutting them open with their bayonets and feasting on them without even bothering to spit out the pips. Joubert devoured three of the large fruit in minutes and rubbed his belly.

Even General Desaix was standing in the water, up to his boot tops, scooping the dirty fluid into his hands, splashing his face and drinking too.

To Lausard it seemed as if the entire river was filled with troops, drinking and washing, swimming or floating and relaxing. Even the sun beating mercilessly down upon them could not quell their joy. When it became too unbearable, the men simply ducked their heads beneath the surface. Lausard saw horses cavorting about in the water like spring lambs, as delighted to be drinking as their riders.

The sergeant had no idea how long he spent in the river, but finally, his stomach distended, he walked up the shore, where he joined Karim and Carbonne, who handed him a piece of water melon. Lausard ate hungrily. He stood on the bank with some of his men watching others thrashing about in the water. Delpierre scooping water into his mouth, Chatillo and Tigana washing their tunics in the muddy river, Charnier from number two squadron lifting a gourd full of water over his head and pouring it down to cool his sun-baked scalp. An air of happiness and relief that had not been witnessed for many months had overtaken the men, and it was an infectious joy, one which even Lausard felt. It was as if all the toil and torture of the desert marches had been worthwhile for just this moment.

Momentarily the men forgot everything: the agony of the blistering sun, the heat that sucked air from their lungs, the searing sunlight that blinded them, the khamsin that scorched their skin and peppered them with hot sand grains. Even the agonies of thirst and hunger were pushed to the back of their minds.

Lausard accepted another piece of water melon from Carbonne and ate it with relish, juice running down his face. As he looked on he noticed amongst the banks littered with discarded uniforms and weapons a number of soldiers lying motionless, some half in, some half out of the water. He crossed to one, an infantry sergeant, and prodded the man with the toe of his boot. The soldier's head fell to one side and Lausard saw that his eyes were staring blindly. The man's belly was swollen up as if he was pregnant, his tongue lolling from one corner of his mouth, and Lausard realized he was dead. There were others in the same condition. To drink so much after having gone without for so long had taken the ultimate toll on these men.

Elsewhere, others, bloated with the amount they had drunk, were crawling out of the water like wriggling, swollen worms, making their way up the bank where the scorching sun rapidly dried their uniforms and once again tortured their flesh. Those who had eaten their fill of water melons were now feeling the painfully uncomfortable beginnings of stomach cramps, but many ignored the pain and continued to gorge themselves. The effects of excessive eating and drinking were as dangerous as the discomfort of thirst and hunger, but as they had flocked towards the Nile and its bounty, none of the men had given a second thought to how their stomachs, deprived of food and water over the past weeks, had shrunk. All they saw was the chance to relieve their suffering and they took it.

Those men who had water bottles were eagerly filling

them with the muddy water, determined not to have to go without fluid again for as long as they had during the desert marches. A canteen full of dirt, it seemed, was preferable to nothing at all. Now that the dragoons had quenched their own thirst, those whose horses hadn't charged into the river of their own accord now led their animals to the Nile to drink. Many of the animals, Lausard noticed, drank with the same abandon as their riders – and many also paid the price. As he strolled up and down the bank Lausard saw more than a dozen of the stricken animals collapsed on the soggy sand or in the water itself. He also saw many of them urinating or defecating into the water, while, all around them, troops still not satiated continued to drink.

Food, water and rest. The three things they had craved so badly for so long were theirs for the time being and Lausard, like so many of the other men in the division, was determined to enjoy this brief respite from suffering. He had no idea how long it would last.

It began with agonizing stomach pains.

To Lausard it felt as if someone had pierced his belly with red-hot hooks and was trying to yank out his insides. The pain was excruciating. It spread slowly to his lower back and his bowels, and as it did he felt a new sensation. Not pain but an unavoidable relaxing of the muscles there.

Others were suffering too. Joubert and Moreau were experiencing the same symptoms, and from the groans rising into the night air Lausard was convinced that most of the army was suffering exactly as he and his companions were. The vile odour of human excrement seemed to clog his nostrils. He saw Gaston doubled up, the young trumpeter vomiting Nile water and water melon on to the sand. And he was not alone. Throughout the division, men were in the grip of this insidious torment – the latest torture they had been forced to endure since arriving in a land with nothing but hardship to offer.

'What curse is this?' Delacor clutched his stomach, feeling his bowels loosen. He looked at Karim accusingly.

'The fruit and the water. You drank too much and you ate more than you needed.'

'How do we stop it?' Lausard asked through clenched teeth.

'Cooked rice or bread usually works – or at least helps.'

'Did the Mamelukes teach you medicine as well as swordplay and horsemanship?' Rocheteau wanted to know, feeling his own stomach contract.

'They taught me many things. I learned the ways of the desert myself for the most part.'

'Bread,' Lausard said, looking around at the hovels of El Rahminaya. 'There is plenty of wheat around here but no flour mills or baking ovens.' He turned to Rocheteau. 'Give me that bag of wheat you took.'

The corporal handed it over without hesitation.

'Fetch me some flat stones,' Lausard instructed. 'And some kindling. We need to build a fire.'

Half a dozen of the dragoons scurried off to fetch what the sergeant had requested, pulling branches from nearby palm trees and stripping them. Sonnier and Gaston returned with five or six large, flat rocks and watched as Lausard poured some of the wheat on to one and began pounding it with another until he had a large quantity of brownish yellow powder. To this he added some water from his canteen, and used a stick to stir the mixture around in a small clay pot Roussard had found in one of the abandoned hovels. Meanwhile, Rocheteau and Giresse lit a fire, using two spare flints the corporal took from his cartouche. When it was ablaze, Lausard poured quantities of the thick wheat and water mixture on to some flat stones and placed them in the fire. After a few minutes a glorious aroma spread from the blaze, and even though the loaves were charred, the men found their mouths watering. Troops nearby also detected the heavenly scent and some wandered over to check it out. But the dragoons stood and faced them, guarding their meal jealously, the pain that racked them making them even more fearsome. The stones were glowing red and Lausard used his bayonet to pick one from the fire, flipping it out, taking the flat, blackened creation baked upon it in his hand. He broke it into several pieces and handed it around to the men closest to him, who ate ravenously.

He did the same with each of the six delicacies as and when they were ready for consumption.

'Glorious!' Joubert declared, chewing on the seared wheat that looked more like a blackened pancake than a loaf, but it was a welcome change from water melon.

'My father would have been proud of you, Alain,' Charvet said, pushing a piece of the bread into his mouth. 'He was a master baker. If I close my eyes I can still imagine the smell of his shop and those loaves he cooked.'

'And a good red wine to go with it,' Giresse added. 'With some onions cooked in oil.'

'And an omelette.' Bonet wiped his mouth with the back of his hand. 'I can't remember the last time I ate eggs. Mind you, I can't remember the last time I ate bread.'

'I haven't eaten any bread since before we left Toulon,' Lausard exclaimed. 'How long ago is that? Time seems to have lost its meaning here.' He rubbed his stomach as he ate, his belly rumbling ominously. He hoped this remedy worked.

'Water melons can be cooked,' Karim informed them. 'If they are, they should be safe.'

Lausard nodded.

'How come you're not afflicted with this disease as we are?' Roussard asked Karim.

'Your stomachs are not used to this kind of diet. That is why you suffer. You have known only pampering for too long.'

'Pampering?' Delacor snarled. 'Fighting for crumbs in the gutters of Paris. Do you call that pampering?'

'It seems you have lost your sense of humour along with the contents of your stomach.' Karim's reply was accompanied by laughter.

'When is this all going to end?' Joubert asked mournfully, his stomach contracting painfully yet again. He groaned.

'The rest of the army is gathered here or close by,' Lausard said. 'The time is near.'

'For what?' Roussard demanded. 'Our deaths at the hands of the Mamelukes?'

'Better a death in battle than to disease, thirst or hunger,' Lausard retorted.

'I don't want death from any*one* or any*thing*,' Roussard announced.

'We could all pray to God to protect us,' Moreau offered.

'The way he's protected us so far?' Lausard sneered. 'Go ahead, you pray if that's what you want, but leave me out of it.'

'Do you believe in God, Karim?' Bonet addressed the Circassian.

'I believe in Allah, all praise to him. That is what I was brought up to believe. That is why the Mamelukes and the Bedouin will resist you. To them this is a holy war. You represent not just a threat to their country but a threat to their religion too. They will not allow that.'

'We'll see,' murmured Lausard, pushing more of the charred bread into his mouth. 'They may not have any choice.'

Twenty-Three

The tent was small compared to Bonaparte's usual dwelling. He had chosen to spend the night in a subaltern's tent rather than his usual 'Marquis' tent, forsaking the hundredweight of canvas and seven-foot supporting ridgepoles for a bivouac usually shared by up to three men. The size of the enclosure didn't bother him though. His mind was on more pressing matters as he pored over the maps laid out before him. Berthier sat at a small table, quill in hand, watching his commander, while Sulkowski and Junot hovered close by the entrance should they be called upon to deliver orders to any of the five divisional commanders.

'Are you sure the information is correct?' Berthier asked, finally breaking a lengthy silence.

Bonaparte looked around at him and smiled. 'The spies who acquired it were well paid. Even now Murad Bey approaches the town of Shubra Khit. Less than eight miles south of here. He has under his command three to four thousand horsemen, several thousand foot soldiers and a flotilla of gunboats. It is the moment I have waited for, Berthier. The chance to confront the *true* enemy. The Mamelukes.'

'What are your orders?'

Bonaparte got to his feet and began pacing back and forth slowly, gazing off into the distance, as if looking through the material of the tent.

'You will instruct Generals Desaix, Reynier, Bon, Dugua and Vial to march on Shubra Khit,' the Corsican began. 'They are to march through the night if necessary and they will manoeuvre by way of the town of Minyet Salama.'

The scratching of quill on parchment became clearly audible inside the tent as Berthier transcribed his commander's words.

'Captain Perrée's flotilla will also converge on that point,' Bonaparte continued. 'Send an order to General Andréossy that he is to go aboard *Le Cerf*, Perrée's flagship, and direct the supporting action from the river. Instruct General Dumas that all non-mounted cavalry are also to board the flotilla. Those men with mounts will take shelter inside each divisional square unless otherwise instructed. The baggage trains will also remain inside the squares. Each division will fight in squares six ranks deep on all four sides, the artillery to be placed at the corners of the squares. It is imperative these orders are followed. The strictest discipline must be maintained during the battle. There is but one way to defeat the Mamelukes and that is to face them with an orderly, immovable front. That is exactly what I intend to do.'

Berthier scribbled away. 'What is the strength of the Moslem flotilla?' he asked.

'As far as my spies could tell they have seven ships. Mostly manned by Greeks and Turks.'

'Seven to our five.'

'The combat will be on the land, not the water. That is merely a diversion.' Bonaparte clapped his hands together and smiled broadly. 'The time has come, Berthier. In a few hours from now we will destroy the Mamelukes once and for all. Our destiny awaits us.'

Lausard sat motionless on his horse and watched as the six horsemen cantered around the perimeter of the square. All of them were large men, their stature increased further by the sheer volume of clothing they wore and the array of weapons they carried. The early-morning sun glinted on their weapons and gilded helmets, the rays accentuating the dizzying variety of colours worn by each of the Mamelukes. Over muslin shirts they wore layers of bright and brilliant silken vests and caftans, more often than not criss-crossed by belts inlaid with jewels, and the entire dazzling ensemble was highlighted by voluminous silken trousers, one leg of which would have comfortably wrapped a man. Their horses too were richly harnessed, some wearing saddle cloths inlaid with gold and precious stones. Even the flat, Oriental stirrups they used were gilt. But these were deadly too, the outer and inner edges sharpened to act as an extra weapon during close-quarters combat. Infantry could be kicked in the face, enemy horses slashed or opposing cavalry cut with one expert kick of those scythe-edged stirrups.

Lausard was mesmerized by the brilliance of these horsemen but also puzzled by their tactics. For more than three hours now, ever since dawn, small detachments of Mameluke horsemen had left their seething lines to the south of Shubra Khit, galloped towards the French, then slowed their magnificent mounts and cantered in and around the network of divisional squares looking at their enemy. They made no attempt to attack but rode past repeatedly as if on some kind of bizarre parade, occasionally speaking to each other and pointing at the squares.

The squares were six deep, as Bonaparte had ordered. The first two lines formed an impenetrable hedge of steel, some of the soldiers kneeling and resting the butts of their muskets on the sand so that the razor-sharp metal pointed upwards towards the Mamelukes. Behind, four more rows of muskets waited to fire at the given order. Two four-pounders had been left at the corner of each square, the gunners sheltering inside until told to man their pieces. They had loaded with case shot in preparation for the Mameluke attack which, at present, didn't seem to be materializing.

The Mameluke battle-line extended in a sickle shape from the Nile at Shubra Khit to the south and west of the French squares. Lausard noticed that although the line didn't move forward it was certainly not stationary. Every now and then, apart from horsemen who rode to inspect the French squares, men would dash forward and gallop at incredible speed from one end of the line to the other, as if to display to their comrades their finery and the majesty of their mount.

Lausard fumbled in his pocket for his telescope and peered more closely at the enemy troops. Behind the cavorting Mamelukes was a mass of foot soldiers, some, he noticed, armed with nothing more than wooden clubs. They were in no particular formation but stood beneath the blazing early-morning sun waiting for the order to advance, while their horsemen continued to display their riding skills in front of each other, apparently oblivious to the waiting French.

Lausard pocketed the telescope again and noticed that another small group of Mamelukes was cantering towards the square. It rode within ten yards of the bristling bayonets, peering curiously at the motionless French and the impenetrable squares. The French troops looked on with a mixture of bewilderment and something close to amusement. They continued to hold their fire.

'What the hell are they doing?' Rocheteau asked Karim.

'Looking for a weakness. This is all new to them. They are not yet sure how to attack.'

'Who are the infantry?' Lausard nodded towards the foot soldiers.

'Mostly Mameluke servants. The rest are Egyptian *fellahin*. They want to be here even less than you do.' Karim smiled.

'I doubt that,' Roussard said, watching as the enemy mass seethed, the sun glinting on all manner of weapons, jewels and precious metals.

'Will the servants fight?' Lausard pressed. 'They don't seem very well equipped.'

'Their only job is to help their masters,' Karim observed. 'The Mamelukes always fight in the same way. They will fire their carbines first then slide them under their thighs. Then they will fire their pistols; some carry up to three pairs. Those they will throw over their shoulders to be collected by their servants. Then they will throw their *djerids* – javelins made from stripped and sharpened palm branches – and, finally, they will charge with their scimitars. Some carry two; they grip the reins in their teeth and slash to right *and* left. And they will take off heads with one blow given the chance.'

Lausard nodded gravely as he listened.

'They know no fear,' the Circassian added. 'And they are rarely captured. For them there is either death or victory. If they are forced to flee they will do so with the same speed with which they attack. They will not allow you to take possession of their riches if they can help it.'

'Riches?' said Delacor, sitting up in his saddle.

'Each Mameluke carries his personal fortune on him, in money belts. Sometimes in the form of coins, sometimes as jewels.'

'Now that *is* interesting,' Delacor mused, rubbing his aching stomach.

'Perhaps we *will* go home rich men if we can get our hands on some of that.' Rocheteau chuckled.

'I wish to God they'd just attack and get it over with,' said Roussard.

'What's your problem?' Carbonne asked. 'We're safe in here.' He gestured around him at the six-rank walls of the square. 'It's the dog-faces who are going to get the worst of it.' He looked at the infantry and grinned.

A corporal in the rear rank heard him and looked round. 'We usually do. You bastards only ride in when the *real* work's been done. You should be thanking us for saving your miserable asses.'

Carbonne ignored him and, like his comrades, continued to gaze at both the detachments of Mamelukes still riding around the squares and the main force of Oriental horsemen, who continued to sway back and forth but made no attempt to advance.

'Perhaps they're waiting for the infantry to break ranks,' Bonet suggested.

'Then they'll be waiting a long time,' Lausard mused.

'Well at least they're prettier than the Austrians,' Rocheteau commented and several men within earshot laughed.

The sound was eclipsed by the sudden and thunderous retort of cannon fire.

All eyes turned in the direction of the blasts, to see that the French and Moslem flotillas on the Nile were exchanging fire. Within minutes, banks of thick smoke enveloped the vessels and began rolling across the water towards the land. It was as though a signal had been given. Lausard looked towards the Mameluke masses as he heard a chorus of high-pitched shrieks and screams. For brief seconds everything seemed to freeze. The horsemen, swords held up high in the air appeared motionless in full gallop, their horses rearing and kicking their hooves. Then the second passed. The full, teeming horde of Mameluke horsemen, screaming oaths and brandishing their glittering weapons, bore down on the French like a tidal wave. Dust from so many churning hooves sent a thick cloud into the air as the horsemen thundered forward. Trailing in their wake came the servants and the *fellahin*, dashing along as fast as they could behind their masters, who were now closing to within one hundred yards of the waiting French. Artillerymen slipped out from the squares to man their pieces and Lausard watched as corporals checked the sights and elevations of the barrels. Portfires were lit and ready. Around every square orders were bellowed to the infantry to hold their fire until told otherwise. Some of the words were lost amid the rumbling caused by the onrushing Mameluke horde, the churning hooves causing the ground to shake.

Lausard noticed there was no formation, no organization to the charge. The sharpened stirrups the Mamelukes used prevented them from riding in close order
for fear of injuring each other. The entire frantic advance
was nothing more than a disordered dash accompanied
by blood-curdling shouts designed to strike terror into
the enemy. But the French remained steady, awaiting
the order to open fire. Some of the dragoons pulled
their carbines to their shoulders, prepared to add their
own firepower to that of the infantry.

The Mamelukes were less than one hundred yards
away now and Lausard could see all manner of weapons
being brandished by some of the leading riders.

Eighty yards.

Bullets sliced through the air as some of the Mamelukes
opened fire.

Seventy yards.

Lausard could see battleaxes, maces, spears, swords
and pikes being held aloft as the massive wave of
horsemen drew ever nearer.

Sixty yards.

'Ready!' roared NCOs.

Fifty yards.

'Fire.'

The sound of so many muskets being discharged at
once was deafening. And with that eruption came the
fury of the cannon, spewing out their case shot into
the onrushing Mamelukes. The volleys of fire and the
salvoes from the cannon were devastating at such close
range. Men and horses went down in bloodied heaps,
riders' magnificent costumes transformed into bloody
rags as bullets tore into them, the superb Arab ponies
turning crimson. The entire battlefield was immediately

shrouded in noxious, sulphurous smoke, and the Mamelukes appeared from the choking clouds shouting their defiance and milling around the squares, seeking some way in.

More volleys of fire, executed with perfect precision by the French, sent more of the enemy crashing to the ground. Some of those who had lost their horses charged the squares on foot, but they were shot down before they could get within twenty yards.

Despite the deafening crackle of musket fire, Lausard could hear an unceasing cannonade coming from the vessels on the Nile. He could also see smoke rising from more than one of them. The ships of the two flotillas were jammed together, some so close that men were fighting hand to hand aboard the flimsy craft. Then a choking cloud of smoke rolled across the square to once more hide the ships from view.

In many places, the Mamelukes withdrew a hundred or so yards and contented themselves with riding around the squares. Other groups charged at opposite sides of the same formation, hoping to find a weakness. More were brought down by the well-drilled fire. Lausard noticed how infantry in squares not under attack would peer across to watch their comrades firing endlessly into the mass of horsemen. Then, as the last of the Mamelukes withdrew to a safe distance, Lausard heard orders being shouted to cease fire.

Smoke drifted thickly across the battlefield as the French waited for the next wave of attack, but the only place where combat seemed to be truly taking place was on the Nile itself. Two of the ships from the French flotilla were now ablaze, thick black smoke rising into the cloudless sky, momentarily blotting out the sunlight over the vessels. Lausard wished that it would do the same inside the square. The temperature seemed to have risen, driven up by the fire from so many muskets. Infantrymen reloaded, their already dry mouths further parched by the coarse black powder from their cartridges and foul smoke that seared their throats.

Officers and NCOs strode around the inside of the formation checking for any gaps, but they found none. Those dragoons who had used their carbines against the Mamelukes were also busy reloading in anticipation of the next attack. But once again the Mamelukes seemed more intent on displaying their magnificent costumes and consummate horsemanship than on renewing combat. Lausard watched one of them riding back and forth waving his scimitar above his head, occasionally hurling it into the air, catching it by the hilt as it fell. He continued doing this for some time and Lausard could not resist a wry smile at the Moslem's theatrics. Sonnier lifted his carbine and prepared to take a shot at the dashing Mameluke, but Lausard raised his hand and pushed the barrel down, giving his companion a disdainful look.

Artillery men were busily preparing their cannon for the next onslaught, their attention distracted occasionally by the thunderous exchange coming from the Nile-bound flotillas. The ships were barely visible now, such was the thickness of smoke pouring from the burning vessels.

'There's some hot work going on there,' Lieutenant Royere commented, gazing across at the battle. 'Most of Bonaparte's *savants* are aboard those ships.'

'Let's see how those preening "pekinese" enjoy some fighting. Perhaps they'll use their brains to work out a way to defeat the Arabs. After all they're all so clever, aren't they? What good will their brains do them when they're blown out of their heads?' Delacor laughed at his own wit, as did a number of the other men.

'They have suffered hardships as we have,' Bonet said. 'And why do you decry them for their intellect? Just because you are an idiot.'

'Watch it, schoolmaster, or I'll spill *your* brains.'

'At least I have some to spill.'

'Shut up, both of you!' Lausard snapped, watching as the battle on the Nile became more frenzied.

The gunfire was incessant and through the swirling, choking smoke, Lausard could see that batteries on both sides of the Nile – French and Moslem – were being brought to bear on the ships. Protected by infantry, the French gunners poured shot into any Moslem ship within range while, from the far bank, more Greek and Turkish troops added their firepower to that already devastating the French flotilla.

'Look,' Morcau said, grabbing Lausard's arm. 'They're withdrawing.' He was pointing to the Mameluke cavalry, who had wheeled away from the French and started retreating in the direction they had come, towards Shubra Khit. Almost immediately, a series of orders was barked out and the squares broke, the infantry hastily forming columns. Captain Milliere and Lieutenant Royere galloped between squares, gathering their men, forming them into small detachments which moved off slightly behind the infantry.

'What about the bodies?' Delacor said, looking down at a dead Mameluke riddled with bullet wounds. 'If they're all carrying money like Karim said . . .'

'This isn't over yet,' Lausard told him, noticing in the distance that the Mameluke cavalry were rapidly re-forming.

'This is no battle,' Rostov said disdainfully. 'They have no stomach for it.'

Lausard didn't answer, but kept his eyes on the glittering horde, aware also of the increasing volume of noise to his left where the water-borne battle continued. Smoke seemed to have virtually consumed the French fleet and Lausard glanced across to see flames leaping from within the choking blanket. Every now and then he could just make out bodies falling into the water, some pushed, some toppling from wounds, others jumping to avoid the hand-to-hand combat that had spilled over on to the decks.

Meanwhile, the advancing infantry had raised standards, as if this show of martial pride might goad the reassembling Mamelukes into another charge, but still the Moslem horsemen seemed content to career about with apparently no purpose, seemingly unconcerned that their enemy was now advancing towards them. A series of demi-brigades was marching towards the Nile with the intention of bringing their own firepower to bear on the attacking enemy flotilla. From somewhere Lausard could hear the familiar strains of 'La Marseillaise', but the continuous cannon fire and the smoke and the dust being raised by so many marching feet made it impossible to detect its source.

Lausard looked towards the Nile once more.

The explosion was enormous.

A thunderous detonation that deafened even those several hundred yards away and sent a concussion blast rolling across both water and sand.

Lausard watched as the Moslem flagship disappeared in a scorching ball of red and yellow fire, lumps of wood, metal, canvas and men flung into the air by the ferocity of the blast. The ship, he reasoned, had to be carrying extra ammunition. No conventional shell hit could cause such incredible destruction. Several secondary blasts confirmed his suspicions, and he looked on as the ship continued to explode even as it was sinking. Those on board who had survived the initial series of blasts were now hurling themselves into the murky waters of the Nile to escape the fury of the inferno.

'Jesus!' Rocheteau murmured, peering through the rolling smoke at the remains of the vessel.

Lausard continued to watch the blazing wreckage until Rostov grabbed his arm to draw his attention to the Mamelukes. They had wheeled their horses and were galloping away from the advancing French, the dust cloud they left behind almost as thick as the belching smoke drifting across from the burning flagship.

'I said they had no stomach for this,' Rostov said, grinning, and several of the men around him began to shout obscenities at the fleeing Moslems. Even the infantry were bellowing abuse at their fleeing foes, some even laughing hysterically as they watched the remains of the flagship being engulfed by flames.

'Look, there's Bonaparte.' Giresse pointed to the commander in chief riding past on a grey horse, accompanied by Berthier, Junot, Sulkowski and several guides.

'He doesn't look too happy for a man who has just won a battle,' Carbonne commented.

'Rostov was right,' Lausard observed. 'This was no battle. Not the victory Bonaparte wanted. This was just a skirmish. All it has proved is that the Mamelukes don't know how to defeat well-trained, disciplined men.'

'Even if half of them *are* blind and suffering from diarrhoea,' Bonet added and a number of the men laughed.

'Let's hope they run as easily *every* time we meet them,' Sonnier said.

'And let's hope we all get a rest now we've beaten them.' Joubert wiped sweat from his face.

'I wouldn't count on it,' Lausard said. 'And perhaps we should be more disappointed they *didn't* fight. Because the longer they run, the further we have to chase them across this stinking desert. I disagree with you, Rostov. I don't think they flee because they have no stomach for a fight. I fear they flee because they know that this country is as much an enemy to us as they are. How long will it be before they stand against us again? Or before we even *see* them? I suspect that is why Bonaparte looks so angry. He is thinking the same thing. We need to *crush* them, not play cat and mouse with them. They are drawing us deeper into *their* land, where we must fight them on *their* terms, on *their* terrain. They are not cowards and they are not fools. Half the army is sick now. Who knows what state we'll all be in by the time we face them again.'

Twenty-Four

'What is the name of this place?' Napoleon Bonaparte asked, looking down from the dunes that surrounded the village.

'Nekleh,' Sulkowski informed him, his eyes riveted to the pandemonium before him.

The village was ablaze. Every single dwelling had been torched by the marauding French troops, who Bonaparte and his staff now watched dashing through it, some on foot, some on horseback. Bodies littered the narrow streets and small squares. Men, women and children had been butchered by the French as their commander in chief looked on, undisturbed by the sight.

'What do you hope to gain by allowing such atrocities?' Berthier asked, looking on with disgust.

'Atrocities?' Bonaparte's eyes never left the burning village. 'This is war, Berthier, and it calls for drastic action. This village had promised to sell us provisions. It would not. I cannot allow that kind of insolence. It has already spread to many other places during our journey. Would you rather I allowed these savages to treat our men as they wish? To deprive them of food and water? Would you prefer our men to die in their place?'

'But these are women and children whose deaths you ordered,' Berthier argued. 'This village has no tactical worth, its inhabitants offer no threat.'

'They offer a threat to order by their treachery. And their determination *not* to sell us provisions indicates to me that they are our enemies, that they would see us starve or die for want of water. What they suffer they bring upon themselves. They and others like them. This army has always survived by foraging, it will continue to do so here.'

'Foraging, not *butchering*,' Berthier challenged. 'We are meant to be winning over the local people by our presence, by our role as liberators from the tyranny of the Mamelukes, and instead we bring them death and torture. Where are the principles of the Republic? Where are *our* principles?'

'Lost in the desert sand. We have pursued the Mamelukes for four days now since Shubra Khit. I have twenty-five thousand men with which to defeat them. Intelligence reports tell me that they await me with almost forty thousand. They are fresh, rested and fighting on ground of *their* choosing. My army is sick, hungry, thirsty and exhausted, and yet still they march because they believe in *me*. They have no doubt that they will be victorious. They know I will give them the victory they need.'

'Is the massacre of innocents what they need in order to?' Berthier persisted, glancing down at the smoking ruins of Nekleh.

'The village was hostile. Do not presume to question me, Berthier. I know what I must do and I am prepared to do it. For the greater glory of France and the Republic, incidents like this, although regrettable, must occur. I will tolerate no resistance.'

'You speak like a conqueror, not a liberator.'

'The two are very similar,' Bonaparte told him. 'Those who welcome us need have no fear. I have tried to be fair throughout this campaign but I am repaid with treachery. I will not stand for that. What some see as kindliness others see as weakness. I cannot allow myself to appear weak before these people. Similarly, what some see as brutal, others view as strength. It is strength that we must show if we are to prevail. Let the name of this village stand as an example to those who would oppose us, but if this example is not sufficient then I will not hesitate to order more action against the locals. They must be taught a lesson. They must learn to welcome us, not oppose us, and if it is by fear that we rule then so be it.'

Lausard sat on the damp sand, gazing into the flames of the camp fire as they flickered and danced in the stillness of the night. The mouth-watering aroma of roasting pigeon, skewered on the ramrod of a carbine and suspended on the makeshift spit over the fire, reached him, although it was accompanied by a number of other less savoury odours. The smell of many unwashed bodies, of excrement – human, horse and camel – also washed over him. The entire army seemed to have been crushed into the smallest area possible, and were crowded all around. And this mêlée of men and animals did not respect rank because officers, even colonels and generals, were hemmed in as comprehensively as ordinary soldiers. The sick, the able-bodied and those somewhere in between were all gathered together unceremoniously.

There were other camp fires close by, men from other units eagerly cooking everything from lentils to water melon. Even though the fruit had caused such ferocious dysentery among the men, they had continued to feast on it during the four-day march from Shubra Khit, mainly because there was little else to fill their bellies or quench their raging thirsts, but an order from Bonaparte himself instructed that provided the fruit was cooked it was safe to consume.

Elsewhere, those who had scavenged through the pitiful provisions of some villages on the march were enjoying meat, rice and even some of the local bread. Lausard himself had taken two sacks of rice from a village only that morning, and some of his haul was now bubbling away over the same fire in a metal bowl Delacor had stolen, along with a chicken now dangling from his saddle. Giresse had taken some cashmere shawls from one of the villages and stuffed them in his portmanteau, assuring his companions that he would trade them for food when he had the chance, but Lausard doubted anyone in the army would swap something edible for a few shawls, regardless of their value. The only things that had *real* worth in the desert were food and drink.

He watched Rocheteau turning the pigeon, his stomach rumbling from both hunger and the ever-present dysentery. The men sitting around the fire seemed subdued, wearied beyond endurance by the rigours of the campaign. Lausard thought particularly of the massacre at Nekleh. His unit had ridden through shortly after the leading infantry units had begun their eradication of the village. Bodies had littered the streets; men, women and

children shot, bayoneted or burned to death. All of the
men had seen death before, Lausard thought, all of them
had killed and would kill again, but the slaughter at
Nekleh was different in its ferocity, and the apparent
relish with which it was carried out. Someone had told
him that over nine hundred Egyptians had been killed in
less than an hour. He marvelled at how men who were
so exhausted and drained by hunger and fatigue could
suddenly find the energy to commit such acts. But they
had, and Lausard had no doubt they would again before
this campaign was over.

Gaston, Roussard and Tigana were busy feeding the
horses with what little they had collected from various
villages during the march. While most of the officers
of other units, cavalry *and* infantry, had allowed their
men to scavenge at will, Milliere had detailed his men
to fetch fodder for the horses along with provisions for
themselves.

Finally, Rocheteau took the cooked pigeon from the
ramrod and set about cutting it up.

'About time,' Joubert said, rubbing his stomach. 'I'm
starving.'

'You're always starving, fat man,' Rocheteau told
him.

Lausard accepted his portion and some of the rice and
chewed thoughtfully.

'Save some for the others,' he instructed, nodding
towards the men feeding the horses. 'They'll need it.'

'We all need it,' Delacor complained.

'Shall I give some to Lieutenant Royere? He's over
there.' Rocheteau gestured towards the officer, who
was stretched out on some straw, his head resting on
a rolled-up blanket.

'I'll take it,' Lausard said, getting to his feet, taking the food and heading off towards the officer.

As Lausard sat down beside the lieutenant and pushed the pigeon and rice towards him, he saw that the officer was studying a map. Several crosses had been drawn on it.

'The Mamelukes await us outside Cairo,' Royere said, chewing a piece of meat. 'Captain Milliere has already been given orders that we move out at two this morning.' He consulted his time piece. 'Less than an hour.'

'To where? To march across more of this desert? To chase the Mamelukes? To try to fight men who do not *want* to fight?'

'If it is any consolation, Lausard, the entire army shares your feelings. There isn't a man here, and that includes some of the officers, who knows what the hell Bonaparte is doing. Perhaps he isn't even sure himself.' The officer exhaled wearily. 'Once it was a new adventure, but I have a feeling that one day this land will swallow us up. Is that sedition?' He smiled. 'Am I betraying the ethics of the Republic?'

'Don't ask *me* about the ethics of the Republic, Lieutenant,' Lausard snapped. 'I know nothing of its ideals and I *care* nothing for them. Perhaps *that* is sedition.'

'What about the ideals of the ordinary soldier?'

'The French soldier no longer has any ideals. Even if he had to begin with. He is not fighting for the culture of the west, or for one form of government which he wants, and not for the Republic. He's fighting for his life.'

Royere shrugged. 'You may be right. But as a soldier, I feel it is my duty to subordinate my own ideals to the principles and ideals of my country, of the Republic.'

'Right or wrong?'

'Possibly. I believe what Bonaparte is trying to do here is right. Don't you?'

'Does my opinion really matter, Lieutenant? To you? To anyone? It certainly doesn't matter to Bonaparte. How many men have we already left back in that desert? How many have died since we first landed here? Thousands? And for what? Are we any closer to subduing the Mamelukes? Are we any nearer taking control of this country? No. Instead we march and we starve and we die.'

'Other men refused to march on. Why didn't you if you feel so strongly about the futility of this campaign?'

'Those men would not do their duty. As soldiers they should. I am bound by something more powerful than duty. I am bound by honour. That is why I will march and fight and obey orders, even if I do find some of them both ridiculous *and* distasteful.'

'You mean Nekleh?'

'That was *one* order, Lieutenant. One idiotic order among hundreds that have been given since we landed, and both of us know there will be more.' He got to his feet, preparing to rejoin his companions.

'And will you obey them, Lausard?'

The sergeant smiled, then disappeared back into the gloom.

Throughout the night march, Lausard could hear the waters of the Nile lapping against its shores. The army rarely moved more than a mile away from its flowing current, keeping the river on its left flank as it trudged through the sand and water melon patches. Palm trees grew in relative abundance along the river bank and the gentle breeze rustled their fronds as the French passed beneath them. The jingle of harnesses and the rattle of equipment also filled the ears of the marching men, who found, to their relief, that the terrain was fairly level.

As dawn broke and the sun rose into the cloudless sky, the heat Lausard and the rest of the army had come to know and detest began to intensify. Flies swarmed around the men with even more frenzy than usual; dressed as most of them were in filthy uniforms, they made even more tempting targets for the bloated insects. Horses flicked their tails to drive away the troublesome pests while many of the men seemed resigned to the flies' presence and allowed them to crawl over their flesh.

Every few yards men broke rank and scuttled off towards the nearest sand dune or clump of trees as their dysentery tormented them. Some didn't even bother to break ranks and merely defecated as they marched.

A strange, subdued air had overtaken the entire army as it moved relentlessly across the sand. A combination, Lausard thought, of weary resignation and dogged determination. The men were clearly exhausted and moved like automatons, some supported by equally weary colleagues, some still suffering from ophthalmia; all still hungry and thirsty. But it was as if, because they had come this far, they were determined not to give up now.

As the day dragged mercilessly on, the sun rose higher in the sky, the heat growing unbearable. At least half a dozen cavalry mounts collapsed and were shot to put them out of their misery. The animals that drew the artillery fared even worse and the gunners had a difficult task guiding their cannon over the numerous dry streams and irrigation canals. Wheels and axles on both guns and their limbers broke with despairing regularity and a number of units were left to repair the equipment on the spot.

Through the shimmering heat, Lausard saw something moving.

It took him only a second to realize that it was a large body of troops, the sun dancing on their bright costumes and numerous weapons. On both sides of the Nile they swarmed back and forth, and Lausard guessed they were less than a mile from the advancing French. As at Shubra Khit, the Mamelukes rode madly about on their magnificent horses, glorying in their opulent appearance, as if that alone would be enough to make the French turn back. Lausard looked on with admiration: they had exhibited great bravery at Shubra Khit and he wondered how effective they would be if that bravery was ever harnessed to correct military discipline and tactics.

He kept his eyes on the seething, threatening mass, glancing occasionally across to the left, at the glittering skyline of domes and minarets that rose above Cairo itself. And beyond the Mameluke battle line to the outlines of the great pyramids, the huge and mysterious objects clearly visible even at ten miles' distance. Bonet too had seen them and seemed to forget momentarily the Arab horsemen before him, so intent was he in gazing at the ancient monuments. Lausard handed him his telescope, allowing the former schoolmaster to see the massive edifices more clearly.

'Magnificent!' Bonet breathed, his voice full of awe. 'Just look at them. A wondrous sight to behold.'

'What are they?' Tabor asked.

'The great pyramids, my friend,' Bonet said, still gazing through the telescope. 'The final resting place of the pharoahs.'

'And who were the pharoahs?' Delacor pressed. 'Are they our enemies like the Mamelukes and every other bastard in this stinking country?'

Bonet chuckled. 'I don't think we have anything to fear from *them*. They have been buried inside the pyramids for thousands of years.'

'You mean those things are graves?'

'Hundreds of feet high,' Bonet said, still marvelling at the sight. 'Built by thousands of slaves as monuments to the greatness of their kings.'

'The Bourbons didn't get anything like that after we'd finished with them, did they?' Delacor cackled. 'All they got was a hole in the ground.'

Some of the other men laughed.

'The pharoahs were buried with all their personal belongings and fortunes,' Bonet continued.

'You mean those things are full of gold?' Delacor suddenly had a new interest in the ancient monuments. 'If we could get inside them we'd be rich.'

Bonet laughed. 'Some of the slaves who helped to build them were killed afterwards so they couldn't tell what kind of treasure was inside.'

'Who cares?' Roussard said agitatedly. 'We're about to be ridden down by those madmen over there and all you're concerned about is some piles of stone.'

'Piles of stone?' Bonet blurted indignantly. 'They are one of the seven wonders of the world, not some fairground side-show.'

'I still think they're too big for gravestones,' said Rocheteau, smiling.

Lausard also grinned and took back the telescope from Bonet, using it himself to sweep the Mameluke battle line.

He turned to Karim. 'Will they attack us as they did at Shubra Khit?'

'They will because they know no other way.'

Lausard looked up and saw Captain Milliere galloping across the sand towards them. He reined in his horse and looked at Lausard.

'Your squadron is to occupy that village,' he pointed to a collection of buildings away to their right. 'General Desaix has ordered it to be held. He is sending some grenadiers to support you.'

'What about the rest of the regiment, sir?'

'They will take up shelter within General Desaix's divisional square as before.'

Lausard looked past the captain and saw that the infantry was no longer in columns. Indeed, across the entire five-mile front, the troops were in the process of forming their squares, the artillery being positioned at each corner as it had been at Shubra Khit. Led by Milliere, Lausard and his squadron cantered across the burning sand towards the collection of buildings that made up the village of Biktil. Behind them, a detachment of grenadiers followed, some glancing worriedly towards the Mamelukes, anxious to reach the relative safety of the houses they were to defend.

Lausard and his unit drove their horses into the small dwellings, then immediately began preparing their carbines in readiness for the attack. Lausard chose a window and pressed his weapon hard into his shoulder, his cartouche open, ready to pull more cartridges free. Sonnier looked up at the flat roof of the house and decided that it would make a better firing platform. With Rostov's help, he scrambled up.

'How do we know they won't run again?' Lausard did

not take his eyes from the Moslem horsemen even as he addressed Karim.

'There is nowhere else *for* them to run.' Karim was carefully wiping the blade of his scimitar with a cloth. 'They are fighting outside the very gates of their capital city. They will destroy you or die in the attempt.'

'Then let them come,' Lausard said through gritted teeth.

Bonaparte swept the battle lines with his telescope, a smile touching his thin lips.

'They hold the upper hand as far as numbers are concerned,' Berthier said, as he too studied the enemy troops. From the relative safety of General Dugua's divisional square, the commander in chief and his staff took careful note of the Mameluke disposition.

'Intelligence has their numbers at over seventy thousand,' Sulkowski said, trying to calm his skittish horse.

'That may be,' Bonaparte murmured. 'That may be. And we are twenty-five thousand, but the Mamelukes have divided their forces.' He pointed towards the right bank of the Nile. 'Over there, Ibrahim Bey is encamped at Bulaq, perhaps because they feared we would try to cross the Nile before attacking them. On this side of the river, Murad Bey has the remainder of their forces.'

'They also have a flotilla on the river itself,' Berthier added.

'Much good it did them at Shubra Khit,' Bonaparte said, still surveying the Moslem troops. 'They are exactly where we would have wished. If they had chosen to await us on the far bank they would have enjoyed an advantage. As it is, they have played into our hands.'

'What about that village?' Berthier motioned towards

the fortified stronghold of Embabeh, which backed on to the Nile. 'They have artillery there. A frontal assault will cost many troops.'

'Intelligence leads me to believe that the guns are on fixed carriages. Once Vial and Bon's men have passed through the initial barrage they should encounter little trouble. We will penetrate through the centre of their line and cut off their retreat.'

'And what if the Mameluke troops on the far bank attempt to cross, to join with their comrades?' Berthier mused.

'Our own flotilla will prevent that and artillery has already been positioned to cover the main landing points should they attempt it.' Bonaparte took the telescope from his eye and snapped it together, looking around at his staff, his eyes blazing. It was as if his entire being was quickened, his veins filled with fire. 'From those monuments yonder,' he gestured towards the pyramids in the distance, 'forty centuries look down upon you.'

Sulkowski glanced at his pocket watch.

'What time is it?' Bonaparte wanted to know.

'Half past three, sir,' Sulkowski told him, looking across towards the right of the French line, where the first wave of Mameluke horsemen was sweeping with incredible speed towards Desaix's division, the torrent of horsemen bearing down with such ferocious haste that it seemed the French would be engulfed before they could form squares.

'What the hell are they playing at?' Berthier said, a note of concern in his voice. 'What is Desaix doing? Hasn't he seen them?'

Bonaparte smiled. 'Where is your faith, Berthier? Desaix is no fool. He will have seen the attack coming. The

Mamelukes will not break through there or anywhere else.' He watched as they galloped madly across the blazing desert, a magnificent, glistening multitude. 'Gentlemen, it begins.'

Twenty-Five

Lausard had never seen cavalry move so fast. He had marvelled at the Mamelukes' horsemanship at Shubra Khit, but the speed with which they now advanced was amazing. The charge was carried out with such incredible speed and impetuousness that it looked as if it might be successful by its sheer audacity. The ground shook beneath his feet as over five thousand Moslem horsemen swept across the desert like a shimmering tide. The brilliant sunlight glinted on their upraised swords and the thunderous pounding of so many hooves was matched by a chorus of blood-curdling yells and oaths. A huge dust cloud chased them, rising skyward, threatening to blot out the sun.

Lausard wiped sweat from his face and pulled his carbine more tightly into his shoulder, watching as the leading riders began to draw perilously close both to the village and also to General Desaix's men, who were hastily forming a square. Lausard knew that if the infantry was caught in open order by the onrushing cavalry, it would be cut to pieces, and it seemed as if the entire division was moving in slow motion as it formed its ranks ten deep to meet this tide of men and horses. But considering their weakened condition, the French troops completed the manoeuvre with great efficiency, and as the Mamelukes drew nearer, they saw that several rows of bayonets and muskets awaited them. Lausard couldn't hear the order to fire, the noise of the churning hooves drowing it out; all he saw was a great flash of fire as the first volley was fired into the Mamelukes, the dull boom of cannon fire accompanying it. Then a second volley from another rank as the square spat flames and lead again and again.

Dozens of horsemen were sent crashing to the ground, some already dead, others badly wounded. Many were killed by the pounding hooves of oncoming horses. After three volleys the square was hidden from view by clouds of black smoke, but the soldiers kept on firing and Lausard could see the man-made fog being periodically ripped asunder by fresh volleys of fire. The Mamelukes couldn't even get close enough to swipe at the infantry with their swords, the impenetrable rows of bayonets ensuring that the men firing were protected as they constantly loaded and reloaded.

The Moslem horsemen divided into three columns, snaking around Desaix's square and coming under fire from Reynier's men. Lausard could see that the ground between Biktil and Desaix's square was already strewn with corpses; dead men and horses lay in untidy heaps close to the tightly packed formations. Elsewhere, wounded men crawled aimlessly on the bloody sand, one or two actually crawling towards the French troops, intent on inflicting damage on them even in the hour of their death. Lausard watched as two Mamelukes staggered to within feet of the hedge of bayonets before three or four grenadiers inside the square shot them down. A riderless horse galloped past, leaping and cavorting wildly. Another charged past dragging its lifeless rider with it, his foot still stuck in the stirrup.

In addition to the thundering of hooves, Lausard now heard the booming of cannon fire from further across the line, and pulling out his telescope he could see that French troops were moving forward towards the village of Embabeh. Moslem cannon fired at them as they advanced and, to the rear of the French positions, mortars hurled shells into the Mameluke mass. Explosions sent more of the enemy flying into the air, and sand and earth were sent spiralling upwards towards the cloudless sky. Smoke and dust rolled across the battlefield.

'They're not going to touch us,' Roussard said excitedly.

'What makes you think that?' Lausard asked.

'They rode past the village,' Roussard continued. 'They could have attacked us but they rode past.'

The Mamelukes had splintered into dozens of smaller groups by now, each flinging itself at a chosen square with little effect. The ocean of horsemen had floundered on the rocks of the French formations. The infantry kept up a steady fire and the rumble of musketry replaced the thunder of hooves as wave after wave of fire poured into the furious horsemen.

'Alain!'

Lausard looked up as he heard his name shouted and he stepped out of the house in which he was sheltering to where he could see Sonnier sitting on the roof. Using a water barrel beside the building, Lausard clambered up.

'Look,' Sonnier said, pointing.

'I see them,' Lausard murmured.

He guessed there must be close to five hundred Mamelukes hurtling towards Biktil, possibly more. They were charging towards the village with the same suicidal fury with which their comrades were flinging themselves against the squares. Lausard looked down into the village and realized that both his own men and the grenadiers would be overrun by this charge. More horsemen were converging from the western side, close to a thousand men intent on slaughtering the defenders of Biktil, eager to vent their rage and frustration on any French troops they could.

'Everyone up on the roofs,' Lausard ordered, glancing around him. 'Hurry!'

Men all over the village scurried to comply with the order, scrambling to haul themselves up. Lausard saw Tabor lifting first Gaston then Bonet up on to the roof of the building next door, then the two men helped the big man heave his massive frame up alongside them.

Moreau and Rostov used their carbines as a makeshift step, allowing Carbonne to put his foot on the weapons before hoisting him up. Everywhere, dragoons and infantry were dragging themselves up on to the roofs, aware from the thundering of hooves that the Mamelukes were drawing closer by the second.

The first dozen or so riders swept into the narrow streets and rode along hurling their *djerids* up towards the Frenchmen, swinging scimitars at them. The French shot down with pistols, carbines and muskets into the growing tide of horsemen.

More and more of the Moslem horsemen poured into the village, others swarming around it, ensuring that none of the French escaped. Lausard watched as a tall Mameluke on a white horse rose in his stirrups and slashed with his scimitar at a grenadier who was still climbing on to a roof. The razor-sharp steel cut easily through the man's leg just below the knee, the severed limb dropping to the ground, the grenadier screaming and losing his grip. As he fell, another devastating blow practically shaved away half his head.

Lausard swung his carbine up to his shoulder and shot the Mameluke in the face.

Sonnier brought another man crashing down, his horse also toppling as it was hit by bullets fired from another roof. The animal brought down several riders following and French troops nearby poured fire into the mêlée of struggling animals and riders. Horses reared, enabling their riders to slash at the French troops who were sheltering a mere twelve or thirteen feet above the furious horsemen. Lausard stepped back as a bullet struck the roof close to his foot, and for a brief moment, he thought it had come from one of the other roofs. A second bullet convinced him that the Mamelukes swarming around the village were firing at the French with their pistols.

Using his horse as a step, one of the Mamelukes tried to scramble up on to the roof. Lausard drove his bayonet forward and skewered the Moslem through the chest, kicking him away, watching as the man fell back into the street. Others were now following suit, and all over the village, the defenders found that their enemies were climbing up to face them hand to hand.

Karim parried a blow with his scimitar then struck at the stomach of his opponent, disembowelling the Mameluke with one blow.

Rocheteau slammed the butt of his carbine into the

face of another attacker, watching as the man reeled backwards, blood and shattered teeth falling from his mouth. As the Mameluke struggled to regain his senses, Rocheteau drove his bayonet into his chest and kicked him off the roof.

Carbonne shouted in pain as a scimitar blow laid open his forearm. He managed to grab the Mameluke by the wrist, pull him towards him, and drive his head hard against the Moslem's nose. He then grabbed the man in a bear hug and held him while Moreau stabbed the Arab repeatedly with his bayonet.

Below them the Mamelukes still swarmed around the buildings and Lausard wondered how long they would continue their attack. It was a non-stop assault and as soon as one group rode off another would come hurtling into the village. All the time, those Moslems outside the village continued to ride around as if waiting their turn to attack.

The narrow streets of Biktil were choked with dead riders. Wounded men crawled into the houses seeking either shelter or somewhere to die. Riderless horses careened back and forth, slamming into the Mamelukes who already rampaged around the dwellings. The stink of black powder and blood was overpowering, and there was so much smoke billowing up from the continual fire of the French troops that it appeared as if the village was ablaze. The pounding of horses' hooves was accompanied by the clanging of metal on metal as swords and scimitars clashed with bayonets.

Lausard knelt on the roof, picking his targets and firing. He repeated the process continuously until his throat was parched, his mouth filled with grains of black powder and his eyes watering from the fumes. He bit the tops from cartridges, poured powder, rammed ball and wadding down the barrel and fired, then did the same again. And again. Nine or ten Mamelukes lay dead or dying around the house, and as Lausard looked down, he saw and smelled burning. Many of the Moslem corpses were now ablaze. The layers of silken clothing were so fine that the blazing wads from French carbines and muskets had ignited the rich garments as the bullets penetrated them. The stench of burning clothing soon gave way to that of burning flesh. Yet still these furious riders swarmed in and around the village.

Lausard saw that a few of the houses had been taken. Mamelukes were on the roof tops, some clutching pistols with which they were now firing at the French. He looked towards one house where three grenadiers had been sheltering and noticed angrily that all three men had been killed, their conquerors each triumphantly holding the severed heads of the infantrymen in one hand and their blood-laced swords in the other. Lausard swung his carbine to bear on the nearest of them and fired, watching with satisfaction as the man toppled backwards. Sonnier added his own fire and shot another in the stomach. The third leaped to the ground, still gripping the severed head. He disappeared amongst the tangle of dead and wounded.

Lausard blinked away sweat from his eyes and looked out across the rest of the battlefield. He could see that groups of Mamelukes were still defiantly attacking the French divisional squares despite the bodies of their dead companions littering the areas around each face of the impenetrable formations. Dead horses were piled like bloodied barricades around the squares. Some Mamelukes whose horses had been killed were running at the squares on foot, while others sought a fresh mount before resuming their suicidal assault.

'They're insane.' Sonnier was also watching the Moslems' fanatical displays of aggression. 'Don't they realize they're beaten?'

Even as he spoke, one of the guns positioned at a corner of Desaix's square let loose with another charge of canister shot, the eruption of sixty-three metal balls weighing between one and two ounces each ripping through the charging horsemen with devastating effect. An entire line went down as if tripped by some invisible wire. Those following became entangled in the bloodied mess and were promptly fired on by the infantry. All over the battlefield the scene was repeated.

Lausard's appraisal of the battle was interrupted when a bullet whizzed past his ear, missing him by inches. He spun round and saw that a Mameluke had fired a pistol at him and was now clambering up on to the roof top. Realizing he had no time to reload, Lausard dropped his carbine and pulled his sword, facing the scimitar-wielding Moslem. Lausard ducked beneath the first sweeping cut, meeting the second with his own sword. A loud clang reverberated as the two weapons smashed together and Lausard felt the power in his opponent's attack. The sergeant took a step back and thrust at his foe.

The size of the Mameluke belied his agility and he neatly side-stepped the probing blade and struck out with his own weapon, catching Lausard a glancing blow with the tip that split the sergeant's left cheek. In anger as much as pain, Lausard struck out with a shuddering back-hand stroke, which the Mameluke parried but could not hold back. Lausard's momentum carried him forward, and as he fell on to his opponent, he drove a fist into the Moslem's face, splitting the man's lip. The two men rolled towards the edge of the roof, the Mameluke clambering to his feet first, raising his scimitar high above his head. Lausard struck out and drove his sword into the big man's genitals, forcing the blade upwards until he had pushed it almost half the length of the three-foot blade. The Mameluke shrieked, dropped his own sword and grabbed at his punctured groin, blood spilling over his lips. Lausard wrenched his sword free as the Mameluke toppled over the edge.

Lausard looked down at the discarded sword of his enemy. It was a magnificent weapon. The pommel was inlaid with gold, the handle had been carved from some kind of animal horn and the blade itself was black steel. Lausard wiped his own sword and sheathed it, then he slid the scimitar into his belt and went to retrieve his carbine.

The fighting in the village seemed to be abating somewhat and Lausard noticed a number of the Mamelukes fleeing. When he looked to his right he saw why. Several hundred infantrymen had taken advantage of a lull in the fighting and, led by an officer and a trumpeter, they were moving towards Biktil, formed into a smaller but just as effective square. A burst of flame erupted from one side as they fired, downing several enemy horsemen. More and more of the Mamelukes now turned and fled, only a handful charging towards the square. The others hurtled off in the opposite direction, leaving a dust cloud in their wake.

Lausard looked across to the house nearest him where Karim and Rocheteau were crouching on the roof, their faces blackened with smoke. Karim raised a hand in the sergeant's direction and Lausard nodded gently.

Looking beyond, he could see that the Mameluke attack had broken. Many were galloping in the direction of Embabeh, itself ablaze. The blazing muzzle flashes of cannon occasionally illuminated a battlefield still shrouded in smoke and dust.

From the rooftops of several houses a number of the grenadiers began singing 'La Marseillaise' and Lausard looked round to see that Moreau, Giresse and Joubert had joined in, the latter waving his carbine triumphantly in the air, watching with delight as the beaten Mamelukes fled towards the Nile.

'There's nowhere for them to run,' Sonnier said, the sweat pouring down his face cutting swathes through his blackened cheeks. 'They cannot cross the river.'

Lausard didn't answer. He touched a hand to the cut on his cheek, looking down at the blood glistening on his fingertips.

'Are you all right, Alain?'

The sergeant looked towards the rapidly flowing river, seeing that many of the Moslem horsemen were plunging desperately into the water while still astride their mounts. Men and horses thrashed helplessly in the water, the Mamelukes weighed down by their equipment and clothes. From the bank, French infantrymen were already shooting into the terrified mass and, in places, the river was turning red.

'Bonaparte has his victory at last,' Lausard said, observing the scene of carnage. 'I hope he's happy.'

For the first time since arriving in Egypt, Lausard noticed that men did not seem to care too much about the appalling conditions. The heat of the day had given way to the miserable dew-soaked night but there were few complaints. The troops had other things on their minds. Lausard had heard that over two thousand Mamelukes had been killed that afternoon, their bodies either scattered over the battlefield or floating in the waters of the Nile.

As Lausard wandered through the scene of devastation, he saw that not one of the corpses had been left untouched. Even as he passed, men were tearing the clothes from those corpses that hadn't already been stripped. Several grenadiers were arguing over a pair of yellow leather boots they had taken from one rider. Two dragoons from his own regiment were struggling back to their squadron carrying a sack of coins so heavy it needed their combined strength to lift it.

Lausard paused beside a dead, half-naked Mameluke and noticed a gold earring that had gone unnoticed by the other pillagers. He pulled it free and dropped it into his pocket before walking on.

The smell of powder and smoke had been replaced by the stench of rotting flesh. The blazing sun had accelerated the decomposition of the dead and everywhere the all-too-familiar swarms of flies feasted. Lausard passed more troops squabbling over some gold-inlaid horse bridles. One of them was wearing a turban he'd taken from a dead Mameluke, the silk wrapped awkwardly around his head so that it looked more like a bandage.

'Not joining them, my friend?'

The voice startled him and he spun round to see Lieutenant Royere wandering across the sand towards him.

'The money they are collecting from the dead Mamelukes may well buy the six acres General Bonaparte promised us,' Royere said and both men laughed. They continued walking across the body-strewn battlefield.

'Captain Milliere has already collected his own booty. Two cashmere shawls, a skull cap inlaid with fifty gold pieces and some ivory-handled daggers.'

'And you, Lieutenant?' asked Lausard. 'What have you taken? I know that thieving is not confined to us so-called common men.'

'Hardly thieving, Lausard. See it as a redistribution of wealth. One of the purest principles of the Republic.' They both grinned. 'I must confess to having liberated some fine china, a number of rugs and some rather fine silverware from the Mamelukes' baggage train. How much of it I will ever manage to transport home to France is a different matter. I doubt if I will have enough left to make me a rich man.'

'Then perhaps you should be grateful for that, Lieutenant. Rich man and Republic do not sit very comfortably together, do they?'

'We are speaking of riches acquired through personal effort not through birthright,' Royere insisted.

'What is the difference? Wealth is wealth, whether acquired or inherited. It is strange how easily the principles of the Republic have been forgotten here tonight. How many men who fought for liberty, to rid France of the rich and privileged do you see on this battlefield now? These men care only for their own wealth.' He watched as a dragoon, unable to remove a large gold ring from a corpse's finger, sliced off the entire digit with a knife then scuttled off into the gloom in search of more riches.

'Would you care for one of these?' Royere held out a handful of sugar-dusted sweets. 'They are very good. Stolen too I might add but that does not diminish their flavour.'

Lausard took two and pushed them into his mouth.

'It is my sensibilities that are affronted,' he said, grinning, 'not my taste buds.'

Royere chuckled and gestured towards the brilliant orange hue that coloured the sky above Cairo.

'Word has it that the Mamelukes set light to three hundred Egyptian vessels in the port before fleeing,' the officer said.

'Perhaps we should be grateful they didn't set fire to the city itself,' Lausard observed, stepping over a naked corpse as he walked. 'Capturing Cairo was Bonaparte's goal, wasn't it? Enough men have died to achieve it.'

'I fear it is just the first of many objectives. He will not rest until he has subdued the entire country.'

'And then what? Where do we follow him after he has conquered Egypt? To India? Or beyond? Do you really think there is a limit to his ambition, Lieutenant?'

'Like you, Lausard, I do as I am ordered and my orders do not include speculation on the motives of our commander in chief. Although I suspect that for most of the men in this army, the only place they wish to follow him to is France. I must confess I share their longing. Don't you?'

'There is nothing for me in France. There hasn't been since I lost my family. Why should I be so eager to return to a land that took from me what I loved most?'

'France is your home.'

'I have no home. Not any more. The army is the only home I know, wherever it goes.'

'Where it goes next I can only guess. General Bonaparte has sent three companies of infantry under General Dupuy to occupy Cairo. I suspect that he will continue to pursue the Mamelukes. They were beaten today, not destroyed.'

'So we continue to march across the desert in pursuit of them? What has this campaign been other than march and fight, march and fight. I realize that is the way in war but at least in Italy it seemed to serve some purpose. Here, all the suffering has so far been for nothing. The Mamelukes' capital is in our hands, we have beaten them in battles and yet they still remain the rulers of this land. The local people resent us as much as they do the Mamelukes and yet we came supposedly as liberators. Does Bonaparte think that presenting a few tricolours to local tribesmen will make these people accept us? They will rejoice with us only when we leave or when we are all dead. Whichever comes first.'

Twenty-Six

For Lausard and the men of his unit life in Cairo gradually undertook a tedious monotony. As soldiers, their purpose was to fight and they soon grew tired of a life without purpose.

Lausard reflected on the conflicting feelings tormenting the men ever since they had left Toulon over five months earlier. During the long voyage from France to Egypt they had wanted nothing more than to feel solid ground under their feet and face their enemy – to use the skills they had been taught and had used to such devastating effect a year earlier in Italy. But upon arriving in Egypt, they had been overcome by its desolation. The desert marches had seen many die – from the effects of thirst and sun, by their own hand and from other ailments peculiar to a country the men found exceptionally hostile. The battles with the Bedouin or the Mamelukes had served to take their minds off their suffering, but they also presented the men with the possibility that they might lose their lives. And yet now, having been billeted in the European quarter of Cairo for more than a month, they craved action once again, even though it might end their lives. They needed combat as a hungry man needs food.

News that the Mamelukes had been fought and beaten at a place called Salalieh had circulated, but the dragoons had not been involved. Cavalry, it seemed, were superfluous to requirements on this campaign. So Lausard and his regiment, like many other troops, had been left to fester in the capital city, surrounded by squalor they could barely have dreamed of. Even as he sat sipping his coffee, Lausard looked around the square of Birket-el-Fil and yet again ran his eyes over the filth. He had long since decided that it was a city which did not deserve its great reputation. Narrow, unpaved, filthy streets, dark houses that appeared to be falling to pieces, public buildings that looked like dungeons, shops that resembled stables; the entire city was redolent of dust and garbage. Blind and half-blind men, and people dressed in rags pressed together in the streets or squatted in the squares or cowered in the entrances of buildings smoking their pipes. For the most part the women were filthy too, their faces covered but their pendulous breasts clearly visible through their torn gowns. Many were accompanied by yellow, skinny children, who were covered with suppuration and devoured by flies. And everywhere there was an unbearable stench – a combination of the dirt, dust and smell of food being fried in rancid oil. Sanitation was virtually unknown, and in most places raw sewage ran through the streets.

At night, the streets were largely impassable, unlit and in places overrun with packs of wild dogs. Even the houses of the rich lacked certain elementary comforts, and the buildings where Lausard and the other men of the squadron were billeted were even more basic. At times, Lausard thought that the stables where the horses were kept were no more uncomfortable.

The days had become almost indistinguishable from each other. Each day dawned with monotonous, scorching regularity and Lausard and his companions found themselves with nothing to do to alleviate their boredom. They had sampled the so-called delights of this city early on. It seemed that its entertainment ran to belly-dancing and snake-charming. Even the prostitutes were old, wizened and, for the most part, horribly diseased.

Lausard took another sip of his coffee and thought, not for the first time, that his time in Cairo had, so far, been one of the most pointless and soul-destroying episodes in his life.

Beside him, Rocheteau was also cradling a cup of coffee, inhaling the aroma. Delacor was sipping a glass of date wine, looking across the table at Joubert, who was chewing hungrily on a pastry. Giresse, using a piece of charcoal, was busily sketching two old Arabs squatting in the middle of the square, oblivious to those who passed them by on either side. Tabor and Gaston sat watching their companion's creation take shape, fascinated by the swift, assured strokes he applied and the image forming on the paper. Bonet was engrossed in the latest edition of the *Courrier de l'Egypte*, one of two newspapers printed in the capital by the members of Bonaparte's Scientific Commission. Karim also glanced at the paper occasionally, between sips of his coffee. He was the only one who still wore his *surtout* buttoned to the neck, the other men having either unbuttoned their top three or four buttons or opened theirs fully. The heat didn't seem to bother Karim. But then again, Lausard had noticed, not much did.

The café where the dragoons had gathered was like many that had sprung up during the French occupation. Some owned and run by merchants, others by members of the more enterprising elements of the army. One man had traded gold he'd confiscated at the battle of the pyramids in exchange for ownership of one of the cafés, which served not just coffee but also wine, rum and brandy, and pastries freshly cooked on the premises. It offered the men a reminder of home, as did the libraries, reading rooms and billiard halls they frequented. But, as Lausard reasoned, the more that was done to make the men feel at home, the more they were reminded how much they missed it.

'It says in here that General Desaix is chasing the Mamelukes all the way into Syria,' Bonet said, jabbing a finger at the newspaper. 'It says that it is only a matter of time before they are completely destroyed.'

'And you believe that, do you, schoolmaster?' Delacor said scathingly.

'And if they *are* destroyed? What then?' Rocheteau wanted to know. 'Does that mean we can go home?'

'I hope so,' Joubert intoned. 'I'm sick of this filthy country and its people. They'd slit our throats if they had the chance.'

'Do you blame them?' Lausard said. 'We have stolen their country from them. How would you feel if it had been they who had invaded France? Would you not have wanted to kill them?'

'We saved them from the Mamelukes, didn't we?' Delacor said.

'You have replaced one form of tyranny with another,' Karim countered, sipping his coffee.

'We have freed them,' Delacor protested.

'We have tried to change Cairo into Paris,' Lausard said. 'Renaming streets after our own, taking over their businesses. I'm not surprised they resent us.'

'This isn't like the Paris *I* can remember,' Rocheteau said, looking round.

'How good is your memory, my friend?' Lausard asked. 'We live in filth here, we lived in filth back in Paris. What's the difference?'

'I'll tell you the difference,' Giresse interjected, still sketching. 'We had women back home.'

The men laughed.

'There are women here,' Joubert offered.

'Not if you are as selective as I am, fat man. I prefer beauty and gentleness in a woman. The women *I* knew back in France were always beautiful. Not like these creatures here. I would not soil myself by lying with them.'

'Nor I,' Delacor insisted.

'When did *you* acquire standards when it comes to women?' Lausard wanted to know.

'You can marry an Egyptian woman if you wish,' Bonet said. 'I know men who have. All you have to do is become a Moslem, speak their words of faith. "There is no God but God and Mohammed is his Prophet." And that is it, you have a wife.'

'If Paris is worth a mass, then eleven words is the worth of a bed mate here.' Lausard grinned.

'It's blasphemy,' Moreau said. 'We are not Moslems, we cannot become Moslems. They worship a different God. Not *our* God.'

'Shut up, your holiness,' Delacor snapped. 'If I thought that speaking eleven words would get me a woman for the night I might just do it.'

'I would speak twenty-two words and have two women,' Giresse added, and once again the men laughed.

'There is an old Turkish proverb,' Karim told them. 'Take a white woman for the eyes and an Egyptian woman for pleasure. Perhaps you should bear that in mind.'

Giresse finished his sketch and held it up for his companions to see.

'Very good.' Bonet admired it. 'You have excellent natural talent, Giresse.'

'There is magic in these fingers,' Giresse said, grinning. 'Ask any of the women I've slept with.'

The men chuckled loudly.

'Perhaps Bonaparte will invite you to join the Scientific and Artistic Commission,' Lausard suggested. 'You can run around drawing these ruins he seems so obsessed with. I'm sure they'll find you a job somewhere. There seems to be more work for civilians out here than soldiers.'

'Those "pekinese" are no use to us.' Delacor's tone was dismissive. 'I don't know why Bonaparte brought them. All they do is get in the way and eat the food *we* should have.'

'There are some brilliant men amongst them,' Bonet confirmed.

'But why are they *here*?' Tabor enquired.

'To study the country and its history,' Bonet told him. 'There is much to be learned from this country.'

'Yes,' Rocheteau rasped. 'Look at what this country has offered us. Dysentery, blindness, thirst, madness, suicide, fever and all manner of other suffering.'

Lausard slapped him on the shoulder. 'Order some more drinks. We cannot change our fate, we can only endure it. All the ills this country and its people throw at us will not break us.'

'I wish I could believe you, Alain,' Giresse said.

'You only need look at what our commander in chief offers us to pass our time,' Lausard said, a wispish smile on his lips. 'How can you doubt his concern for us? Theatrical shows with men playing women's parts. Jugglers. Puppet shows. I even heard that a club is to be opened and balls organized. And if we tire of those diversions, we can always visit the pyramids again or go ostrich hunting. How can you miss France when you have such a wealth of activities at your disposal?' There was a strong note of scorn in his voice. 'Perhaps one day, Bonaparte will remember we are soldiers, perhaps he will let us fight again.' Lausard raised his cup in salute. 'To that day, my friends.'

Other receptacles were raised in salute.

'What is the toast?' Rocheteau asked.

'Women,' Giresse said.

'Food,' Joubert offered.

'Home,' Rocheteau added.

'Survival,' Lausard concluded.

The men drank.

Napoleon Bonaparte walked around like a man in a trance, passing from one room to another in the sumptuous surroundings of the palace of Mohammed Bey el-Elfi. He had taken up residence in the magnificent building in Esbekiya Square upon entering Cairo, struck by its opulence, impressed that the building – unlike many of those owned by the upper classes of the Moslem caste – was truly fit for a conqueror like himself. The windows boasted glass panes, the staircases were of marble, alabaster and polished granite from Aswan, the floors covered by mosaics. There was a bath on every floor and, to complete the vision, the main reception room boasted a monumental ornamental fountain.

But at this moment the Corsican cared nothing for this show of wealth. He cared nothing for his victories or anything to do with this country. He paced back and forth in one of the smaller state rooms, hands clasped behind his back, his head bowed.

'Your generals are waiting,' Berthier told him, his voice gentle, almost consoling.

'Let them wait.' Bonaparte continued pacing.

'I can send them away if you wish. The meeting can be held—'

'Just let them wait,' Bonaparte repeated, finally stopping his relentless march back and forth. He looked directly at Berthier, something close to bewilderment in his eyes. 'Why did she betray me? She was the world to me. Could she not see that? Did she not realize the spell she cast upon me?' He crossed to a nearby chaise-longue and sat down heavily. 'It is the end of my world, Berthier. Without Josephine there is nothing for me. All I have achieved here is meaningless. My whole *life* is meaningless.' He sat back, gently stroking his forehead with his fingers.

Major Junot cleared his throat somewhat theatrically and took a step forward.

'Sir, I feel that *I* am to blame for your melancholy,' the aide-de-camp said. 'Had I not let it slip out that your wife had been indiscreet then—'

'Indiscreet! The word barely captures the nature of her treachery. And as for keeping this news from me, you would have done me no favours, Junot. Josephine is *my* wife. Don't you feel I have a right to know what the whole of Paris society has known for some time? If I am to be a cuckold then I want no whispered indignities behind my back. This was no indiscretion, this was betrayal – and for what? The attentions of some common soldier? This dog is nothing more than a dandified hussar, and yet his charms, it would appear, rank more highly in the eyes of my wife than do my own achievements. To conquer countries, to destroy armies, to extend the boundaries of the Republic is not enough for her. She seeks more in a husband perhaps. And yet, if this is so, why should she content herself with a mere hussar?' His voice had risen both in volume and vehemence. He exhaled deeply, the weariness returning to his tone. 'I am weary of humanity,' he said quietly. 'I need solitude and isolation. Greatness bores me. My feelings are dried up. Glory is stale when one is twenty-nine. I have exhausted everything, there is nothing left for me but to become really and completely selfish.'

He got to his feet and crossed to the nearest window, looking out over the city.

'Have you ever loved someone with such consuming energy, Berthier?'

'My young Mistress Visconti. Not a minute passes that I don't think of her.'

'But she has not betrayed you. It is a sad thing to concentrate all one's feelings on a single person, in a single heart. Especially when that love is not returned.' Bonaparte shrugged. 'It is nearly two months since I discovered this betrayal and yet still it tortures me. I fear it will never end, this pain I feel, and yet how can I dwell on my own disappointments when the army relies on me?'

'It is only natural you are still affected,' Berthier consoled him. 'Love does unspeakable things to men. As cruel as anything a battlefield can offer. But at least in combat a wound to the heart means certain death; in love a wound to the heart means a lifetime of suffering.'

Bonaparte nodded sagely, his entire demeanour changing from self-pity to grim determination.

'Send in the others,' he ordered, watching as Junot opened the doors leading to the state room. A number of officers walked in, led by General Dupuy. Behind him came Murat, a huge white ostrich feather in his bicorn and his feet adorned by yellow leather boots. General Caffarelli stomped in behind him, his wooden leg thumping loudly on the marble floor. Bonaparte waited until the men were settled, then he looked at each one in turn.

'Where do I begin, gentlemen?' he said. 'We came to this country as liberators, prepared to accept the ways of those we encountered. Tolerant of their religion and their ways – and how do they repay us? By rising against us. In nearly every town and village we have occupied the populace has risen against us. *That* is their thanks to us for bringing them freedom. In the Menzala region of the Nile we are faced with what amounts to guerilla war. The leader of those guerillas, Hassan Tubar, is in constant contact with Ibrahim Bey who, even as we speak, is being pursued by General Desaix and his men. The population massacred the garrison at El Mansura and, every day, fresh reports reach me of more risings, all of which I have given orders should be dealt with summarily. Even here in Cairo itself there is still resistance. I order five or six people beheaded every day in this city.' He exhaled deeply.

'What news from Desaix?' Murat asked.

'He pursues the Mamelukes into Syria. When he catches them he fights and beats them, but his men are suffering from sickness, as are the men all over Egypt.'

'I heard that fifteen per cent of the troops were in hospital,' Caffarelli said.

'That is true,' Bonaparte agreed. 'Men who cannot be replaced. Not since that cursed Englishman Nelson destroyed our fleet at Aboukir bay. We have been separated from our homeland, we are in a hostile country that fights us either openly or behind our backs while we still chase an enemy whose only concern is to run. Our men are sick and dying. And on top of all that, the Sultan of Turkey has declared war on us. But, I promise you, we will still prevail.'

'I hope your optimism is well founded,' Murat remarked. 'How are we to stand against a Turkish army when we cannot even control the Egyptian peasants?'

'I thought the Turks were our allies,' Dupuy said.

'The Sultan has issued a *firman*, declaring a holy war against us. I have already devised plans for the defence of Egypt.'

'We are to defend a country that isn't even ours yet.' Murat snorted.

'The Turks plan a pincer movement. According to my intelligence, one pincer will be formed by the Army of Rhodes. This is to be transported by sea, with the assistance of the English.'

'Always the English,' Berthier murmured.

'Just so,' Bonaparte said, smiling. 'But they will not influence the outcome of this venture. The second pincer is formed by the Army of Damascus, who will advance by way of Palestine and the Sinai desert.'

'So how do you propose to stop them?' Murat wanted to know.

'I intend to leave ten thousand French troops, supported by local militia, to control Egypt. I will lead the remainder of the army across the desert into Palestine, defeat the Army of Damascus then double back to meet the Army of Rhodes and crush *them*.'

The other officers listened in silence.

It was Murat who finally spoke. 'We cannot control Egypt with *thirty* thousand men. How do you propose to do it with just ten thousand? This entire country has risen against us.'

'Then each revolt must be met with sterner punishment,' Bonaparte snarled. 'For every Frenchman killed, I want ten Arabs executed. I have shown them mercy and they have thrown it back in my face. They will not be allowed to do that again.'

'If it is reprisals you wish to see, then put your chief of police in command,' Dupuy said. 'The man is a maniac.'

'Would you prefer the lawlessness we found when we first arrived here?' Bonaparte challenged. 'The Janissary companies work well.'

'They are supposed to be highly trained,' Dupuy protested. 'They are riff-raff. Turks, Greeks, Moors, and commanded by that butcher Bartholomew they are little better than those they seek to subdue. He presented me with a sackful of severed Bedouin heads less than a week ago as I was about to eat dinner. Am I to assume that he is also responsible for the slaughter of those prostitutes who were beheaded and tossed into the Nile?'

'The problem was out of hand,' Bonaparte said

dismissively. 'Every one of them was infected with syphilis. I could not allow such a plague to spread through the troops.'

'Four hundred were killed and disposed of,' Dupuy persisted.

'We have more pressing problems than dead prostitutes, Dupuy.'

'Have you heard any news from the Directory?' Caffarelli questioned Bonaparte. 'Do they know of our predicament? They should be sending us food, supplies and reinforcements or are they content to let us rot here in this godforsaken hole?'

'The English Navy is blockading the approaches to Alexandria,' Bonaparte said. 'Nelson and his ships control the seas. We are forced to deal with our problems in our own way.'

'So the Directory has abandoned us?' Caffarelli continued. 'I always suspected they would. I told you they were no better than the Bourbons they replaced. They care nothing for this army now, or for what becomes of it. They only supported you because they felt that this country was rich pickings. That is why they instigated this invasion.'

'This was, from first to last, *my* idea,' Bonaparte snarled. 'I did not need some fool in the Directory to tell me the advantages of conquering Egypt. *I* saw its worth. I made *them* see. We came to this country because *I* decreed it, not the Directory.'

'So, should the men blame *you* for their predicament here?'

Bonaparte put an arm around Caffarelli's shoulder. 'Max,' he said quietly, 'we have been alone ever since we landed here with nothing but our wits and our courage to sustain us. They have been good enough so far, they will see us through whatever else is to come. We do not *need* the Directory. We never have.'

'When was the last time you received any communication from them?' Murat wanted to know.

'As I said, the English fleet has blockaded the harbours,' Bonaparte stalled. 'This has prevented the exchanging of information, but this very day I received word that the ship *L'Anemone* was beached at Marabout. There is a courier on board carrying despatches from the Directory.'

'Then where is he?' Caffarelli demanded.

'He and twenty-five other passengers were taken prisoner by Bedouin tribesmen. They are demanding a ransom for their release. I want those prisoners back. I want those despatches. But I will not pay these savages one sous.'

'The hostages are probably dead already,' Murat said dismissively.

'I cannot take that chance. I must have the despatches the courier is holding.'

'So what do you propose to do, send another army back to Marabout to free these men? To fragment an army that is already in pieces?'

'Sometimes stealth is to be preferred to force,' Bonaparte told him. 'This matter requires the services not of an army but of a small unit of troops. A detachment of your cavalry, Murat. That should be sufficient.'

Berthier stepped forward. 'General, I thought your policy was to pacify the local population. To win them over. If you send troops against them you will defeat your own objectives.'

'Berthier, no one has gone farther than I in attempting to appease these savages,' Bonaparte said bitterly. 'I have tried to coax them on to my side. I assured them that we came not to destroy their religion but to preserve it. But that religion has been the chief obstacle to unity here. I could tell these people three times a day that neither myself nor my men are Christians. That we had imprisoned the Pope and closed the churches and that we respected Islam. But it would not matter. All the rhetoric and charlatanry in the world will not change the fact that to these people we are Infidels and we always will be. Why do you think they have risen against us in so many places? Against forces who seek to bring only order to a disordered land.' He exhaled loudly. 'I never wished to destroy their religion, only their apathy, their submissiveness to a fate they believed could not be altered. I have tried to drag them from their feudalism into our modern world and they have repaid me with treachery and disrespect. I will play their games no longer. I have tried mercy, perhaps they will respond better to tyranny.'

Berthier nodded slowly.

'Now these hostages.' Bonaparte addressed Murat. 'I want them freed as soon as possible.'

'And what of their captors?'

'If they can be bargained with, so be it. If not, destroy them.'

'It is a dangerous mission,' Murat observed.

Bonaparte took a step towards him, his piercing eyes looking deeply into those of the cavalry general.

'Then make sure you pick the right men.'

Twenty-Seven

'This is like retreating,' Delacor complained. 'How long did it take us to cross this stinking desert in the first place? And now, we are retracing our own footsteps just for the sake of some bastard "pekinese".'

'It isn't the same route,' Bonet observed. 'We didn't follow the path of the Nile when we first landed.'

'Who cares? We're still going back to where we started, aren't we?' Delacor glanced up at the cloudless sky. 'Three days in this godforsaken desert already and for what?'

Lausard, riding a couple of lengths ahead, turned briefly in his saddle.

'Delacor, why don't you shut up? Save your energy. You're going to need it. You were bored in Cairo, now's your chance to do something.'

'Like what?' Roussard wanted to know. 'Get killed by the Arabs. I'd rather be in Cairo.'

Lausard turned back in his saddle, his eyes fixed on Captain Milliere, Lieutenant Royere and four other troopers who rode about thirty or forty yards ahead of the column of dragoons. The squadron had made good time since leaving Cairo, stopping just twice for water and food. They carried sufficient hard rations for a week and there was enough fodder for the horses at each outpost they stopped at. The length of the Nile was patrolled by French troops garrisoned in places like Wardan and El Rahmaniya. In fact, Lausard had noticed, the troops in these more distant outposts seemed much more cheerful than the men stationed in the larger towns and cities. They seemed to get on better with the local population, those who hadn't fled into the desert, and at Wardan the French troops had taught the Arabs how to use the baking ovens they had been supplied with. Lausard and his men had picked up loaves as well as supplies of wine and brandy made with dates.

'From what I hear, we're better off out of Cairo at the moment,' Rocheteau remarked. 'I was talking to a grenadier back in Wardan and he said they'd heard that the locals had risen against Bonaparte. Over two hundred of our men were killed in the city and nearly three thousand of theirs.'

'You can't trust these bastards, I always said that,' Delacor said.

'A revolt in Cairo will be followed by more elsewhere,' Lausard commented. 'This whole country will explode one of these days.'

'And we'll be right in the middle of it,' Roussard said uneasily. 'It's because of men like *him*.'

His words were directed at the silver-haired individual riding alongside Lausard. The man tried to ignore Roussard's comments but Lausard could see him shift uncomfortably in his saddle.

'It's your friends we're supposed to rescue, isn't it?'

Roussard continued. 'Risk our lives for a bunch of chemists.'

Citizen Gustav Caminarro glanced at his critic and considered retaliating, but the fierce look in the eyes of Roussard and those who flanked him told him that silence was the better option.

Caminarro was in his early thirties. A thin-faced, distinguished-looking man who had been all too eager to join the expedition to Egypt and more than happy to accept Caffarelli's invitation when the gathering of scientists and other thinkers had begun. He had experienced the same hardship and privations as the troops, but his arrival in Egypt had not, as it had for most of the army, been the beginning of another chapter of suffering – it had been the fulfilment of his dream and his duty.

'So, what do you do here?' Lausard asked him. 'Why did you come on this expedition?'

'I am a geologist. I have been working under the supervision of Berthollet to find a way of purifying Nile water, but I have also been studying the rocks and minerals of this region.'

'A rock is a rock, isn't it?' Rocheteau said and some of the other men laughed.

'The geological features of this country are unlike those I've seen anywhere else. They are quite fascinating.'

'So while we've been dying of thirst and hunger, fighting the Mamelukes and trying to subdue the Arabs, you've been crawling around collecting stones?' Delacor's tone was dismissive.

'I would imagine that the work has been very interesting,' Bonet said. 'I myself went to look at the pyramids and I was amazed by them. It is the history of this country that I find so fascinating.'

'Shut up, schoolmaster,' said Delacor. 'Perhaps you should join Bonaparte's "pekinese" if you're so impressed with this stinking place.'

'I wouldn't expect you to appreciate the beauties of this land. Only educated men like Citizen Caminarro and myself are capable of that.'

'The only things I want to appreciate are a good woman and some good wine,' Giresse said, smiling.

'Or some good food,' Joubert added.

'What could you find here that you couldn't find anywhere else?' Lausard asked.

'This country is rich in treasures,' Caminarro told him. 'All kinds of natural treasures. Their study will benefit all of mankind eventually.'

Delacor hawked and spat. 'Who cares?'

'Why do you hate men of learning like myself?' Caminarro enquired. 'We have done you no harm and yet you insult us constantly. You show us no respect.'

'Respect has to be earned,' Rocheteau reminded him. 'If you could use a sword and a pistol, men like Delacor would be more likely to accept you.'

'I am not a fighting man. Not unless I have to be. But I fought at Shubra Khit. I and many of my colleagues were on the ships the Moslems attacked. A number of them were killed. And now more will die unless you rescue them from the Bedouin who hold them captive."

'Are all the hostages from the Scientific Commission?' Lausard pressed.

'Most of them, but I believe that there are a handful of men who are representatives of the Directory.'

'Even more reason to let them die then,' Carbonne grunted.

'How will you free them?' Caminarro asked.

Lausard shrugged. 'Captain Milliere said that we were to bargain with them if possible. If not, we are to destroy them. They are Bonaparte's orders. Remember, citizen, we do not have the luxury of choice here. We do as we are ordered and we were ordered to recover the hostages.'

'You must have been chosen for your abilities, for your bravery.'

Lausard smiled wanly. 'The reason we were chosen is because we are expendable.'

'That's right,' Rocheteau added. 'No one cares about a few ex-prisoners.'

'You are criminals?' Caminarro's expression darkened.

'Not all of us,' Karim said, grinning.

'No, not our Circassian here,' Lausard said. 'He is not like us. He fights for revenge, don't you, Karim? And Lieutenant Royere up ahead, he is driven by idealism. We all have different motives, citizen, but that need not concern you. All you need to worry about is whether or not we can free your companions.'

'And can you?'

Lausard did not answer the geologist. His attention had been caught by the sight of two riders approaching the column from the north-west. Even from a distance he knew that they were Rostov and Moreau. Captain Milliere had despatched them in the direction of Marabout nearly an hour earlier.

'Why the hell couldn't Kléber have sent some of his men to rescue these "pekinese"?' Roussard demanded. 'Why drag *us* halfway across this stinking desert?'

'I told you,' Lausard reminded him. 'We're expendable.'

'What is the name of the place we are going?' Tabor asked.

'What does it matter?' Delacor snapped. 'Every stinking place in this whole filthy country looks and smells the same.'

'Marabout is where we landed, isn't it?' Rocheteau said.

Lausard nodded. 'All these months of marching, fighting, suffering and dying, and we're back where we started.'

Milliere lowered the telescope then looked across at Lausard who, from his vantage point up on the ridge, was also peering at the Bedouin encampment. He could see twenty or thirty tents, dozens of horses, camels and donkeys wandering unhindered through the encampment, and well over a hundred tribesmen. The sinking sun cast long shadows over the camp and tinged everything that moved with the crimson hue of fresh blood. Even the sea beyond looked as if someone had dyed it the same vivid colour. Some of the Bedouin were lighting fires as the night crept across the land, still an hour or two away but announcing its approach by the discoloration of the sky. Lausard held his horse by its bridle, the animal tossing its head skittishly every now and then, finally calmed by a soothing pat on its neck.

Caminarro had also dismounted, his backside and legs sore from the long journey, and he accepted the telescope that Milliere handed him, squinting through the eyepiece at the Arab encampment. He could see no sign of the hostages, only the bustle of animals and Bedouin. He handed the telescope back to Milliere.

'What are you supposed to bargain *with*, citizen?' Milliere asked. 'How much will it take to keep your comrades alive?'

'I have a bag of fifty gold pieces with me.'

'Don't say that too loudly or you'll be robbed by the squadron before you can free the hostages,' Lausard advised. 'Why should the Bedouin be interested in gold anyway? They have no need of money.'

'They will take it,' Karim said. 'They will see it as a sign that they have the power to force the Infidel to do their will.'

'You're very sure of that, Karim?' Milliere said.

'I know how their minds work.'

Milliere nodded. 'Very well. Citizen Caminarro, myself, you Lausard, Rocheteau and Gaston will ride into the village and meet with their leaders. Karim will act as interpreter.'

'Captain, I do not think that taking the boy with us will help,' Karim offered. 'The Bedouin may wish to keep him. You all know too well their fondness for youth. The boy will be safer if he remains with the squadron. The Mamelukes have fought battles over the possession of young boys, the Bedouin are the same.'

'Let Joubert come with us then,' Milliere said. 'Surely even the most depraved mind could not find *him* a worthy prize.'

The men laughed.

Lausard mounted his horse and motioned to Rocheteau and Joubert to join him. Milliere turned to Lieutenant Royere.

'If they will not bargain,' he instructed, 'if they try to kill us on the way into the camp, while we are in it or during our exit, then attack. And spare no one.'

Royere nodded, watching as the small procession set off down the sandy ridge towards the Bedouin camp.

As they drew nearer, Lausard could hear the sound of

voices raised excitedly. He could hear the neighing of horses, the snorting of camels, the braying of donkeys, even the sounds of sheep and goats. A light breeze had sprung up and one of the Bedouin tents flapped gently, the noise adding to the overall cacophony. As well as the aural assault, a profusion of smells accosted them. The stench of excrement, human and animal, was prevalent, as was the odour of unwashed bodies.

The small party of Frenchmen was now no more than fifty yards from the outer perimeter of the camp and Lausard saw several Arabs watching them intently as they drew closer. Eventually, one turned and sprinted off into the heart of the camp.

Caminarro shifted uncomfortably in his saddle, the sweat running down his face not just the product of the early-evening heat. He could feel his heart thudding ever faster and he found it increasingly more difficult to control his breathing as he saw more and more Bedouin stop to watch the approach of the dragoons.

A mounted Arab rode towards them slowly, circling them with his pony. The troops did their best to ignore him but Caminarro could barely contain his fear and watched the Arab's every movement with mounting terror. He fumbled beneath his saddle cloth, one hand hovering over his pistol.

'Leave it alone,' Lausard ordered without looking at him.

They were past the outer perimeter now, heading towards the very centre of the camp. It seemed that every Arab present had turned to watch their steady progress. One stepped towards the horse ridden by Karim and ran a hand along its hindquarters, muttering something in Arabic. Karim ignored the remark, even the cackling laugh that followed. Another Bedouin spat in the path of Lausard's horse, barking something angrily. The sergeant glared at the Bedouin from beneath the peak of his brass helmet and the look was enough to make the man step back a pace.

Caminarro glanced behind him and saw that the other Bedouin had formed a tight circle around the dragoons. He paused momentarily, his heart hammering against his ribs.

'Keep going,' Lausard murmured through gritted teeth.

Another Arab pulled his robe aside and exposed his genitals to Rocheteau, who edged his horse sideways slightly and almost knocked the man to the ground.

He shouted something in his anger.

Rocheteau turned to Karim. 'What did he say?'

'He called you a jackal.'

'He must know you,' Joubert commented.

'Shut up!' Milliere snapped, also looking around at the gathering of tribesmen.

Lausard was sure that there were well over two hundred Bedouin gathered around, looking on with curiosity as the dragoons reached a particularly large tent in the centre of their camp. But it was what stood before the tent that caught the attention of Lausard and his companions.

'Oh my God!' Caminarro gasped, his hand across his mouth. He felt his stomach contract.

Three long stakes were embedded in the sand outside the largest tent. On top of each was a severed head. The eyes of the one in the centre were still open and Caminarro swallowed hard, transfixed by the lifeless orbs. Lausard saw him pull more tightly on his reins, and for a second the sergeant feared that Caminarro might try to gallop away. He edged his horse closer to the geologist. The horde of Arabs had drawn in even more tightly around the dragoons and one of them was tugging at Lausard's shabraque. The sergeant glared down at him, flicking out one boot to push the man back. Rocheteau rested one hand on the hilt of his sword but Lausard noticed and shook his head.

Two Arabs emerged from the tent. Big men, one sporting a large growth of beard. The remainder of his face was pitted and swarthy, and he regarded the dragoons with a mixture of distaste and amusement.

'Tell him I want to see the hostages,' Milliere said to Karim. 'Tell him we have his ransom.' The dragoons looked on as the Circassian translated.

The bearded Arab shouted something towards the tent and the flap opened.

Lausard and the others saw half a dozen naked figures being pushed out into the blazing sunshine. Their Bedouin guards were pushing them, kicking those who lost their footing, herding them towards the waiting dragoons. The men looked terrified and, Lausard noticed, many bore bruises on most parts of their bodies. The tribesmen nearby were spitting and shouting at them, some grabbing the men as they passed.

'Please God, help us,' said the leading Frenchman, looking up imploringly at the dragoons. 'They will kill us all. Get us out of here.' He pointed towards the three severed heads. 'We will all end up like that if you do not save us.'

'When did they do that?' Milliere asked.

'This morning. They will kill us all.'

'Which of you is the courier from the Directory?'

'It is I.' One of the men stepped forward. 'My name

is Lesimple. I carry despatches for General Bonaparte from the Directory. It is vital that he gets them.'

'Do you still have them?' Milliere pressed. 'These savages haven't stolen them, have they?'

'They took everything else of value,' Lesimple said. 'Our clothes, shoes, personal belongings, but they didn't seem interested in the papers I carried.'

'Where are the other hostages?'

'Inside that tent,' Lesimple told Milliere, gesturing behind to the canvas cover.

One of the Arabs suddenly stepped between Lesimple and Milliere and began raving, gesturing wildly at the tent, Lesimple and also at the dragoons.

'He says they want the ransom now,' Karim informed Milliere. 'Otherwise they will kill the hostages and us too.'

'Let them try,' Rocheteau hissed, glaring at the bearded Arab.

'Not yet,' Lausard murmured.

'Shall I give him the gold?' Caminarro wanted to know.

'How many hostages are left?' Milliere asked Lesimple.

'Including myself, twenty-two. They killed three, as you can see. Another man was wounded when we beached; he died last night.'

The leading Arab was still speaking excitedly in his native tongue.

'He says that unless you pay now, the rest of the hostages will be executed immediately,' Karim said, without taking his eyes from the Arab, who suddenly drew his sword and pressed it against the throat of the hostage standing closest to him. The man yelped in fear, his face draining of colour.

'For the love of God give him what he wants,' Lesimple urged.

'Tell him to release the hostages and we'll pay,' Milliere instructed Karim.

Karim relayed the instructions, nodding as the Arab snarled back at him angrily.

'No gold, no hostages,' the Circassian informed his officer.

'If we give them the gold they'll kill the hostages anyway,' Lausard said.

'Then what do you suggest, Sergeant?'

'Give him half now,' Lausard advised Milliere. 'Tell them to release half the hostages and that he'll get the rest of the gold when *we've* got the other hostages.'

'I don't think we're in a position to bargain,' Milliere said, looking around at the large number of Arabs surrounding them.

'Please get us out,' Lesimple begged.

'You have to give them the gold,' Caminarro insisted.

'Tell them that unless they release the hostages we'll kill them all,' Lausard said, looking first at Karim then at Milliere.

'There are six of you,' Caminarro blurted. 'How can you hope to fight this many? Are you insane?'

'Tell him, Karim,' Lausard insisted.

The Circassian looked at Milliere for confirmation.

'They don't know our strength, Captain,' Lausard persisted. 'They won't stand against organized troops, we saw that at Barada.'

'But in the time it takes us to bring the rest of the squadron back, they could have killed all the hostages,' the officer said.

'They're going to kill them anyway, you know that.'

'We have to retrieve those papers from the Directory.'

'What about us?' Lesimple protested. 'Do not speak of us as if we were not here. How dare you play with our lives?'

'You will *have* no life without our help,' Lausard reminded him.

'Offer him half,' Milliere said. 'Half now and the other half when the rest of the hostages are released.' He nodded towards Karim who translated.

The Arab spat on the sand in front of Milliere's horse. He then babbled something that Karim listened to intently before turning again to Milliere.

'He says they will release ten of the hostages now for half the gold. They will release five more tomorrow for the other half. They will keep seven for themselves.'

'You cannot let them do that,' Lesimple said, his face turning white with terror. 'You don't know what foul torments these heathens have put us through already.'

'Tell them they must release *all* the hostages,' Milliere said.

Karim repeated the instructions and received a tirade in return.

'He says they will keep seven.'

'Any ideas, Lausard?' Milliere turned to the sergeant. 'If we return to Cairo without hostages *and* despatches I don't think General Bonaparte will be the happiest man in Egypt.'

'They have no idea of our strength, Captain . . .' Lausard began.

'But they hold the trump card, Lausard. We must get those despatches back.'

'And these men,' Caminarro protested.

'We can get both,' Lausard suggested, 'if we attack in the right way. You forget, Captain, you command a squadron of criminals. Men of cunning as well as courage. I think both will be needed here.'

Milliere nodded.

'Give him half the gold now, tell him we'll be back to pick up the other hostages in the morning.'

'All of them?' Milliere asked.

'All they will release. Fifteen is better than none.'

'You cannot play with our lives this way,' Lesimple said, tugging at the bridle of Lausard's horse.

'Get away from me, you fool,' Lausard snapped. 'If you trust us you might *all* get away from here with your lives.'

'Give him half,' Milliere instructed Caminarro and he watched as the engineer counted out twenty-five pieces of gold and handed them to the Arab. 'The rest tomorrow.'

The officer wheeled his horse and raised a hand, beckoning his troops to follow him.

'We go,' he said. 'There is nothing more we can do here.'

'You can't leave these men,' Caminarro shouted.

'If you want to come with us you ride out now,' Lausard said simply. 'If not, then stay with your friends.'

'Don't leave us,' Lesimple wailed, his mournful cry echoed by some of the other hostages.

The dragoons guided their horses through the wall of Arabs, determinedly looking straight ahead, refusing to be distracted by the shouts and jeers of the leering Bedouin. Behind them they could still hear the terrified yells of the hostages, shrieks of despair and cries for help, but none looked back, not even Caminarro. Gradually those mournful shrieks were drowned by the raucous laughter of the Arabs, who gathered around their captives once more.

As the group reached the perimeter of the camp, a Bedouin ran across towards Rocheteau's horse and shouted something at the corporal.

'He called us cowards,' Karim explained as the Arab repeated the words and made an expansive gesture with his arm designed to encompass all the riders.

'I find it hard to disagree with him,' Caminarro snapped. 'You have abandoned those men to God knows what fate. You were sent here to free them and yet you give them gold and for what? They will all die because of you—'

Lausard grabbed his arm. 'We've abandoned no one. It is just a matter of time.'

'Time before what? Before they are all butchered?'

'This is *our* business now. I suggest you leave it to us.'

Behind them, the laughter of the Bedouin grew louder.

Twenty-Eight

Lausard felt uncomfortably exposed beneath the dull white glow of the full moon. The impenetrable blackness that normally covered the desert at night existed only in the shadows. Elsewhere, the landscape was illuminated by a silvery sheen. Every now and then the sergeant glanced up towards the sky, hoping that the wisps of cloud driven by the easterly breeze would grow and form thicker banks to envelop the moon and give him the darkness he wanted. In the meantime, he continued to crawl across the sand like some nocturnal hunter, his eyes fixed on the low range of sand dunes fifty feet ahead. Beyond them was the Bedouin camp.

Lausard could see the tips of the closest tents poking upwards as if thrusting out of the sand itself. Ten yards to his right, Rocheteau was also hauling himself across the sand, a knife gripped in one hand. To Lausard's left, Giresse crawled a few more feet, then raised himself up on to his haunches and sprinted for the nearest dune, throwing himself down behind it. He crouched nervously, waiting for Lausard and Rocheteau to join him. Behind them, moving with a little more ease, came Gaston. He crawled with surprising speed, his red trumpeter's tunic looking black in the cold light of the moon. He carried a pistol and his sword but he also carried his trumpet, slung around one shoulder by its braided strap. If Lausard's plan was to work, the instrument would be as integral a part of events as any blade or bullet.

The dragoons reached the dunes and paused, Lausard edging up to the rim of the sandy ridge, peering over. The nearest Bedouin tent was about ten yards away, the others dotted across the sand in no particular formation. Many had ponies or camels tethered outside but the bulk of the horses were gathered together away to the left, about fifty yards from where the dragoons now sheltered. Between the dragoons and the animals were five or six tents, two of which had small fires burning outside them, one still bearing the remains of a charred goose on a makeshift spit. The fires had died down, glowing dimly in the night, but for Lausard and his companions that would be sufficient.

Lausard ducked down as he saw an Arab emerge from one of the tents and peer around in the gloom. Lausard wondered if the Bedouin could possibly have heard their approach but reasoned that it was impossible. The dragoons had used stealth of which the tribesmen themselves would have been proud. Lausard's thoughts were confirmed when he saw the Arab pull up his robe and squat down, his back to the dragoons. He grunted and began to defecate. The sergeant nudged Rocheteau and indicated towards the Arab. He watched as the corporal scurried across the sand, caught the Arab around the jaw and, with one swift, skilful movement, drew the knife across his throat. Rocheteau held on to his victim

to prevent any sound escaping the man's lips, and finally
released the body, allowing it to slump back on the sand,
blood jetting darkly from the gashed throat.

Lausard and the other two dragoons hurried over to
join him, the sergeant using his sword to slice off several
lengths of canvas from the dead Bedouin's tent. Then,
closely followed by Giresse and Gaston who were mim-
icking his actions, he hurried towards the nearest fire.
All three men placed the ends of the canvas in the dying
embers, watching as the material caught fire, then they
swiftly yanked the burning streamers free. A number of
the horses begin to whinny, alerted and alarmed by the
activity going on so close by. Lausard knew that their
frightened reaction would soon stir the Bedouin; he and
his men had to act quickly. Each of them ran towards
the tents and dropped two lengths of burning canvas
on to them. The flames erupted quickly, devouring the
dry material with relish. Three of the makeshift shelters
caught fire within moments, and shouts of alarm began
to rise from inside.

Lausard wrapped one of the burning streamers swiftly
around the end of his sword and ran towards the horses,
touching the flame to the flanks of several mounts. They
reacted with the fury he'd expected, kicking out and
whinnying in pain and fear. More than fifty horses
began to move away from the source of the fire, anxious
to escape it. They swung right, crashing into several
more tents whose occupants were now stumbling out
to see what was happening. Two were ridden down
immediately by the terrified horses. Another drew his
sword and ran at Lausard, who ducked beneath the
clumsy swing and drove his sword into the Bedouin's
back, the blazing canvas still attached to the point. The

steel pierced his kidneys and the cloth ignited the robe he wore, rapidly transforming the tribesman into a human torch. He shrieked in agony as he rolled on the sand in an attempt to snuff out the flames that devoured him.

Elsewhere Rocheteau had ignited other tents. More and more Arabs were spilling out into the night, aware that they were under attack but unsure of the source. They saw their horses stampeding away, other tents burning, the occupants of some staggering about as fire enveloped them. Figures dashed to and fro in the flame-lit hell, the dragoons able to move easily amongst their bewildered enemies. Lausard struck down two more tribesmen with his sword. Giresse dispatched another with a blow to the skull that practically split the man's cranium. Even Gaston drove his blade into the belly of an Arab, forcing the sword so deep he had to kick the Arab away to free the bloodied steel.

Moving with speed and purpose, the dragoons made their way towards the centre of the camp, setting other tents ablaze, leaving more fires in their wake. Many of the Bedouin seemed more concerned with regaining their horses or camels than with the attackers in their midst, and a large number had dashed off into the desert in pursuit of their mounts. Others had simply fled, thinking that such a venomous assault must be the work of many foes. If they had known there were just four Frenchmen among them they may well have stayed and fought.

The camp had been transformed into a scene of utter chaos. Men rushed back and forth, some seeking their enemies, others trying to retrieve belongings or animals, most dazzled by the leaping flames from the burning tents, many more swept away by the stampeding or terrified horses. Very few even saw the dragoons making their way towards the tent that housed the hostages. The four men were further hidden by the dense smoke. Lausard felt the heat from the flames on his cheeks and the smoke stung his eyes, but he raced on. As he reached the large tent he pulled a pistol from his belt and forced his way inside. The Arab who confronted him froze momentarily, transfixed by the sight of the dragoon. Lausard raised his pistol and fired at point-blank range, shooting the man in the face and ignoring the blood that spurted on to him.

Giresse met one of the other Arabs in the tent with a powerful back-hand swipe that caught the man across the shoulder, shattering his collar bone. As he dropped to his knees, blood flowing from the savage wound, Giresse drove his sword through the Bedouin's throat.

Rocheteau grabbed the third man by the hair, simultaneously bringing his knife upwards, driving it through the Arab's bottom jaw and on into the roof of his mouth.

'Take them out the back way,' Lausard instructed, and Gaston began hacking at the canvas of the tent with his sword. 'Move!' Lausard shouted at the terrified hostages, who rushed towards the hole that Gaston had hacked in the rear of the tent.

'Alain, look,' Giresse said, peering out through the tent flap into the camp, which was now illuminated by fire.

Lausard saw half a dozen Arabs running towards the large tent.

He nodded to Giresse and Rocheteau to follow the hostages and Gaston out into the night. Then he pulled a cartridge from his cartouche, bit off the end, spat the ball down the pistol barrel, rammed down the wadding and thumbed back the hammer. He fired off the shot then turned and scurried after his men.

As they spilled out into the night, Giresse and Rocheteau guided the terrified hostages towards a sand dune about thirty yards away. They urged them on, occasionally pushing the frightened men to speed their escape. Fortunately for the Frenchmen, the majority of the Bedouin were too preoccupied with saving their possessions to give chase, but the Arabs Giresse had spotted running towards the large tent continued to give chase. Lausard faced them, joined by Rocheteau.

The sergeant killed the first of the attackers with a single thrust to the chest, his sword passing cleanly between ribs as he drove the steel in deep. He slid the blade free and spun round to face the next man. Rocheteau, meanwhile, drove a boot into the groin of his first opponent, the man doubling up in agony. The corporal brought his sword down on to the back of the Arab's neck and he sprawled in the sand at his feet, blood spreading around him. Another of the Bedouin turned and fled. Of the two who remained, one tugged a pistol from inside his robe and shoved the barrel to within inches of Lausard's face. Everything seemed to freeze for the sergeant. Then the Bedouin pulled the trigger and the hammer slammed down. Nothing happened. Instantly Lausard realized that either the powder was damp or the flint had worn smooth. The smile the Arab had been wearing vanished and he stood motionless, unable to believe his bad luck. Lausard reacted with devastating speed, striking so powerfully with his sword that he severed the Arab's arm just below the elbow. The tribesman dropped to his knees, shrieking in agony until Lausard caught him with another back-hand swipe that shattered his jaw and sent several teeth flying across the sand. The remaining Arab turned to flee, but before he had taken two paces, Rocheteau skewered him twice in the back.

Lausard turned to Gaston and nodded.

'Now!' he shouted.

Gaston raised the trumpet to his lips, knowing what he had to do. Summoning every ounce of strength, mustering every breath in his body, he began to blow the notes that signalled the charge. Among the hostages, Lesimple heard the familiar sound and looked on with bewilderment. Then, suddenly, they began to feel the ground shake beneath them. The accompanying sound originated from the eastern edge of the Bedouin camp and it grew like rolling thunder.

To the ridge away to the east, illuminated by the cold brilliance of the moon, first one, then two lines of horsemen appeared, followed by a third, all with swords raised, all driving on their mounts with ferocious speed. Lausard could make out the figure of Captain Milliere leading the charge, Lieutenant Royere close behind him, urging the men on, and as the horsemen hurtled towards the already panic-stricken Arabs, Gaston continued to blow the charge. It was as if the notes he delivered spurred the charging dragoons on to even greater speeds. They crashed through the outer perimeter of the encampment, riding through the remains of tents, hacking down Bedouins as they tried to flee. Those not killed by sword cuts were trampled beneath the churning hooves of the big Breton horses. Few tried to fight back. Their only objective was escape, many dashing off into the desert on foot. Some of the men in the third line of dragoons broke off to pursue them, but for the most part they were allowed to run.

Lesimple and the other hostages watched in awe as the dragoons crashed through what remained of the camp. Many of them were now reining in their mounts, some slipping from their saddles to inspect what the Arabs had left behind.

Milliere and Royere rode towards Lausard, who raised his sword in salute.

Rocheteau patted Gaston on the back and the youth smiled.

As the two officers drew nearer, Lausard could see that they were closely followed by Caminarro, who nodded towards the sergeant.

'Forgive me for doubting you,' he said flatly. 'Are *all* the hostages safe?'

Lausard nodded. 'All they've lost are their clothes and a little pride.'

He was aware of someone standing close to him and turned to see Lesimple clutching a sheaf of papers close to his chest.

'These are the despatches sent by the Directory,' he said, holding them out towards Caminarro. 'I must get them to General Bonaparte. I have guarded these with my life.'

'We'll camp here for the night,' Milliere told the courier. 'At first light we set out for Cairo.' He dismounted and crossed to Lausard, shaking the sergeant's hand. 'You did well.' He looked at Rocheteau, Gaston and Giresse. 'All of you did. Well done. I suggest you join your colleagues. They are busy trying to find anything of value the Arabs might have left behind.'

Rocheteau, Giresse and Gaston scuttled off, while Lausard wiped his sword with a piece of cloth and sheathed it.

'And when we return to Cairo, Captain, what then?' Lausard asked.

'Who knows?' the officer said. 'Your guess is as good as mine. All we can do is await orders.'

'And find out where our General decides to send us next? What mission will he have for us, I wonder?'

'There may be some instructions in those despatches,' Royere mused.

'I doubt it,' Lesimple said. 'I know what these despatches contain. When the Directory entrusted me to deliver them they also informed me of their contents.'

Lausard and Milliere exchanged glances.

'Is that usual procedure when urgent political documents are involved?' Lausard queried.

'It wasn't a matter of procedure. I am a close friend of Citizen Sieyès who occupies a position on the Directory. It was he who told me of the contents of these despatches. Since you risked your lives to save my life *and* the despatches, I feel you have a right to know what they contain.'

'Are we to march on India after conquering Egypt?' Lausard demanded, his voice thick with scorn. 'Are the despatches instructions for the further expansion of the Republic?'

'They contain congratulations on the capture of Malta.' Lesimple was almost apologetic. 'Nothing more.'

The dragoons looked disbelievingly at the courier for a second then at each other.

'Bonaparte sent us halfway across Egypt for nothing,' Milliere said.

'I felt you had a right to know,' Lesimple continued.

Lausard laughed but it had a hollow ring.

Royere kicked out angrily at a small mound of sand.

'I suspect that General Bonaparte will be as disheartened as you when he receives the despatches,' Lesimple said quietly.

Milliere nodded his agreement.

'They care nothing for us,' Lausard said. 'The Directory has more pressing issues, such as lining its own pockets. It has left us here to rot, but if the truth is told, did we ever really expect anything else?' He turned and began walking away towards what remained of the Bedouin camp.

'Where are you going, Lausard?' Milliere called after him.

Lausard turned briefly, a crooked smile on his lips. 'The same place as you and everyone else in the French army, Captain. Hell, eventually.'

The darkness swallowed him up.

Twenty-Nine

During the campaign Lausard had thought often how
time can play tricks with a man's mind. The sheer
monotony of a long march, coupled with lack of food and
water and searing heat caused even the most level-headed
soldier to lose track of time. Hours passed like days, and
days themselves seemed to stretch out indefinitely. But
at least the four-day return trip to Cairo from Marabout
was more favourable than the outbound journey. The
provisions he and his companions had taken from the
Bedouin camp had been plentiful, more than enough to
sustain them during the trek across the desert, and he
reasoned that the sensation of time elongating affected
him less with a full belly. But even with the relative wealth
of supplies, several horses had died from exhaustion and
two or three dragoons had been struck down. The
freed *savants* seemed to have endured with remarkable
strength, Lausard thought, but compared to the horrors
they had been subjected to at the hands of their Bedouin
captors, a desert march was a favourable alternative.

The squadron had kept the Nile in sight on its left

during the entire return journey. The odd patrol from French-occupied towns had been encountered along the way, but other than that the men had seen no one. Certainly no roving Bedouins. As they crested another ridge of sand, Lausard saw the spires and minarets of Cairo glinting in the searing midday sun. He also spotted something else.

Three large white tents were set up outside the walls of Cairo, each one about fifty feet long and fifteen feet high. Above each one an imposing black flag fluttered.

'Hospital tents,' Lausard murmured, spotting the black standards.

'But why *outside* the city?' Rocheteau questioned.

He was not the only one to notice several sentries with fixed bayonets gathered twenty or thirty yards from the tents. As the squadron drew nearer, the infantrymen lowered their weapons as if the dragoons were enemies, musket barrels aimed at them, bayonet points sparkling in the sunlight.

'Ride on,' a tall corporal ordered, waving the dragoons past.

'What's happening here?' Milliere demanded.

'If you've got any sense you'll ride on,' the corporal repeated. 'The men inside are all infected.'

Milliere looked puzzled.

'Oh my God,' Karim muttered. 'It's the plague.'

The corporal nodded.

'Bubonic plague,' Karim said quietly. 'It kills more Egyptians a year than starvation and thirst combined.'

'The men in these tents are dying,' the corporal told them. 'More than fifteen a day, inside *and* outside the city. General Bonaparte has set up these quarantine measures to prevent it spreading any further. Some of the officers won't leave their houses in the city. They give orders through hatches cut in the doors and they won't receive any paper unless it is soaked in vinegar first. They think that helps.' He smiled wanly. 'Any man complaining of a fever is sent to one of these tents and not allowed within four hundred yards of his comrades. Their rations are placed one hundred yards from their tents, those well enough to reach them usually live, those who can't die anyway.' He sighed wearily. 'Like I said, I'd ride on if I were you. We're here only because we're on a punishment detail. We stole from one of the mosques. The officers don't care if we live or die, they're too busy trying to keep on the right side of these stinking Moslems.' He hooked a thumb over his shoulder in the direction of Cairo. 'This plague has broken out in Alexandria and Damietta too. It'll probably kill the whole army in a matter of weeks.'

'What treatment is there?' Lausard asked.

'How the hell do I know? You're welcome to come inside and ask one of the surgeons if you like.'

'There is no cure,' Karim told the sergeant. 'I have seen this plague before, many times. It begins with a fever then growths form under the arms or in the groin. Sometimes it takes less than twenty-four hours to kill a man.'

'You have seen it, you have survived it,' Lausard said. 'How?'

'No one knows what causes it so no one knows who is more likely to catch it. I have seen men survive it, but not often. If they live beyond four days then they have a chance, but it isn't usual.'

'Everyone's panicking,' the corporal interjected. 'Some surgeons are refusing to treat those who are infected.

There is talk that those wounded in skirmishes with the Bedouin are put into beds previously occupied by plague victims, that orderlies are selling the clothes of the dead instead of burning them. No one knows what to do to survive. Some of the bodies were buried so shallow the dogs in the city dug them up and devoured them. The whole city is falling apart and yet still Bonaparte talks of conquest. He is marching into Syria even now. Those who have gone with him are lucky. The rest of us sit around with our thumbs stuck up our backsides waiting to die.'

Milliere jerked on the reins of his horse and turned the horse away, Lausard and the rest of the dragoons following him.

'I don't want to die of some terrible disease,' said Joubert. 'If I have to die I'd sooner it was on a battle-field.'

'I don't want to die at *all*,' Roussard commented.

'Nor I,' Sonnier added.

'*Vive Bonaparte*,' Delacor said cynically.

'You can't blame him for *this*,' Bonet admonished.

'He brought us here, didn't he? I'll blame him if I want to.' Delacor rounded on Moreau. 'Where is your God now when we need him?'

'It won't be a God, *anyone's* God, who decides whether you live or die now,' Lausard said.

'I've always been lucky, I hope my luck holds out.' Rocheteau looked at Lausard. 'You always said we were better off away from Paris, Alain, better off away from a life in the gutter or in prison. Do you still believe that?'

Lausard didn't answer.

*　　*　　*

An unearthly stillness filled the house where the dragoons were billeted; a silence that came with fear and foreboding. Those who could slept. Others sat on their makeshift pallets of straw-stuffed rags staring into the gloom or talking quietly, almost reverentially.

Lausard sat on his mattress, using an oily rag to clean the blade of his sword, a single candle providing an island of light in an ocean of blackness. Beside him, Rocheteau lay on his back, arms crossed behind his head.

'If I was to return to France now and sell all the gold, silver and precious stones I've collected since we got here,' the corporal pointed out, 'I could be a very rich man.'

'Then perhaps you should be thankful you are here,' Lausard told him. 'Being a rich man in France hasn't been much of a pastime these past ten years, has it? You should know, you saw enough people go to the guillotine.'

'No, you're missing the point,' Rocheteau insisted. 'What I'm trying to say is that I could have anything I wanted now and yet I'll probably end up dying here of plague, or even if I don't, I can't see how any of us will ever get back home. What with the English blockading the ports and everything else that's going on.'

'So all your gold and jewels are no good to you then? Do you want me to take them for you?'

Rocheteau smiled. 'I think I'll take my chances.'

Lausard finished cleaning his sword and slid it back into the scabbard.

'We *are* going to die, aren't we, Alain?'

'Every man dies,' Lausard said. 'It's just a matter of when and how. But not every man truly lives.'

'And you think *we* have?'

'We have been more alive during the past two years than we ever were stealing and scraping a living in the gutters of Paris. At least the army gave us something. A reason to go on. A chance to die as free men. That is more valuable than all the gold and jewels in the world.'

Lausard glanced up to see a figure in the doorway at the far end of the room. A man dressed, like himself, in the dragoon uniform. The trooper was looking around the billet, squinting into the gloom. He finally took a few faltering steps inside, passing men who glanced quizzically at him. He looked at each puzzled face, his gaze finally alighting on Lausard's. The private crossed to the sergeant and drew himself to attention.

'You are Sergeant Lausard,' he said and it sounded more like a statement than a question. 'I was sent to find you.'

'Who sent you? What's the charge this time?'

The private looked perplexed. 'I have something for you.' He reached into his pocket.

Lausard watched as the man withdrew a gleaming object and held it out to him. It glinted dully in the light cast by the candle and the sergeant could make out that it was a snuff box.

'Who is sending me gifts?'

'It is from Corporal Charnier of the third squadron. He asked me to bring it to you. He said he wanted you to have it as he would have no further use for it himself. He said you were a man of honour, that you would appreciate this gift.'

'Where is Charnier?' Lausard demanded.

'He is in one of the hospital tents outside the city. He's been there for the last four days. He has the plague.'

Lausard was on his feet in an instant. 'Take me to him,' he instructed.

'Alain, don't be a fool.' Rocheteau grabbed his companion's arm. 'You'll end up the same way as the others. You heard what he said. Plague. This isn't something you can stand up and fight like you would one of the enemy. Charnier knows that too.'

Lausard shook his arm free. 'Charnier is a good man. I'm not going to leave him to rot in that plague tent. Would you leave *me* to die like some miserable dog?'

Rocheteau shook his head.

'Karim said that if a man survived beyond four days then he might recover,' Lausard reminded the corporal. 'If there is a chance that Charnier can be saved by taking him out of that place then I will do it.'

'And what about your own life?' Rocheteau asked. 'By going there you risk catching the plague yourself.'

'Why should I worry about losing my life?' the sergeant snapped, then he turned to the private. 'Take me to him. Now!'

'I will not go back inside that place again. Charnier gave me that snuff box when he first caught the fever. I promised to give it to you but that was all I promised. I will not risk my life again.'

Lausard snatched the snuff box from him. 'Which tent is he in?'

The private told him and Lausard was already striding towards the door.

'Alain,' Rocheteau called after him but the sergeant didn't stop.

'He's a fool,' the private said dismissively.

'Better a fool than a coward,' Rocheteau said scathingly.

*　　*　　*

As Lausard rode he was surprised at how quiet and dark the city was. Very little light filtered into the narrow streets from the buildings on either side and some of the men he passed were barely visible in the blackness. Only as he reached the outer walls did the night seem to come alive. He heard the barking of wild dogs, the rustling of a breeze through the branches of palm trees; even the low mutterings of sentries seemed to echo in the stillness as he passed through the main gate and out into the desert. He rode at a steady pace, eyes fixed ahead, his horse cantering evenly as he guided it across the sand. Up ahead, looming white like phantoms in some fevered dream, he could make out the shapes of the hospital tents.

'Halt.'

He obeyed the order and saw an infantryman advancing towards him, Charleville pressed to his shoulder.

'Turn back,' the private instructed. 'No one is allowed beyond this point, by order of General Bonaparte.'

'I must get through,' Lausard told him.

'You know what lies beyond? In those tents? The men inside are dying of plague. Do you wish to join them?'

'Step aside,' Lausard persisted.

'I have orders to shoot anyone who tries to pass this point,' the private said, aiming the musket at Lausard's chest.

The dragoon edged his horse a couple of steps nearer, his eyes fixed on those of the sentry.

'Then shoot,' the sergeant challenged.

The private thumbed back the hammer on his musket, the sound echoing in the stillness. Lausard extended his arms on either side, pushing out his chest as if to give the infantryman a clearer target. For long moments the two men faced each other, the musket wavering slightly. Lausard remained in the saddle like a statue, his expression fixed, his eyes boring into the private. One slip of the man's finger and Lausard knew that the Charleville would blast him from point-blank range. With only a couple of feet between the two men, the private couldn't miss. The only sound to punctuate the delicate impasse was the occasional snorting of Lausard's horse as it pawed at the sand with its hoof.

Then, without a word, the infantryman lowered his musket and stepped aside, allowing Lausard to ride on.

Another minute and Lausard was outside the tent housing Charnier. He glanced up at the black flag of warning, flapping wildly in the breeze.

Lausard dismounted, leaving his horse watching patiently, sniffing the air. Like Lausard it could smell the foul odour emanating from the hospital tent, an odour that became almost intolerable as Lausard pulled aside the flap and entered the makeshift hospital. The place reeked of death and disease. The stench of excrement mingled with a more cloying, nauseating smell of pus, all exacerbated by the heat. Very little sound came from inside and many of the men who lay on the rough beds did not move.

Lausard passed among them, peering at the dimly lit faces on either side of him as he made his grim trek through the seemingly endless lines of wretches. Here and there bodies were covered with rags to hide their faces, a last attempt at dignity in a world that had stripped men of their humanity. Bowls beside some of the beds were filled with water, blood or vomit dependent upon the stage of the disease the occupant had reached. The water was usually brackish and stank as much as the blood.

Lausard moved slowly through the hall of suffering, wondering what kind of care these men were receiving. It seemed to be very little. One man was lying half in and half out of his bed, burbling incoherently. Lausard crossed to him, ready to help him back in. He studied the man's features. The milk white complexion, the dark rings beneath the eyes, the sweat that slicked the man's face and most of his upper body. And, beneath both arms, he saw three swollen, purulent growths. Almost as big as eggs. The man opened his eyes and, for precious seconds, looked directly into Lausard's. Whether the man realized he was being helped Lausard had no idea but, briefly, a smile touched the man's lips. He tried to speak as Lausard laid him back on his bed but he could not manage to get any words out. Instead he gripped the sergeant's hand and squeezed with a strength Lausard would have thought impossible. He knelt beside the man for a moment longer, watching him attempting to mouth something. Lausard could smell the rancid breath and the awful putrescent stench that rose from the body; it was as if the man was beginning to decompose before death had even taken him.

As Lausard rose, the man gripped his hand even more tightly, and the sergeant understood. He nodded gently and extended one hand, touching it to the man's fevered brow, stroking his hair gently. He would not leave this poor wretch now. Not at the point of death. The man looked at him once more and his eyes seemed to clear. There seemed to be an instant of incredible clarity and the smile that Lausard had felt sure he'd seen grew wider. A single tear rolled from the man's eye and trickled down his cheek, and Lausard felt the grip on his hand slowly released. The man's eyes remained open and Lausard waited for long moments before carefully closing them. He pulled the filthy sheet that covered the soldier over his head and stepped away.

Lausard had no idea how many men the hospital tent was home to but he kept walking, looking at each tortured face. Some had found the oblivion of sleep, some the even greater release of death. Flies buzzed around the bodies of dead and living alike, crawling over them gleefully. They welcomed the corpulence, the open wounds and the weeping sores. To his right someone moaned softly in their sleep. He looked round and saw that it was a boy in his late teens, his body wasted and ravaged by plague.

In the bed next to him was Charnier.

Lausard knelt beside him and gently shook him, allowing the corporal time to wake from his troubled slumber. He opened his eyes slowly and, it seemed, with difficulty.

'Charnier. It's me, Lausard. I came to return your gift.'

Charnier tried to sit up but the effort was too much. He pressed a hand to his head and sucked in a deep, polluted breath.

'Alain,' he said, clearing his throat. 'How did you get here?'

'I'm taking you out of here. I will not let you die in this place.' He reached into his pocket and pulled out the snuff box, holding it up for Charnier to see. 'I want to return this. You will have need of it. Not I.'

'I fear I will have need of *nothing* any more. The surgeons told me they could do nothing for me.'

'You're still alive.'

'God knows how. I've seen enough poor devils die of

367

this stinking plague during the last four days. Perhaps it's just as well I didn't trust those surgeons. Look.' He lifted up the shirt he wore and revealed the bloodied mess beneath one arm. 'I had two growths there, they call them buboes. Another in my groin. The doctors said it would do no good to lance them. Perhaps I was wrong, but I opened them myself. That was two days ago. There have been no more. I thought that if I released the poison I would feel better. Perhaps *I* should have been a doctor.' He managed a smile.

'Can you stand?' Lausard asked.

With Lausard's help, Charnier struggled to his feet, swaying uncertainly for a second, then he nodded.

'My uniform is under the bed. Unless those damned orderlies have sold it. That is what they do with most of the clothes around here.'

'Where *are* the orderlies and the doctors?'

'They ride back into the city every night at sun-down and return at daybreak. They care nothing for our suffering because they can do nothing to help us.'

Lausard helped him dress quickly then supported him as they made their way towards the far end of the tent, out into the night air.

'Alain, I can't ride.'

'Get up.' Lausard indicated his horse. He held the animal still while Charnier hauled himself up into the saddle, then Lausard climbed up behind him, gripping the reins with one hand and snaking his arm around his companion with the other, holding him tightly. Charnier gripped the mane of the horse as Lausard put spurs to it and headed back towards the city.

The sentries they passed paid them little heed, even those at the main gates of Cairo simply nodded as

Lausard rode past with his companion slumped across the pommel of his saddle. Once inside the city both men dismounted, the sergeant helping Charnier, who smiled and stamped his feet on the rough cobbled street.

'Do you think I will die, Alain?'

'I don't think there has been a bullet, blade or shot made that will snuff out your worthless life, you old pirate. Certainly not a disease.' He handed the snuff box to Charnier, who took it and dropped it into his pocket.

'Alain,' he began, 'you saved my life. If I had remained in that tent I . . .'

'Return to your squadron, my friend,' Lausard said, preparing to remount his horse. He extended his right hand and Charnier shook it warmly.

'I owe you my life,' the corporal repeated.

'You owe me nothing. You saved yourself. Besides, many years ago I abandoned some people I should have protected. I allowed them to die to save my own life. I hid like a snivelling dog while my own family was slaughtered. I can never wipe out the memory of my failings, of my cowardice. What I *can* ensure is that it never happens again. It is I who should thank you, my friend.' Lausard saluted and rode off, the sound of his horse's hooves echoing on the road. They gradually disappeared, dying away in the darkness like forgotten dreams.

Thirty

'Can a man lose time as easily as he loses money?'

Lausard looked up, puzzled by the comment, amused slightly at its source.

He and a dozen of his companions were watering their horses in the muddy water of the Nile, the animals lathered and weary after the ride. Lausard guessed that the patrol had been out for close to an hour. The sun was beating down with its customary ferocity and most of the dragoons had undone their tunics in an attempt at relief from the sweltering temperature. But, after so long in such a hostile and unforgiving land they should, Lausard reasoned, have all known better.

'What the hell are you going on about?' Delacor looked across at Tabor, who was gazing out towards the endless desert. 'How can you *lose* time, you idiot?'

'I think we've all lost time since we came to this country,' Rostov commented. 'How long have we been here now? Fourteen months? And for what?'

'I heard that Bonaparte himself is thinking of returning

to France,' Bonet said. 'War with Austria has begun again. The Directory needs him.'

'Who told you that?' Delacor demanded.

'A private of hussars I spoke to the other day. He was with Bonaparte right through Syria and Palestine. He was at the siege of El Arish and at Acre. He said that at the siege of Acre the artillery were so short of shells that they had to collect those fired by the enemy. They were paid for each ball they retrieved. Twelve sous for a twenty-four-pound ball, nine sous for an eighteen-pound ball and—'

'Is he the same one who told you Bonaparte is leaving Egypt?' Lausard interrupted.

'I have no reason to doubt him, he is a good man.'

'And when he leaves, how many of *us* leave with him? Certainly not those he ordered poisoned at Jaffa. Did your hussar tell you *that* story?'

'Bonaparte ordered our own men poisoned?' Rocheteau was aghast.

'Plague victims who couldn't be moved,' Lausard continued. 'Rather than let them fall into the hands of the Turks he ordered them killed. Perhaps there was mercy behind his thinking.'

'I wish he'd show some mercy to us and let us go home,' Roussard said mournfully.

'If there is war against Austria he will have need of troops,' Bonet offered. 'Let us just hope that we are among those he needs. He knows of our abilities.'

'There'll be no room for us when he leaves,' Delacor hissed, 'but you can be sure that he'll take his "pekinese" with him. His poets, his artists and his writers. He values them more than he does his soldiers.'

'I wonder how much France has changed since we left?' Rostov mused.

'You mean how much the Directory has changed it,' Lausard corrected. 'They will not be eager to see Bonaparte return, war or no war. Here he is no threat to them. Back in France they fear him.'

'Do you think the people here will ever forgive us for what we have done, or forget us?' Tabor asked.

'In a year they will not even remember you were here,' Karim said, smiling.

'And when we return, Karim, will you return with us?' Lausard asked.

'I am one of you now. As long as I wear the same uniform I fight at your side.'

'And when we return, do we get our six acres of land that Bonaparte promised us?' Rocheteau muttered.

Lausard smiled and swung himself into his saddle, followed rapidly by the other men.

'Your six acres, Rocheteau,' he said, pointing out towards the desert. 'There they are. Yours, mine and every man's in this whole disease-riddled, hungry, exhausted army. Bonaparte promised us land and wealth but all *he* ever wanted was glory. The problem is that the pursuit of glory is a meaningless chase.' He wheeled his horse and rode off, watched for a second by the other men, his broad back silhouetted against the horizon, the heat haze hanging like a shimmering blanket over the scorched land. Rocheteau spurred his horse and followed the sergeant, as did the other men, dust rising behind them.

Lausard looked at his pocket watch and noted that it was approaching noon. They would stop for food, what little they had, in another hour and try to find shelter from the searing sun just as they did every day and would continue to do until otherwise ordered. The patrols usually lasted three or four hours. Any longer was unbearable for both men and horses. Lausard glanced again at his watch and shook it. It had stopped. Dust had probably clogged the delicate inner workings, he thought. The timepiece was useless now, the hands frozen for ever. Perhaps this was final confirmation that time truly had no relevance in this land. He dropped the watch, allowing it to fall into the soft sand. The horses following galloped over it.

The patrol rode on.

High above them in the cloudless sky the sun blazed.

BONAPARTE'S SONS

Richard Howard

With the Bourbon monarchy a distant memory, confusion reigns in the French republic of 1795 . . .

Crushing the resistance of the Paris mob at the guillotine, but facing annihilation on three European fronts, the ruling Directory resorts to enlisting condemned prisoners into the army. Alongside the murderers, rapists and thieves emerge men like Alain Lausard, a miltary-educated aristocrat forced to live as a peasant during the hysteria of The Terror.

Cheating execution for salvation on the battlefield, Lausard turns hardened criminals into a ruthless cavalry unit, spearheading – with stunning victories over the Austrian army – Napoleon Bonaparte's relentless drive through Piedmont and Northern Italy.

Yet tensions between the ranks remain, and when the regiment falls under the command of the despotic Cezar, a mission behind enemy lines threatens to push the mutinous atmosphere to the very brink of anarchy . . .

THE CONQUEST

Elizabeth Chadwick

When a comet appears in the sky over England
in the spring of 1066, it heralds a time of
momentous change for Ailith, a young saxon
wife. Newly pregnant, she has developed
a friendship with her Norman neighbour,
Felice, who is also with child. But when
Felice's countrymen come not as friends but as
conquerors, they take all that Ailith holds dear.

Rescued from suicidal grief by Rolf, a handsome
Norman horse-breeder, Ailith is persuaded
to become nurse to Felice's son, Benedict,
but the situation soon becomes fraught with
tension. Ailith leaves Felice's household for
Rolf's English lands and, as his mistress,
bears him a daughter, Julitta. But the Battle of
Hastings has left a savage legacy which has bitter
repercussions, not only for Rolf and Ailith but
for the next generation, Benedict and Julitta.

From bustling London streets to the windswept
Yorkshire Dales, from green Norman farmland
to the rugged mountains of the Pyrenees and
the Spain of El Cid, this is an epic saga of love
and loss, compassion and brutality, filled with
unforgettable characters

Other bestselling Warner titles available by mail:

☐ Bonaparte's Son	Richard Howard	£5.99
☐ The Conquest	Elizabeth Chadwick	£5.99
☐ The Champion	Elizabeth Chadwick	£5.99
☐ Disordered Land	Helen Cannam	£6.99
☐ Kingdom of Shadows	Barbara Erskine	£6.99
☐ Waterfront	Richard Woodman	£5.99

Ⓦ

WARNER BOOKS

WARNER BOOKS
CASH SALES DEPARTMENT, P.O. BOX 11, Falmouth, Cornwall,
TR10 9EN
Tel: +44 (0) 1326 372400, Fax: +44 (0) 1326 374888
Email: books@barni.avel.co.uk.

POST AND PACKING:
Payments can be made as follows: cheque, postal order (payable
to Warner Books)
or by credit cards. Do not send cash or currency.
U.K. Orders   **FREE OF CHARGE**
E.E.C. & Overseas   25% of order value

Name (Block Letters) _____

Address _____

_____

_____

Post/zip code: _____

☐ Please keep me in touch with future Orbit publications
☐ I enclose my remittance £_____
☐ I wish to pay by Visa/Access/Mastercard/Eurocard

Card Expiry Date

☐☐☐☐☐☐☐☐☐☐☐☐☐☐☐☐ _____